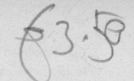

Praise for Boris Akunin

'Whether in skittish or sombre mood, Akunin is immensely readable (and excellently translated by Andrew Bromfield); the beguiling, super-brainy, sexy, unpredictable Fandorin is a creation like no other in crime fiction' *The Times*

'Fandorin [is] a debonair combo of Sherlock Holmes, D'Artagnan and most of the soulful heroes of Russian literature . . . Andrew Bromfield's translation is key to maintaining the entertaining period pastiche . . . Fandorin is very much a figure from the time of his creation: an all-knowing yet taciturn functionary with a past in espionage and a love of Japanese martial arts working in a Russia beset by internal division' *Sunday Telegraph*

'This . . . demonstrates Akunin's underlying seriousness of purpose in writing the Fandorin novels, whose clever devices and mischievous tricks disguise a determination to strip bare the extremes of human behaviour' *Sunday Times*

'Intricate, incredible, pleasurable' *Literary Review*

'A double treat for fans' *Time Out*

'An excellent read' *Guardian*

'The perfect Sunday afternoon read' *Scotland on Sunday*

Boris Akunin is the pseudonym of Grigory Chkhartishvili. He has been compared to Gogol, Tolstoy and Arthur Conan Doyle, and his Erast Fandorin books have sold over eighteen million copies in Russia alone. He lives in Moscow.

By Boris Akunin

SPECIAL ASSIGNMENTS

The Further Adventures of Erast Fandorin

BORIS AKUNIN

Translated by Andrew Bromfield

PHOENIX

A PHOENIX PAPERBACK

First published in Great Britain in 2007
by Weidenfeld & Nicolson
This paperback edition published in 2007
by Phoenix,
an imprint of Orion Books Ltd,
Orion House, 5 Upper St Martin's Lane,
London WC2H 9EA
An Hachette Livre UK company

First published in Russian as *Osobye Porucheniya: Pikoviy Valet,
Dekorator* by Zakharov Publishers, Moscow, Russia and
Edizioni Frassinelli, Milan, Italy. All rights reserved.

Published by arrangement with Linda Michaels Limited,
International Literary Agents.

3 5 7 9 10 8 6 4 2

Copyright © Boris Akunin 1999
Translation © Andrew Bromfield 2006

A CIP catalogue record for this book
is available from the British Library.

ISBN 978-0-7538-2348-4

Typeset by Input Data Services Ltd, Frome

Printed and bound in Great Britain by Clays Ltd, St Ives plc

The Orion Publishing Group's policy is to use papers that
are natural, renewable and recyclable products and
made from wood grown in sustainable forests. The logging
and manufacturing processes are expected to conform to
the environmental regulations of the country of origin.

www.orionbooks.co.uk

THE JACK
OF SPADES

CHAPTER I

The Jack of Spades
Oversteps the Mark

No one in the whole wide world was more miserable than Anisii Tulipov. Well, perhaps someone somewhere in darkest Africa or Patagonia, but certainly not anywhere nearer than that.

Judge for yourself. In the first place, that forename – Anisii. Have you ever heard of a nobleman, a gentleman of the bed-chamber, say, or at the very least, the head of some official department, being called Anisii? It simply reeks of icon-lamps and priests' offspring with their hair slicked with nettle oil.

And that surname, from the word 'tulip'! It was simply a joke. He had inherited the ill-starred family title from his great-grandfather. When Anisii's forebear had been studying in the seminary, the father rector had had the bright idea of replacing the inharmonious surnames of the future servants of the Church with names more pleasing to God. For the sake of simplicity and convenience, one year he had named all the seminarians after Church holidays, another year after fruits, and great-grandfather had found himself in the year of the flowers: someone had become Hyacinthov, someone Balzamov and someone else Buttercupov. Great-grandfather never did graduate from the seminary, but he had passed the idiotic surname on to his progeny. Well, at least he had been named after a tulip and not a dandelion.

But never mind about the name! What about Anisii's appearance! First of all, his ears, jutting out on both sides like the handles of a chamber pot. Tuck them in under your cap and they just turned rebellious, springing back so that they could stick out like some kind of prop for your hat. They were just too rubbery and gristly.

There had been a time when Anisii used to linger in front of the mirror, turning this way and that way, combing the long hair that he had grown specially at both sides in an attempt to conceal his lop ears – and it did seem to look a bit better, at least for a while. But when the pimples had erupted all over his physiognomy – and that was more than two years ago now – Tulipov had put the mirror away in the attic, because he simply couldn't bear to look at his own repulsive features any more.

Anisii got up for work before it was even light – in winter time you could say it was still night. He had a long way to go. The little house he had inherited from his father, a deacon, stood in the vegetable garden of the Pokrovsky Monastery, right beside the Spassky Gates. The route along Pustaya Street, across Taganskaya Square, past the ominous Khitrovka district, to his job in the Department of Gendarmes took Anisii a whole hour at a fast walk. And if, like today, there was a bit of a frost and the road was covered with black ice, it was a real ordeal – your tattered shoes and worn-out overcoat weren't much help to you then. It fair set your teeth clattering, reminding you of better times, your carefree boyhood, and your dear mother, God rest her soul.

A year earlier, when Anisii had become a police agent, things had been much better: a salary of eighteen roubles, plus extra pay for overtime and for night work, and occasionally they might even throw in some travel expenses. Sometimes it all mounted up to as much as thirty-five roubles a month. But the unfortunate Tulipov hadn't been able to hold on to his fine, lucrative job. Lieutenant-Colonel Sverchinsky himself had characterised him as a hopeless agent and in general a ditherer. First he'd been caught leaving his observation post (he'd had to: how could he not slip back home for a moment when his sister Sonya hadn't been fed since the morning?). And then something even worse had happened: Anisii had let a dangerous female revolutionary escape. During the operation to seize a conspirators' apartment he'd been standing in the back yard, beside the rear entrance. Because Tulipov was so young, just to be on the safe side they hadn't let him take part in the actual arrest. But then, didn't the arresting officers, those experienced bloodhounds, let a female student get away from them? Anisii saw a young lady in spectacles running towards him, with a frightened, desperate look on her face. He shouted 'Stop!' but he couldn't bring himself to grab her – the young lady's hands looked so terribly frail. He just stood there like a stuffed dummy, watching her run away. He didn't even blow his whistle.

For that outrageous dereliction of duty they had wanted to throw Tulipov out of the department altogether, but his superiors had taken pity on the orphan and demoted him to courier. Anisii's job now was a lowly, even shameful one for an educated man with five classes of secondary school. And worst of all, it had absolutely no prospects. Now he would spend his entire life rushing about like an errand boy, without ever earning a state title.

To give up on yourself at the age of twenty is no easy thing for anyone, but it wasn't even a matter of ambition. Just you try living on twelve and a half roubles. He didn't really need much for himself, but there was no way to explain to Sonya that her younger brother's career was a failure. She wanted butter, and cream cheese, and she had to be treated to a sweet every now and then. And wood to heat the stove – that cost a rouble a yard now. Sonya might be an idiot, but she still moaned and cried when she was cold.

Before he slipped out of the house, Anisii had managed to change his sister's wet bed. She had opened her piggy little eyes and babbled, 'Nisii, Nisii.'

'You be good now; don't get up to any mischief,' Anisii told her with feigned severity as he rolled over her heavy body, still hot from sleep. He put a coin on the table, the ten kopecks he had promised to leave for their neighbour Sychikha, who kept an eye on the cripple. He chewed hastily on a stale bread-bun, following it with a gulp of cold milk, and then it was time to head out into the darkness and the blizzard.

As he trudged across the snow-covered vacant lot towards Taganskaya Square, with his feet constantly slipping, Tulipov felt very sorry for himself. It was bad enough that he was poor, ugly and untalented, but his sister Sonya was a burden for the rest of his life. He was a doomed man; he would never have a wife, or children, or a comfortable home.

As he ran past the Church of Consolation of All the Afflicted, he crossed himself as usual, facing towards the icon of the Mother of God, lit up by its little lamp. Anisii had loved that icon since he was a child: it didn't hang inside where it was warm and dry but out there on the wall, exposed to the elements, only protected from the rain and the snow by a small canopy, with a wooden cross above it. The little flame was burning, unquenchable in its glass cover; you could see it from a long way away. And that was good, especially when you were looking at it from out of the cold darkness and howling wind.

What was that white shape, up on top of the cross?

A white dove. Sitting there preening its little wings with its beak, and it couldn't care a straw for the blizzard. It was a sure sign – his dear departed mother had been a great authority on signs – a white dove on a cross meant good fortune and unexpected happiness. But where could good fortune come from to him?

The low wind swirled the snow across the ground. Oh, but it was cold.

Today, however, Anisii's working day could hardly have got off to a better start. You could say that Tulipov had a real stroke of luck. Egor Semenich, the collegiate registrar in charge of deliveries, cast a dubious glance at Anisii's unconvincing overcoat, shook his grey head and gave him a nice warm job, one that wouldn't have him running all over the place across the boundless, wind-swept city: all he had to do was deliver a folder of reports and documents to His Honour Mr Erast Petrovich Fandorin, the Deputy for Special Assignments to His Excellency the Governor-General. Deliver it and wait to see if there would be any return correspondence from Court Counsellor Fandorin.

That was all right – Anisii could cope with that. His spirits rose. He'd have the folder delivered quick as a flash before he even had time to start feeling chilled. Mr Fandorin's apartments were close by, right there on Malaya Nikitskaya Street, in an outbuilding on Baron von Evert-Kolokoltsev's estate.

Anisii adored Mr Fandorin – from a distance, with timid reverence, without any hope that the great man would ever notice Tulipov even existed. The Court Counsellor had a special reputation in the Department of Gendarmes, even though he served in a different department. His Excellency Efim Efimovich Baranov himself, Moscow's chief of police and a lieutenant-general, considered it no disgrace to request confidential advice or even solicit patronage from the Deputy for Special Assignments.

And that was only natural – anyone who knew anything at all about high Moscow politics knew that the father of Russia's old capital, Prince Vladimir Andreevich Dolgorukoi, favoured the Court Counsellor and paid attention to his opinions. All sorts of things were said about Mr Fandorin: for instance, he was supposed to have a special gift for seeing right through anybody and spotting even his very darkest secret in an instant.

The Court Counsellor's duties made him the Governor-General's eyes and ears in all secret Moscow business that came under the aegis of the gendarmes and the police. That was why the information that Erast Petrovich required was delivered to him every day from General Baranov and the Department of Gendarmes, usually to the Governor's house on Tverskaya Street, but sometimes to his home, because the Court Counsellor's work routine was free, and he had no need to go to the office if he did not wish.

That was the kind of important person Mr Fandorin was, but even so he had a simple manner with people and he didn't put on airs. Twice Anisii had delivered packages to him at Tverskaya Street and been completely overwhelmed by the courteous manners of such an influential individual: he would never humiliate the little man, he always spoke respectfully, always offered you a seat.

And it was very interesting to get a close look at an individual about whom the most fantastic rumours circulated in Moscow. You could see straight away that he was a special man: that handsome, smooth, young face, that raven-black hair touched with grey at the temples; that calm, quiet way of speaking, with the slight stammer, but every word to the point, and he obviously wasn't used to having to say the same thing twice. An impressive kind of gentleman, no two ways about it.

Tulipov had not been to the Court Counsellor's home before and so, as he walked in through the openwork cast-iron gates with a crown on the top and approached the stylish single-storey outhouse, his heart was fluttering slightly. Such an exceptional man was bound to live in a special kind of place.

He pressed the button of the electric bell. He had prepared his first phrase earlier: 'Courier Tulipov from the Department of Gendarmes with documents for His Honour.' Then he remembered and tucked his obstinate right ear in under his cap.

The carved-oak door swung open. Standing there in the doorway was a short stocky oriental – with narrow little eyes, fat cheeks and coarse, spiky black hair. The oriental was dressed in green livery with gold braiding and, rather oddly, straw sandals.

The servant gazed in annoyance at the visitor and asked: 'Wha' you wan'?'

From somewhere inside the house a rich woman's voice said: 'Masa! How many times do I have to tell you! Not "What you want?" but "What can I do for you"!'

The oriental cast an angry glance back into the house and muttered unwillingly to Anisii: 'Wha' can do f'you?'

'Courier Tulipov from the Department of Gendarmes with documents for His Honour.'

'All righ', come,' the servant invited him, and moved aside to let him through.

Tulipov found himself in a spacious hallway. He looked around curiously and for a moment was disappointed: there was no stuffed bear with a silver tray for calling cards, and how could a gentleman's apartment not have a stuffed bear? Or did no one come calling on the Deputy for Special Assignments?

But even though there was no bear to be seen, the hallway was furnished very nicely indeed, and there was a glass cupboard in the corner with some peculiar kind of armour, all made out of little metal plates, with a complicated monogram on the chest and a helmet with horns like a beetle's.

An exceptionally beautiful woman glanced out through the door leading to the inner rooms – into which, of course, a courier could not be admitted. She was wearing a red dressing gown that reached right down to the floor. The beauty's thick, dark hair was arranged in a complicated style, leaving her slim neck exposed; her hands were crossed over her full breasts and her fingers were covered with rings.

The lady gave Anisii a disappointed look from her huge black eyes, wrinkled up her classic nose slightly and called out: 'Erast, it's for you. From the office.'

For some reason Anisii felt surprised that the Court Counsellor was married, although in principle there was nothing surprising in such a man having a lovely spouse, with a regal bearing and haughty gaze.

Madame Fandorin yawned aristocratically, without parting her lips, and disappeared back through the door, and a moment later Mr Fandorin himself came out into the hallway.

He was also wearing a dressing gown, not red, but black, with tassels and a silk belt.

'Hello, T-Tulipov,' said the Court Counsellor, fingering a string of green jade beads, and Anisii was simply overwhelmed with delight; he had never have expected Erast Petrovich to remember him, especially by name – there must be plenty of petty minions who delivered packages to him – but there it was.

'What's that you have there? Give it to me. And go through into the drawing room, sit down for a while. Masa, take M-Mr Tulipov's coat.'

Anisii walked timidly into the drawing room, not daring to gape all around, and sat down modestly on the edge of a chair upholstered with blue velvet. It was only a little while later that he started gazing stealthily around him.

It was an interesting room: all the walls were hung with coloured Japanese prints, which Anisii knew were very fashionable nowadays. He also spotted some scrolls with hiero-glyphs and two curved sabres, one longer and one shorter, on a lacquered wooden stand.

The Court Counsellor rustled the documents, occasionally marking something in them with a little gold pencil. His wife paid no attention to the men and stood at the window, looking out into the garden with a bored air.

'My dear,' she said in French, 'why don't we ever go anywhere? It really is quite intolerable. I want society, I want to go to the theatre, I want to go to a ball.'

'Addy, you yourself s-said that it's inappropriate,' replied Fan-dorin, looking up from his documents. 'We might meet acquaintances of yours from Petersburg. It would be awkward. For me, personally, it's all the same.'

He glanced at Tulipov, and the courier blushed. Well, he wasn't to blame – was he? – if he understood French, even with some difficulty.

So it turned out that the beautiful lady was not Madame Fandorin at all.

'Ah, forgive me, Addy,' Erast Petrovich said in Russian. 'I haven't introduced Mr Tulipov to you; he works in the Depart-ment of Gendarmes. And this is Countess Ariadna Arkadievna Opraksina, my g-good friend.'

Anisii had the impression that the Court Counsellor hesitated slightly, as if he weren't quite sure how to describe the beautiful woman. Or perhaps it was simply the stammer that made it seem that way.

'Oh, God,' Countess Addy sighed in a long-suffering voice, and walked rapidly out of the room.

Almost immediately her voice rang out again: 'Masa, get away from my Natalya immediately! Off to your room with you right now, you vile girl! No, this is simply unbearable!'

Erast Petrovich also sighed and went back to reading the documents.

At that point Tulipov heard the tinkling of the doorbell, muffled by the noise of voices from the hallway, and the oriental he had seen earlier came tumbling into the drawing room like a rubber ball. He started jabbering away in some foreign mumbo-jumbo, but Fandorin gestured for him to be quiet.

'Masa, I've told you: when we have visitors, speak to me in Russian, not Japanese.'

Promoted to the rank of visitor, Anisii assumed a dignified air and peered curiously at the servant.

'From Vedisev-san,' Masa declared curtly.

'From Vedishchev? From Frol Grigorievich? Show him in.'

Anisii knew who Frol Grigorievich Vedishchev was all right. He was a well-known character, nicknamed 'the Grey Cardinal'. He had been with Prince Dolgorukoi since his childhood, first as an errand boy, then as an orderly, then as a manservant, and for the last twenty years as his personal valet – since Vladimir Andreevich had taken the ancient city into the tight grip of his firm hands. The valet might seem to be small fry, but it was well known that the clever and cautious Dolgorukoi never took any important decisions without first consulting his faithful Frol. If you wanted to approach His Excellency with an important request, first you had to cajole and convince Vedishchev, and then you could consider the job already half-done.

An energetic fellow in the Governor's livery walked or, rather, ran into the drawing room and started jabbering from the doorway.

'Your Honour, Frol Grigorievich wants you to come. He insists you must come to see him as a matter of great urgency! It's a real rumpus, Erast Petrovich, a real rumpus! Frol Grigorievich says we can't manage without you! I'm in the Prince's sleigh; we'll be there in an instant.'

'What kind of "rumpus" is this?' the Court Counsellor asked with a frown, but he stood up and took off his dressing gown to reveal a white shirt and black tie. 'All right, let's go and t-take a look. Masa, my waistcoat and frock coat, and look lively!' called Fandorin, stuffing the documents into the folder. 'And you, Tulipov, will have to ride along with me. I'll finish reading these on the way.'

Anisii was quite willing to follow His Honour anywhere at all, as he demonstrated by hastily leaping up off his chair.

This was something the courier Tulipov had never imagined – that one day he would take a ride in the Governor-General's closed sleigh.

It was a noble sleigh, a genuine carriage on runners. Inside it was upholstered in satin, the seats were Russian leather, and in the corner there was a little stove with a bronze flue, though it wasn't lit. The servant sat on the coachbox and Dolgorukoi's foursome of dashing trotters set off at a spanking pace.

As Anisii was swayed smoothly, almost gently, to and fro on the soft seat intended for far more noble buttocks, he thought to himself: Ah, no one will ever believe this.

Mr Fandorin cracked the sealing wax as he opened some despatch. He wrinkled his high, clear forehead. How very handsome he is, Tulipov thought with no envy, in genuine admiration, glancing sideways to observe the Court Counsellor tugging on his slim moustache.

After rushing them to the big house on Tverskaya Street in five minutes, the sleigh did not turn to the left, towards the office, but to the right, towards the formal entrance and the personal chambers of Vladimir Andreevich Dolgorukoi, 'the Great Prince of Moscow' (which was by no means the only nickname the all-powerful Governor had acquired).

'I beg your pardon, Tulipov,' Fandorin said hurriedly as he opened the little carriage door, 'but I can't let you go just yet. I'll jot down a couple of lines for the c-colonel later. But first I must sort out this little rumpus.'

Anisii followed Erast Petrovich out of the sleigh and into the grand marble palace, but then immediately dropped behind, intimidated by the sight of the imposing doorman with the gilded mace. Tulipov suddenly felt terribly afraid of being humiliated, concerned that Mr Fandorin would leave him to cool his heels below stairs, like some little puppy dog. But he overcame his pride and prepared to forgive the Court Counsellor: after all, how could you take a man into the Governor's apartments in a coat like this and a cap with a cracked peak?

'What are you doing stuck back there?' Erast Petrovich asked impatiently, turning round. He was already halfway up the stairs.

'Don't fall behind. You can see what a devil of a mess we have here.'

It was only then that Anisii finally realised that there really was something quite extraordinary going on in the Governor's house. If you looked closely, even the exalted doorman had an air that was not so much grand as confused. There were some brisk, rough-looking fellows carrying trunks, boxes and crates with foreign lettering on them into the hallway from the street. Was someone moving then?

Tulipov hopped and skipped up the stairs to the Court Counsellor and tried to keep within two paces of him, which meant that at times he had to trot in an undignified manner, because His Honour walked with a long and rapid stride.

Oh, how beautiful it was in the Governor's residence! Almost like in a church: variegated columns (perhaps they were porphyry?), brocade door curtains, statues of Greek goddesses. And the chandeliers! And the pictures in gold frames! And the parquet gleaming like a mirror, with those inlaid patterns!

Looking round at the parquet, Anisii suddenly noticed that his disgraceful shoes were leaving a dirty, wet trail on the wonderful floor. Oh Lord, don't let anyone notice that, he thought.

In a spacious hall that was completely deserted but had armchairs standing along the walls, the Court Counsellor said: 'Sit here. And hold the folder.'

He set off towards the tall, gilded doors, but they suddenly swung open to meet him. First there was a confused hubbub of voices in heated conversation, and then four men came out into the hall: a stately general, a lanky individual who did not look Russian wearing a check coat with a cape, a bald, skinny old man with absolutely immense sideburns and a civil functionary in uniform, wearing spectacles.

Recognising the general as Prince Dolgorukoi himself, Anisii quivered and drew himself up to attention.

From close up His Excellency did not look as fresh and sprightly as he appeared when viewed from a crowd: his face was covered with immensely deep wrinkles, his curls were unnaturally luxuriant, and the chestnut-brown of his long moustache and sideburns was too rich for a man of seventy-five.

'Erast Petrovich, just in time!' exclaimed the Governor. 'He mangles his French so badly you can't understand a thing, and he hasn't got a single word of Russian. You know English. So please explain what he wants from me! And how he was ever admitted! I've been trying to make sense of him for the best part of an hour, but it's a waste of time!'

'Your Excellency, how could we not have admitted him, when he's a lord and he visits the house,' the functionary in spectacles whined plaintively, clearly not for the first time. 'How could I have known . . .'

At this point the Englishman also started speaking, addressing the new man and indignantly waving some piece of paper covered with seals in the air.

Erast Petrovich began translating dispassionately: 'This is a dishonest game; they don't do things like this in civilised countries. I was with this old gentleman yesterday; he signed a bill of sale for the house and we sealed the agreement with a handshake. And now, you see, he has decided not to move out. His grandson, Mr Speier, told me that the old gentleman was moving to a home for veterans of the Napoleonic Wars; he will be more comfortable there, because the care is good, and this mansion was for sale. This kind of dithering does him no credit, especially when the money has already been paid. And a large sum, too – a hundred thousand roubles. Here is the bill of sale!'

'He's been waving yon piece of paper around for ages, but he won't let us have it,' remarked the bald old man, who had so far remained silent. Obviously he must be Frol Grigorievich Vedishchev.

'I'm Speier's grandfather?' the Prince babbled. 'They're putting me in an almshouse?'

The functionary stole up to the Englishman from behind, stood on tiptoe and managed to sneak a glimpse at the mysterious sheet of paper.

'It really does say a hundred thousand, and it's been witnessed by a notary,' he confirmed. 'And it's our address: the house of Prince Dolgorukoi, Tverskaya Street.'

Fandorin asked: 'Vladimir Andreevich, who is this Speier?'

Prince Dolgorukoi mopped his scarlet brow with a handkerchief and shrugged. 'Speier is a very pleasant young man with excellent references. He was presented to me at the Christmas ball by . . . mmm . . . who was it now? Ah, no, now I remember. It wasn't at the ball. He was recommended to me in a special letter by His Highness the Duke of Saxen-Limburg. Speier is a very fine, courteous young fellow, with a heart of gold, and very unfortunate. He was in the Kushka campaign, wounded in the back, and since then he can't move his legs. He gets around in a wheelchair, but he hasn't let it get him down. He does charitable work, collects contributions for orphans and contributes huge sums himself. He was here yesterday morning with this mad Englishman, who he said was the well-known British philanthropist Lord Pitsbrook. He asked me to allow him to show the Englishman round the mansion, because His Lordship is a connoisseur and lover of architecture. How could I refuse poor Speier such a trifling request? Innokenty here accompanied them.' Dolgorukoi jabbed his finger angrily towards the functionary, who threw his hands up in the air despairingly.

'Your Excellency, how could I have . . . You told me yourself to be as helpful as I possibly could . . . '

'Did you shake Lord Pitsbrook's hand?' asked Fandorin, and Anisii thought he caught the glint of a spark in the Court Counsellor's eyes.

'Why, naturally,' the Prince said with a shrug. 'First Speier told him something about me in English, then the lanky fellow beamed and reached for my hand to shake it.'

'And d-did you sign some kind of document before that?'

The Governor knitted his brows as he tried to remember. 'Yes, Speier asked me to sign the speech of welcome for the newly re-opened Catherine the Great Girls' Home. Such sacred work – re-educating juvenile harlots. But I didn't sign any bill of sale! You know me, dear fellow: I always read everything I sign very carefully.'

'And then what did he do with the address?'

'I think he showed it to the Englishman, said something and put it in a folder. The folder was lying in his wheelchair.' Dolgorukoi's face, already menacing, turned as dark as a storm cloud. 'Ah, *merde*! Could he really ...'

Erast Petrovich addressed the lord in English, apparently succeeding in winning the son of Albion's complete confidence, because he was given the mysterious sheet of paper to study.

'All drawn up in due form,' the Court Counsellor muttered, running his glance over the bill of sale. 'With an official seal and a stamp from the "Möbius" notary's office and the signature ... What on earth!' An expression of extreme perplexity appeared on Fandorin's face. 'Vladimir Andreevich, look here! Look at the signature!'

The Prince took hold of the piece of paper disdainfully, as if it were a toad, and held it as far away as he could from his long-sighted eyes. He read out loud: '"Jack of Spades" ... I beg your pardon, what does this "Jack" mean?'

'Well, well, well ...' Vedishchev drawled. 'That's clear then. The Jack of Spades again. Well, well. Our Lady in Heaven, what a turn-up this is.'

'The Jack of Spades?' said His Excellency, still unable to make any sense of anything. 'But that's the name of a band of swindlers – the ones who sold the banker Polyakov his own trotters last month, and helped the merchant Vinogradov pan for gold dust in the River Setuni at Christmas. Barabanov reported to me about them. We're looking for them, he said, the villains. I laughed at the time. But have they really dared try to swindle me – me, Dolgorukoi?' The Governor-General tore open his gold-embroidered collar and his face took on such a terrible expression that Anisii pulled his head back down into his shoulders.

Vedishchev fluttered across to the furious Prince like a startled hen and started clucking: 'Vladim Andreich, everyone makes mistakes sometimes; why distress yourself so? I'll get your valerian drops and call the doctor to let your blood! Innokenty, give me a chair!'

However, Anisii was first to reach the Governor with a chair.

They sat the overwrought Prince down on the soft seat, but he kept struggling to stand up and pushing away his valet.

'Like some petty merchant or other! Do they take me for a boy? I'll give them the almshouse!' he cried incoherently. Vedishchev made all sorts of reassuring sounds and once even stroked His Excellency's dyed – or perhaps false – curls.

The Governor turned to Fandorin and said plaintively: 'Erast Petrovich, my friend, what is going on here? They've got completely out of hand, these bandits. In my person they have insulted, abased and mocked the whole of Moscow. Call out all the police and the gendarmes, but find the villains. I want them tried! Sent to Siberia! You can do anything, my dear fellow. From now on, regard this as your most important job, a personal request from me. Baranov won't be able to manage on his own; he can assist you.'

'We can't possibly use the police,' the Court Counsellor replied thoughtfully. There were no sparks glittering in Fandorin's eyes now; his face expressed nothing except concern for the reputation of the authorities. 'If the word spreads, the entire c-city will split its sides laughing. We can't allow that to happen.'

'I beg your pardon,' said Dolgorukoi, growing furious again. 'Then what are we supposed to do – just let these "Jacks" get away with it?'

'Under no circumstances. I shall handle this m-matter. But confidentially, with no publicity.' Fandorin thought for a while and continued: 'Lord Pitsbrook's money will have to be repaid out of the municipal t-treasury and we shall have to apologise to him, but not explain anything about the "Jack". We'll say it was all a misunderstanding. Your grandson took too much upon himself.'

On hearing his name mentioned, the Englishman agitatedly asked the Court Counsellor about something.

Fandorin replied briefly and turned back to the Governor: 'Vedishchev will think of something that will satisfy the servants' curiosity. And I'll start searching.'

'But how can you find such a set of rogues all on your own?' the valet asked doubtfully.

'Yes, it will not be easy. But it is not desirable to extend the circle of people who know about this.' Fandorin glanced at the secretary in spectacles, whom the Prince had called Innokenty, and shook his head. Innokenty was obviously not suitable as an assistant. Then he turned towards Anisii, and Anisii's blood ran cold at the sudden keen awareness of how unpresentable he appeared: young and skinny with ears that jutted out, and covered in pimples as well.

'I won't ... I won't say a word,' he babbled. 'My word of honour.'

'And who is this?' roared His Excellency the Governor, who had apparently only just noticed the pitiful figure of the courier. 'Why is he here?'

'This is Tulipov,' explained Fandorin, 'from the Department of Gendarmes. An experienced agent. It is he who is going to assist me.'

The Prince ran his glance over the cowering Anisii and knitted his brows menacingly. 'Now, you listen here, Tulipov. Make yourself useful, and I'll make a man of you. Make a mess of things and I'll grind you into dust.'

As Erast Petrovich and the dumbfounded Anisii walked towards the stairs, they heard Vedishchev say: 'As you wish, Vladim Andreich, but there's no money in the treasury. A hundred thousand is no joke. The Englishman will have to make do with an apology.'

Outside there was another shock in store for Tulipov. As he pulled on his gloves, the Court Counsellor suddenly asked him: 'Is it true what I've been told – that you support an invalid sister and have refused to give her into public care?'

Anisii had not expected such detailed knowledge of his domestic circumstances, but in his stunned condition, he was less surprised than he ought to have been. 'She can't go into public care,' he explained. 'She'd pine away. The poor simpleton is far too used to me.'

That was when Fandorin really astounded him. 'I envy you,' he sighed. 'You're a fortunate man, Tulipov. At such a young age you already have reason to respect yourself – something you can be proud of. The Lord has given you a firm core for the whole of your life.'

Anisii was still trying to grasp the meaning of these strange words when the Court Counsellor continued: 'Do not be concerned about your sister. Hire a nurse for her for the period of the investigation. At public expense, naturally. From this moment on until the case of the Jack of Spades is closed you will be at my disposal. We shall be working together for a while. I hope you won't find it too b-boring.'

This was his unexpected happiness, Tulipov suddenly realised. This was his good fortune.

Praise be for the white dove!

CHAPTER 2

The Science of Life
According to Momos

In recent years he had changed his name so often that he had almost forgotten the original one, the one he had been born with. And in his own mind he had long since referred to himself as 'Momos'.

Momos is the name of a spiteful ancient Greek jester, the son of Nyx, the goddess of night. In a prophecy of the 'Egyptian Pythia', the same name is given to the jack of spades, a bad card that promises a meeting with a scoffing fool or a malicious trick of fortune.

Momos was fond of cards and even had a profound respect for them, but he didn't believe in fortune-telling and the meaning he invested in his chosen name was quite different.

It is well known that every mortal plays a game of cards with destiny. The cards that are dealt do not depend on man; you have to take what you are given: some will get nothing but trumps, others nothing but twos and threes. Nature had dealt Momos middling cards – rubbish, you could say: tens and jacks. But a good player will make a fight of it even with cards like that.

In terms of the human hierarchy, too, it was the jack that suited him best. Momos's assessment of himself was a sober one: he was no ace, of course, and no king, but he was no worthless card either. So he was a jack. But not some boring old jack of clubs or respectable jack of diamonds or – God forbid – sentimental, drooling jack of hearts, but a special jack, the jack of spades. Spades were a complex suit, the most junior suit in all the games except for bridge, in which they outranked clubs and hearts and diamonds. The conclusion was: decide for yourself what game you are going to play with life, and your suit will be the main one.

In his early childhood Momos had been obsessed by the Russian saying about chasing two hares at once. Why, he used to wonder in bewilderment, was it not possible to catch both of them? Did you just have to abandon one of them, then? Little Momos (he wasn't Momos yet; he was still Mitenka Savvin) definitely did not agree with that. And he had turned out to be absolutely right. The saying had proved to be a stupid one, designed for the dull-witted and lazy. On occasions Momos had managed to catch not just one or two long-eared, fluffy grey animals at once, but many of them. For that he had his own psychological theory, which he had developed specially.

People had invented many sciences, and most of them were of no benefit to a normal man, but they carried on writing treatises, defending their master's and doctoral dissertations, becoming members of academies. Ever since he was very little, Momos had been able to sense with his very skin, his bones, his spleen that the most important branch of learning was not arithmetic or Latin, but *the ability to please.* That was the key with which it was possible to open any door. It was strange, though, that this most important knowledge was never imparted by tutors or grammar-school teachers. He had had to discover its laws for himself. But if you thought about it for a moment, that was actually to his advantage. The boy had shown a talent for this most important branch of learning early on, and he could only thank God that others were unaware of the advantages of this discipline.

For some reason ordinary people failed to pay this crucial activity the serious attention it deserved. They thought: If someone likes me, that's good; if they don't, then that's just too bad – you can't force anyone to like you. Oh yes, you can, Mitenka thought as he grew up, you certainly can. And once you've made someone like you, managed to find the key that fits him, that person is yours to do with as you like.

It turned out that you could make anyone like you, and very little was required to do it – just to understand what kind of

21

person they were, how they saw the world, what they were afraid of. And once you'd understood that, you could play them like a reed pipe, and choose your own melody. A serenade if you liked, or a polka.

Nine out of ten people would tell you everything about themselves if you were just willing to listen. The astounding thing was that nobody listened to anybody else properly. In the best case, if people were well brought up, they would wait for a pause in the conversation before mounting their own hobbyhorse again. But you could find out so many important and interesting things if you just knew how to listen!

Listening properly was a kind of art. You had to imagine that you were an empty bottle, a transparent vessel connected with the person you were talking to via an invisible tube, and let the contents of the other person flow into you a drop at a time, so that you were filled with liquid that was the same colour and strength, the same composition – to stop being yourself for a while and become him. And then you would come to understand that person's essential being, and you would know in advance what he was going to say and what he was going to do.

Momos mastered his science gradually and in his early years he applied it in a small way, for limited gain, but mostly for purposes of checking and experimenting: to obtain a good mark at his grammar school without having learned the lesson; then later, at military school, to win the respect and affection of his comrades; to make a girl fall in love with him.

Later, when he had joined the regiment and his skill and control had grown rather more sure, the benefits that it brought became more significant. For instance, you could clean out a man with money at cards, and he would sit there calmly and not take offence at this fine young chap, the Cornet Mitya Savvin. And he wouldn't stare at your hands any more than necessary. That was not bad, surely?

But all this had only been gymnastic exercises for developing the muscles. His knowledge and talent had come in genuinely useful six years earlier, when destiny had offered the future

Momos his first real Chance. He hadn't yet known at that time that a Chance ought not to be fished for, but created. He had kept waiting for good fortune to swim into his hands of its own accord, and the only thing he had been afraid of was that he might let it slip.

He hadn't.

At the time things in general were looking pretty mouldy for the young cornet. The regiment had been stationed in the provincial city of Smolensk for more than a year, and every opportunity to apply his talents had already been exhausted. He had won money at cards from everyone he could; everything he could borrow had been borrowed long ago; the colonel's wife loved Mitya with all her heart, but she was tight-fisted with money, and her jealousy exhausted him. And then there was his little slip with the remount money: Cornet Savvin had been sent to the horse fair at Torzhok, where he had got quite carried away and spent more than was permitted.

The general outlook was that he could either be taken to court, or make a run for it, or marry the merchant Pochechuev's pimply daughter. The first option, of course, was out of the question, and the capable young man was hesitating between the second and the third.

Then suddenly fortune had tossed him a trump widow card that might well be just enough for him to save his doomed hand. His great-aunt, a Vyatka landowner, bequeathed her estate to her favourite nephew. Once, when he was still a cadet, Mitenka had spent an extremely boring month with her and, for lack of anything better to do, had practised his science of life a little. Afterwards he had completely forgotten the old woman and never thought of her, but his aunt had not forgotten the dear, quiet little boy. It was certainly no vast latifundium that Mitya had inherited: only a miserable thousand acres, and that in some back-of-beyond province where it was shameful for a respectable man to spend even a week.

How would an ordinary, unexceptional little cornet have behaved if he had had such a stroke of luck? He would have sold the inheritance from his great-aunt to cover the shortfall in the remount money, paid off some of his debts and carried on living in the same old way, the stupid fool.

Well, how else? you may ask.

Allow me to set you a little problem. You have an estate that is worth at best twenty-five, perhaps thirty thousand roubles. But you have debts amounting to a full fifty thousand. And, most important of all, you are sick to death of counting the kopecks, you want to live a decent life, with a good carriage, in the finest hotels; you want life always to taste sweet: you don't want to be kept by the colonel's fat wife, you want to acquire a fine, fragrant buttonhole of your own, a tuberose with tender eyes, a slim waist and a lilting laugh.

I've had enough of drifting along the river of life like a splinter of wood, Mitenka decided; it's time to take destiny by its long swan neck. And that was when the science of psychology came in truly useful.

He did not spend just a week or even two in that remote province; he lived there for three whole months. He rode around visiting the neighbours and succeeded in making each of them like him in their own way. With the retired major, a churlish recluse and boor, he drank rum and hunted a bear (and that really gave him a fright). With the collegiate counsellor's wife, a thrifty widow, he made jam out of paradise apples and wrote down advice about farrowing pigs in a little book. With the district marshal of the nobility, who had never graduated from the Corps of Pages, he discussed the news of the great world. With the justice of the peace he visited the gypsy camp on the other side of the river.

He was rather successful: at one and the same time he was a simple chap, a wild character from the capital, a serious young man, a bold spirit, a 'new man', a devotee of the old times and also a certain candidate for a bridegroom (in two families unacquainted with each other).

And when he decided that the soil had been sufficiently manured, he carried the entire business off in just two days.

Even now, years later, when you might think he had plenty of other things to remember and be proud of, Momos enjoyed going over the memory of his first genuine 'operation' – especially the episode with Euripides Callistratovich Kandelaki, who had a reputation among the local landowners as the greatest skinflint and addict of lawsuits ever to walk the earth. Of course, he could have got by without Kandelaki, but Mitenka was young and passionate then; he enjoyed the challenge of cracking tough nuts.

The niggardly Greek was a retired revenue officer. There's only one way to make a man of that sort like you: create the illusion that he can turn a profit at your expense.

The bold cornet galloped up to his neighbour's house on a lathered horse, flushed bright red, with tears in his eyes and his hands trembling. From the doorway he howled: 'Euripides Callistratovich, save me! You are my only hope! I confide in you as my confessor! They've summoned me back to the regiment, to the auditor! I embezzled some money! Twenty-two thousand!'

He really did have a letter from the regiment – concerning the indiscretion with the remount funds. The colonel had lost patience with waiting for Savvin to return from leave.

Mitya took out the envelope with the regimental seal and one other document as well. 'In a month's time I am due to receive a loan of twenty-five thousand from the Nobles' Land Bank secured against my aunt's estate. I thought,' he sobbed, knowing perfectly well that the Greek could not possibly be moved to pity, 'that I would get the money and cover the shortfall. But I won't have enough time! The shame of it! There's only one thing left for me – a bullet in the forehead! Save me, Euripides Callistratovich, my dear fellow! Give me twenty-two thousand, and I'll have a power of attorney drawn up for you to receive the loan. I'll go back to the regiment, make amends, save my honour and my life. And in a month you'll receive twenty-five thousand. Profit for you and salvation for me! I implore you!'

Kandelaki put on his spectacles, read the ominous letter from the regiment and carefully studied the mortgage agreement with the bank (also genuine, drawn up in due, correct form) chewed on his lips for a while and offered fifteen thousand. He finally settled on nineteen.

The scene in the bank a month later must have been truly remarkable, when the owners of the eleven powers of attorney issued by Mitya all turned up at once. His profits were pretty good, only after that, of course, he had had to change his life in the most radical manner. But to hell with his former life; he didn't regret it at all.

The former Cornet Savvin was not afraid of any difficulties with the police. The Empire, thank the Lord, was a big one, there were plenty of fools in it and more than enough rich towns. A man of imagination and spirit would always find scope for his ingenious pranks. And a new name and papers were a trifling matter. He could call himself whatever he wanted. He could be whoever he wanted.

As for his appearance, that was where Momos had been exceptionally lucky. He was very fond of his own face and could spend hours admiring it in the mirror. Hair a wonderful pale blondish-brown colour, like the overwhelming majority of the indigenous Slavonic population. Small, expressionless features, small grey-blue eyes, a nose of indefinite shape, a weak, characterless chin. All in all, absolutely nothing to hold the eye's attention. Not a physiognomy, but a blank canvas – paint whatever you like on it.

Average height, with no distinguishing features. The voice, it is true, was unusual – deep and resonant; but Momos had learned to control this instrument with consummate skill: he could boom in a deep bass and beguile in a charming tenor, squeak in a falsetto and even squeal a little in a female soprano.

In order to change one's appearance and become unrecognisable, it is not enough simply to dye one's hair and glue on a beard. A man is made up of his facial expressions, his way of walking and sitting down, his gestures, intonations, the special little words he uses in conversation, the force of his glance. And, of course, his ambience – the clothes, the first impression, the name, the title.

If actors had earned big money, Momos would certainly have

become a new Shchepkin or Sadovsky – he could sense that he had it in him. But no one paid the kind of sums he wanted, not even to leading actors in the theatres of the capital. And in any case, it was so much more interesting to act out plays not on the stage, with fifteen-minute intervals, but in real life, every day, from morning till night.

Who had he not played during the last six years? – it was impossible to remember all the roles. And what was more, every play had been entirely his own creation. Following the manner of military strategy, Momos referred to them as 'operations', and before the beginning of a new adventure he liked to imagine himself as Maurice of Saxony or Napoleon. But, of course, these were not sanguinary battles that he planned, but diverting amusements. That is, the other dramatis personae might not perhaps fully appreciate the wittiness of the plot, but Momos himself was always left entirely satisfied.

Many performances had been played out – both small and large, genuinely triumphant and less successful – but so far there had not been a single flop followed by booing and whistling.

At one time Momos had developed an interest in immortalising the memory of national heroes. The first time, after losing at whist on a Volga steamer and going ashore in Kostroma without a single kopeck to his name, he had tried collecting contributions for a bronze monument to Ivan Susanin. But the local merchants had been stingy, the landed gentry had tried to make their contributions in butter or rye, and the outcome had been a mere trifle – less than eight thousand. In Odessa, though, the contributions paid for a monument to Alexander Sergeevich Pushkin had been generous, especially from the Jewish merchants, and in Tobolsk the fur traders and gold miners had stumped up seventy-five thousand to the eloquent 'member of the Imperial Historical Society' for a monument to Yermak Timofeevich, the conqueror of Siberia.

The year before last the Butterfly Credit Union had proved a great success in Nizhny Novgorod. The idea had been simple and brilliant, designed for that extremely common breed of people whose belief in free miracles is stronger than their natural caution. Butterfly had taken loans from the locals at a fantastically high rate of interest. The first week, only ten people put their money in (nine of them decoys, hired by Momos himself). However, next Monday, when they all received ten kopecks for every rouble invested – the interest was paid out weekly – the town seemed to go insane. A queue three blocks long formed at the company's office. A week later Momos again paid out ten per cent, after which he had to rent another two offices and hire twelve new assistants to take in the money. On the fourth Monday the doors of the offices remained locked. The rainbow-winged Butterfly had fluttered on its way, quitting the banks of the Volga for ever in search of pastures new.

For any other man the pickings from Nizhny Novgorod would have been enough to last the rest of his life, but Momos never hung on to money for very long. Sometimes he imagined that he was a windmill fed by a broad stream of bank notes and jingling coins. The windmill waved its broad sails through the air, knowing no respite, transforming the money into the fine flour of diamond tie pins, thoroughbred trotters, wild sprees that lasted for days, breathtaking bouquets for actresses. But the wind always kept on blowing, and the flour was scattered into the boundless distance, and not a single speck remained.

Well, let it scatter, there was enough 'grain' to last Momos for ever. There would always be grist for the miraculous windmill.

He had made a thorough tour of all the trade fairs and provincial towns, constantly developing his skill. Last year he had reached the capital, St Petersburg, and cleaned up quite handsomely. The suppliers to the royal court, crafty bankers and commercial counsellors would not soon forget the Jack of Spades.

It was only quite recently that Momos had thought of declaring his exceptional gift to the public. He had succumbed to the blandishments of the imp of vanity, and begun to feel slighted. All those incomparably talented capers he had thought up, all that imagination and skill and passion he had invested, and there was no recognition for it. The blame was always lumped on to some band of swindlers, or Jewish plots, or the local authorities.

And the good people of Russia were unaware that all these elaborate *chefs-d'œuvre* were the work of a single master.

Money was no longer enough for Momos; he wanted fame. Of course, it was much riskier to work with a trade mark, but fame was never won by the faint-hearted. And just you try to catch him, when he had his mask prepared for every operation! Who were you supposed to catch? Who should you be searching for? Had anyone ever seen Momos's genuine face? Well then . . .

'Gasp and gossip and laugh in farewell' was Momos's mental valediction to his fellow-countrymen. 'Applaud a great artist, for I shall not be with you for ever.'

No, he wasn't preparing to die – not at all; but he had begun thinking seriously about parting with the Russian expanses that were so dear to his heart. There was just the old capital to work over, and then the time would be exactly right for Momos to make his debut on the international stage – he could feel that he was already strong enough to do it.

The wonderful city of Moscow. The Muscovites were even more stupid than the Petersburgians, more open-hearted and less callous, and they had just as much money. Momos had been based here since the autumn and had already pulled off several elegant swindles. Another two or three operations and it would be 'Farewell, my native land!' He ought to take a stroll around Europe and a look at America. They said many interesting things about the North American states. His instinct told him he would find the space to spread his wings there. He could launch a campaign to dig some canal, organise a stockholding company to construct a trans-American railroad or, say, to search for Aztec gold. And then again, German princes were in great demand just then, especially in the new Slav countries and on the South American continent. That was something worth thinking about. Indeed, in his prudent manner, Momos had already taken certain measures.

But for the time being, he had business in Moscow. He could go on shaking the apples off this tree for a long time yet. Give him time, and the writers of Moscow would be writing novels about the Jack of Spades.

The morning after the amusing caper with the English lord and the old governor, Momos woke late, with a headache – he had been celebrating all evening and half the night. Mimi just adored celebrations; they were her natural element, so they had had glorious fun.

The mischievous girl had transformed their deluxe suite in the Metropole Hotel into a Garden of Eden: tropical hothouse plants in tubs, the chandelier completely covered with chrysanthemums and lilies, the carpet littered with rose petals, baskets of fruit from Eliseev and bouquets from Pogodin everywhere. A python from Morselli's menagerie was looped round the palms in patterned coils, imitating the original Serpent Tempter – not very convincingly, however: because it was winter, the serpent dozed all the time and never once opened its eyes. But Mimi, in her role as Eve, was on top form. As he remembered, Momos smiled and rubbed his aching temple. That cursed Veuve Clicquot. When, after the fall had already taken place, Momos was luxuriating in the spacious porcelain bath tub, surrounded by floating Wanda orchids (at fifteen roubles apiece), Mimi had showered him with champagne from huge bottles. He had obviously been too zealous in striving to catch the frothing stream in his lips.

But yesterday even Mimi had worn herself out with her gambolling. Look at the way she was sleeping – you couldn't have woken her up if there was a fire. Her slightly swollen lips were half open, she had put both hands under her cheek in the way she usually did, and her thick golden locks were scattered across the pillow.

When they'd decided that they would travel together, Momos had told her: 'A man's life, my girl, is the same as he is. If he is cruel, then life is cruel. If he is timid, then it is terrifying. If he is sour, then it is sad. But I am a jolly man and my life is jolly, and so will yours be too.'

And Mimi had fitted into the jolly life as if she had been created especially for it, although he had to assume that in her twenty-two years she must have tasted more than her share of bitter radish and mustard. But Momos had not asked her about that – it was none of his business. If she wanted to tell him, she would. But she wasn't one of those girls who cling to bad memories and she certainly wouldn't try to appeal to his pity.

He had picked Mimi up the previous spring in Kishinev, where she was passing herself off as an Ethiopian dancer in a variety show and was wildly popular with the local fast livers. She had blackened her skin, dyed and frizzed her hair, and she leapt around the stage wearing nothing but garlands of flowers, with bracelets on her arms and legs. The Kishinevians took her for an absolutely genuine Negress. That is, at first they had had their doubts, but a visiting Neapolitan merchant who had been to Abyssinia had confirmed that Mamselle Zemchandra really did speak Ethiopian, and so all doubts had been dispelled.

It was precisely this detail that had first delighted Momos, who appreciated the combination of impudence with meticulous attention to detail in hoaxes. With those blue eyes the colour of harebells and that absolutely Slavonic little face, dark as it may be, to claim to be an Ethopian – that required great daring. And to learn Ethiopian into the bargain!

Later, when they were already friends, Mimi told him how it had happened. She'd been living in Peter, all washed up after the operetta went bankrupt, when she'd managed by chance to get a job as a governess for twins, the children of the Abyssinian ambassador. The Ethiopian prince – or Rass, in their language – simply had not been able to believe his good fortune: an obliging, cheerful young lady, content with a small salary, and the children adored her – they were always whispering with her about some secrets or other, and they had begun behaving like little angels. One day the Rass had been strolling through the Summer Gardens with State Secretary Morder, discussing difficulties in Italian–Abyssinian relations, when he'd suddenly seen a crowd of people. He'd walked over to it and – Lord God of Ethiopia! – there he'd seen the governess playing an accordion and his own little son and daughter dancing and singing. The audience had been gawking at the little blackamoors, clapping and throwing

31

money into a turban made out of a twisted towel, and it was given unstintingly, from the heart.

Anyway, Mimi had been obliged to make her escape from Russia's northern capital with all possible haste – with no luggage and no residence permit. She wouldn't have minded, she sighed, but she felt so sorry for the children. Poor little Mariamchik and Asefochka – their life was probably very boring now.

But then, I'm not bored with you here, thought Momos, gazing lovingly at the shoulder protruding from under the blanket, with those three moles that formed a neat equilateral triangle.

He put his hands behind his head and gazed round the suite into which they had moved only the previous day in order to cover their tracks – a superb set of apartments, with a boudoir, a drawing room and a study. The gilded moulding was slightly overdone, a little too much in the merchant taste. The apartments in the 'Loskutnaya' had been more elegant, but it been time to move out of there – in a perfectly official manner, of course, doling out generous tips and posing for a sketch artist from the *Moscow Observer*. It would do no harm to appear on the cover of a well-respected illustrated journal in the guise of 'His Highness' – you could never tell when it might come in useful.

Momos glanced up absent-mindedly at the gilded Cupid with fat, round cheeks who had ensconced himself under the canopy of the bed. The plaster mischief-maker was aiming his arrow straight at the guest's forehead. The arrow was not visible, though, because Mimi's 'flaming heart' lacy drawers were dangling on it. How had they got up there? And where had they come from? After all, Mimi had been playing the part of Eve. It was a mystery.

Something about the astounding drawers intrigued Momos. There ought to be an arrow underneath them, and nothing more – that was obvious. But what if there was no arrow there, but something else? What if the little Cupid was cocking a snook, with his plump little fingers folded into a contemptuous gesture that was held out like an arrow beneath the bright piece of material?

Yes, yes, he could make out the outline of something.

Forgetting his aching temples, Momos sat up on the bed, still staring at the drawers.

Anyone would have expected there to be an arrow underneath them, because an arrow was what was required by Cupid's official function and capacity; but what if there really was no arrow, only a contemptuous snook?

'Wake up, my girl!' he said, slapping the sleeper on her rosy cheek. 'Look lively! Paper and a pencil! We're going to compose an announcement for the newspaper!'

Instead of replying, Mimi pulled the blanket up over her head. Momos sprang out of bed, his feet landed on something rough and cold on the carpet and he shouted out in horror: the dozy python, the Tempter of Eden, was lying there, coiled up like a garden hose.

CHAPTER 3

A Cunning Rogue

Apparently you could spend your time at work in quite different ways.

As a police sleuth – standing out in the bushes under the pouring rain for hours, watching the second window from the left on the third floor – or trudging along the street after the 'mark' who had been passed on for you to take your turn, without knowing who he was or what he had done.

Or as a courier, dashing around the city with your tongue hanging out, clutching an official satchel crammed with packages.

Or even as a temporary assistant to His Honour the Governor's Deputy for Special Assignments . . . Anisii was supposed to arrive at the outhouse on Malaya Nikitskaya Street at ten. That meant he could walk at a normal pace, not dashing through the dark side streets, not hurrying, but in a dignified manner, in the light of day. Anisii was also issued money for a cab, so he had no need to spend an hour on the journey; he could arrive at work in a carriage, like a lord. But it was all right, he didn't mind walking, and the extra fifty kopecks would always come in handy.

The door was always opened by the Japanese servant Masa, whom Anisii had already got to know well. Masa bowed and said, 'Goomorn, Tiuri-san,' which meant 'Good morning, Mr Tulipov.' The Japanese found it hard to pronounce long Russian words, and he could not manage the letter 'l' at all, so 'Tulipov' was transformed into 'Tiuri'. But Anisii did not take offence at Fandorin's valet, and their relations had become perfectly friendly, one might even say conspiratorial.

The first thing Masa did was to inform Anisii in a low voice about 'the state of the atmosphere' – that was how Anisii referred to the mood pervading the house. If the Japanese said 'Cam,' it meant everything was calm, the beautiful Countess Addy had woken in a serene mood and was singing, billing and cooing with Erast Petrovich, and she would regard Tulipov with a distracted but benevolent glance. In that case, he could enter the drawing room quiet fearlessly. Masa would serve him coffee and a roll, Mr State Counsellor would launch into cheerful banter and his favourite jade beads would clack cheerfully and briskly in his fingers.

But if Masa whispered 'Lou,' which meant 'loud', Anisii had to slip through into the study on tiptoe and set to work immediately, because the atmosphere in the house was stormy. It meant that Addy was sobbing again and screaming that she was bored, that Erast Petrovich had ruined her life by taking her away from her husband, the most worthy and most noble of men. I'm sure you're very easy to lead, thought Anisii, leafing through the newspapers as he listened timidly to the peals of thunder.

That was his job in the morning now: to study the printed publications of the city of Moscow. It was pleasant work: you rustled the pages smelling of ink, reading about the rumours of the city and examining the tempting advertising announcements. There were sharp-pointed pencils on the desk, blue for ordinary marks, red for special notes. Yes indeed, Anisii's life was quite different now.

And by the way, the pay for such wonderful work was also twice as much as he had received before, and he had been promoted in the state rankings too. Erast Petrovich had dashed off a couple of lines to the department and Tulipov had immediately been made a candidate for a formal title. When the first vacancy arose, he would sit a trifling examination and that would be it – the former courier would be an official, Mr Collegiate Registrar.

This was how it had all begun.

On that memorable day when the white dove appeared to

Anisii, he and Court Counsellor Fandorin went straight from the Governor's house to the notary's office that had registered the bill of sale with the scoffing signature. Alas, behind the door with the bronze plaque that read *Ivan Karlovich Möbius*, they found nothing. The titular counsellor's wife Kapustina, whose house it was, had opened the locked door with her own key and testified that Mr Möbius had rented the ground floor two weeks earlier and paid for a month in advance. He was a thorough and reliable man and he had printed very prominent announcements about his office in all the newspapers. She had been surprised when he had not appeared at the office the previous day.

Fandorin listened, nodding his head and occasionally asking brief questions. He ordered Anisii to make a note of the description of the vanished notary's appearance. 'Average height,' Tulipov's pencil recorded with a studious squeak. 'Moustache, little goatee beard. Mousy hair. Pince-nez. Rubs his hands and laughs all the time. Polite. Large brown wart on right cheek. Looks at least forty. Leather galoshes. Grey coat with black roll collar.'

'Don't write about the g-galoshes and coat,' said the Court Counsellor, glancing briefly at Anisii's notes. 'Only the physical appearance.'

Behind the door there was a perfectly ordinary office: in the reception room there was a writing desk, a safe with its door half open and shelves with files. The files were all empty, mere cardboard shells, but in the safe on the metal shelf, in the most obvious spot, there was a playing card: the jack of spades. Erast Petrovich took the card, examined it through a magnifying glass and dropped it on the floor.

He explained to Anisii: 'It's just an ordinary card, the same as they sell everywhere. I can't stand cards, Tulipov, and especially the jack of spades (which they also call Momos). I have some extremely unpleasant memories associated with it.'

From the office they went to the English consulate to meet Lord Pitsbrook. On this occasion the son of Albion was accompanied by a diplomatic translator, and so Anisii was able to record the victim's testimony himself.

The British citizen informed the Court Counsellor that the 'Möbius' notary office had been recommended to him by Mr Speier as one of Russia's most respectable and oldest legal firms. In confirmation of this assertion, Mr Speier had shown him several newspapers, each of which carried a prominent advertisement for 'Möbius'. The lord did not know any Russian, but the year of the company's foundation – sixteen hundred and something – had made a most favourable impression on him.

Pitsbrook also showed them one of the newspapers, the *Moscow Provincial Gazette* which, in his English manner, he called the *Moscow News*. Anisii stretched his neck to peer over Mr Fandorin's shoulder and saw a huge advertisement covering a quarter of the page:

MÖBIUS

Notary's Office
Ministry of Justice
registration certificate No. 1672

**Wills and bills of sale drawn up,
powers of attorney witnessed,
mortgages secured,
representation for the recovery of debts,
and other sundry services**

They took the British citizen to the office of ill-fame, and he gave a detailed account of how, having received the paper signed by 'the old gentleman' (that is, His Excellency the Governor-General) he had set out to come here, to the 'office'. Mr Speier had not gone with him, because he was not feeling very well, but he had assured him that the head of the firm had been informed and was expecting his titled foreign client. The lord had indeed been received very courteously and offered tea with 'hard round biscuits' (spice cakes, perhaps?) and a good cigar. The documents had been witnessed very promptly and the notary had taken the money – a hundred thousand roubles – for safe keeping and put it in the safe.

'Yes indeed, safe keeping,' Erast Petrovich muttered, and asked something, pointing at the safe.

The Englishman nodded, opened the unlocked iron door and hissed an oath.

The lord was unable to add anything substantial to the portrait of Ivan Karlovich Möbius; he simply kept repeating that he had a wart. Anisii even remembered the English word for it.

'A distinctive feature, Your Honour. A large brown wart on the right cheek. Perhaps we'll find the rogue after all?' said Tulipov, expressing his sound idea with timid reserve. He had taken the Governor-General's words about being ground into dust very much to heart. He wanted to prove useful.

But the Court Counsellor did not take Anisii's contribution seriously and said absent-mindedly: 'That's nothing, Tulipov. A psychological trick. It's not difficult to give yourself a wart or, say, a birthmark that covers half your cheek. Usually witnesses only remember a striking feature like that, and pay less attention to the others. Let us focus instead on the protector of juvenile harlots, "Mr Speier". Did you note down his portrait? Show it to me. *Height uncertain, because in wheel-chair. Dark blondish-brown hair, short at the temples. Soft, gentle expression.* (Hmm . . .) *Eyes apparently light-coloured.* (That is important, we shall have to question His Excellency's secretary again.) *Open, pleasant face.* So, there is nothing to give us a lead. We shall have to trouble His Highness the Duke of Saxen-Limburg. Let us hope he knows something about this "grandson", since he provided him with a special letter of recommendation to the "grandfather".'

Erast Petrovich went to the Loskutnaya Hotel on his own, dressed up in his uniform, to see the royal prince. He was gone for a long time and returned with a face darker than a thunder cloud. At the hotel he had been told that His Highness had left the previous day to take the Warsaw train, but the tall passenger had failed to show up at the Bryansk Station.

That evening the Court Counsellor held a consultation with Anisii, which he called an 'operational analysis', to sum up the results of the long day. This procedure was new to Tulipov. Later on, when he was already used to the idea that every day concluded with an 'analysis', he began to get a little bolder, but that first evening he said nothing for most of the time, afraid of blurting out something stupid.

'Right, let's be rational about this,' the Court Counsellor began. 'The notary Möbius, who is not a notary at all, has gone, evaporated. That is one.' A jade bead on the rosary clicked loudly. 'The invalided philanthropist Speier, who is not a philanthropist at all, and unlikely to be an invalid, has also gone, disappeared without trace. That is two. (And once again – click!) What is especially intriguing is that the duke has also mysteriously disappeared, and unlike the "notary" and the "invalid", he would appear to have been genuine. Of course, Germany is just full of little crowned princes, far too many to keep track of, but this one was received in Moscow with full honours, the n-newspapers wrote about his arrival. And that is three (click!). On the way back from the station I dropped into the offices of *The Week* and the *Russian Herald* and asked how they had heard about the forthcoming visit by His Highness the Duke of Saxen-Limburg. It turned out that the newspapers had received the information in the usual manner, by telegraph from their St Petersburg correspondents. What do you make of that, Tulipov?'

Anisii immediately broke into a nervous sweat and said uncertainly: 'Who knows, Your Honour, who it was that actually sent them – those telegrams.'

'That's what I think too,' the State Counsellor said approvingly, and Tulipov instantly breathed a sigh of relief. 'Anyone at all who knew the names of the St Petersburg correspondents could have sent a telegram from anywhere at all ... Oh, and by the way. Don't call me "Your Honour"; we're not in the army, after all. First name and patronymic will do, or ... or just call me "Chief" – it's shorter and easier.' Fandorin smiled grimly at something or other and continued with the 'analysis'. 'Look here – we're getting somewhere. A certain cunning individual, who has simply found out the names of a few correspondents (which requires no more than leafing through the newspapers), sends off telegrams to the newspaper offices about the arrival of a German prince, and after that everything simply follows its own course. Reporters meet "His Highness" at the station, *Russian Thought* prints an interview, in which the honoured guest expresses extremely bold opinions on the Baltic question, categorically distancing himself from Bismarck's political line, and there you have it. Moscow is conquered, our patriots accept the duke with open arms. Ah, the press – how few people in Russia realise how powerful it really is ... Right, then, Tulipov; now we move on to our conclusions.'

When the Court Counsellor, or 'Chief', paused, Anisii felt afraid that he would have to draw the conclusions, and the poor courier's head was suddenly full of formless mist.

But no, Mr Fandorin managed without Anisii's assistance. He strode energetically across the study, clattered his beads rapidly and then clasped his hands behind his back.

'The membership of the Jack of Spades gang is unknown. There are at least three men involved: "Speier", the "Notary" and the "Duke". That is one. They are brazenly insolent, highly inventive and incredibly self-assured. That is t-two. There are no tracks to follow. That is three . . .' Erast Petrovich paused for a moment and concluded quietly, almost even stealthily: 'But there are certain clues, and that is four.'

'Really?' Anisii asked eagerly. He had been feeling dejected, expecting a quite different conclusion: *This is hopeless, Tulipov, so you can go back to your courier's job.*

'I think so. The "jacks" are firmly convinced that they have got away with it, and most likely that means they will want to play another prank or two. That is one. Even before this business with Lord Pitsbrook they managed to pull off two highly successful and extremely daring hoaxes. Both times they came away with plenty of money, both times they had the effrontery to leave their calling card, but they never even thought of gathering

up their substantial trophies and leaving Moscow. So now ...
Would you like a cigar?' The Court Counsellor clicked open the
lid of an ebony casket standing on the desk.

Although, for reasons of economy, Anisii did not use tobacco,
he could not resist and took one – the slim, neat, chocolate-
coloured cigars looked so very appetising, with their red and
gold labels. Imitating Erast Petrovich, he smacked his lips as he
kindled the flame into life and prepared to experience a heavenly
bliss that was the exclusive prerogative of rich gentlemen. He
had seen cigars like this on Kuznetsky Most, in the window of
Sychov's Colonial Shop – at one and a half roubles apiece.

'The next point,' Fandorin continued, 'is that the "jacks" use
the same methods repeatedly. That is two. In both the business
with the "Duke" and the episode with the "notary" they
exploited the natural human propensity to trust the printed
word. Well, all right, never mind His Lordship. The English are
used to t-trusting everything that *The Times* p-prints. But look
what fine informants our Moscow newspapers are ... First they
inform the citizens of Moscow about "His Highness's" arrival,
then they go on to create a ballyhoo and fill everyone's head
with nonsense ... Tulipov, you don't inhale a cigar!'

But it was too late. Having completed his thoroughgoing
preparations Anisii breathed in and filled his chest with the
astringent smoke that was prickling the roof of his mouth. The
light dimmed and poor Tulipov felt as if his insides had been
ripped open with a file. He doubled up, coughing and choking
and feeling that he was about to die on the spot.

Having revived him (with the help of water from the carafe
and energetic slaps to Anisii's skinny back), Fandorin summed
up briefly: 'Our job is to keep our eyes peeled.'

And now Tulipov had been keeping his eyes peeled for a week.
In the morning, on the way to his most enviable job, he bought
a full set of Moscow's various newspapers. He marked everything that was remarkable or unusual in them and reported to
his 'chief' over lunch.

Lunch deserves a special mention. When the Countess was in

good spirits and came to the table, the food served was exquisite –
dishes delivered from the Ertèle French restaurant: some kind
of *chaud-froid* with snipe and truffles, *salat Romain*, macedoine
in melon and other culinary miracles that Anisii had never even
heard of before. But if Addy had spent the morning feeling
miserable in her boudoir or had gone out to unwind in the
haberdashery and perfumery shops, then Masa seized power in
the dining room, and things assumed a quite different com-
plexion. Fandorin's valet went to the Japanese and Chinese shop
on the Petrovsky Lanes and brought back unsalted rice, marin-
ated radishes, crunchy seaweed that tasted like paper and sweet
fried fish. The Court Counsellor ate all this poison with obvious
relish, and Masa gave Anisii tea, a fresh bagel and sausage. To
tell the truth, Tulipov greatly preferred this kind of meal, because
in the presence of the lovely but capricious Countess, he was so
completely overwhelmed that he was unable to appreciate the
wonderful delicacies properly anyway.

Erast Petrovich listened attentively to the results of Tulipov's
morning research. He dismissed the greater part out of hand
and agreed to bear the remainder in mind. In the afternoon
they separated to verify the facts: Anisii checked the suspicious
announcements and his chief checked the important individuals
who had arrived in Moscow (on the pretext of bringing them
greetings from the Governor-General; he took a close look to
make sure they were not impostors).

So far it had all come to nothing, but Anisii was not dispirited.
He would gladly have carried on working like this for ever.

That morning Sonya had a stomach ache – she must have
been gnawing the lime from the stove again – and so Tulipov
had no time for breakfast at home. He wasn't given any coffee
in the Chief's house either – it was a 'loud' day. Anisii sat quietly
in the study, leafing through the newspapers and, as luck would
have it, his eyes kept stumbling across advertisements for all
kinds of food.

'Safatov's shop on Sretenka Street has received a delivery of
the exceptionally tender salted beef known as "Entrecôte", he
read, even though the information was of no use to him. 'At 16

kops a pound, all lean meat, it can replace ham of the very highest sort.'

All in all, he barely survived until lunch, and he wolfed down his bagel as he reported on the day's catch to Erast Petrovich.

On that day, 11 February 1886, the number of new arrivals was small: five military generals and seven counsellors of state. The Chief marked down two to be visited: the head of the naval quartermaster service, Rear-Admiral von Bombe, and the head of the state treasury, Privy Counsellor Svinin.

Then Tulipov moved on to the more interesting subject of unusual announcements.

'By decision of the Municipal Duma,' he read out, with significant pauses, 'two shop-owners from the Municipal Arcade on Red Square are to be invited to a consultation on the establishment of a joint-stock company for the purpose of rebuilding the Municipal Arcade and erecting on its current site an emporium with a glass dome.'

'Well, what do you f-find suspicious about that?' asked Fandorin.

'It doesn't make sense, does it – why does an emporium need a glass dome?' Anisii remarked reasonably. 'And anyway, Chief, you told me to point out to you any announcements that invite people to contribute money, and this is a joint-stock company. Perhaps it's a swindle?'

'It isn't,' the Court Counsellor reassured him. 'The Duma really has decided to demolish the Municipal Arcade and build an enclosed three-storey gallery in the Russian style in its place. Go on.'

Tulipov set aside the rejected article from the *Moscow Municipal Gazette* and picked up the *Russian Word*.

'Chess Tournament. At two o'clock this afternoon in the premises of the Moscow Society of Chess Lovers, M. I. Chigorin will play a tournament against ten opponents. Mr Chigorin will play *à l'aveugle*, without looking at the board or writing down his moves. The stake for a game is 100 roubles. An entry ticket costs 2 roubles. All who wish to attend are welcome.'

'Without looking at the board?' Erast Petrovich asked in

surprise, and made a note in his little book. 'All right. I'll go along and play.'

Cheered by this, Anisii went on to read an announcement from the *Moscow Municipal Police Gazette*.

'*Unprecedented real estate lottery.* The international evangelical society "The Tears of Jesus" is holding its first *monumental charitable lottery* in Moscow to support the construction of the Chapel of the Shroud of the Lord in Jerusalem. *Fantastically valuable prizes*, donated by benefactors from all over Europe: apartment houses, villas in the finest European cities. *Prizes are confirmed on the spot!* One standard ticket for 25 roubles. Hurry, the lottery will only be in Moscow for *one week*, and then it will move on to St Petersburg.'

Erast Petrovich was intrigued. 'A monumental lottery? A very creative idea. The public will take to it. No need to wait for the draw; you learn if you've won anything straight away. Interesting. And it doesn't look like a swindle. Using the *Police Gazette* f-for a hoax is too bold a move altogether. Although we can expect anything from the "jacks" ... I think you'd better go there, Tulipov. Here's twenty-five roubles. Buy a ticket for me. Go on.'

'*News!* I have the honour to inform the respected public that in recent days my museum, located opposite Solodovnikov's Passage, has taken delivery from London of an extremely lively and cheerful *chimpanzee with a baby.* Entrance 3 roubles. F. Patek.'

'And what has the chimpanzee done to displease you?' the Chief asked with a shrug. 'What do you s-suspect her of?'

'It's unusual,' Anisii mumbled. In all honesty, he had simply wanted to take a look at this great marvel, especially since it was so 'lively and cheerful'. 'And the entrance charge is too high.'

'No, that's not ambitious enough for the Jack of Spades,' said Fandorin, shaking his head. 'And you can't disguise yourself as a chimpanzee. Especially a baby one. Go on.'

'*Missing dog.* On 28 January this year a male dog, a large mongrel by the name of Hector, went missing. He is black, with a crooked rear left leg and a white patch on his chest. Anyone who returns him will receive 50 roubles. Bolshaya Ordynka

Street, the house of Countess Tolstaya, ask for Privat-Docent Andreev.'

The Chief sighed at this announcement too: 'You seem to be in the mood for fun this morning, Tulipov. What would we want with "large mongrel"?'

'But it's fifty roubles, Erast Petrovich! For a common mongrel! That's really suspicious!'

'Ah, Tulipov, people love that kind of beast, with crooked legs, more than the handsome ones. You don't understand a thing about love. Go on.'

Anisii sniffed resentfully, thinking: And you know so much about love, don't you? That's why the doors slam in your house in the morning and they don't serve my coffee.

He read out the next item of the day's harvest: 'Male impotence, weakness and the consequences of the sins of youth cured with electrical discharges and galvanic baths by Doctor of Medicine Emmanuel Straus.'

'An obvious charlatan,' Erast Petrovich agreed. Only it's rather petty for the "jacks", isn't it? But go and check anyway.'

Arnsii returned from his expedition shortly after three in the afternoon, tired and with nothing to show for it, but in a good mood which, as a matter of fact, had been with him all through the preceding week. He was looking forward to the most enjoyable stage of the work: the analysis and discussion of the events of the day.

'I see from the absence of any gleam in your eyes that your nets are empty,' the perspicacious Erast Petrovich said in greeting. He had evidently only got back recently himself – he was still wearing his uniform and the crosses of his decorations.

'And what do you have, Chief?' Tulipov asked hopefully. 'What about the generals? And the chess player?'

'The generals are genuine. And so is the chess player. A truly phenomenal gift: he sat with his back to the boards and didn't take any notes. He won nine games out of ten and only lost one. Not bad business, as the traders say nowadays. Mr Chigorin took in nine hundred roubles and paid out a hundred. A net profit of eight hundred, and all in about an hour.'

'And who did he lose to?' Anisii asked curiously.

'Me,' his chief replied. 'But that's not important; the time was wasted.'

Wasted, was it? thought Tulipov. A hundred roubles' worth!

He asked respectfully: 'Do you play chess well?'

'Terribly badly. It was pure luck.' Looking in the mirror, Fandorin adjusted the already ideal wings of his starched collar. 'You see, Tulipov, in my own way I am also something of a phenomenon. The gambler's passion is unknown to me, I loathe all games, but I always have the most fantastic luck in them. I grew used to it a long time ago and it no longer surprises me. It even happens in chess. Mr Chigorin got his squares confused and ordered his queen to be moved to f5, instead of f6, right beside my rook, and he was so upset that he decided not to continue. Playing ten games without looking is really extremely difficult, after all. But what have you got to tell me?'

Anisii gathered himself, because at these moments he felt as if he were taking an examination. But it was an enjoyable examination, not like a real one. Nobody gave him poor marks or failed him here, and quite often he won praise for his keen observation or quick-wittedness.

Today, it was true, he had nothing special to boast about. Firstly, Tulipov's conscience was not entirely clear: he had taken himself off to Patek's museum after all, spent three roubles of public money and gaped for half an hour at the chimpanzee and her baby (they really were both exceptionally lively and cheerful, the advertisement had not lied), although this was of absolutely no benefit to the job in hand whatsoever. He had also gone round to Bolshaya Ordynka Street, out of sheer professional zeal, had a word with the owner of the mongrel with the crooked leg and listened to his heart-breaking story, which had concluded in restrained manly sobbing.

Anisii did not really feel like telling the Chief all the details about the electrical doctor. He started, but then became embarrassed and broke off. In the line of duty he had had to submit to a shameful and rather painful procedure, and even now it still felt as if he had needles pricking his crotch.

'Straus, that doctor, is a repulsive character,' Anisii tattled to Erast Petrovich. 'Very suspicious. Asks all sorts of foul questions.' And he concluded spitefully: 'There's someone the police ought to look into.'

Erast Petrovich, a man of delicate sensibilities, did not inquire into the details. He said with a serious air: 'It was praiseworthy of you to subject yourself to the electrical procedure, especially since in your case any "consequences of the sins of youth" are scarcely possible. Self-sacrifice for the sake of the cause deserves every encouragement, but it would have been quite enough to restrict yourself to a few questions. For instance, how much this doctor charges for a session.'

'Five roubles. Here, I even have a receipt,' said Anisii, reaching into the pocket where he kept all his financial records.

'No need,' said the Court Counsellor, waving the paper aside. 'The "jacks" would hardly bother getting their hands dirty for the sake of five roubles.'

Anisii wilted. That accursed pricking had begun spreading so fast across his electrically tormented body that he actually squirmed on his chair and, in order to undo the unfavourable impression created by his foolishness, he began telling Erast Petrovich about the monumental lottery.

'A respectable institution. Only one word for it: Europe. They're renting the first floor in the building of the Tutelary Council for the Care of Orphans. The queue goes all the way down the stairs, people of every rank and class, even quite a few from the nobility. I stood there for forty minutes, Erast Petrovich, before I reached the counter. Russian people are certainly responsive to an appeal for charity.'

Fandorin twitched one sable eyebrow vaguely. 'So you think it's all above board? Not a whiff of any swindle?'

'Oh no, not at all! There's a constable at the door, with a shoulder belt and sword. He salutes everyone respectfully. When you go in, there's a counter, and behind it there's a very modest, pretty young lady with a pince-nez, all in black, with a white headscarf and a cross hanging round her neck. A nun or a lay sister, or perhaps just a volunteer – you can't tell with those foreigners. She takes the money and lets you spin the drum. She speaks fluent Russian, only with an accent. You spin it yourself and take the ticket out yourself – it's all fair and square. The drum's made of glass, with little folded pieces of cardboard in it – blue for twenty-five roubles and pink for fifty roubles – that's for those who want to contribute more. No one took any pink ones while I was there, though. You open up the ticket right there, in front of everyone. If you haven't won, it says: "May the Lord save you." Here, look.' Anisii took out a handsome piece of blue cardboard with Gothic lettering on it. 'And anyone who's won anything goes in behind the counter. There's a desk in there, with the chairman of the lottery sitting at it, a very impressive, elderly clerical gentleman. He confirms the prizes and does the paperwork. And the young lady thanks the people who don't win most cordially and pins a beautiful paper rose on their chests as a sign of their charity.'

Anisii took out the paper rose that he had carefully tucked away in his pocket. He was thinking of taking it to Sonya; she would be delighted.

Erast Petrovich inspected the rose and even sniffed it. 'It smells of "Parma Violets",' he observed. 'An expensive perfume. You say the young lady is modest?'

'She's a really nice girl,' Tulipov confirmed. 'And she has such a shy smile.'

'Well, well. And do people sometimes win?'

'I should say so!' Anisii exclaimed! 'When I was still standing in the queue on the stairs one fortunate gentleman came out who looked like a professor. All flushed, he was, waving a piece of paper with seals on it – he'd won an estate in Bohemia. Five hundred acres! And this morning, they say, some official's wife drew a tenement house actually in Paris. Six storeys! Just imagine that kind of luck! They say she had quite a turn; they had to give her smelling salts. And after that professor who won the estate, lots of people started taking two or three tickets at once. Who minds paying twenty-five roubles a time for prizes like that? Ah,

I didn't have any money of my own with me, or I'd have tried my luck too.'

Anisii squinted up dreamily at the ceiling, imagining himself unfolding a piece of cardboard and finding ... What would it be? Well, for instance, a chateau on the shores of Lake Geneva (he had seen the famous lake in a picture – oh, it was so beautiful).

'Six storeys?' the Court Counsellor asked, off the subject. 'In Paris? And an estate in B-Bohemia? I see. You know what, Tulipov: you come with me, and I'll play this lottery of yours. Can we get there before it closes?'

So that was his cool, god-like self-control – and he said the gambler's passion was unknown to him.

They barely got there in time. The queue on the stairs had not grown any shorter; the lottery was open until half past five, and it had already struck five o'clock. The clients were feeling nervous.

Fandorin walked slowly up the steps until he reached the door and then said politely: 'Excuse me, ladies and gentlemen, I'd just like to take a look – out of curiosity.'

And – would you believe it! – he was allowed through without a murmur. They'd have thrown me out, for sure, thought Anisii, but they'd never think of doing that to someone like him.

The constable on duty at the door, a fine, upstanding young fellow with a dashing curl to his ginger moustaches, raised his hand to his grey astrakhan cap in salute. Erast Petrovich strolled across the spacious room divided into two by a counter. Anisii had taken a look round the lottery office the last time, and so he immediately fixed his envious gaze on the spinning drum. But he also kept glancing at the pretty young lady, who was just pinning a paper flower on the lapel of a distraught student and murmuring something consoling.

The Court Counsellor inspected the drum in the most attentive manner possible and then turned his attention to the chairman, a fine-looking, clean-shaven gentleman in a single-breasted jacket with an upright collar. The chairman was clearly bored and he even yawned briefly once, delicately placing his open hand over his mouth.

For some reason Erast Petrovich pressed a single white-gloved finger to the plaque bearing the legend 'Ladies and gentlemen who buy a pink ticket are allowed through ahead of the queue' and asked: 'Mademoiselle, could I please have one pink ticket?'

'Oh, yes, of course; you are a real Christian,' the young lady said in agreeably accented Russian, at the same time bestowing a radiant smile on this benefactor and tucking away a lock of golden hair that escaped from under her headscarf as she gladly accepted the fifty-rouble note proffered by Fandorin.

Anisii held his breath as he watched his chief casually reach into the drum, take hold of the first pink ticket he came across between his finger and thumb, pull it out and unfold it.

'It's not empty, surely?' the young lady asked in dismay. 'Ah, I was quite certain that you were sure to win! The last gentleman who took a pink ticket won a genuine palazzo in Venice! With its own mooring for gondolas and a front porch for carriages! Perhaps you would like to try again, sir?'

'With a porch for carriages. My, my,' said Fandorin, clicking his tongue as he examined the little picture on the ticket: a winged angel with its hands folded in prayer and covered with a piece of cloth that was obviously intended to symbolise a shroud.

Erast Petrovich turned to face the queue of customers, doffed his top hat respectfully and declared in a loud, resolute voice: 'Ladies and gentlemen, I am Erast Petrovich Fandorin, His Excellency the Governor-General's Deputy for Special Assignments. This lottery is hereby declared under arrest on suspicion of fraud. Constable, clear the premises immediately and do not admit anyone else!'

'Yes, Your Honour!' the constable with the ginger moustaches barked, without the slightest thought of doubting the resolute gentleman's authority.

The constable proved to be an efficient fellow. He flapped his arms as if he were herding geese and drove the agitated, clamouring customers out through the door with great alacrity. No sooner had he rumbled 'If you please, if you please, you can see what's happened for yourselves' than the room cleared and the guardian of order drew himself erect at the entrance, ready to carry out the next order.

The Court Counsellor nodded in satisfaction and turned towards Anisii, who was standing there with his mouth hanging open at this unexpected turn of events.

The elderly gentleman – the pastor or whoever he was – also seemed to be quite perturbed. He stood up, leaned over the counter and froze, blinking goggle-eyed.

But the modest young lady reacted in an absolutely amazing manner. She suddenly winked one blue eye at Anisii from behind her pince-nez, ran across the room and leapt up on to the broad window sill with a cry of 'Hup-la!' Then she clicked open the catch and pushed the window open, letting in the fresh, frosty smell from the street outside.

'Hold her!' Erast Petrovich shouted in a despairing voice.

With a sudden start, Anisii went dashing after the agile maiden. He reached out a hand to grab her skirt, but his fingers simply slid across the smooth, resilient silk. The young lady jumped out of the window and Tulipov slumped across the window sill, just in time to see her skirts expand gracefully as she glided downwards.

The first floor was high above the ground, but the dare-devil jumper landed in the snow with the agility of a cat, without even falling. She turned round and waved to Anisii, then lifted her skirt high to reveal a pair of shapely legs in high galoshes and black stockings, and went dashing off along the pavement. A moment later, and the fugitive had slipped out of the circle of light cast by the street lamp and disappeared into the rapidly gathering twilight.

'Oh, my gosh!' I said Anisii, crossing himself as he scrambled up on to the window sill. He knew as a matter of absolute certainty that he was about to hurt himself, and he would be lucky just to break a leg, but it could easily be his back. He and Sonya would make a fine pair then: the paralysed brother and the idiot sister – a wonderful couple.

He squeezed his eyes shut, preparing to jump, but the

Chief's firm hand grabbed hold of him by the coat-tails.

'Let her go,' said Fandorin, watching the young lady's receding figure with amused bewilderment. 'We have the main culprit here.'

The Court Counsellor walked unhurriedly across to the chairman of the lottery, who threw up his arms as if in surrender and without waiting for any questions, started jabbering: 'Your, Your Excell— I just accepted a small emolument ... I have no idea what is going on, I just do what they tell me ... There's the gentleman over there – ask him ... the one pretending to be a constable.'

Erast Petrovich and Tulipov turned in the direction indicated by the trembling hand, but the constable was not there. There was just his uniform cap, swaying gently to and fro on a hook.

The Chief dashed towards the door, with Anisii following him. Once they saw the dense, agitated crowd on the stairs, they knew there was no way they could force their way through it. Fandorin grimaced violently, rapped himself on the forehead with his knuckles and slammed the door shut.

Meanwhile Anisii was examining the astrakhan cap that the fake constable had left behind. It was just an ordinary cap, except that that there was a playing card attached to its lining: a coyly smiling page-boy wearing a plumed hat, under the sign of the suit of spades.

'But how on earth –? How did you –?' Anisii babbled, gazing in amazement at his infuriated chief. 'How did you guess? Chief, you're an absolute genius!'

'I'm not a genius, I'm a blockhead!' Erast Petrovich retorted angrily. 'I fell for it, hook, line and sinker! I went for the puppet and let the leader get away. He's cunning, the rogue, oh, he's cunning ... You ask me how I guessed? I didn't have to guess. I told you I never l-lose at any game, especially if it's a matter of luck. When the ticket didn't win, I knew straight away it was a swindle.' He paused for a moment and added: 'And anyway, who ever heard of a Venetian palazzo with a porch for carriages? There aren't any carriages in Venice, only boats ...'

Anisii was about to ask how the Chief had known that the

Jack of Spades was behind everything, but before he could, the Court Counsellor roared in fury: 'Why are you still examining that damned cap? What's so interesting about it?'

CHAPTER 4

One Good Turn Deserves Another

If there was one thing he simply could not stand, it was the mysterious and inexplicable. Every event, even the sudden appearance of a pimple on your nose, had its own prehistory and immediate cause. Nothing in the world ever happened just like that, entirely out of the blue. But suddenly here, by your leave, an excellently planned, elegant and – why indulge in false modesty? – *brilliant* operation had simply collapsed for no obvious reason whatever.

One half of the study door swung open slightly with a repulsive squeak and Mimi's cute little face appeared in the crack. Momos grabbed a leather slipper off one foot and flung it furiously, aiming at that golden fringe – keep out; don't interrupt when I'm thinking. The door hastily slammed shut. He ruffled up his hair furiously, sending curling papers flying in all directions, clamped his teeth on his chibouk and started scraping the copper nib of his pen across a sheet of paper.

The accounts looked abominable.

At an approximate calculation, the earnings from the lottery at the end of the first day came to seven or eight thousand. The till had been confiscated, so that was a complete loss.

Over the week, the lottery ought to have gathered speed at an increasing rate, bringing in sixty thousand at the most conservative estimate. It couldn't have been dragged out any longer than that – some impatient owner of a villa in Paris would have gone to admire his winnings and seen that the object concealed beneath the 'flaming heart' drawers – that is, under the shroud – was not at all what he had thought it was. But they could have gone on gathering honey for a week at least.

So their unearned profit came to sixty thousand, and that was the *minimum minimorum*.

And what about the non-recoverable expenditure on the preparations? It was a mere trifle, of course. Renting the first floor, printing the tickets, equipment. But this was a matter of principle – Momos had been left with a loss!

Then, they'd arrested the stooge. Admittedly he didn't know a thing, but that was bad; it was untidy. And he felt sorry for the old fool, an actor from the Maly Theatre who had taken to drink. He'd be feeding the fleas in the lock-up now for his miserable thirty roubles advance.

But he felt sorriest of all for his magnificent idea. A monumental lottery – it was so delightful! What was the worst thing about those overplayed swindles called lotteries? First the client paid his money, and then he had to wait for the draw. A draw, note, that he himself wouldn't see. Why should he take anyone's word that everything was honest and above board? And how many people actually liked to wait? People were impatient – everybody knew that.

This had been different, however: pick out your own beautiful, crisp little ticket to heaven with your own fair hand. The little angel entices you, seduces you: have no doubts, dear Mr Blockhead Idiotovich. What could there possibly be behind this alluring little picture but absolute delight for you? Unlucky? Well, never mind; why don't you try again?

The details had been important, of course – so that it wouldn't be just an ordinary charitable lottery but a European, evangelical lottery. The Orthodox believers weren't over-fond of members of other creeds, but where money was concerned they trusted them more than their own – that was a well-known fact. And organising it not just anywhere, but at the Tutelary Council for the Care of Orphans! And advertising it in the *Police Gazette*! In the first place, it was a paper the people of Moscow loved and enjoyed reading, and in the second, who would ever suspect anything crooked there? And then there was the constable at the entrance!

Momos tore off his curling papers and tugged a lock of hair down from his forehead to his eyes – the ginger colour was almost gone. He only had to wash it once more and it would be fine. It was a pity that the ends of his hair had faded and split – that was from dying it so often. There was nothing to be done about that; it was part of his profession.

The door squeaked again and Mimi said quickly: 'Pussy cat, don't throw anything. A man's brought what you told him to.'

Momos roused himself. 'Who? Sliunkov?'

'I don't know; he's repulsive, hair slicked over a bald patch. The one you cleaned out at whist at Christmas.'

'Send him in!'

The first thing Momos always did when he was preparing to conquer new territory was acquire a few useful people. It was like going hunting. When you came to a rich hunting ground, you took a look around, checked the forest paths, spied out convenient hidey-holes, studied the habits of the game; and in Moscow Momos had his own informants in various key positions. Take this Sliunkov, for instance: a man with a lowly position, a clerk from the secret section of the Governor's chancellery, but he could be so useful. He'd come in handy in that business with the Englishman, and he was just what was needed now. Reeling in the clerk couldn't possibly have been any easier: Sliunkov had lost three and a half thousand at cards and now he was bending over backwards to get his IOUs back.

The man who came in had sleeked-down hair and flat feet, with a document folder under his arm. He spoke in a half-whisper, constantly glancing round at the door: 'Antoine Bonifatievich' – he knew Momos as a French citizen – 'in the name of Christ the Lord, this is a hard-labour offence. Be quick, don't ruin me. I'm shaking in my shoes.'

Momos pointed without speaking: Put the folder on the desk, his gesture said. Then he waved his hand, still without speaking: Now wait outside the door.

The folder bore the following heading:

At the top left there was a stamp:

Office of the
Governor-General of Moscow.
Secret records

And then, written by hand: *'Top secret'*.
There was a list of documents pasted inside the cardboard cover:

Service record
Confidential references
Personal information

Well now, let's take a look at this Fandorin who's appeared to taunt us.

Half an hour later the clerk left on tiptoe with the secret file and a cancelled IOU for five hundred roubles. For a good turn like that, Momos could have handed back all his IOUs, but he might still come in useful again.

Momos strolled thoughtfully round the study, toying absent-mindedly with the tassel of his dressing gown. So that was him: an unmasker of conspiracies and master of secret investigations? He had more orders and medals than a bottle of champagne. A Knight of the Japanese Orders of the Chrysathemums – that was remarkable. And he'd distinguished himself in Turkey, and Japan, and travelled on special assignments to Europe. Yes indeed, a serious gentleman.

What had it said there in the references? – 'Exceptional abilities in the conduct of delicate and secret matters, especially those requiring skills of investigative deduction.' Hmm. He would like to know how the gentleman had deduced the nature of the lottery on the very first day.

Well never mind, my scary Japanese wolf; it still remains to be seen whose tail will end up in the trap, Momos warned his invisible opponent. But he shouldn't put his entire trust in official documents, no matter how secret they might be. The information on Mr Fandorin needed to be supplemented and 'fleshed out'.

The fleshing-out of the information took three days. During that time Momos undertook the following actions.

Having transformed himself into a manservant looking for a position, he befriended Prokop Kuzmich, the yard-keeper of Fandorin's landlord at the estate. They took a drop of vodka together, with pickled mushrooms, and had a chat about this and that.

He visited Korsh's Theatre and observed the box where Fandorin was sitting with his lady-love, the fugitive wife of the St Petersburg Usher of the Chamber, Opraksin. He did not look at the stage, on which, as chance would have it, they were performing Mr Nikolaev's play *Special Assignment*, but only at the Court Counsellor and his current flame. He made excellent use of his Zeiss binoculars, which looked like opera glasses, but had a magnification factor of 10. The Countess was, of course, a perfect beauty, but not to Momos's taste. He knew her kind very well and preferred to admire their beauty from a distance.

Mimi also made her contribution. In the guise of a milliner, she made the acquaintance of the Countess's maid Natasha and sold her a new serge dress at a very good price. In the process they drank coffee with cakes, chatted about women's matters and gossiped a little.

By the end of the third day the plan of the counter-attack was ready. It would be subtle and elegant – exactly what was required.

The operation was set for Saturday, 15 February.

The military action unfolded precisely according to the planned dispositions. At a quarter to eleven in the morning, when the curtains were drawn back at the windows of the outhouse on Malaya Nikitskaya Street, a postman delivered an urgent telegram addressed to the Countess Opraksina.

Momos was sitting in a carriage diagonally across from the estate, keeping an eye on his watch. He noticed some kind of movement behind the windows of the outhouse and even thought he could hear a woman shouting. Thirty minutes after the delivery of the message, Mr Fandorin himself and the Countess hastily emerged from the house. Trotting along behind them, tying up her headscarf, came a ruddy-cheeked young woman – the aforementioned maid Natasha. Madame Opraksina was in a state of obvious agitation. The Court Counsellor was saying something to her, apparently trying to calm her down, but the Countess evidently did not wish to be calmed. But then, he could understand how Her Excellency must be feeling. The telegram that had been delivered read: 'Addy, I am arriving in Moscow on the eleven o'clock train and coming straight to you. Things cannot go on like this. You will either leave with me or I shall shoot myself before your very eyes. Yours, insane with grief, Tony.'

According to information received from the maid, Madame Opraksina might have abandoned her legal spouse, the Privy Counsellor and Usher of the Chamber Count Anton Apollonovich Opraksin, but she still called him Tony. It was perfectly natural that Monsieur Fandorin would decide to spare the lady an unpleasant scene. And, of course, he would accompany her as she was evacuated, since Ariadna Arkadievna was highly strung and would need to be consoled at length.

When Fandorin's conspicuous sleigh with its cavern of fluffy American bearskin had disappeared round the corner, Momos unhurriedly finished his cigar, looked in the mirror to check that his disguise was in order and, at precisely twenty minutes past eleven, jumped out of the carriage. He was wearing the uniform of an usher of the chamber, complete with ribbon, star and sword, and a three-cornered hat with a plumage on his head. For a man who had come straight from the train, of course, it was a strange outfit, but it ought to impress the oriental servant. The important thing was to be swift and decisive – to give him no chance to gather his wits.

Momos walked through the gates with a determined stride,

crossed the yard at a half-run and hammered loudly on the door of the wing, although he could see the bell clearly enough.

The door was opened by Fandorin's valet, a Japanese subject by the name of Masa, who was absolutely devoted to Fandorin. This information, and also the previous day's close study of Mr Goshkevich's book on Japanese manners and customs, had been of assistance to Momos in determining how he ought to comport himself

'Aha, Monsieur Fandorin!' Momos roared at the slanty-eyed short-ass, rolling his eyes in a bloodthirsty manner. 'Abductor of other men's wives! Where is she? Where is my adored Addy? What have you done with her?'

If Mr Goshkevich could be trusted (and why not trust such a highly respected scholar?), there was nothing worse for a Japanese than a shameful situation and a public scandal. And furthermore, the yellow-skinned sons of the Mikado had a highly developed sense of responsibility to their suzerain and lord and, for this round-cheeked chappy, Court Counsellor Fandorin was his suzerain.

The valet was genuinely alarmed. He bowed from the waist and muttered: 'Apowogy, apowogy. I at fawt. I steal wife, cannot weturn.'

Momos did not understand the oriental's mutterings or what it had to do with anything, but one thing was clear: as befitted a Japanese vassal, the valet was prepared to accept responsibility for his master's guilt.

'Ki me, I at fawt,' the faithful servant said with a bow and backed inside, gesturing for the menacing visitor to follow.

Aha, he doesn't want the neighbours to hear, Momos guessed. Well, that suited his own plans perfectly.

Once inside the hallway, Momos pretended to look more closely and realise his mistake: 'Why, you're not Fandorin! Where is he? And where is she – my beloved?'

The Japanese backed away to the door of the drawing room, bowing all the time. Realising that he could not pass himself off as his master, he straightened up, folded his arms across his chest and rapped out: 'Massa no hea. Gon way. Foweva.'

'You're lying, you rogue,' Momos groaned, dashing forward and pushing Fandorin's vassal aside.

Sitting in the drawing room, cowering in his chair, was a puny, lop-eared, pimply creature in a shabby frock coat. His presence was no surprise to Momos. This was Anisii Tulipov, a lowly employee of the Department of Gendarmes. He dragged himself all the way here every morning, and he'd been at the lottery.

'Aha-a!' Momos drawled rapaciously. 'So that's where you are, Mr Libertine.'

The puny, lop-eared creature leapt to his feet, gulped convulsively and babbled: 'Your ... Your Excellency ... I don't, actually ...'

Aha, Momos concluded, that means the boy is aware of his superior's personal circumstances – he'd realised immediately who'd come calling.

'How, how, did you lure her away?' Momos groaned. 'My God, Addy,' he roared at the top of his voice, gazing around, 'what did this ugly freak tempt you with?'

At the word 'freak', the puny creature flushed bright scarlet, clearly taking offence. Momos had to switch tactics in mid-stride.

'Could you really have yielded to this wanton gaze and these voluptuous lips!' he howled, addressing the innocent Addy. 'This lustful satyr, this "knight of the chrysanthemums" only wants your body, but I cherish your soul! Where are you?'

The puny youth drew himself erect. 'Sir, Your Excellency. I am only aware of the delicate circumstances of this situation by pure chance. I am not Erast Petrovich Fandorin, as you seem to have thought I was. His Honour is not here. Nor is Ariadna Arkadievna. And so there is absolutely no point in your—'

'What do you mean, not here? Momos interrupted in a broken voice, slumping on to a chair in exhaustion. 'Then where is she, my little kitten?' When he received no reply, he exclaimed: 'No, I don't believe you! I know for certain that she is here!'

He set off round the house like a whirlwind, flinging open the doors, thinking to himself on the way: A fine apartment, and furnished with taste. When he came to the room with the dressing table covered with little jars and crystal bottles, he froze and sobbed: 'My God, it's her casket. And her fan.' He lowered his face into his hands. 'And I was still hoping, still believing it wasn't true . . .'

The next trick was intended for the Japanese snuffling behind him. It was something he ought to like. Momos pulled his short sword out of its scabbard and with a face contorted by passion, he hissed: 'No, better death. I cannot endure such shame.'

Spotty-faced Tulipov gasped in terror, but the valet looked at the disgraced husband with unconcealed admiration.

'Suicide is a grave sin,' the little sleuth said, pressing his hands to his chest in great agitation. 'You will destroy your soul and condemn Ariadna Arkadievna to eternal suffering. This is love, Your Excellency; there is nothing to be done. You should forgive. Act like a Christian.'

'Forgive?' the miserable usher of the chamber muttered, perplexed. 'Like a Christian?'

'Yes!' the boy exclaimed passionately. 'I know it's hard, but it will lighten the burden of your soul, you'll see!'

Momos wiped away a tear, dumbfounded. 'To truly forgive and forget . . . Let them laugh, let them despise me. Marriages are made in heaven. I shall take my darling away. I shall save her!' He raised his eyes prayerfully to the ceiling, and large, genuine tears flowed down his cheeks – that was another miraculous gift that Momos possessed.

The valet suddenly came to life. 'Yes, yes. Take way, take way home, awtogeweh,' he said, nodding. 'Vewy ansom, vewy nobuw. Why hawakiwi, no need hawakiwi, not wike Chwischan!'

Momos stood there with his eyes closed and his brows knitted in suffering. The other two waited with bated breath to see which feeling would win out: wounded pride or nobility.

It was nobility.

Momos shook his head decisively and declared: 'Very well, so be it. The Lord has preserved me from mortal sin.' He thrust the sword back into its scabbard and crossed himself with vigorous sweeps of his hand. Thank you, my dear man, for saving a Christian soul from damnation.' He held his hand out to the puny creature, who clutched it and held on to it, squeezing Momos's fingers with tears in his eyes.

The Japanese asked nervously: 'Take wady's fings home? Awtogeweh?'

'Yes, yes, my friend,' Momos said with a nod of noble sadness. 'I have a carriage. Take her things and put them in it, her clothes, her tri–tri–trinkets.' His voice trembled and his shoulders began to shake. The valet dashed away and began stuffing trunks and suitcases, afraid the mournful husband might change his mind. The pimply boy dragged the luggage out into the yard, puffing and panting. Momos walked round the rooms again and admired the Japanese prints. Some of them were most entertaining, with indecent details. He stuffed a couple of the more savoury ones inside his jacket – to amuse Mimi. In the master's study he took a set of jade beads, as a souvenir. And he left something in their place, also as a souvenir. It took less than ten minutes to load everything.

The valet and the pimply sleuth both saw the 'Count' to his carriage and even helped him up on to the footboard. The carriage had sunk considerably lower on its springs under the weight of Addy's luggage.

'Drive,' Momos told the coachman in a melancholy voice, and rode away from the field of battle.

He held the Countess's jewellery box in his hands, lovingly fingering the glittering stones. It was actually not a bad haul at all. Pleasure had been combined with business in a most satisfactory fashion. The sapphire diadem alone – the one he had already taken note of in the theatre – was probably worth a good thirty thousand. Or should he give it to Mimi, to go with her lovely blue eyes?

As he drove along Tverskaya Street, a familiar sleigh came rushing along in the opposite direction. The Court Counsellor was alone, with his fur coat unbuttoned and a resolute look on his pale face. He was on his way to have things out with the ferocious husband. Most praiseworthy – he was a brave man. But it was Madame Addy to whom the dear fellow would have to make his explanations now and, according to the information that Momos possessed and his own personal impressions, those explanations would not be easily made. Addy is going to give you hell, Momos thought, delighted at the prospect. That will teach you to spoil Momos's fun, Mr Fandorin. One good turn always deserves another.

CHAPTER 5

A Grouse Hunt

The meeting to consult on the case of the Jack of Spades was limited to a narrow circle: His Excellency Prince Dolgorukoi, Frol Grigorievich Vedishchev, Erast Petrovich Fandorin and, like a quiet little mouse in the corner, the humble servant of God, Anisii.

It was evening time and the lamp under its green shade illuminated only the Governor's writing desk and its immediate surroundings, so that candidate-for-a-state-rank-title Tulipov was as good as invisible in the soft shadows that filled the corners of the study.

The speaker's voice was low, dry and monotonous, and His Excellency the Governor seemed to be almost dozing off: his wrinkled eyelids were closed and the long wings of his moustache were trembling in time to his slow, regular breathing.

Meanwhile the report was approaching its most interesting part: the conclusions.

'It would be reasonable t-to assume,' Fandorin stated, 'that the gang consists of the following members: the "Duke", "Speier", the "Notary", the "Constable", the girl with exceptional gymnastic abilities, "Count Opraksin" and his coachman.'

At the words 'Count Opraksin', one corner of the Court Counsellor's mouth turned down in suffering, and a tactful silence filled the study. However, when Anisii looked a little closer, he saw that he was the only one actually maintaining a tactful silence and everyone else was simply saying nothing without being the slightest bit tactful. Vedishchev was smiling openly in glee, and even His Excellency opened one eye and gave an eloquent grunt.

In fact the outcome of the previous day's events had been very far from funny. After the Chief discovered the jack of spades (on the malachite paperweight in the study, where his jade beads had been lying), his perennial sangfroid had deserted him. Admittedly, he hadn't said a word of reproach to Anisii, but he had berated his valet ferociously in Japanese. Poor Masa had been so affected by it that he wanted to do away with himself and had even gone running into the kitchen to get the bread knife. It had taken Erast Petrovich a long time to calm the poor fellow down afterwards.

But that had been just the beginning; the real fireworks had begun when Addy came back. Recalling what had happened then, Anisii shuddered. The Chief had been presented with a stern ultimatum: until he returned her toiletries, scent and jewellery, Ariadna Arkadievna would wear the same dress and the same sable cloak; she would apply no scent and keep the same pearl earrings on. And if that should make her ill, then Erast Petrovich would be solely and completely to blame. Tulipov had not heard what came after that, because he had taken the coward's way out and withdrawn but, if the Court Counsellor's pale face and the dark circles under his eyes were anything to go by, he had not got any sleep last night.

'I warned you, my dear fellow, that nothing good would come of this escapade of yours,' Prince Dolgorukoi declared in a didactic tone, 'nothing good at all. A respectable lady, from the highest echelon of society, a husband with a very substantial position. I even received complaints about you from the Court Chancellery. As if there aren't enough women without husbands, or at least of more modest rank.'

Erast Petrovich flushed and Anisii was frightened he might say something more than could be permitted to his high-ranking superior, but the Court Counsellor took himself in hand and carried on talking about the case as if nothing out of the ordinary had been said: 'That was how I imagined the membership of the gang as late as yesterday. However, after analysing what my assistant has told me about yesterday's . . . events, I have changed my opinion. And entirely thanks to Mr Tulipov, who has rendered the investigation invaluable assistance.'

Anisii was most surprised by this declaration and Vedishchev, the spiteful old man, interposed venomously. 'Why, of course, he's a well-known agent. Anisii, why don't you tell us how you carried the suitcases out to the carriage and took the Jack by the elbow and helped him in so that he wouldn't, God forbid, miss his step.'

Tulipov blushed bright red in torment, and wished the earth would simply swallow him up.

'Frol Grigorievich,' said the Chief, interceding for Anisii, 'your gloating is out of place. All of us here have been made fools of, each in his own way . . . begging your pardon, Your Excellency.' The Governor had started dozing again and gave no response to the apology, and Fandorin continued. 'So let us try to make allowances for each other. We have a quite exceptionally strong and audacious opponent.'

'Not opponent – opponents. An entire gang,' Vedishchev corrected him.

'What Tulipov told me has made me doubt that.' The Chief slipped his hand into his pocket, but immediately jerked it back out, as if he'd burned his fingers. He was going to take out his beads, Anisii guessed, but the beads aren't there.

'My assistant remembered what the "Count's" carriage looked like and described it to me in detail, in particular the monogram "ZG" on the door. That is the sign of the Zinovy Goder company, which rents out carriages, sleighs and fiacres, both with coachmen and without. This morning I visited the company's office and was able without any difficulty to locate the very carriage: a scratch on the left door, crimson leather seats, a new rim on the rear right wheel. Imagine my surprise when I learned that yesterday's "important gentleman" in uniform and wearing a ribbon took the carriage with a coachman!'

'Well, and what of it?' asked Vedishchev.

'Oh come now! It meant that the coachman was not an

accomplice, not a member of the gang of jacks, but a complete outsider! I found that coachman. Admittedly, I did not profit greatly from talking to him: we already had a description of the "Count" without him, and he was unable to tell me anything else that was useful. The things were delivered to the Nikolaevsky Station and deposited at the left-luggage office, following which the coachman was let go.'

'And what did you find at the left-luggage office?' asked Prince Dolgorukoi, suddenly awake again.

'Nothing. An hour later a cabby arrived with the receipts, took everything and left for an unknown destination.'

'Well then, and you say Anisii rendered assistance,' said Frol Grigorievich with a dismissive wave of his hand. 'It was a total flop.'

'Far from it,' said Erast Petrovich, almost reaching for his beads again and stopping himself with a frown of annoyance. 'What does this give us? Yesterday's "Count" arrived alone, without any accomplices, even though he has an entire gang of them, and all outstanding actors. They would have been able to manage the simple role of a coachman somehow. And yet the "Count" complicates the plan by involving an outsider. That is one. "Speier" was recommended to the Governor by the "Duke", but by letter, not in person. That is to say, the "Duke" and his protégé were never seen together. The question is, why? Surely it would have been simpler for one member of the gang to introduce another in person? That is two. Now, gentlemen, can you explain to me why the Englishman went to see the "Notary" without "Speier"? It would have been more natural to complete the deal with both sides present. That is three. Let us go on. In the case of the lottery caper, our Jack of Spades made use of a decoy chairman who was also not a member of the gang. He was simply a pitiful drunk who had been told nothing, hired for a small fee. That is f-four. And so we see that in each of these episodes we are faced with only one member of the gang: either the "Duke" or the "Invalid" or the "Notary" or the "Constable" or the "Count". And from this I conclude that the Jack of Spades gang consists of only one individual. Probably the only permanent assistant he has is the young woman who jumped out of the window.'

'Quite impossible,' rumbled the Governor-General, who had a rather strange way of dozing without missing anything of importance. 'I didn't see the "Notary", the "Constable" and the "Count", but the "Duke" and "Speier" can't be the same person. Judge for yourself, Erast Petrovich. My self-styled "grandson" was pale and puny; he had a high voice, a flat chest and a stoop, with thin black hair and a quite distinctive duck's-bill nose. Saxen-Limburg is a fine, handsome fellow: broad in the shoulders, with a military bearing and a voice trained to command. An aquiline nose, thick sandy sideburns, a rollicking laugh. Absolutely unlike "Speier"!'

'And how t-tall was he?'

'Half a head shorter than me. So he was average.'

'And our lanky Lord Pitsbrook described the "Notary" as being "just above his shoulder", so he was average height too. So was the "Constable". And how about the "Count", Tulipov?'

Fandorin's bold hypothesis had thrown Anisii into a fever. He leaped to his feet and exclaimed: 'I should say he was average too, Erast Petrovich. He was slightly taller than me, by about one and a half *vershoks*.'

'Height is the one part of a person's appearance that is difficult to alter,' the Court Counsellor continued. 'It is possible to use high heels, but that is too obvious. True, in Japan I did encounter one individual from a secret sect of professional killers who deliberately had his legs amputated so that he could change his height at will. He could run on his wooden legs better than on real ones. He had three sets of artificial limbs – short, medium and tall. However, such selflessness in one's profession is only possible in Japan. As far as our Jack of Spades is concerned, I believe I can describe his appearance to you and provide an approximate psychological portrait. His appearance, however, is largely irrelevant, since this man changes it with ease. He is a man without a face, always wearing one mask or another. Nonetheless, let me try to describe him.'

Fandorin stood up and began walking around the study with his hands clasped behind his back.

'Well then, this man's height is . . .' – the Chief glanced briefly at Anisii's upright figure – '. . . two *arshins* and six *vershoks*. His natural hair colour is light – dark hair would be more difficult to disguise. And his hair is probably also brittle and bleached at the ends from the frequent use of colouring agents. His eyes are blue-grey, rather close-set. His nose is average. The face is unremarkable, so perfectly ordinary that it is hard to remember and pick out in a crowd. This man must often be confused with someone else. And now for his voice . . . The Jack of Spades controls it like a true virtuoso. To judge from the fact that he can easily mimic a bass or a tenor with any specific modulations, his natural voice must be a sonorous baritone. His age is hard to guess. He can hardly still be youthful, since he obviously has experience of life, but he is not elderly – our "constable" disappeared into the crowd very n-nimbly indeed. The ears are a very important detail. Criminological science has demonstrated that they are unique to each individual and their form is impossible to change. Unfortunately, I have only seen the Jack in the guise of the "constable", and he was wearing a cap. Tell me, Tulipov, did the "Count" remove his cocked hat?'

'No,' Anisii replied curtly. He tended to take any reference to the subject of ears – especially to their uniqueness – personally.

'And you, Your Excellency – did you pay any to attention to what kind of ears the "Duke" and "Speier" had?'

Dolgorukoi answered sternly: 'Erast Petrovich, I am the Governor-General of Moscow, and I have plenty of other matters to concern me apart from examining someone's ears.'

The Court Counsellor sighed: 'A pity. That means we won't be able to squeeze much out of his appearance . . . Now for the criminal's personality traits. He comes from a good family; he even knows English. He is an excellent psychologist and a talented actor – that much is obvious. He possesses uncommon charm and is very good at winning the trust of people he hardly even knows. He has lightning-fast reactions and is very inventive. An original sense of humour.' Erast Petrovich glanced severely at Vedishchev to make sure he didn't giggle. 'In general, clearly an exceptional and highly talented man.'

'We could use talents like that to populate Siberia,' Prince Dolgorukoi muttered. 'Why don't you stick to the point, my dear chap, without the glowing testimonials? We're not proposing Mr Jack of Spades for a decoration. Can he be caught – that's the important question.'

'Why not? – anything is possible,' Fandorin said thoughtfully. 'Let us size things up. What are our hero's vulnerable points? He is either excessively greedy or fantastically extravagant – no matter how much he gets away with, it is never enough for him. That is one. He is vain and longs for admiration. That is two. The third point – and the most valuable for us – is his excessive self-assurance and tendency to underestimate his opponents. That gives us something to work on. And there is a fourth point. Despite the precision with which he acts, he still sometimes makes mistakes.'

'What mistakes?' the Governor asked quickly. 'He seems as slippery as an eel to me – no way to grab hold of him.'

'There have been at least two mistakes. Why did the "Count" mention the Knight of the Orders of Chrysanthemums to Anisii yesterday? I do happen to be a Knight of the Japanese Orders of the Greater and Lesser Chrysanthemums; however, in Russia I do not wear them, I do not boast about them to anyone, and you will not learn anything about these regalia of mine from my servants. Certainly, the genuine Count Opraksin, as a man of some standing in the state who has access to higher spheres, might have been able to discover such details, but the Jack of Spades? Where from? Only from my personal file and service record, which lists my decorations. Your Excellency, I shall require a list of all the functionaries in the secret section of your chancellery, especially those who have access to p-personal files. There are not so very many, are there? One of them is connected with the Jack. I think an internal informant must also have been required in the fraudulent transaction with the English lord.'

'It's unimaginable,' Prince Dolgorukoi exclaimed indignantly, 'for one of my people to play me such a dirty trick!'

'Nothing easier, Vladim Andreich,' Vedishchev put in. 'How

many times have I told you you've got a fine crop of spongers and toadies.'

Unable to restrain himself, Anisii asked quietly: 'And what was the second mistake, Chief?'

Erast Petrovich answered in a steely voice: 'Making me really angry. This was a professional matter, but now it's personal.'

He strode along the front of the desk with a springy step, suddenly reminding Tulipov of the African leopard in the cage beside the unforgettable chimpanzee.

But then Fandorin stopped, took hold of his own elbows and started speaking in a different tone of voice, thoughtful and even rather dreamy: 'Why don't we play M-Mr Jack of Spades, alias Momos, at his own game?'

'We could play him all right,' commented Frol Grigorievich, 'only where are you going to find him now? Or do you have some idea where he is?'

'No, I don't,' the Chief snapped, 'and I don't intend to go looking for him. Let him come and seek me out. It will be like a grouse hunt with a decoy. You put a plump papier-mâché grouse hen in a spot where it's easy to see, the male grouse c-comes flying up and – bang! – it's all over.'

'Who's going to play the grouse hen?' asked Dolgorukoi, half-opening a cautious eye. 'Could it perhaps be my favourite Deputy for Special Assignments? After all, you are also a master of disguise, Erast Petrovich.'

It suddenly struck Tulipov that the few comments the old prince made were almost always exceptionally precise and to the point. Erast Petrovich, however, did not seem to find Dolgorukoi's perspicacity surprising in the least.

'Who else should dress up as the stuffed bird, if not me, Your Excellency. After what happened yesterday, I will not yield that honour to anyone.'

'And just how is he going to find the grouse hen?' Vedishchev asked with lively curiosity.

'Just as he should in a grouse hunt: he will hear the call of the hunter's whistle. And for our hunter's whistle, we shall employ the same means as Momos himself.'

'If a man is accustomed to duping everyone he wishes, it is not so very difficult to trick him too,' the Chief said to Anisii when they had returned to Malaya Nikitskaya Street and secluded themselves in the study for an 'analysis'. 'It simply never occurs to a swindler that anyone would have the nerve to out-trick the trickster and rob the thief. And in particular he can scarcely anticipate such perfidious guile from an official personage, especially one of such high rank.'

As he listened reverently, Anisii thought at first that by 'an official personage of high rank', the Court Counsellor meant himself. However, as subsequent events demonstrated, Erast Petrovich was aiming far higher than that.

Having propounded his initial, theoretical thesis, Fandorin paused for a while. Anisii sat there motionless – God forbid that he might interrupt his superior's thinking process.

'We need the kind of decoy that will have Momos drooling at the mouth and also – even more importantly – provoke his vanity. He has to be lured not just by a large haul, but also by the prospect of great fame. He is far from indifferent to fame.'

The Chief fell silent again, pondering the next link in the chain of logic. After seven and a half minutes (Anisii counted them on the huge clock, obviously an antique, in the form of London's Big Ben) Erast Petrovich declared: 'Some gigantic precious stone ... Say, from the legacy of the Emerald Rajah. Have you ever heard of him?'

Anisii shook his head, looking his chief straight in the eye.

For some reason the Court Counsellor seemed disappointed: 'Strange. Of course, that business was kept secret from the general public, but some rumours did leak out into the European press. They must have reached Russia, surely. But then, what am I thinking of? When I took that memorable voyage on the *Leviathan*, you were still a child.'

'Did you say you took a voyage on a leviathan?' asked Anisii, unable to believe his ears, picturing Erast Petrovich sailing across the stormy waves on the broad back of the legendary whale-fish monster.

'It doesn't matter,' Fandorin said dismissively. 'Just an old investigation that I was involved in. It's the idea that's important here: an Indian rajah and an immense diamond. Or a sapphire or emerald? It doesn't matter which. That will depend on the mineralogical collection,' he muttered in a totally incomprehensible closing remark.

Anisii blinked in puzzlement, and the Chief felt it necessary to add something (which still failed to introduce any clarity): 'It's a bit crude, of course, but for our Jack it ought to b-be just the thing. He should take the bait. Right then, Tulipov, enough idle gaping. To work!'

Erast Petrovich opened the latest number of the *Russian Word*, immediately found what he wanted and started reading out loud:

A Visitor from India

Truly, there is no counting the diamonds that lie concealed in the caves of stone, especially if those caves lie on the lands owned by Ahmad-Khan, the heir to one of Bengal's richest rajahs. The prince has arrived in old Mother Moscow on his way from Teheran to St Petersburg and will be a guest of the city of golden domes for at least a week. Prince Vladimir Andreevich Dolgorukoi is according our high-ranking visitor every appropriate honour. The Indian prince is staying at the Governor-General's villa on the Sparrow Hills and tomorrow evening the Assembly of Nobles is hosting a ball in his honour. The cream of Moscow society is expected to gather, eager for a glimpse of the prince from the East, and even more of the famous 'Shakh-Sultan' emerald that adorns Prince Ahmad's turban. It is said that this gigantic stone once belonged to Alexander the Great himself. We have been informed that the prince is travelling unofficially and almost incognito, with no retinue or pomp and ceremony. He is accompanied only by his devoted old wet-nurse Zukhra and his personal secretary Tarik-bei.

The Court Counsellor nodded in approval and put the newspaper down.

'The Governor-General is so angry with the Jack of Spades that he has sanctioned the holding of a b-ball and will take part in this performance himself. I believe he will actually quite enjoy it. For the "Shakh-Sultan" they have issued us a faceted beryl from the mineralogical collection of Moscow University. It is impossible to distinguish it from an emerald without a special magnifying glass, and we are not likely to allow anyone to inspect our turban through a special magnifying glass, are we, Tulipov?'

Erast Petrovich opened a hat box and took out a white brocade turban with an absolutely immense green stone and turned it this way and that, so that the facets glinted blindingly.

Anisii smacked his lips together admiringly – the turban really was a joy to behold. 'But where are we going to get Zukhra from? And that secretary – what's his name – Tarik-bei. Who's going to be them?'

The Chief looked at his assistant with something between reproach and pity, and Anisii suddenly understood. 'No, how could you?' he gasped. 'Erast Petrovich, have mercy! What kind of Indian would I make! I'll never agree, not even to save my life!'

'I think we can assume that you will agree, Tulipov,' sighed Fandorin, 'but Masa will require a little more persuasion. He's not likely to find the role of an old wet-nurse to his liking ...'

On the evening of 18 February the whole of Moscow high society really did convene at the Assembly of Nobles. In the jolly, devil-may-care atmosphere of Pancake Week, the people of the city, weary after the long, cold winter, celebrated almost every day, but the organisers of today's festivities had made a really special effort. The snow-white staircase of the palace was entirely covered in flowers, the footmen in powdered wigs and pistachio camisoles positively flung themselves at people to catch the fur coats and cloaks as they slipped off the ladies' and gentlemen's shoulders, and from the dining room there came the alluring tinkle of crystal and silver as the tables were laid for the banquet.

In his role as host of the ball, the Lord of Moscow, Prince Vladimir Andreevich Dolgorukoi, was smart and fresh, genial with the men and gallant with the ladies. However, the genuine centre of gravity in the marble hall today was not the Governor-General but his Indian guest.

Everyone took a great liking to Ahmad-Khan, especially the ladies, young and old. The nabob was wearing black tails and a white tie, but his head was crowned by a white turban with a quite immense emerald. The oriental prince's jet-black beard was trimmed in the latest French fashion and his brows were pointed arches, but the most impressive features of his swarthy face were the bright-blue eyes (it had already been ascertained that His Majesty's mother was French).

Standing modestly slightly behind and to one side of him was the prince's secretary, who also attracted no small attention. Tarik-bei was not as handsome as his master, and his figure was not very impressive, but on the other hand, unlike Ahmad-Khan, he had come to the ball in genuine eastern costume: an embroidered robe, white shalwars or loose trousers and golden slippers with curving, pointed toes and open backs. It was a pity that the secretary did not speak a single civilised language and his only reply to all questions and greetings was to press his hand either to his heart or to his forehead and give a low bow.

All in all, the two Indians were quite wonderfully fine.

Anisii, who had not hitherto been unduly spoiled by the attentions of the fair sex, froze completely rigid on finding himself at the centre of a bevy of beauties. The young ladies twittered gaily, discussing the details of his costume without the slightest embarrassment, and one, the extremely pretty Georgian Princess Sofiko Chkhartishvili, even called Tulipov 'a lovely little Moor'. A phrase that was often repeated was 'poor thing', which set Anisii blushing deeply (thank God, no one could see that under his Brazil-nut make-up).

In order to clarify the matter of the make-up and the comments about the 'poor thing', we shall have to turn the clock back a few hours, to the moment when Ahmad-Khan and his faithful secretary were preparing for their first grand social entrance . . .

Erast Petrovich, already sporting a pitch-black beard, but still in his household dressing gown, made Anisii up himself. First he took a little bottle of dark chocolate-coloured liquid and explained that it was an infusion of Brazil nut. He rubbed the thick, odorous oil into the skin of Anisii's face, ears and eyelids. Then he glued on a thick black beard and pulled it off again. He stuck on a different one, something like a goatee, but rejected that too.

'No, Tulipov, we can't make a Moslem out of you,' the Chief told him. 'I was too hasty with Tarik-bei. I should have said you were a Hindu. Some kind of Chandragupta or other.'

'Can't I just have a moustache, without a beard?' asked Anisii. It was an old dream of his to have a moustache, but the way his own grew was unconvincing somehow, in little clumps.

'It's not done. In oriental etiquette that is too dandified for a secretary,' said Fandorin. He turned Anisii's head to the left, then to the right and declared: 'There's nothing else for it; we'll have to make a eunuch of you.' He mixed up a little yellow grease and started rubbing it into Anisii's cheeks and under his chin – 'to loosen the skin a bit and gather it into a fold'. He inspected the result and was satisfied: 'A genuine eunuch. Just what we need.'

But that was not the end of Tulipov's torments. 'Since you're a Moslem now, the hair has to go' – the Court Counsellor passed sentence implacably.

Already crushed by his transformation into a eunuch, Anisii bore the shaving of his head without a murmur. The shaving was carried out deftly by Masa, with an extremely sharp Japanese dagger. Erast Petrovich rubbed the smelly brown infusion into Anisii's naked cranium and told him: 'It shines like a cannon ball.' He took a little brush, tinkered with Anisii's eyebrows a little and approved his eyes: brown, with a slight slant, just right.

He made Anisii put on the broad silk trousers and some sort of short, patterned woman's jacket, then the robe, and finally jammed a turban on his bald pate and unfortunate ears.

Anisii walked across to the mirror with slow, reluctant steps, expecting to see some hideous monstrosity – and instead was pleasantly astonished: staring out at him from the bronze frame was a picturesque Moor – no sign at all of pimples or protruding ears. What a pity it was he couldn't stroll around Moscow like that all the time!

'You're done,' said Fandorin. 'Just rub some make-up into your hands and neck. And don't forget your feet and ankles – you'll be wearing loose slippers . . .'

The gilded morocco sandals, which Erast Petrovich referred to so unromantically as slippers, caused Anisii problems, because he wasn't used to them. They were the reason why Anisii stood absolutely stock-still at the ball. He was afraid that if he moved from the spot one of them was bound to fall off – it had already happened on the staircase. When the lovely Georgian lady asked in French if Tarik-bei would care to dance a waltz with her, Anisii became flustered and, instead of following instructions and replying silently with an oriental bow, he whispered quietly: '*Non, merci, je ne danse pas.*'

Thank God, the other girls didn't seem to have caught what he muttered, or the situation would have become complicated. Tarik-bei was not supposed to understand a single white man's language.

Anisii turned anxiously to his chief, who had been talking for several minutes to a dangerous guest, the British Indologist Sir Andrew Marvell, an exceedingly boring gentleman wearing spectacles with thick lenses. A little earlier, when Ahmad-Khan had been exchanging bows with the Governor-General on the upper landing of the staircase, Dolgorukoi had whispered excitedly (Anisii had heard snatches of the exchange): 'Why the devil did he have to turn up? . . . And he would have to be an Indologist! . . . I can't turn him out, he's a baronet . . . What if he sees through your disguise?'

However, to judge from the calm way in which the prince and the baronet were conversing, Fandorin was in no danger of being seen through. Anisii did not know English, but he heard he often-repeated words 'Gladstone' and 'Her Britannic Majesty'.

When the Indologist blew his nose loudly into a handkerchief and walked away, the prince summoned his secretary to him with a brief, imperious gesture of a swarthy, ring-bedecked hand and hissed to him: 'Wake up, Tulipov. And be more affectionate with her; don't look so surly. Only don't overdo it.'

'More affectionate? Who with?' Anisii asked in an astonished whisper.

'Why, with that Georgian. Can't you see that it's her? The window-jumper.'

Tulipov looked round and was struck dumb. It was her! Why hadn't he realised it straight away! Yes, the white-skinned young lady from the lottery now had swarthy skin, the hair that had been golden was black and woven into two plaits, her eyebrows had been painted out as far as her temples, and a delightful mole had somehow appeared on her cheek. But it was her, definitely her! And the sparkle in her eyes was exactly the same as that other time, just before her reckless leap from the window ledge.

The bait had been taken! The grouse was circling round the decoy hen.

Gently, now, Anisii, you mustn't go frightening him off.

He pressed his hand to his forehead, then to his heart, and bowed to the starry-eyed charmer with true oriental gravity.

CHAPTER 6

Platonic Love

But was he a charlatan? – that was the first thing that had to be checked. The last thing he needed was to bump into some professional colleague on tour, come to pluck the plump Moscow geese. An Indian rajah, the Shakh-Sultan emerald – there was more than a whiff of the operetta about all these oriental delights.

He had checked. And the very last person His Bengali Highness resembled was a crook. Firstly, from close up it was immediately obvious that he came from a genuine royal blood line: from his bearing, his manners, from the benevolent languor of his gaze. Secondly, Ahmad-Khan had struck up such a highly intellectual conversation with 'Sir Andrew Marvell', the well-known Indologist who had happened so opportunely to be in Moscow – all about the internal politics and religious confessions of the Indian Empire – that Momos had been afraid he might give himself away. The prince's polite question about his opinion of the practice of *suttee* and whether it reflected the true spirit of Hinduism had obliged him to change the subject to the health of Her Majesty Queen Victoria, feign a sudden attack of sneezing and beat a hasty retreat.

But the most important thing was that the emerald shone with such seductive conviction that not a trace of doubt remained. How he longed to detach that glorious green cobblestone from the noble Ahmad-Khan's turban, saw it up into eight substantial gemstones and sell off each one for something like twenty-five thousand. Now that would be just the job!

Meanwhile Mimi had been working on the secretary. She

said that although Tarik-bei was a eunuch, that didn't stop him shooting keen glances into a lady's décolleté, and he was clearly not indifferent to the female sex in general. Mimi could be trusted in such matters; there was no way to fool her. Who could say how eunuchs felt about such things? Perhaps the natural desires never went away even when the means of satisfaction had been lost?

The plan for the forthcoming campaign, which in his own mind Momos had already dubbed the 'Battle for the Emerald', had taken shape of its own accord.

The turban was always on the Rajah's head. But surely we could assume that he removed it when he went to bed?

Where did the Rajah sleep? In the mansion on the Sparrow Hills. That meant Momos had to go there.

The Governor-General's villa was intended for use by honoured guests. There was a wonderful view of Moscow from that spot on the hills, and there were not so many idle onlookers to annoy the visitors. It was good that the house was rather out of the way. But the villa was guarded by a gendarme post, and that was bad. Clambering over walls in the night and then high-tailing it to the shrilling tones of a police whistle was in bad taste, not Momos's style.

Ah, if only the secretary weren't a eunuch, the whole thing could not have been simpler. The Georgian princess, driven to desperation by her passion, would have paid Tarik-bei a secret night-time visit and, once she was in the house, she would have found some way of wandering into the Rajah's bedroom to see whether the emerald might be persuaded to leave that boring turban in search of new adventures. After that it would be a purely technical matter, and Momos knew all about that sort of thing.

But this line of thought, entirely speculative as it was, set a black cat's sharp claws scraping at Momos's heart. For an instant he imagined Mimi in the embraces of a handsome, broad-shouldered young fellow with a luxuriant moustache who was no eunuch but quite the opposite, and he did not like what he saw. It was nonsense, of course, sentimental drivel, but – would you believe it! – he suddenly realised that he would not have gone down this most simple and natural route, even if the secretary's means had been a match for his desires.

Stop! Momos jumped off the desk on which he had been sitting until that moment, dangling his legs (his thoughts moved more nimbly like that) and walked across to the window. Stop-stop-stop . . .

The coaches and fours, and the sleighs, and the carriages on their spiked winter wheels were pouring down Tverskaya Street in an unbroken stream. Soon spring would arrive, bringing slush. It was Lent, but today the sun still shone without warming, and the main street of Moscow looked smart and full of life. It was four days since Momos and Mimi had moved out of the Metropole and into the Dresden. Their suite was a little smaller, but it had electric light and a telephone. They couldn't have stayed in the Metropole any longer. Sliunkov had come to see him there several times, and that was dangerous. That little fellow was too unreliable altogether. With a responsible, in fact secret job like that, he still dabbled at cards, and didn't even know his own limits. What if the ingenious Mr Fandorin or some other chief of his were to take hold of him by the lapels and give him a good shaking? No, God looked after those who looked after themselves.

Anyway, the Dresden was a very fine hotel, and located exactly opposite the Governor's palace, which was like home to Momos now, after the business with the Englishman. It gave him a warm feeling just to look at it.

The previous day he'd seen Sliunkov in the street and deliberately moved up close to him, even nudged him with his shoulder, but the clerk still hadn't recognised the Marseilles merchant Antoine Bonifatievich Darioux, a long-haired dandy with a waxed moustache, as Momos. Sliunkov had simply muttered, 'Pardon,' and trudged on, hunched over under the powdery falling snow

Stop-stop-stop, Momos told himself again. He had an idea: why couldn't he kill two birds with one stone as he usually did? – or, to be more precise, kill the other man's bird and keep his own away from the stones; or to put it another way, have his cake and eat it. Yes that was exactly the way it would be: innocence preserved and capital acquired.

And why not? – it could very well work! And things were coming together well. Mimi had said that Tarik-bei understood a little French, and 'a little' was exactly the amount that was required.

From that moment on the operation had a new title. It was called 'Platonic Love'.

He knew from the newspapers that after dinner His Indian Highness liked to stroll along the walls of the Novodevichy Convent, where the winter amusements and rides were laid out. There was ice-skating, and wooden slides, and all sorts of sideshows – plenty for the foreign visitor to look at.

As we have already said, it was a genuine Shrovetide day – light and bright with a touch of frost – and so, after strolling round the frozen pond for an hour, Momos and Mimi were chilled through. It wasn't so bad for Mimi. Since she was playing a princess, she was wearing a squirrel-skin coat, with a pine-marten hood and a muff – only her cheeks were ruddy and flushed. But Momos was frozen through to the bone. For the good of the cause he had decked himself out as an elderly oriental chaperone, gluing on thick eyebrows that ran together across the bridge of his nose, deliberately leaving his upper lip unshaved and blackening it and sticking an extension like the bowsprit of a frigate on his nose. His headscarf, with the plaits of false hair streaked with grey dangling from under it, and the short rabbit-fur jacket over his long beaver coat did little to keep him warm; his feet were freezing in their soft felt shoes, and still the damned Rajah did not show up. To amuse Mimi and avoid getting bored himself, from time to time Momos intoned in a soaring contralto with a Georgian accent: 'Sofiko, my darling little chick, your old nurse is absolutely frozen,' or something else of the same kind, and Mimi giggled and stamped her chilly feet in their pretty scarlet boots.

His Highness eventually deigned to arrive. Momos spotted

the closed sleigh upholstered in blue velvet from a distance. There was a gendarme in a greatcoat and dress-uniform helmet with a plume sitting on the box beside the coachman.

The prince, wrapped in sables, strolled unhurriedly along beside the skating rink in his tall white turban, casting curious glances at the amusements of these northerners. Trotting along behind His Highness was a low, squat figure in a sheepskin coat that reached down to the ground, a shaggy round cap and a yashmak – presumably the devoted wet nurse Zukhra. The secretary Tarik-bei, in an overcoat of woollen cloth, beneath which his white shalwars could be seen, kept falling behind, gaping eagerly at a gypsy with a bear, or stopping beside a man selling hot spice tea. The pompous gendarme with the grey moustache brought up the rear, in the role of guard of honour. That was helpful: he could take a good look at the ladies who would come visiting that night.

The public showed tremendous interest in the colourful procession. The simpler among them gaped open-mouthed at the infidels, pointing their fingers at the turban and the emerald and the old oriental woman's covered face. The respectable, washed public behaved with greater tact, but also evinced great curiosity. Momos waited until the people of Moscow had had their fill of ogling 'the Indians' and returned to their former amusements, then gave Mimi a gentle nudge in the ribs: it was time.

They set off towards the others. Mimi curtseyed lightly to His Highness and he nodded graciously. She beamed joyfully at the secretary and dropped her muff. The eunuch did what he was supposed to do and rushed to pick it up. Mimi also squatted down and she and the oriental bumped foreheads in a most charming fashion. Following this small, entirely innocent incident, the length of the procession quite naturally increased, with the prince still striding along at the front in regal solitude, followed by his secretary and the princess, and then the two elderly eastern women, with the sniffling, red-nosed gendarme bringing up the rear.

The princess twittered away in lively French and kept losing her footing all the time, providing a pretext for clutching at the secretary's arm as often as possible. Momos tried to make friends with venerable Zukhra, attempting to express his sympathy to her in gestures and exclamations. Zukhra, however, proved to be a genuine virago. The bitch refused to get to know him and merely cackled from under her chaddar and waved her stubby-fingered hand about, as if to say: Go away, I keep to myself. A genuine savage, in fact.

Mimi and the eunuch, on the other hand, were getting along like a house on fire. Momos waited until the oriental finally mellowed and offered the young lady permanent support in the form of his crooked arm and decided that was enough for the first time. He caught up with his young ward and intoned sternly: 'Sofiko-o, my little dove, it's time to go home for tea and bread-cakes.'

The following day 'Sofiko' was already teaching Tarik-bei how to skate (for which the secretary demonstrated quite outstanding ability). In general, the eunuch proved quite compliant: when Mimi lured him behind a fir tree and seemingly by accident set her plump lips right in front of his brown nose, he didn't shy away, but obediently kissed them. Afterwards she told Momos: 'You know, Momochka, I feel so sorry for him. I put my arms round his neck, and he was trembling all over, the poor thing. It's really atrocious to mutilate people like that.'

'The Lord gave the cussed cow no horns,' the callous Momos replied flippantly. The operation was set to take place the following night.

During the day everything went as smooth as butter: driven insane by passion, the princess completely lost her head and promised her platonic admirer that she would pay him a visit during the night. In promising, she emphasised the exalted nature of her feelings and the union of two loving hearts in the highest sense, with no crude vulgarity. She could not tell how much of this the oriental understood, but he was clearly over-joyed at the prospect of the visit and explained in broken French that he would open the garden gate at precisely midnight. 'But I shall come with my nanny,' Mimi warned him. 'I know what you men are like.'

At that Tarik-bei hung his head and sighed bitterly. Mimi felt so sorry for him she almost cried.

That Saturday night there was a moon and stars, perfect for platonic love. After letting his coachman go outside the gates of the Governor's suburban villa, Momos took a look around. Ahead of him, beyond the mansion, was the steep drop to the River Moscow; behind him stood the fir trees of the Sparrow Park; to his right and his left he could see the dark silhouettes of expensive dachas. They would have to leave on foot afterwards: through the Acclimatic Garden to the Knacker's Quarter. There they could hire a troika at the inn on the Kaluga road at any time of day or night. And then a sleigh ride with bells jingling along the Kaluga highroad! Never mind the biting frost – the emerald would be warm against his heart.

They gave the secret knock at the gate and the little door opened immediately. The impatient secretary was obviously already standing there, waiting. He gave a low bow and beckoned for them to follow. They walked through the snow-covered garden to the entrance of the house. The three gendarmes on duty in the vestibule were drinking tea with hard, dry bread rings. They gave the secretary and his nocturnal visitors a curious glance; the sergeant-major with the grey moustache grunted and shook his head, but he didn't say anything. What business was it of his?

In the dark corridor Tarik-bei pressed a finger to his lips and pointed somewhere upstairs, then folded his hands together, put them against his cheek and closed his eyes. Aha, that meant His Highness was already sleeping – excellent.

The drawing room was lit by a candle and smelled of some kind of oriental incense. The secretary seated the chaperone in an armchair, set a bowl of sweetmeats and fruits in front of her and muttered something incomprehensible, but it was not hard to guess the significance of his request.

'Ah, children, children,' Momos purred placidly, and wagged a finger in warning. 'But no nonsense, mind.'

The enamoured couple took each other by the hand and went

out through the door and into the secretary's room to devote themselves to their exalted, platonic passion. He'll slobber all over her, the Indian gelding, Momos thought with a frown. He sat and waited for a while, to give the eunuch time to get carried away. He ate a juicy pear and tried some halva. Right, that should be long enough.

He had to assume that the master's chambers were over there, behind that white door with the moulding. Momos went out into the corridor, squeezed his eyes shut and stood like that for about a minute to let his eyes grow accustomed to the darkness. But after that he moved quickly, without making a sound.

He opened one door a little: it was the music room. Another – that was the dining room. A third – still not the right one.

He recalled that Tarik-bei had pointed upwards. That meant he had to go up to the first floor.

He slipped out into the vestibule and ran silently up the carpet-covered staircase – the gendarmes didn't even glance round. Another long corridor with another row of doors.

The bedroom turned out to be the third on the left. The moon was shining into the window and Momos could easily make out the bed, the motionless silhouette under the blanket and – hoorah! – the little white mound on the small bedside table. A moonbeam fell on the turban, and a bright ray was reflected from the glittering stone, straight into Momos's eye.

Momos approached the bed, walking on tiptoe. Ahmad-Khan was sleeping on his back, with his face covered by the edge of the blanket – all that could be seen was a head of short-trimmed, spiky black hair.

'Hushaby, hushaby,' Momos whispered gently as he placed a jack of spades right on the sleeper's stomach.

He reached out cautiously for the stone. When his fingers touched the smooth, gleaming surface of the emerald, a strangely familiar hand with short fingers suddenly shot out from under the blanket and seized Momos's wrist in a tight grip.

He squealed in surprise and jerked away with a start, but it was pointless: the hand had taken a firm hold on him. The blanket had slipped down, and gazing out at Momos from under

87

its corner was the fat-cheeked physiognomy of Fandorin's valet, with its unblinking slanty eyes.

'I've been d-dreaming of meeting you for a long time, Monsieur Momos,' a low, mocking voice said behind his back. 'Erast Petrovich Fandorin at your service.'

Momos swung his head round like a trapped animal and saw that there was someone sitting in the tall Voltaire chair in the dark corner, with one leg crossed over the other.

CHAPTER 7

The Chief Is Amused

'Dzi-ing, dzi-ing!'

The piercing, monotonous ringing of the electric bell penetrated Anisii's drifting consciousness from somewhere far away, on the other side of the world. Tulipov did not even realise at first what this new phenomenon could be that had supplemented the picture of God's wonderful world, already so incredibly enriched. However, a whisper of alarm from the darkness roused the sleuth from his state of bliss.

'*On sonne! Qu'est que c'est?*'

Anisii jerked upright, immediately remembered everything and freed himself from a gentle, but at the same time remarkably tenacious, embrace.

The signal! The trap had been sprung! Oh, this was bad! How could he have forgotten his duty?

'*Pardon,*' he muttered, '*tout de suite.*'

In the darkness he felt for his Indian robe, shuffled on his slippers and dashed to the door without turning back to answer the insistent voice that was still asking questions. Bounding out into the corridor, he locked the door with two turns of the key. There, now she wouldn't be flitting off anywhere. It was no ordinary room: it had steel bars on the windows. When the key scraped in the lock, he felt a sickening scraping sensation in his heart as well, but duty is duty.

Anisii shuffled smartly along the corridor in his 'bedroom slippers'. On the upper landing of the staircase the moon peeped in through the corridor window, plucking out of the darkness a white figure running towards him. The mirror!

Tulipov froze for a moment, trying to make out his own face in the gloom. Was it true? Was this him – little Anisii, the deacon's son, the imbecile Sonya's brother? If the happy gleam in the eyes were anything to go by (and in any case, he couldn't see anything else), it wasn't him at all, but someone quite different, someone Anisii didn't know at all.

He opened the door into 'Ahmad-Khan's' bedroom and heard Erast Petrovich's voice.

'. . . You will pay in full for all your pranks, Mr Jester. For the banker Polyakov's trotters, and for the merchant Patrikeev's "river of gold", and for the English lord, and for the lottery. And also for your cynical escapade directed against me, and for obliging me to smear myself with tincture of Brazil nut and walk around in an idiotic turban for five days.'

Tulipov already knew that when the Court Counsellor stopped stammering, it was a bad sign – Mr Fandorin was either under extreme stress or damnably angry. It this case it was obviously the latter.

The stage in the bedroom was set as follows: the elderly Georgian woman was sitting on the floor beside the bed, with her monumental nose strangely skewed to one side. Towering up over her from behind, with his sparse eyebrows knitted in a furious frown and his hands thrust bellicosely against his sides, was Masa, dressed in a long white nightshirt. Erast Petrovich himself was sitting in an armchair in the corner of the room, tapping on the armrest with an unlit cigar. His face was expressionless, his voice was deceptively languid, but its suppressed rumblings of thunder made Anisii wince.

The Chief turned to his assistant and asked: 'Well, how is our little bird?'

'In the cage,' Tulipov reported, waving the key with the double bit.

The 'chaperone' looked at the agent's hand raised in triumph and shook his head sceptically.

'A-ah, Mr Eunuch,' the crooked-nosed woman said in such a resonant, rolling baritone that Anisii started. 'A bald head suits you.' And the repulsive hag stuck out her broad, red tongue.

'And women's clothes suit you,' retorted Tulipov, stung. He instinctively raised a hand to his naked scalp.

'B-Bravo,' said Fandorin, approving his assistant's quick wit. 'I would advise you, Mr Jack, to show less bravado. You are in real trouble this time; you have been caught red-handed.'

Two days earlier, Anisii had been confused at first when the 'Princess Chkhartishvili' had shown up for a stroll in the company of her chaperone. 'Chief, you said there were only two of them – the Jack of Spades and the girl, and now some old woman has turned up as well.'

'You're an old woman yourself, Tulipov,' the 'prince' had hissed through his teeth as he bowed graciously to a lady walking in the opposite direction. 'That's him: our friend Momos. A virtuoso of disguise – give him his due. Except that his feet are a little large for a woman, and his gaze is rather too stern. It's him all right, my dear fellow. Couldn't be anyone else.'

'Shall we take him in?' Anisii had whispered excitedly, pretending to be brushing the snow off his master's shoulder.

'What for? The girl, now – well she was at the lottery, and we have witnesses. But nobody even knows what he looks like. What can we arrest him for? For dressing up as an old woman? Oh no, I've been looking forward to this; we have to be able to throw the book at this one: caught red-handed at the scene of the crime.'

To be quite honest, at the time Tulipov had thought the Court Counsellor was being too clever by half. But, as always, things turned out as Fandorin had said they would. The grouse had gone for the decoy and they had him bang to rights. There was no way he could wriggle out of it now.

Erast Petrovich struck a match, lit his cigar and began talking in a harsh, dry voice: 'Your greatest mistake, my dear sir, was deciding to joke at the expense of those who do not take kindly to being mocked.'

Since the prisoner said nothing, concentrating on setting his nose back in place, Fandorin felt it necessary to explain: 'I mean, firstly, Prince Dolgorukoi and, secondly, myself. No one has ever had the insolence to scoff at my personal life so impudently. And with such unpleasant consequences for myself.'

The Chief wrinkled up his brow in an expression of suffering. Anisii nodded in sympathy, remembering how things had been for Erast Petrovich before they were able to move from Malaya Nikitskaya Street to the Sparrow Hills.

'Certainly, it was pulled off very neatly, I won't deny it,' Fandorin continued, in control of himself once again. 'You will, of course, return the Countess's things, without delay, even before the trial begins. I will not charge you with that – in order not to drag Ariadna Arkadievna's name through the courts.'

At this point the Court Counsellor began pondering something, then nodded to himself as if he were taking a difficult decision and turned to Anisii. 'Tulipov, if you would be so kind, check the things against the list drawn up by Ariadna Arkadievna ... send them to St Petersburg. The address is the house of Count and Countess Opraksin on the Fontanka Embankment.'

Anisii merely sighed, not daring to express his feelings in any bolder manner. And Erast Petrovich, evidently angered by the decision that he himself had taken, turned back to his prisoner: 'Well then, you have had some good fun at my expense. But everyone knows that pleasures must be paid for. The next five years, which you will spend in penal servitude, will allow you plenty of time to learn some useful lessons about life. From now on you will know who can be joked with and who cannot.'

From the flatness of Fandorin's tone, Anisii realised that his chief was absolutely raging furious.

'If you will permit me, my dear Erast Petrovich,' the 'chaperone' drawled in a familiar fashion. 'Thank you for introducing yourself at the moment of my arrest, or I would still have believed you to be an Indian prince. But I am obliged to wonder how you have arrived at the figure of five years' penal servitude. Let us check our arithmetic. Some trotters or other, some river of gold, an English lord, a lottery – all sheer guesswork. What has all of that got to do with me? And then, you mention some things belonging to a countess? If they belong to Count Opraksin, then what where they doing in your home? Are you cohabiting with another man's wife? That's not good. Although, of course, it's none of my business. But if I am being accused of something, then I demand formal charges and proof. There absolutely has to be proof.'

Anisii gasped at this insolence and glanced round anxiously at his chief. Fandorin chuckled ominously. 'And perhaps you would be so good as to tell me what you are doing here? – in this strange costume, at such a late hour?'

'It was just a bit of foolishness,' the Jack replied with a sniff of regret, 'a foolish hankering after the emerald. But this, gentlemen, is what is known as "provocation". You even have gendarmes on guard downstairs. This is an entire police conspiracy.'

'The gendarmes don't know who we are,' said Anisii, unable to resist a chance to boast. 'And they're not part of any conspiracy. As far as they're concerned, we're orientals.'

'It doesn't matter,' the rogue said dismissively. 'Just look how many of you there are – servants of the state, all lined up against one poor, unfortunate man whom you deliberately led into temptation. In court any decent lawyer will give you a whipping that will leave you itching for ages afterwards. And if I'm right, that stone of yours is worth no more than ten roubles at best. One month's detention at the most. And you talk to me about five years' penal servitude, Erast Petrovich. My arithmetic is more accurate.'

'And what about the jack of spades that you placed on the bed in front of two witnesses?' the Court Counsellor asked, angrily stubbing out his unfinished cigar in the ashtray.

'Ah, yes, that was a bit unnecessary,' said the Jack, hanging his head repentantly. 'I suppose you could say it was cynical. I wanted to shift the blame on to the "Jack of Spades" gang. They're the talk of Moscow at the moment. I suppose they'll probably add a church penance to my month of detention for that. Never mind; I'll redeem my sin through prayer.' He crossed himself piously and winked at Anisii.

Erast Petrovich jerked his chin, as if his collar were too tight, although the wide neck of his white shirt embroidered with oriental ornament was not fastened.

'You have forgotten your female accomplice. She can't get out of the lottery charge. And I don't think she will agree to go to prison without you.'

'Yes, Mimi likes company,' the prisoner willingly agreed. 'Only I doubt that she'll sit quietly in your cage. Mr Eunuch, would you be so good as to let me take another look at that key?'

Anisii glanced at his chief, tightened his grip on the key and showed it to the Jack from a distance.

'Yes, I wasn't mistaken,' Momos said with a nod. 'An absolutely primitive, antiquated "grandmother's trunk" style of lock. Mimi can have one of those open in a second with a hairpin.'

The Court Counsellor and his assistant were up and away in the same instant. Fandorin shouted something to Masa in Japanese – it must have been 'Keep a close eye on him' or something else of the sort. The Japanese took a tight grip of the Jack's shoulders, and Tulipov didn't see what happened after that, because he had already darted out through the door.

They ran down the staircase and dashed across the vestibule, past the astounded gendarmes.

Alas, the door of 'Tarik-bei's' room was standing ajar. Their little bird had flown!

Erast Petrovich groaned as if he had toothache and went dashing back into the vestibule, with Anisii on his tail.

'Where is she?' the Court Counsellor barked at the sergeant-major.

The gendarme's jaw dropped at the shock of suddenly hearing the Indian prince speak in perfect Russian.

'Answer me, quickly now!' Fandorin shouted at the serviceman. 'Where's the girl?'

'Well now . . .' Just to be on the safe side the sergeant-major stuck on his helmet and saluted. 'She went out about five minutes ago. And she said her chaperone would stay on for a while.'

'Five minutes!' Erast Petrovich repeated agitatedly. 'Tulipov, let's get after her! And you, keep your eyes peeled!' They ran down the steps of the porch, dashed through the garden and bounded out through the gates.

'I'll go right, you go left!' the Chief ordered.

Anisii hobbled off along the fence. One slipper immediately got stuck in the snow and he had to hop along on one foot. The fence came to an end, and there was the white ribbon of the road, the black trees and bushes. Not a soul. Tulipov started spinning round on the spot, like a chicken with its head chopped off. Where should he look? Which way should he run?

Below the steep bluff, on the far side of the icy river, the gigantic city lay spread out in an immense black bowl. It was almost invisible, with just occasional bright strings of street lights in the darkness, but the darkness was not empty, it was clearly alive: something down there was breathing drowsily, sighing, groaning. A brief gust of wind swept the fine white snow across the ground, piercing Anisii's light robe and chilling him to the marrow of his bones.

He had to go back. Perhaps Erast Petrovich had had better luck?

They met at the gates. Unfortunately, the Chief had returned alone too.

Shivering from the cold, the two 'Indians' ran back into the house.

Strange – the gendarmes were not at their post; but from upstairs, on the first floor, they could hear a loud clattering, swearing and shouting.

'What the devil!' Still winded from their run along the street, Fandorin and Anisii dashed up the stairs as fast as their legs would carry them.

In the bedroom everything had been turned upside down. Masa was squealing in rage, with two gendarmes hanging on to his shoulders, and the sergeant-major was wiping a red ear with his sleeve but keeping his revolver trained on the Japanese.

'Where is he?' asked Erast Petrovich, gazing around.

'Who?' the sergeant-major asked in bemusement, spitting out a broken tooth.

'The Jack!' Anisii shouted. 'That is, I mean, that old woman!'

Masa babbled something in his own language and the gendarme with the grey moustache stuck the barrel of his gun in his stomach: 'You shut it, you heathen swine! Well then, Your . . .' The serviceman hesitated, unsure of how to address this strange superior. 'Well then, Your Hinduness, we're standing downstairs, keeping our eyes peeled, as ordered. Suddenly upstairs a woman starts shouting. "Help," she screams, "murder! Save me" So we come up here, and we look and see this slanty-eyed devil's got the old woman who was with the young lady down on the floor and taken her by the throat. The poor woman's screeching: "Save me. This Chinese robber broke in and attacked me!" He's muttering away in his own heathen tongue, something like: "Nowoma, nowoma!" He's a strong devil – look here, he knocked my tooth out and he stove in Tereshchenka's cheekbone too.'

'Where is she – the old woman?' asked the Court Counsellor, grabbing the sergeant-major by the shoulders, obviously very hard – the gendarme turned as white as chalk.

'She's here somewhere,' he hissed. 'Where could she have got to? She's got frightened and hidden away in a corner somewhere. She'll turn up. Ow, would you mind . . . That hurts!'

Erast Petrovich and Anisii exchanged glances without speaking.

'Is it back to the chase, then?' Tulipov asked eagerly, thrusting his feet deeper into his slippers.

'No, we've done enough running for Mr Momos's amusement,' Fandorin replied in a crestfallen voice.

The Chief released his grip on the gendarme, sat down in an armchair and let his arms dangle lifelessly. A strange, incomprehensible change came over his face. A deep, horizontal crease appeared across his smooth brow; the corners of his lips slowly crept downwards; his eyes closed. When his shoulders began to shudder, Anisii felt afraid that Erast Petrovich was about to burst into tears.

Then suddenly Fandorin slapped himself on the knee and broke into soundless peals of irrepressible, carefree laughter.

CHAPTER 8

'La Grande Opération'

Momos held up the hem of his skirt as he dashed along the fences, past the empty dachas in the direction of the Kaluga highway. Every now and then he glanced round to see if there was anyone in pursuit, if he ought to dive into the bushes which – the Lord be praised! – grew thickly along both sides of the road.

As he ran past a snowy grove of fir trees, a pitiful little voice called to him: 'Momchik, there you are at last! I'm frozen already.'

Mimi peeped out from under a spreading fir, rubbing her hands together pitifully. He was so relieved he sat down right there on the edge of the road, scooped up a handful of snow and pressed it against his perspiring brow.

The false nose slid completely to one side and Momos finally tore the damn thing off and flung it into a snowdrift. 'Oof,' he said. 'It's a long time since I've run so hard.'

Mimi sat down beside him and lowered her head on to his shoulder. 'Momochka, there's something I have to confess to you . . .'

'What is it?' he asked cautiously.

'It wasn't my fault, honestly . . . The thing is . . . He wasn't a eunuch after all.'

'I know,' Momos muttered, furiously brushing the green needles off her sleeves. 'It was our acquaintance Mr Fandorin and his gendarme Leporello. They really took me for a ride. First class all the way.'

'Are you going to get your own back?' Mimi asked timidly, looking up into his face.

'Oh, to hell with them. We need to clear out of Moscow. And the sooner the better.'

But in fact they didn't clear out of inhospitable Moscow, because the following day Momos had the idea for the grandiose scheme that he appropriately named 'La Grande Opération'. The idea occurred to him by pure chance, through a most amazing confluence of circumstances.

They were retreating from Moscow in strict order, taking every conceivable precaution. At the crack of dawn Momos had gone to the flea market and bought the equipment required for a total sum of three roubles, seventy-three and a half kopecks. He had removed all the make-up from his face, donned a five-sided cap with a peak, a quilted jacket and high boots with galoshes, transforming himself into an entirely unremarkable petty tradesman. Things had not been so simple with Mimi, because the police already knew what she looked like. After a little thought he had decided to turn her into a boy. In a sheepskin cap with earflaps, a greasy sheepskin jacket and huge felt boots she became absolutely indistinguishable from the kind of light-fingered Moscow juveniles to be found darting around the Sukharev Market – better watch out for your pocket!

In fact, Mimi really could rifle through other people's pockets quite as briskly as any regular market thief. Once, when they had found themselves all washed up in Samara, she had deftly relieved a rich merchant's waistcoat pocket of his grandfather's turnip watch. The watch was rubbish, but Momos knew it had sentimental value for the merchant. The inconsolable provincial had offered a reward of a thousand roubles for the family heirloom and been most voluble in his thanks to the girl student who found the watch in a roadside ditch. With those thousand roubles, Momos had opened up a Chinese pharmacy in that peaceful town and done a very good trade in herbs and roots for treating the various ailments suffered by merchants.

But what was the point in recalling former successes, when here they were, retreating from Moscow like the French, downcast and despondent? Momos assumed that there would be agents watching for them at the stations and he had taken appropriate measures.

First of all, in order to mollify the dangerous Mr Fandorin, he had sent all of Countess Addy's things to St Petersburg. He had, admittedly, been unable to resist adding a postscript to the accompanying receipt: 'To the Queen of Spades from the Jack of Spades.' He had sent the jade beads and the prints he had borrowed back to Malaya Nikitskaya Street via the municipal post, but without any postscript, preferring in this case to err on the side of caution.

He had decided not to put in an appearance at any railway station, but despatched his suitcases to the Bryansk Station in advance, to be loaded on to the following day's train. He and Mimi were going on foot. Once past the Dorogomilovskaya Gates, Momos was intending to hire a driver and ride in his sleigh as far as the first railway station, in Mozhaisk, where he would be reunited with his baggage on the following day.

He was in a sour mood, but meanwhile Moscow was still celebrating. It was Forgiveness Sunday, the final day of wild Pancake Week. At dawn the next day the fasting and praying would begin, the coloured globes would be taken down from the street lamps, the brightly painted fair booths would be dismantled and the number of drunks would sharply decrease; but today the people were still finishing up their revels, their food and their drink.

At the Smolensk market they were riding in 'diligences' down an immense wooden slope, everybody laughing and whistling and squealing. Everywhere you looked, they were selling hot pancakes – with herring heads, with buckwheat, with honey, with caviar. A Turkish conjuror in a red fez was cramming crooked yataghans into his white-toothed maw. An acrobat was walking on his hands and jerking his legs about in an amusing fashion. Some swarthy-faced, bare-chested fellow in a leather apron was belching tongues of flame out of his mouth.

Mimi turned her head this way and that like a genuine little urchin. Entering into her role, she asked Momos to buy her a poisonous red sugar rooster on a stick and delighted in licking

100

the wretched treat with her sharp little pink tongue, although in real life she preferred Swiss chocolate, of which she could devour as many as five bars a day.

But the people on the brightly decorated square were not only making merry and guzzling down pancakes. There was a long line of beggars sitting along the wall of the rich merchants' Church of the Mother of God of Smolensk, bowing their heads down to the ground, asking forgiveness from the Orthodox faithful and granting them forgiveness in return. This was an important day for the beggars, a profitable day. Many people approached them with offerings – some brought a pancake, some a half-bottle of vodka, some a kopeck.

Some big shot or other in an unbuttoned mink coat and with his bald head uncovered came striding heavily out of the church on to the porch. He crossed his puffy, repulsive features and shouted out in a loud voice: 'Forgive me, good Orthodox people, if Samson Eropkin has done you wrong!'

The beggars began bustling about and cackling discordantly: 'And you forgive us, little father! Forgive us, our benefactor!'

They were clearly expecting offerings, but no one pushed himself forward. Instead they all lined up briskly into two rows, clearing the way through to the square, where the big shot's magnificent open sleigh was waiting for him – lacquered wood lined with fur.

Momos stopped to see how a fat-face like this would go about buying his way into Paradise. It was obvious from his face that he was as vicious a bloodsucker as the world had ever seen, but even he was aiming for the Kingdom of Heaven. Momos wondered just what price he put on the entrance ticket.

A massive, black-bearded hulk with the face of an executioner came striding out after the pot-bellied benefactor, towering up over him by a head and a half. The hulk had a long leather whip wound round his right hand and elbow, and in his left hand he was carrying a canvas pouch. Every now and then the master turned to his massive lackey, scooped money out of the pouch and presented it to the beggars – one coin to each of them. When a little old man with only one leg lost patience and reached for the alms out of turn, the bearded hulk gave a menacing bellow and in a single, lightning-swift movement untwined the whip and lashed the cripple across the top of his grey head with the very tip of it – how the old fellow gasped!

Every time the mink-coated benefactor thrust a coin into one of the outstretched hands, he intoned: 'I give not to you, you pitiful drunks, not to you – but to the Lord God All-Merciful and the Mother of God, the Intercessor, for forgiveness of the sins of the servant of God, Samson.'

Momos looked harder and was able to satisfy his curiosity: as he ought to have expected, the fat-faced distributor of alms was buying his escape from the fires of hell rather cheaply, giving the beggars one copper kopeck each.

'Evidently the sins of the servant of God, Samson, are not so very great,' Momos muttered aloud, preparing to continue on his way.

A voice roughened and hoarse from alcohol mumbled right in his ear: 'They're great, right enough, son, oh they're great. You can't be from Moscow, then, if you don't know the famous Eropkin?'

Standing beside Momos was a skinny, sinewy ragamuffin with a nervous, twitching, yellowish face. The ragamuffin reeked of stale, cheap alcohol, and his gaze, directed past Momos at the niggardly donor, was filled with a fierce, burning hatred.

'That Samson sucks the blood of nigh on half of Moscow,' the jittery fellow explained to Momos. 'The dosshouses in Khitrovka, the taverns in Grachi, at the Sukharev Market, and in Khitrovka again – they're almost all his. He buys up stolen goods from the Khitrovka "dealers" and lends money at huge rates of interest. In short, he's a vampire – a cursed viper, he is.'

Momos glanced at the repulsive fat man, who was already getting into his sleigh, with more interest now. Well, well, what colourful characters there did seem to be in Moscow.

'And he cares nothing for the police?'

The ragamuffin spat. 'What police! He hangs about in the apartments of the Governor himself, Prince Dolgorukoi. But of course, Eropkin's a general now! When they were building the

Cathedral he put up a million out of his profits, and for that he got a ribbon from the Tsar, with a big star and a position in a charitable institution. He used to be Samson the Bloodsucker, but now he's "Your Excellency". He's a thief, an executioner, a murderer.'

'Well now, I don't expect he's actually a murderer,' Momos said doubtfully.

'You don't?' said the drunkard, looking at the other man for the first time. 'Of course, Samson Kharitonovich Eropkin wouldn't get his own hands bloody. But did you see that mute, Kuzma? What about that whip? He's not a man; he's a wild beast, a guard dog on a chain. He won't just kill anyone; he'll tear them limb from limb while they're still alive. And he's done it too – there have been cases! Ah, son, the things I could tell you about what they get up to!'

'Well come on, you tell me. We'll sit for a while, and I'll pour you a glass,' Momos invited him. He was in no hurry to get anywhere, and he'd obviously run into an interesting sort of fellow. You could learn all sorts of useful things from people like that. 'Just let me give my little boy twenty kopecks for the carousel.'

They took a seat in the tavern. Momos asked for tea and rusks; the drinking man took a half-bottle of gin and salted bream.

The man with the story to tell took a slow, dignified drink, sucked on a fish tail and began working his way up to his subject: 'You don't know Moscow, so I suppose you've never heard about the Sandunovsky Baths?'

'Of course I have – those baths are famous,' Momos replied, topping up the other man's glass.

'That's just it: they're famous. I used to be the top man there in the gentlemen's department. Everybody knew Egor Tishkin. Let your blood for you, and trim a corn, and give you a first-rate shave – I could do it all. But what I was really famous for was the massage business. Clever hands, I used to have. The way I used to drive the blood through their veins and stretch their bones had all the counts and the generals purring away like kittens. And I could treat all sorts of ailments too – with various

103

potions and decoctions. Some months I raked in as much as fifteen hundred roubles! I had a house, and a garden too. I had a widow who came round to see me – her husband used to be a clergyman.'

Egor Tishkin downed his second drink with no ceremony, in one, and didn't bother to take a sniff at his fish.

'That louse Eropkin singled me out. He always used to ask for Tishkin. The number of times I was even called out to his house. As good as at home there, I was. I used to shave his ugly, bumpy face, and squeeze out his fatty tumours and cure his impotence for him. And who was it saved him from his kidney stones? Who put his hernia back in? Ah, Egor Tishkin used to have golden fingers then. And now he's a naked, homeless beggar. And all because of him, all because of Eropkin! I tell you what, son: get me another drop. My soul's burning up.'

When he'd calmed down a bit, the former bathhouse master continued: 'He's superstitious, Eropkin. Worse than an old countrywoman. He believes in all sorts of signs: black cats, and cocks crowing and the new moon. And let me tell you, my dear man, that Samson Kharitonovich used to have this amazing wart in the middle of his beard, right smack in his dimple. All black, it was, with three ginger hairs growing out of it. He used to really pamper it, used to say it was his special sign. He deliberately let the hair grow on his cheeks, but he had his chin shaved to make the wart more obvious. And it was me that took that special sign of his away . . . I wasn't feeling too well that day – had too much drink the night before. I didn't use to indulge very often – only on holidays – but my mother had just passed away, and I'd been taking comfort, the way you do. Anyway, my hand was shaking, and that was a sharp razor – Damascene steel. And I sliced Eropkin's damned wart clean off. Blood everywhere, and the screams! "You've destroyed my good fortune, you cack-handed devil!" And Samson Kharitonovich starts sobbing and trying to stick it back on, but it won't hold – it just keeps falling off. Eropkin went absolutely wild and called Kuzma. First he works me over with that whip of his, but that's not enough for Eropkin. "Your hands should be torn off," he says, "all your crooked fingers torn out one by one." Kuzma grabs hold of my right hand, sticks it in the crack of the door and slams it shut and there's this terrible crunch . . . I shout out: "Father, don't destroy me, you'll leave me without a crust of bread, at least spare the left one." But it was pointless: he mangled my left hand too . . .'

The drunk waved one hand in the air and for the first time Momos noticed the unnatural way his fingers stuck out without bending.

Momos poured the poor fellow more drink and patted him on the shoulder. 'This Eropkin's a really ugly brute,' he said slowly, recalling the benefactor's bloated features. He really disliked people like that. If he hadn't been leaving Moscow, he could have taught the swine a little lesson. 'So tell me: do his taverns and dosshouses bring in a lot of money?'

'Reckon it at something like thirty thousand a month,' answered Egor Tishkin, angrily brushing away his tears.

'Oh, come on. You're exaggerating there, brother.'

The bathhouse attendant sat up suddenly: 'I ought to know! I tell you, his house was like my own home. Every day God sends, that Kuzma of his goes off to the Hard Labour and the Siberia, and the Transit Camp, and the other drinking establishments Eropkin owns. He collects up to five thousand in a day. On Saturdays they bring it to him from the dosshouses. There's four hundred families living in the Birdcage alone. And what about the pickings from the street girls? And the loot, the stolen goods? Samson Kharitonovich puts all the money in a simple sack and keeps it under his bed. That's his way. He once arrived in Moscow as a country bumpkin with that sack, and he thinks he came by his wealth because of it. In other words, he's just like an old woman – believes in all sorts of nonsense. On the first day of every month he gets his earnings out from under the bed and drives them to the bank. Driving along in a carriage and four with his dirty sack, as pleased as Punch. That's his most important day. The money's secret, from illegal dealings, so on the last day he has trained bookkeepers sitting there drawing up false documents for the whole bundle. Sometimes he takes thirty thousand to the bank, sometimes more – it depends how many days there are in the month.'

'He keeps that sort of money at home, and no one's robbed him?' Momos asked in amazement, becoming more and more interested in what he heard.

'Just you try robbing him. There's a brick wall round the house, dogs running around in the yard, the menservants – and then there's that Kuzma. That whip of Kuzma's is worse than any devolver: he'll slice a mouse running past in half for a bet. None of the "businessmen" ever bother Eropkin. They'd only come off worse. There was one time – five years ago it was – when one hothead tried it. They found him later in the knacker's yard. Kuzma had torn all his skin off in strips with his whip. Neat as a whistle. And no one said a word; everyone kept mum. You can be sure Eropkin has the police in his pocket. The amount of money he has, there's no counting it. Only his wealth won't do him any good, the tyrant – he'll die of stone fever. He's got kidney stones, and with Tishkin gone there's no one to cure him. You don't think the doctors know how to dissolve a stone, do you? Samson Kharitonovich's people came to see me. "Come on, Egorushka," they said, "he forgives you. He'll give you money too – just come back and treat him." I didn't go. Maybe he forgives me, but he'll never have my forgiveness!'

'So tell me: does he often hand out alms to the beggars?' asked Momos, feeling the blood beginning to course recklessly through his veins.

Mimi glanced into the tavern, looking bored, and he gave her a sign: Don't interfere, this is business.

Tishkin propped his sullen head on his hand and his unsteady elbow slithered across the dirty tablecloth. 'Often. From tomorrow, when the Lenten Fast begins, he'll be coming to Our Lady of Smolensk every day. The bastard has an office here, on Pliushchikha Street. He'll get out of his sleigh along the way, hand out a rouble in kopecks and then ride on to rake in the thousands.'

'I tell you what, Egor Tishkin,' said Momos: 'I feel sorry for you. You come along with me. I'll get you a place to sleep for the night and give you a bit of money for a drink. You can tell me about your bitter life in a bit more detail. So you say he's highly superstitious, this Eropkin?'

It's just downright unfair, Momos thought as he led the stumbling martyr to the door. What sort of bad luck is this at the very last moment! It was February, the shortest little month of all! Only twenty-eight days! There'd be thirty thousand less in the sack than in January or in March. But at least it was already the twenty-third. Not too long to wait until the end of the month, but still enough time to prepare properly. Only he'd have to get the luggage from the train.

There was an immense operation taking shape: he could wipe out all his Moscow fiascos in a single stroke.

The following day, the first day of the Week of the Adoration of the Cross, Smolenskaya Square was unrecognisable, as if the sorcerer Chernomor had shot by above the square in the night and with a single pass of his broad hands swept all the sinners, drunks, singers and shouters off the face of the earth, whisked away the spiced-tea men, piemen and pancake men, carried off the bright-coloured pennants, the paper garlands and the balloons, leaving behind only the empty fairground booths, only the black crows on the snow gleaming wetly in the sun, only the beggars on the porch of the Church of Our Lady of Smolensk.

Matins had been sung in the church while it was still dark, and the long, dignified fast, intended to last seven weeks, had begun. The church elder had already walked through the fasting congregation three times, collecting offerings, and three times carried a dish heavy with copper and silver into the sanctuary, when the most important parishioner of all, His Excellency Samson Kharitonovich Eropkin, arrived. He was in an especially mellow mood today: his broad, flabby face was cleanly washed, his sparse hair was combed in a neat parting and his long sideburns were slicked with oil.

Samson Kharitonovich positioned himself directly opposite the Holy Doors of the sanctuary and spent about a quarter of an hour bowing down to the ground and crossing himself with broad gestures. The priest came out with a candle, waved the censer at Eropkin and muttered: 'Lord, Master of my life, purify me, a sinner . . .' And then up walked the elder with an empty dish. The praying man got up from his knees, parted the fabric flaps of his coat and put three hundred-rouble notes in the elder's dish – that was Samson Eropkin's established custom on the Monday of the Cross.

The generous man came out on to the square, where the poor beggars were already waiting, holding out their hands, bleating, jostling each other. But Kuzma simply swayed his whip slightly and the jostling immediately stopped. The paupers lined up in two ranks, like soldiers on parade. A solid mass of coarse grey cloth and tatters, except that on the left side near the middle there was something white.

Samson Kharitonovich Eropkin screwed up his puffy little eyes and saw a fine-looking boy standing among the beggars. The boy had large, bright-blue eyes. He had fine features and his face was clean. His golden hair was cut pudding-basin style (oh, what an outcry there'd been: Mimi had at first absolutely refused to have her lovely locks trimmed so short). The miraculous youth was dressed in nothing but a snow-white shirt – but he didn't seem to feel the cold at all (why, of course not: under the shirt there was a fine sweater of the best-quality angora, and Mimi's delicate bust was tightly wrapped in warm flannel). He had velveteen trousers, and bast sandals, and his light-coloured foot wrappings were unstained.

As he gave out his kopecks, Eropkin glanced now and then at the unusual beggar, and when he got close to the boy, he held out not one coin, but two, and told him: 'Here you are, pray for me.'

The golden-haired youth did not take the money. He raised his clear eyes to the sky and declared in a ringing voice: 'You give too little, servant of God. The dues you offer Our Lady of Sorrow are too small.' He looked Eropkin straight in the eye and the venerable believer was strangely disturbed by that stern, unblinking glance. 'I see your sinful soul. There is a bloody stain on your heart, and filthy decay within you. It must be pu-urged, it must be pu-urged,' the holy fool sang. 'Or else the stench and

108

decay will devour you. Does your belly pain you, Samson? Does your kidney torment you with agony? That's from the filth; it must be pu-urged.'

Eropkin stopped dead in his tracks. And with good reason! His kidneys really were in a terrible state, and he had a large wine-coloured birthmark on the left side of his chest. The information was accurate, all right; it had come from Egor Tishkin.

'Who are you?' His Excellency gasped in fright.

The boy did not answer. He raised his blue eyes to the sky again and began moving his lips gently.

'He's a holy fool, benefactor,' eager voices told Eropkin from both sides. 'It's his first day here, father. Nobody knows where he came from. He talks in riddles. His name's Paisii. Not long since he had a falling fit, and foam came out of his mouth, but it smelt like heaven. He's one of God's own.'

'Then here's a rouble for you, if you're one of God's own. Pray for the forgiveness of my grievous sins.'

Eropkin took a paper rouble out of his wallet, but again the holy fool did not accept it. He said in a quiet voice: 'Do not give it to me. I don't need it: the Mother of God will feed me. Give it to him.' And he pointed to an old beggar known to the whole market, the legless Zoska. 'Your lackey offended him yesterday. Give it to the cripple, and I'll pray to the Mother of God for you.'

Zoska rolled up eagerly on his little trolley and held out his huge, knotty hand. Eropkin squeamishly thrust the rouble into it.

'May the Most Holy Virgin bless you,' the boy declared in a ringing voice, stretching out his slim hand towards Eropkin. And then a miracle happened that was remembered for a long time afterwards in Moscow.

From out of nowhere a huge raven flew up and landed on the holy fool's shoulder. The beggars in the crowd gasped out loud. But when they noticed that the black bird had a gold ring on its leg, everything went quiet.

Eropkin stood there, numb with fright, his thick lips trembling, his eyes starting out of his head. He tried to raise his hand to cross himself, but he couldn't do it.

Tears began flowing from the holy fool's eyes. 'I pity you, Samson,' he said, taking the ring off the bird's leg and holding it out to Eropkin. 'Take it, it's yours. The Holy Virgin does not accept your rouble; she is paying you back. And she sent a raven because your soul is black.'

The man of God turned and walked quietly away.

'Stop!' Samson Kharitonovich shouted, gazing at the glittering ring in confusion and dismay. 'You, you wait! Kuzma! Put him in the sleigh! We'll take him with us!'

The black-bearded hulk overtook the boy and took hold of his shoulder.

'Let's go to my house, do you hear? What's your name? ... Paisii!' Eropkin called to him. 'Live with me for a while, warm yourself.'

'I cannot live in a palace of stone,' the boy replied sternly, looking back. 'It blinds the soul. But you, Samson, do this. Tomorrow, when matins has been sung, come to Iverskaya Street. I shall be there. Bring a pouch of gold coins, and be sure it's full. I wish to entreat the Virgin for you again.'

Everybody watched as the holy fool walked away, with the black raven pecking at his shoulder and cawing hoarsely.

(The raven's name was Balthazar. He was a trained bird, bought at the famous Bird Market. The clever creature had quickly mastered a simple trick: Mimi stuffed millet into the shoulder seam of her shirt, Momos released Balthazar and he flew to the white shirt – at first from five paces, then from fifteen, and then from thirty.)

He came, the bloodsucker. Just as he'd been told to. And he brought the pouch too. Not actually a pouch, but a big, heavy leather purse. Kuzma was carrying it for his master.

During the night, as was only to be expected, the charitable general had been tormented by doubts. No doubt he had tried the Holy Virgin's ring with his teeth, and even tested it with acid. Have no doubts, Your Bloodsuckerness, it's an excellent ring, fine old work.

The holy fool Paisii was standing slightly to one side of the chapel – standing there calmly, with a cup for offerings hanging round his neck. When people put in enough money, he went and gave it away to the cripples. There was a crowd of people standing round the boy, at a respectful distance, eager for a miracle. After the previous day's occurrence the rumour had spread round the churches and the porches of a miraculous sign, a raven with a gold ring in its beak (the story had changed in the telling and retelling).

Today it was overcast and colder, but the holy fool was still only wearing a white shirt, except that his throat was wrapped in a piece of cloth. He did not glance at Eropkin or greet him when he approached.

From his position, of course, Momos could not hear what the bloodsucker said to him, but he assumed it was something sceptical. Mimi's task was to lead Eropkin away from all the places crowded with people. There had been enough publicity; it was no longer needed now.

Then the man of God turned to go, gestured for the paunchy general to follow and set off straight across the square, on a path directly towards Momos. Eropkin hesitated for a moment and set off after the holy fool. The curious onlookers were about to swarm after them, but the black-bearded janissary cracked his whip a couple of times and the idlers fell back.

'No, not this one; he has no sanctity in him,' Momos heard Mimi's crystal-clear voice say as she stopped for a moment beside a crippled soldier.

Beside a twisted hunchback the holy fool said: 'And not this one, his soul's asleep.'

But when he reached Momos, who had taken up a position slightly apart from the other female beggars, the boy stopped, crossed himself and bowed down to his feet. He told Eropkin: 'Give the pouch to this unfortunate woman. Her husband has passed on, and the little children are asking for food. Give it to her. The Holy Virgin pities such people.'

Momos began screeching in a piercing falsetto from under the woman's headscarf that was pulled almost right down to his

111

nose: 'What's this "give"? What's this "give"? Whose boy are you, eh? How do you know about me?'

'Who are you?' asked Eropkin, leaning down to the widow.

'I'm Marfa Ziuzina, father,' Momus sang in a sweet voice now, 'a wretched widow. Our provider passed away, and I've got seven to feed, each one smaller than the last. If you gave me ten kopecks, I could buy them some bread.'

Eropkin snorted and looked at the widow suspiciously. 'All right, Kuzma, give it to her. But make sure Paisii doesn't run off.'

The black-bearded hulk handed the purse to Momos – it wasn't so very heavy.

'What's this, father?' the little widow asked in fright.

'Well?' said Eropkin, turning to the holy fool without answering. 'Now what?'

The boy mumbled something incomprehensible. He dropped to his knees and beat his forehead three times against the cobblestones of the road. Then he pressed his ear to the stone, as if he were listening to something. Then he stood up.

'The Holy Virgin says tomorrow at first light come to the Neskuchny Gardens. Dig in the earth under the old oak tree beside the stone arbour. Dig where the oak is overgrown with moss. And you will have your answer, servant of God.' The holy fool added quietly, 'Come there, Samson, and I will come too.'

'Ah, no!' Eropkin exclaimed craftily. 'What kind of fool do you take me for? You're going with me, brother. Take him, Kuzma. You'll be all right in a stone palace for one night; you won't melt. And if you've cheated me – you're for it. I'll have my gold coins back out of your throat.'

Momos crept back and away, quietly, without getting up off his knees, then straightened up and darted off into the labyrinth of streets around Okhotny Ryad.

He untied the purse and put his hand in. There weren't many imperials after all – only thirty. Samson Kharitonovich Eropkin had decided to be mean; he'd been tight-fisted with the Holy Virgin. But never mind, the Mother of God wouldn't be stingy with her own faithful servant!

112

When it was still dark, Momos dressed with plenty of warm padding, took a flask of cognac with him and assumed his position at the spot he had spied out in advance: in the bushes, with a good view of the old oak tree. In the twilight he could make out the vague outlines of the white columns of the rotunda. At the hour of dawn there was not a single soul in the Neskuchny Gardens.

Momos's combat position was thoroughly equipped and prepared. He had just eaten a pork sandwich (never mind about the Lenten fast) and taken a drink from the lid of his Shustov cognac, when Eropkin's sleigh came rolling up along the alley.

The first to get there was the mute, Kuzma. He peered cautiously all around (Momos ducked down), walked around the oak for a moment and waved. Samson Kharitonovich walked across, holding the holy fool Paisii tightly by the hand. Another two men stayed sitting on the coachbox.

The boy walked up to the oak, bowed to it from the waist, and pointed to the agreed spot: 'Dig here.'

'Get the spades!' Eropkin shouted, turning towards the sleigh.

The two strong young fellows walked across, spat on their palms and started pounding away at the frozen earth. The earth yielded with wonderful ease, and very soon there was a clang (Momos had been too lazy to bury the treasure very deep).

'There's something here, Samson Kharitonovich!'

'What is it?'

'Seems like something metal.'

Eropkin dropped to his knees and started raking the clods of earth away with his hands. Grunting with the effort, he pulled up a copper vessel, green with age, out of the ground (it was an old saucepan, clearly from before the Fire of Moscow – bought from a junkman for fifty kopecks). Something glimmered faintly in the semi-darkness, catching the light from the sleigh's lantern.

'Gold!' gasped Eropkin. 'A lot of gold!'

He tipped the heavy, round coins on to his palm and held them up in front of his eyes. 'They're not my imperials! Kuzya, light a match!'

He read out loud: '"An-na, emp-ress and au-to-crat ..." It's

113

old treasure! There must be at least a thousand gold pieces here!'

Momos had tried to get hold of something a bit more intriguing, with Jewish letters, or at least Arabic script, but that had worked out too expensive for each coin. He'd bought gold two-rouble pieces from the reign of the Empress Anna and *lobanchiks* from the reign of Catherine the Great for twenty roubles apiece. He hadn't bought a thousand, but he'd bought plenty; there was lots of this old stuff in the antique shops at the Sukharev Market. Samson Kharitonovich would count the coins afterwards – he was bound to – and the number was a special one, not accidental; it would have its effect later.

'Things are bad with you, Samson,' the boy sobbed. 'The Holy Virgin doesn't forgive you; she's paying you back.'

'Eh?' asked Eropkin, crazed by the shimmering of the gold.

It's a great thing, a whole lot of gold coins all at once. It doesn't add up to such an astronomical sum in paper money, but it's spellbinding. It can make a greedy man lose his wits completely. This wasn't the first time Momos had exploited this strange property of gold. The important thing now was not to give Eropkin time to draw breath. The skinflint's head had to start spinning, swirling his brains around. Come on now, Mimi, this is your benefit performance.

'Either you gave too little again, or there's no forgiveness for you at all,' the holy fool declared in a piteous voice. 'You'll rot alive, you wretched orphan.'

'How's that, no salvation?' Eropkin exclaimed anxiously, and even from the bushes, twelve yards away, Momos could see the gleaming beads of sweat spring to his forehead. 'If it wasn't enough, I'll give more. I've more money than I can count. How much do I have to give, tell me!'

Paisii swayed from side to side on the spot and did not answer.

'I see . . . I see a dark chamber. Icons on the walls, an icon-lamp burning. I see a feather mattress, swan's-down pillows, many pillows . . . Under the bed is darkness, the darkness of Egypt. The golden calf is there . . . A bast sack, crammed full with pieces of paper. That is the source of all the evil!'

The mute Kuzma and the men with the spades moved right

up close to the boy; their faces were dazed, and Eropkin's shaven chin was trembling.

'Our Mother in Heaven does not want your money,' the young man of God intoned in a strange, ululating voice (she's using those modulations from *La Bayadère*, Momos realised). 'What our Intercessor wants is for you to purge yourself – for your money to be purged. It's dirty, Samson, and that's why it brings you no happiness. A righteous man must bless it, bless it with his sinless hand, and it will be purged. A great and righteous man, a holy man with a blind eye and a withered arm and a lame leg.'

'Where can I find someone like that?' Eropkin whined, shaking Paisii by his thin shoulders. 'Where is there a righteous man like that?'

The boy inclined his head to one side, listened to something and said in a soft voice: 'A voice . . . A voice will speak to you . . . out of the ground . . . Do what it says.'

And then Mimi pulled a strange trick: in her usual soprano voice, she suddenly launched into a French chansonette from the operetta *Jojou's Secret*. Momos grabbed hold of his head in despair – she'd overdone it now, the little imp! She'd ruined everything!

'He's singing with the voice of an angel!' one of the men gasped, and crossed himself quickly. 'Singing in a heavenly language, the language of the angels!'

'That's French, you fool,' Eropkin croaked. 'I've heard it sometimes happens that holy fools start talking in foreign tongues they've never known in their lives.' And he crossed himself too.

Paisii suddenly collapsed on to the ground and started thrashing about in convulsions. A thick stream of foam bubbled out his mouth.

'Hey!' Samson Kharitonovich shouted, frightened. He bent down over the boy. 'Wait a bit with your fit! What kind of voice is it? And what does it mean – this holy man's going to purge my money? Will the money disappear? Or will it be returned with interest?'

But the boy only arched up his back and hammered his feet on the cold earth, shouting: 'A voice . . . out of the ground . . . a voice!'

Eropkin turned to his ruffians in astonishment and told them: 'He really does give off a sweet smell, a heavenly smell!'

I should think so, Momos chuckled to himself. The Parisian soap, 'L'arôme du paradis', one and a half roubles for a tiny little bar.

However, the pause could not be dragged out any longer: it was time for the specially prepared star turn of the entire performance. It wasn't for nothing that the evening before he'd spent the best part of an hour laying a garden hose under the fallen leaves and sprinkling earth over it. One end with a wide funnel was now in Momos's hand, and the other, with a wider funnel, was precisely positioned between the roots of the oak. To conceal the secret, it was covered with wire mesh, and the mesh was covered with moss. It was a reliable system, experimentally tested; he just had to fill his lungs right up to the top with air.

And Momos tried his very best: he breathed in, pressed the tube tightly against his lips and boomed: 'At midnight . . . Come . . . To the Varsonofiev Chapel . . .'

It sounded very convincing – almost too impressive. In fact, the impression produced was so strong that it caused a problem. When the sepulchral voice boomed out from under the ground. Eropkin squealed and jumped, his henchmen shied away as well, and they didn't hear the most important thing: where to take the money.

'. . . near the Novopimenovksy Monastery,' Momos boomed to make things clearer, but that cloth-eared blockhead Eropkin was so stunned he still didn't hear.

'Eh? What monastery?' He asked the ground fearfully. He looked around and even stuck his nose into a hollow in the oak.

Now what was Momos supposed to do? The Supreme Power wouldn't repeat everything ten times for the deaf dolt! That would turn the whole thing into a cheap comedy. This was a predicament.

Mimi solved his difficulty She sat up and babbled in a quiet voice: 'The Varsonofiev Chapel, near the Novopimenovsky Monastery. The holy hermit is there. Take the sack to him. At midnight tonight.'

People in Moscow said bad things about the Varsonofiev Chapel. Seven years earlier the small gate church near the entrance to the Novopimenovsky Monastery had been struck by a bolt of lightning that had knocked down its holy cross and cracked its bell. What kind of house of God was it, if it could be struck by lightning?

The chapel had been boarded up and the clergy and the pilgrims and the simple public had started to avoid it. At night shrieks and terrible, inhuman groans were heard from inside the thick walls. It was either cats fornicating, with the echo under the stone vaults amplifying their howls, or there was something far worse than that taking place in the chapel. The father superior had held a prayer service and sprinkled the place with holy water, but it hadn't helped; people only became even more afraid.

Momos had spotted this wonderful place before Christmas and been thinking it might come in useful ever since. And now it had; it was just the thing.

He had considered the setting carefully and prepared the stage effects carefully. 'La Grande Opération' was approaching its finale, and it promised to be absolutely stunning.

'The Jack of Spades has outdone himself!' – that was what the newspapers would have written the following day, if only there had been genuine openness and freedom of speech in Russia.

When the small bell in the monastery gave a dull clang and began chiming midnight, there was the sound of cautious footfalls outside the double doors of the chapel. Momos imagined Eropkin crossing himself and reaching out a hesitant hand towards the gilded panel. The nails had been pulled out of the boards – one gentle tug and the door would open with a heart-stopping creak.

And now it had opened, but it was not Samson Kharitonovich Eropkin who glanced in; it was the mute Kuzma. The cowardly bloodsucker had sent his devoted slave on ahead.

The jaw under the black beard dropped open and the coiled whip slid off Kuzma's shoulder like a dead snake.

And indeed, eschewing all false modesty, there was something here worth gaping at.

Standing at the centre of the square space was a table of rough boards, with four candles flickering on it, one at each corner. There was also an old man in a white surplice, with a long grey beard and long, silky hair tied round on his forehead with string. He was sitting on a chair, hunched over an old book in a thick leather binding (*Travels Into Several Remote Parts Of The World. In Four Parts. By Lemuel Gulliver, First a Surgeon, And Then A Captain Of Several Ships*, published in Bristol in 1726 – bought at a book stall for its thickness and impressive appearance). One of the hermit's eyes was covered by a black patch and his left arm was in a sling. The sage did not appear to have noticed the man who had come in.

Kuzma gave a low grunt, turning away, and Eropkin's pale features appeared from behind his broad, massive shoulder.

Then, without looking up, the holy hermit spoke in a clear, resonant voice: 'Come here, Samson. I have been expecting you. You are mentioned in the secret book.' And he jabbed his finger at an engraving showing Gulliver surrounded by Houyhnhnms.

Stepping carefully, the entire honourable company entered the chapel: the most venerable Samson Kharitonovich, clutching the boy Paisii tightly by the hand, Kuzma and the same two men as before, who lugged in a plump bast sack.

The sage pierced Eropkin with a menacing glance from his single eye under its matted eyebrow and held up a finger in admonition. In response to this gesture, one of the candles suddenly hissed and went out. The bloodsucker gasped and let go of the boy's hand – which was the required effect.

The trick with the candle was a simple one, but impressive. Momos himself had invented it for use when he ran into difficulties at cards: the candles looked like ordinary ones, but the wick slid freely inside the wax. It was an unusually long wick, threaded though a crack in the table underneath the candle. Jerk your left hand under the table, and the candle went out (of course, Momos had the dolly to control the wicks hanging on his sling).

'I know, I know who you are and what kind of man you are,' the hermit said with an ominous laugh. 'Give me that sack of yours, stuffed full of blood and tears; put it there . . . Not on the table, not on the magic book!" he shouted at the two men. 'Toss it under the table, so I can set my lame leg on it.'

He nudged the sack gently with one foot – it was damned weighty. Must be all one-rouble and three-rouble notes. At least three stones. But never mind – what's your own isn't heavy.

Eropkin was superstitious and none too sharp-witted, but he wasn't going to give away his sack that simply. Miracles alone weren't enough. Psychology was required: sudden pressure, rapid surprises. He mustn't be allowed to gather his wits, and think, to take a close look. So giddy up, now!

The old sage wagged his finger at Eropkin in warning, and immediately a second candle went out.

Samson Kharitonovich crossed himself

'Don't you go crossing yourself here!' Momos barked at him in a terrifying voice. 'Your hands will wither and fall off! Or don't you know who you've come to see, you fool?'

'I kn— I know, father,' Eropkin hissed: 'a holy hermit.'

Momos threw back his head and laughed malevolently – just like Mephistopheles played by Giuseppe Bardini.

'You are a stupid man, Samson Eropkin. Did you not count the coins in the treasure?'

'I did . . .'

'And how many were there?'

'Six hundred and sixty-six.'

'And where did you hear the voice from?'

'From under the ground . . .'

'Who speaks from under the ground, eh? Don't you know that?'

Eropkin sat down, horrified – his legs had clearly given way under him. He was about to cross himself, but suddenly felt afraid and hastily hid his hands behind his back – then looked round at his men to make sure they weren't crossing themselves either. They weren't, but they were trembling.

'I need you, Samson,' said Momos, switching into a more cordial tone and shifting the sack ever so slightly towards himself with his foot. 'You are going to be mine. You are going to serve me.'

He snapped his fingers with a loud crunch; a third candle went out, and the darkness under the gloomy vaults immediately grew thicker.

Eropkin backed away.

'Where are you going? I'll turn you to stone!' Momos growled, and then he played on contrast once again, speaking ingratiatingly. 'Don't be afraid of me, Samson. I need men like you. Do you want a mountain of money that would make your lousy sack look like a heap of dust?' He gave the sack a derisive kick. 'You'll keep your sack; stop trembling over it. But how would you like me to give you a hundred like it? Or is that not enough for you? Do you want more? Do you want power over humankind?'

Eropkin gulped, but he didn't say anything.

'Pronounce the words of the Great Oath, and you will be mine for ever! Agreed?' Momos roared out the last word so that it echoed back and forth between the old walls.

Eropkin pulled his head down into his shoulders and nodded.

'You, Azael, stand here at my left hand,' the old man ordered the boy, who ran behind the table and stood beside him.

'When the fourth candle goes out, repeat what I say, word for word,' the mysterious old man instructed Eropkin. 'And don't gawp at me – look up.'

Once he was sure that all four future servants of the Evil One had obediently thrown back their heads, Momos extinguished the final candle, squeezed his eyes shut and nudged Mimi in the ribs: Don't look!

The voice rang out again in the darkness: 'Look up! Look up!'

He pulled the sack towards himself with one hand and prepared to press the button with the other.

Up above, where the light of the candles had not reached, even when they were still burning, Momos had installed a magnesium *Blitzlicht*, the very latest German invention for photography. When its unendurable white flash blazed out in the pitch darkness, Eropkin and his cut-throats would be left totally blind for about five minutes. And in the meantime, the jolly trio – Momos, Mimi and the Money – would slip out through the back door, which had been oiled in readiness.

Outside the door there were a light American sleigh and a fleet little horse who was probably already weary of waiting. Once that sleigh darted away, then you, Samson Kharitonovich Eropkin, might as well try to catch the wind. This was no operation, it was a work of art.

It was time!

Momos pressed the button. Something fizzed, but he didn't see any bright flash from behind his closed eyelids.

Of all things, a misfire, just at that very moment! So much for the vaunted achievements of technical progress! At the rehearsal everything had been just perfect, but now the premiere had been turned into a fiasco!

Swearing silently to himself, Momos picked up the sack and tugged on Mimi's sleeve. They backed away towards the exit, trying not to make any noise.

But just then the accursed *Blitzlicht* came to life: it hissed, gave a dull flash, belched out a cloud of white smoke, and the chapel was illuminated with a feeble, flickering light. Four figures could clearly be made out, frozen motionless on one side of the table, and two others creeping away on the other.

'Stop! Where are you going?' Eropkin squealed. 'Give me my sack! Hold them, lads; they're Freemasons! Ah, the stinking rats!'

Momos made a dash for the door, since the light had faded, but then something whistled through the air and a noose tightened round his throat. That damned Kuzma and his cursed whip! Momos dropped the sack and clutched at his throat with a croak.

'Momchik, what's wrong?' Mimi asked, puzzled. She grabbed hold of him: 'Let's run!'

But it was too late. Rough hands emerged from the darkness, grabbed Momos's collar and threw him to the floor. Terrified and choking without air, he lost consciousness.

When consciousness returned, the first thing he saw was crimson shadows swaying across the black ceiling and the smoke-blackened frescoes. There was a lighted lantern flickering on the floor; it must have been brought from the sleigh.

Momos realised that he was lying on the floor with his hands tied behind his back. He turned his head this way and that, trying to assess the situation. The situation was awful; it couldn't possibly have been worse.

Mimi was squatting on her haunches, huddled up into a tight ball, with the mute monster Kuzma towering up over her, lovingly caressing his whip, the very sight of which made Momos twitch. The raw skin on his throat still stung.

Eropkin himself was sitting on a chair, bright crimson and sweaty. His Excellency had evidently been making a great deal of noise while Momos was in a state of blissful oblivion. The two minions were standing on tiptoe on the table, arranging something there. When Momos looked more closely, he saw two dangling ropes, and he didn't like the look of the arrangement at all.

'Well, my darlings,' Samson Eropkin said in an amiable voice when he saw that Momos had come round, 'wanted to clean out Eropkin himself, did we? You're cunning, you devils, cunning. Only Eropkin's smarter. Wanted to make me the laughing-stock of all Moscow, did we? But never mind,' he drawled with relish. 'Now I'll give you something to laugh about. There's a vicious fate in store for anyone who tries to take a bite at Eropkin, a terrible fate – to teach the others a good lesson.'

'Why this melodrama, Your Excellency,' Momos said with a grin, putting on a brave front. 'It really doesn't become you. A full state counsellor, a bulwark of piety. After all, there is the court, the police. Let them punish us; why should you get your hands dirty? And then, after all, my dear fellow, you have lost nothing. Haven't you acquired an old gold ring? You have. And the treasure too. Keep them, as compensation, so to speak, for the injury.'

'I'll give you compensation,' said Samson Kharitonovich, smiling with just the corners of his mouth. There was a soft, frightening glow in his eyes. 'Well, is it ready?' he shouted to his men.

They jumped down on to the floor. 'It's ready, Samson Kharitonovich.'

'Go on then, string him up.'

'I beg your pardon, how do you mean – "string him up"?' Momos asked indignantly when he was lifted off the floor with his feet upwards. 'This is beyond all – Help! Help! Police!'

'Shout away, shout away,' Eropkin told him. 'If there's anyone walking by in the middle of the night, he'll just cross himself and take to his heels as fast as he can.'

Then Mimi suddenly started wailing piercingly: 'Fire! We're burning! Good people, we're burning.'

She'd come up with the right idea: a passer-by wouldn't be frightened by a shout like that; he'd come running to help or dash to the monastery to sound the alarm bell.

Momos joined in with her. 'Fire! We're burning! Fire!'

But they weren't allowed to carry on shouting for long. The black-bearded mute tapped Mimi gently on her head with his fist and the delicate little swallow simply slumped over, landing face-down on the floor. The stinging serpent of the whip wound itself round Momos's throat once again and his howl was reduced to a croak.

The torturers lifted up the bound man and dragged him on to the table. They tied one ankle to one rope and the other ankle to the other, pulled, and a moment later Momos was dangling above the rough-planed boards like a letter Y. His grey beard hung downwards, tickling his face; his surplice slid down, exposing legs in narrow breeches and boots with spurs. Once out in the street, Momos had been intending to tear off his grey hair, pull off his loose robe and transform himself into a dashing hussar – no one would ever have recognised him as the 'hermit'.

He ought to have been sitting in the troika now, with Mimi on one side and the sack with all that money in it on the other, but instead of that he'd been ruined by that dastardly German invention, and here he was, dangling in the air with his face towards that near but unreachable door that led out into the snowy night, to the sleigh, salvation, good luck and life.

He heard Eropkin's voice behind him: 'Tell me, Kuzya, how many blows would it take you to split him in half?'

Momos began twisting round on the ropes, because he was interested in the answer to that question too. When he twisted right round, he saw the mute holding up four fingers. Then he thought for a moment and added a fifth.

'Well, no need to do it in five,' Samson Kharitonovich said, to make his wishes quite clear. 'We're not in any hurry. Better do it gently, a little bit at a time.'

'Honestly, Your Excellency,' Momos said hastily, 'I've already learned my lesson and I've been badly frightened – honestly I have. I have some savings. Twenty-nine thousand. I'd be glad to pay them as a fine. You're a man of business. What's the point of giving way to emotions?'

'And I'll deal with the lad later,' Eropkin said thoughtfully, with obvious pleasure, as if he were talking to himself.

Momos shuddered, realising that Mimi's fate would be more terrible than his own. 'Seventy-four thousand!' he shouted, for that was exactly how much he had left from his previous Moscow operations. 'But the boy's not to blame: he's feeble-minded.'

'Go on, show him your skill,' ordered Eropkin.

The whip gave a predatory whistle. Momos gave a sickening screech, because something cracked and crunched between his outstretched legs. But there was no pain.

'You've unpicked his trousers very neatly there,' Eropkin said approvingly. 'Now go in little bit deeper. Just half a *vershok*. To make him howl. And then keep on going in by the same amount until we have two halves dangling on two ropes.'

Momos felt a cold draught on the most vulnerable, most delicate part of his body and realised that with his first virtuoso stroke Kuzma had slit open his breeches along the seam without touching him.

Oh Lord, if you exist, prayed the man who had never prayed in his life, the man who had once been called Mitenka Savvin, *send me an archangel, or even your shabbiest little angel. Save me, Lord. I swear that henceforth I'll only turn over low snakes like Eropkin and no one else. Honestly, on my word of honour, Lord.*

At that moment the back door opened. The first thing Momos saw in the opening was the night, with streaks of wet snow slanting down across it. Then the night retreated and became the background as its place was taken by the silhouette of a slim figure wearing a long, waisted coat and tall top hat, and carrying a walking cane.

CHAPTER 9

The Letter of the Law or the Spirit of Justice?

Anisii had scoured his features with soap, and pumice and even sand – but still the swarthiness had not completely gone. Erast Petrovich still had it too, but it looked well on a handsome devil like him, rather like a dense tan. On Tulipov, however, the nut colouring had distributed itself across his face in little islets as it faded, and now, with his patchy skin and thin neck, he looked like an African giraffe – only not so tall. But every cloud has a silver lining: his pimples had disappeared completely . . . absolutely, as if they had never even existed. In two or three weeks his skin would be clear – the Chief had promised. And the cropped hair would soon grow back – no two ways about that.

The morning after they had caught the Jack red-handed with his female accomplice (whom Anisii could not recall without a languorous sigh and a sweet thrill in various parts of his soul and his body) and then let them go again, he and the Court Counsellor had had a brief but important conversation.

'Well now,' Fandorin said with a sigh. 'You and I, Tulipov, have made fools of ourselves, but we may assume that the Jack of Spades' Moscow tour is now at an end. What are you thinking of doing now? Do you wish to return to the department?'

Anisii gave no reply and merely blenched a deadly shade of white, although that could not be seen under his swarthy stain. The thought of returning to his miserable career as a courier after all the wonderful adventures of the last two weeks seemed absolutely unbearable.

'Naturally, I will give you the most flattering references possible for the Chief of police and Sverchinsky. It is not your fault that I was not up to the job. I shall recommend that you be transferred to the investigative or operational unit – whichever you wish. But I also have another proposition for you, Tulipov . . .'

The Chief paused and Anisii, already shaken by the brilliant prospect of a triumphant return to the gendarmerie, strained forward, sensing that something even more breathtaking was about to be said.

'. . . Provided, of course, that you have nothing against working with me on a permanent basis, I can offer you a position as my assistant. My own position entitles me to a permanent assistant, but so far I have not made any use of this right and preferred to manage on my own. However, I think you would suit me. You are lacking in knowledge of people, you are inclined to ponder things for too long and have insufficient faith in your own abilities; but in our business those very qualities could be extremely useful, if they are turned in the necessary direction. Your scant knowledge of people frees you from making stereotyped judgements, and in any case it is a short-coming that can be remedied. To hesitate before taking a decision is also useful – provided only that afterwards, once having decided, you do not delay. And lack of faith in your own abilities protects you from pointless bravado and acting heedlessly. It can develop into a salutary prudence. Your main virtue, Tulipov, is that your fear of finding yourself in a shameful situation is stronger than your physical fear, which means that in any situation you will attempt to conduct yourself in a worthy fashion. That suits me very well. And you really do think rather well for someone with five classes of ordinary secondary school. What do you say?'

Anisii said nothing: he had been struck dumb and he was terrified even to move a muscle – what if this marvellous dream suddenly evaporated? What if he rubbed his eyes and saw his squalid little room, and Sonya snivelling because she was wet, and the cold sleet outside the window, and it was time to go running off to work and start delivering documents round the city?

Seeming suddenly to recall something, the Court Counsellor said in a guilty voice: 'Ah, yes, I haven't named the terms; I sincerely beg your pardon. You will immediately be granted the title of collegiate registrar. Your position will have a long title: "Personal Assistant to the Deputy for Special Assignments of the Governor-General of Moscow". The salary is fifty roubles a month and some other kind of quarterly emoluments – I don't remember exactly. You will be paid moving expenses and provided with an apartment at public expense, for I shall require you to live nearby. Of course, the move might not be convenient, but I promise that the apartment will be comfortable and well suited for your family circumstances.'

He means Sonya, Anisii guessed, quite correctly.

'Since I am ... hmm ... returning to the bachelor life,' the Chief said with an indeterminate gesture, 'Masa has been ordered to find new servants: a cook and a maid. Since you will be living nearby, they can also serve you.'

I mustn't start bawling now, Tulipov thought in a panic; that would be just too embarrassing altogether.

Fandorin spread his arms wide in puzzlement: 'Well, I don't know what else to tempt you with. Would you like ...'

'No, Your Honour,' Anisii howled, coming to his senses. 'I don't want anything else. That's already more than enough for me. When I didn't say anything, I only meant ...' He broke off, not knowing how to finish.

'Excellent,' Erast Petrovich said with a nod. 'We would appear to be in agreement. And your first task will be as follows: just to be on the safe side – for God takes care of those who take care of themselves – keep a close eye on the newspapers for a week or two. And I'll give instructions for the office of the chief of police to send you the "Police Summary of Municipal Events" to look through every day. Take note of anything exceptional, unusual or suspicious and report to me. This Momos might possibly be even more impudent than we imagine.'

A day or two after this historical conversation that marked such a decisive change in Anisii Tulipov's life, he was sitting at the writing desk in his chief's study at the house, looking through the marks he had made in the newspapers and the 'Police Summary' as he prepared to report.

It was already after eleven, but Erast Petrovich had still not emerged from the bedroom. Just recently he had been rather listless and taciturn in general and shown no real interest in Tulipov's discoveries. He would listen in silence, wave his hand and say: 'You can go, Tulipov. The office is closed for today.'

Today Masa had looked in to see Anisii and whisper with him. 'Ver' bad,' he said. 'At nigh' no sleep, in day no eat, no do zazen or rensu.'

'What doesn't he do?' Anisii asked, also in a whisper.

'Rensu – this . . .' The Japanese made some rapid, abrupt movements with his hands and swung one foot up above his shoulder in a single movement.

'Ah, Japanese gymnastics,' said Tulipov, recalling that on previous mornings, while he was reading the newspapers in the study, the Court Counsellor and his valet would go into the drawing room, move the tables and chairs aside, and then crash and clatter for a long time, every now and then emitting harsh screeching sounds.

'Zazen – this,' said Masa, continuing his explanation. He flopped down on to the floor, pulled his legs in under him, fixed his eyes on the leg of a chair and made an expressionless face. 'Unnerstan', Tiuri-san?'

When Anisii shook his head, the Japanese made no attempt to explain any more. He said anxiously: 'Need woman. With woman bad, without woman worse. I think go good brothel, talk with madam.'

Tulipov also felt that Erast Petrovich's melancholy was connected with the disappearance of Countess Addy from the house, but in his opinion it would be best to refrain from such a radical measure as appealing for help to the madam of a brothel.

Just as the consultation in the study was at its height, Fandorin entered. He was in his dressing gown, with a smoking cigar clenched in his teeth. He sent Masa to bring coffee and asked Anisii in a bored voice: 'Well, what have you got there, Tulipov? Are you going to read me the advertisements for the latest technical wonders again? Or about the theft of a bronze lyre from the tomb of Count Khvostov, like yesterday?'

Anisii hesitated in embarrassment, because he actually had marked out a suspicious advertisement in the *Week* that glorified the properties of a 'self-propelled wonder-bicycle' with some mythical kind of 'internal combustion engine'.

'Oh, no, Erast Petrovich,' he protested with dignity, seeking out something more impressive. 'There's a curious announcement here in yesterday's "Summary". They say there are rumours going round Moscow of some magical black bird that flew down from the heavens to Full State Counsellor Eropkin, gave him a gold ring and spoke with him in a human voice. And they also mention some holy fool, a miraculous boy whom they call either Paisii or Pafnutii. There's a note from the chief of police: "Inform the Consistory, so that the parish priests can explain to their flocks the harmfulness of superstitious beliefs."'

'Eropkin? A black b-bird?' the Chief asked in surprise. 'Samson Kharitonovich Eropkin himself? Strange. Very strange. And tell me, is it a persistent rumour?'

'Yes, it says here that everyone mentions the Smolensk Market.'

'Eropkin is a very rich and very superstitious man,' Erast Petrovich said thoughtfully. 'I would suspect some kind of swindle in this, but Eropkin has such a reputation that none of the Moscow rogues would dare to tangle with him. He's as vicious a villain as the world has ever seen. I've had him in my sights for a while, but unfortunately Vladimir Andreevich has ordered me not to touch him. He says there are plenty of villains, you can't put them all in jail, and this one gives generously to the municipal budget and charity. So a bird spoke to him in a human voice? And it had a gold ring in its beak? Let me have a look.'

He took the 'Police Summary of Municipal Events' from Tulipov and started reading the circled article.

'Hmm. In every case mention is made of a "blessed youth, with a, bright, clean face and golden hair, in a shirt whiter than snow". When did you ever hear of a holy fool with a bright, clean face and a shirt whiter than snow? And look at this, what it says here: "It is difficult to dismiss this rumour as a total invention in view of the remarkable amount of detail, which is not usually typical of such idle inventions." I tell you what, Tulipov: you take two or three agents from Sverchinsky and put Eropkin's house and his movements under secret surveillance. Don't explain the reason why; just say it's an order from His Excellency. Jack or no Jack, I sense some cunning intrigue in this. Let's get to the bottom of these holy miracles.'

The Court Counsellor pronounced this last phrase in a distinctly major key. The news of the magical black bird had produced a miraculous effect on Erast Petrovich. He stubbed out his cigar, and when Masa came in with the coffee things, he said: 'Give the coffee to Tulipov over there. You and I haven't done any sword training for a long time.'

The Japanese beamed brightly, dumped the tray on the desk, sending drops of black liquid flying into the air, and rushed headlong out of the study.

Five minutes later Anisii was standing at the window and wincing as he observed two figures, naked except for loincloths, trampling through the snow in the courtyard on slightly bent legs. The Court Counsellor was slim and muscular; Masa was as solid as a barrel, but without a single fold of fat. Each opponent was holding in his hands a stout stick of bamboo with a round guard on the hilt. You wouldn't kill anyone with a thing like that, of course, but you could very easily cripple them.

Masa held his hands out with his 'sword' pointing upwards, gave a blood-curdling howl and jumped forward. A loud crack of wood against wood, and once again the opponents were circling through the snow. 'Br-r-r-r,' Anisii said with a shudder, and took a sip of hot coffee.

The Chief dashed at the short Japanese, the clash of the sticks fused into a continuous crackling, and they began flashing about so fast that Tulipov's eyes were dazzled.

However, the fight did not last long. Masa slumped down on to his backside, clutching the top of his head, with Fandorin standing over him, rubbing a bruised shoulder.

'Hey, Tulipov,' he shouted merrily, turning towards the house, 'how would you like to join us? I'll teach you Japanese fencing!'

Oh no, thought Anisii, hiding behind the curtain. Some other time.

'You don't want to?' asked Erast Petrovich, scooping up a handful of snow and rubbing it into his sinewy midriff with evident pleasure. 'Off you go then; get on with the job. No more time-wasting!'

How do you like that? As if Tulipov had spent two days in a row sitting around in his dressing gown!

His Honour
Mr Fandorin
26 February, second day of observation

I apologise for my handwriting – I am writing with a pencil and the sheet of paper is on agent Fedorov's back. The note will be delivered by agent Sidorchuk, and I have put the third agent, Latzis, on watch in a sleigh in case the mark departs suddenly.

Something strange is happening to the mark.

He has not been in his office either yesterday or today. We know from his cook that the holy fool, the boy Paisii, has been living in the house since yesterday morning. He eats a lot of chocolate and says that's all right, chocolate is not forbidden during the fast. Early this morning, when it was still dark, the mark went somewhere on his sleigh, accompanied by Paisii and three servants. On Yakimanka Street he got away from us and left in the direction of the Kaluga Gates – he has a very fine troika. We don't know where he went. He came back soon after seven, carrying an old copper saucepan that he held at arm's length. It looked quite heavy. The mark appeared agitated and even frightened. According to information received from the cook, he took no breakfast but locked himself in his bedroom and made jangling sounds there for a long time. There are whispers in the house about some 'huge great treasure' the master is supposed to have found. And a piece of total nonsense about the Holy Virgin herself supposedly appearing to E., or a burning bush speaking to him.

Since midday the mark has been here, in the Church of the Mother of God of Smolensk, praying furiously, bowing down to the ground in front of the Holy Icon. The boy Paisii is with him. The holy fool looks exactly as he was described in the summary. I would only add that he has a keen, lively gaze, not like holy fools have. Come quick, Chief, something is going on here. I'll send Sidorchuk now and go back into the church for communion.

Written at five hours forty-six and a half minutes in the afternoon.

A.T.

Erast Petrovich appeared in the church soon after seven, when the interminable 'Most Blessed Among Women' was already coming to an end. Tulipov (wearing blue spectacles and a ginger wig, so that he wouldn't be taken for a Tatar because of his shaved head) felt a touch on his shoulder. It was a swarthy-faced, curly-haired gypsy in a long fur coat, with an earring in his ear.

'Right, son, hand on the light of God,' the gypsy said, and when Anisii, astounded at such familiarity, took the candle from him, he whispered in Fandorin's voice: 'I see Eropkin, but where's the boy?'

Tulipov blinked, recovered his wits and pointed carefully.

The mark was kneeling on the floor, muttering prayers and bowing incessantly. There was a black-bearded man who looked like a bandit kneeling behind him but not crossing himself, just looking bored. Once or twice he even yawned widely, exposing the glint of his handsome white teeth. A pretty-looking youth was sitting to the right of Eropkin, with his hands folded into a cross and his eyes raised in sorrow, singing something in a thin voice. He was wearing a white shirt, but not actually as snow-white as the rumours had claimed – he clearly had not changed it for a long time. Once Anisii saw the holy fool fall face down on the floor in the ecstasy of prayer and quickly stuff a chocolate into his cheek. Tulipov was terribly hungry himself, but duty is duty. Even when he went outside to write his report he hadn't allowed himself to buy a smoked-sturgeon-belly pie on the square, although he had really wanted to.

'Why are you made up as a gypsy?' he asked the Chief in a whisper.

'And who else do you think I can make myself up as with that Brazil-nut infusion still on my fizzog? A Moor, perhaps? A Moor has no business with the Mother of God of Smolensk.'

Erast Petrovich looked at Anisii reproachfully and suddenly, without the slightest stammer, he said something that made poor Tulipov's jaw drop: 'I forgot one substantial failing that is hard to transform into a virtue. You have a weak visual memory. Don't you see that the holy fool is a close, one might even say intimate, acquaintance of yours?'

'No!' exclaimed Anisii, clutching at his heart. 'It can't be!'

'Just look at her ear. I told you that every person's ears are unique. You see that short pink lobe, and the general outline – a perfect oval: that's rare, and the most distinctive detail – the slightly protruding antitragus. It's her, Tulipov, it is: the Georgian Princess. That means the Jack really is more impudent than I thought.'

The Court Counsellor shook his head as if in amazement at the mysteries of human nature. Then he began speaking curtly, in brief fragments: 'The very best agents. Definitely Mikheev, Subbotin, Seifullin and another seven. Six sleighs and horses good enough not to fall behind Eropkin's sleigh again. The strictest secrecy, following the "enemies all around" system, so that the pursuit will not be evident to the mark, or even to the public. It's quite possible that the Jack himself is hanging about somewhere near here. We don't know what his face looks like, and he hasn't shown us his ears. Quick march to Nikitskaya Street. Look lively!'

Anisii gazed like a man enchanted at the 'boy's' slim neck, and the ideal oval ear with that antitragus, and the thoughts that crept into the mind of the candidate for a state title were entirely inappropriate for a church, especially during the Lenten Fast.

He started, crossed himself and began making his way through to the exit.

Eropkin remained praying and fasting in the church until late and only arrived home after ten. From where the agent Latzis was freezing on the roof of the next house, people could be seen starting to harness horses into a closed sleigh. It seemed that, despite the late night hour, Samson Kharitonovich was not intending to take to his bed.

But Fandorin and Anisii had everything ready. There were three ways to drive away from Eropkin's house in Mertvy Lane: towards the Church of the Asssumption on the Graves, towards Starokoniushenny Lane, and on to Prechistenka Street, and there were sleighs standing unobtrusively at each crossroads.

The Full State Counsellor's sleigh – squat and covered with dark fabric – drove out of the oak gates at a quarter past eleven and set off towards Prechistenka Street. There were two strong-looking fellows in sheepskin jackets sitting on the coachbox, and the black-bearded mute was at the back, on the footboard.

The first of the two sleighs on duty at the entrance to Prechistenka Street set off in unhurried pursuit. The other five lined up behind and set off, keeping a respectful distance behind 'number one' – that was what the front echelon of the surveillance team was called in the jargon. At the back of number one there was a lighted red lantern that the sleighs behind could see from a long distance away.

Erast Petrovich and Anisii rode in a light sleigh, hanging back about a hundred and fifty yards behind the red lantern. The other numbers stretched out in a string behind them. There were peasant sleighs, and a coachman's troika, and a priest's twosome, but even the most unkempt-looking wooden sledges were solidly put together, on steel runners, and the horses had been specially selected to match – they might not be much to look at, but they had speed and stamina.

After the first turning (on to the embankment of the River Moscow), following instructions, number one fell back and, at Fandorin's signal, number two moved up, while number one fell in at the very end of the tail. Number two trailed the mark for exactly ten minutes by the clock, and then turned off to the left, making way for number three.

In this case the strict observance of instructions proved far from excessive, because the black-bearded bandit on the footboard was wide awake; he was smoking a cigar and the thick-skinned brute wasn't bothered at all by the weather – he hadn't even covered his shaggy head with a cap, although a wind had come up and there were large wet flakes of snow fluttering down from the heavens.

Beyond the Yauza the sleigh turned left, but number three went straight on, giving way to number four. The Court Counsellor's sleigh was not included in the sequence of numbers, constantly maintaining second position.

And so they trailed the mark to his destination: the walls of the Novopimenovsky Monastery, with its squat towers glowing white in the night.

From a distance they saw one, two, three, four, five figures detach themselves from the sleigh. The last two were carrying something – either a sack or a human body.

'A body!' gasped Anisii. 'Maybe it's time to take them.'

'Not so fast,' the Chief replied. 'We need to work out what's going on first.'

He set sleighs with agents on all the strategic routes and only then gestured to Tulipov to follow him at the double.

They approached the abandoned chapel cautiously and walked round it. On the far side, by a modest, rusty little door, they came across a sleigh and a horse tethered to a tree. It reached out its shaggy face to Anisii and gave a quiet, pitiful whinny – it had clearly been standing in the same spot for a long time and was feeling bored.

Erast Petrovich pressed his ear against the door; then, to test it, he pulled gently on the handle. The door unexpectedly opened slightly, without making the slightest sound. A dull light glimmered in the narrow crack and he heard a resounding voice uttering strange words: 'Where are you going? I'll turn you to stone!'

'Curious,' whispered the Chief, closing the door hastily. 'The hinges are rusty, but they've been lubricated recently. All right, let's wait and see what happens.'

Five minutes later there was a loud commotion and rumbling inside, but almost immediately everything went quiet again. Fandorin put his hand on Anisii's shoulder: Not now; it's too soon.

Another ten minutes went by and suddenly a woman's voice started screeching: 'Fire! We're burning! Good people, we're burning!'

Immediately a man's voice took up the cry: 'Fire! We're burning! Fire!'

Anisii made a desperate rush for the door, but fingers of steel seized him by the half-belt of his greatcoat and pulled him back. 'I assume that so far this is just the first scene, and the main action is yet to come,' the Chief said quietly. 'We have to wait for the finale. It is no accident that the door has been oiled, and no coincidence that the horse is loitering outside. You and I, Tulipov, have taken up a key position. And one should only hurry in those cases when to delay is quite impossible.' Erast Petrovich raised a finger in admonition and Anisii could not help admiring the velvet glove with the silver press-studs.

The Court Counsellor had dressed like a dandy for the night operation: a long cloth coat lined with beaver fur, a white scarf, a silk top hat and a walking cane with an ivory knob. Anisii may have been wearing a ginger wig, but he had dressed up for the first time in his functionary's greatcoat with buttons bearing official crests and put on his new cap with a lacquered peak. Beside Fandorin, however, he was as dowdy as a sparrow beside a drake.

The Chief was about to say something else equally instructive, but suddenly there was such a bloodcurdling howl from behind the door, filled with such genuine suffering, that Tulipov also screamed at the shock of it.

Erast Petrovich's face tensed up; he clearly did not know if he ought to wait a little longer, or if this was the very case in which to delay was impossible. He twitched the corner of his mouth nervously and inclined his head to one side, as if he were listening to some voice that Anisii could not hear. The voice evidently told the Chief to act, because Fandorin resolutely swung the door open and stepped inside.

The scene that met Anisii's gaze was truly astonishing.

An old man with a grey beard, dressed in a hussar's uniform and a white robe that had slipped down towards his head, was hanging above an empty wooden table with his legs parted and attached to two ropes. Behind him, swinging a long, coiled whip, stood Eropkin's black-bearded cut-throat. Eropkin himself was sitting a bit further away, on a chair. There was a tightly stuffed sack lying at his feet, and the two sturdy young fellows who had travelled on the coachbox earlier, were squatting down by the wall, smoking.

But Tulipov only took all this in, out of the corner of his eye, in passing because his attention was immediately caught by the frail figure lying face-down and unmoving, lifeless. In three bounds Anisii rounded the table, colliding on his way with some weighty folio but keeping his footing and going down on his knees beside the recumbent woman.

When he turned her over on to her back with trembling hands, the blue eyes opened on the pale face and the pink lips muttered: 'Oh, how ginger . . .'

Thank God, she was alive!

'What kind of torture chamber is this we have here?' Erast Petrovich's calm voice asked behind him, and Anisii straightened up, recalling his duty.

Eropkin switched his dumbfounded gaze from the dandy in the top hat to the nimble functionary and back. 'And who are you?' he asked menacingly. 'Accomplices? Right, Kuzma.'

The black-bearded mute made an imperceptible movement with his hand and a long shadow went slicing swiftly through the air towards the Court Counsellor's throat. Fandorin threw up his cane and the furiously swirling end of the whip wrapped itself round the lacquered wood. A single short movement, and the whip was jerked out of Kuzma's huge, bear-like paws and landed in Erast Petrovich's hands. He unhurriedly unwound the tight leather tail and without any apparent effort, using just his fingers, began tearing the whip into tiny pieces. As more and more scraps went flying to the floor, Kuzma seem to deflate visibly. He lowered his shaggy head into his massive shoulders and backed against the wall.

'The chapel is surrounded by police agents,' Fandorin said, when he had completely demolished the whip. 'This time, Eropkin, you will answer for your defiance of the law.'

However, the man sitting on the chair was not frightened by this announcement. 'That's all right,' he said with a grin; 'the purse will take care of it.'

The Court Counsellor sighed and blew his silver whistle. There was a high, ear-splitting trill, and the police agents instantly came tramping in.

'Take these to the station,' said the Chief, indicating Eropkin and his accomplices. 'Draw up a report. What's in the sack?'

'The sack's mine,' Eropkin said hastily.

'What's in it?'

'Money – two hundred and eighty-three thousand, five hundred and two roubles. My money, income from trade.'

'Such a substantial sum in a sack?' Erast Petrovich asked coldly. 'Do you have financial documents for it? The sources of income? Has the duty been paid?'

'You, sir – will you, just for a moment . . . step to one side . . .' Eropkin leapt up off his chair and dashed towards the Court Counsellor. 'I know the way things are done, you know . . .'

He started whispering. 'Let's say there's exactly two hundred thousand, and the rest is at your discretion.'

'Take him away,' ordered Fandorin, turning away. 'Draw up a report. Count the money and register it in due order. Let the excise department deal with it.'

When the four prisoners had been taken out, a cheerful, if somewhat hoarse voice suddenly spoke up: 'Of course, that's very noble – to refuse bribes; but how much longer am I going to hang here like a sack myself? I'm seeing stars already.'

Anisii and Erast Petrovich took hold of the dangling man's shoulders and the young lady, now completely recovered – Mimi, wasn't that her name? – climbed up on the table and untied the ropes.

They sat the tormented victim on the floor. Fandorin pulled off the false beard and grey wig, revealing a quite unremarkable, absolutely ordinary face: close-set blue-grey eyes; light-coloured hair, whitish at the ends; a characterless nose; a slightly crooked chin – everything just as Erast Petrovich had described. The rush of blood had turned the face scarlet, but the lips immediately extended into a smile.

'Shall we introduce ourselves?' the Jack of Spades asked merrily. 'I don't believe I've had the honour ...'

'Then it wasn't you at the Sparrow Hills,' the Chief said with an understanding nod. 'Well, well.'

'Which hills did you say?' the rascal asked insolently. 'I am retired Cornet of Hussars Kuritsyn. Shall I show you my residence permit?'

'L-Later,' the Court Counsellor said with a shake of his head. 'Very well, I shall introduce myself again. I am Erast Fandorin, Deputy for Special Assignments of the Governor-General of Moscow, and no great lover of audacious jests. And this is m-my assistant, Anisii Tulipov.' From the fact that the stammer had reappeared in the Chief's speech, Anisii concluded that the intense action was over now and he allowed himself to relax and steal a glance at Mimi.

She turned out to be looking at him too: 'Anisii Tulipov. That's beautiful. You could act in a theatre with a name like that.'

Suddenly the Jack – for, of course, despite all the casuistry, it was he – winked at Anisii in the most familiar fashion and stuck out a tongue that was as broad as a spade and quite amazingly red.

'Well now, Mr Momos, how am I going to deal with you?' asked Erast Petrovich, watching as Mimi wiped her accomplice's forehead, which was covered with fine beads of sweat. 'According to the dictates of the law or the spirit of justice?'

The Jack thought for a moment and said: 'If you and I, Mr Fandorin, had not met for the first time today, but had a certain history of acquaintance, I would naturally throw myself wholly and entirely on your mercy, for it is immediately clear that you are a sensitive and noble man. You would undoubtedly take into consideration the moral and physical torments that I have suffered, and also the unappetising character of the party with whom I attempted so unsuccessfully to jest. However, circumstances are such that I have no need to exploit your humane inclinations. It seems to me that I have no reason to fear the stern embrace of the law. His Porcine Excellency Samson Kharitonovich Eropkin is unlikely to take me to court for this innocent prank. It would not be in his interest.'

'In Moscow the law is His Excellency Prince Dolgorukoi,' Erast Petrovich answered the insolent scoundrel in the same tone. 'Or do you, Mr Jack, seriously believe in the independence of the judiciary? P-Permit me to remind you that you have offended the Governor-General most cruelly. And what are we to do with the Englishman? The city has to return his hundred thousand.'

'My dear Erast Petrovich, I really have no idea what Englishman you are talking about,' said the rescued man with a broad shrug. 'I have the most genuine and profound respect for His Excellency – and especially for his dyed grey hair. If Moscow is in need of money, then see how much I have obtained for the municipal treasury – an entire sack full. It was greed that made Eropkin blurt out the money was his, but when he cools down he'll disown it again. I don't know a thing, he'll say, about anything. And a certain sum of money of unknown provenance

141

will go to meet the needs of the city of Moscow. To be fair, I really ought to get a few per cent myself.'

'Well now, that is reasonable enough,' the Court Counsellor said thoughtfully. 'And then again, you did return Ariadna Arkadievna's things. And you didn't even forget my beads ... All right – according to the dictates of the law it is. You won't regret spurning the spirit of my justice?'

A slight hesitation was visible on the gentleman's unremarkable face. 'Thank you most kindly, but you know, I am used to relying on myself most of the time.'

'Well, as you wish,' Fandorin said with a shrug, and added without the slightest pause: 'You can g-go to the devil.'

Anisii was stunned, but the Jack of Spades hastily jumped to his feet, evidently afraid that the Governor's deputy would change his mind.

'Thank you! I swear I shall never set foot in this city again. And I'm thoroughly bored with my Orthodox homeland too. Come, Mimi, let us not detain Mr Fandorin any further.'

Erast Petrovich spread his arms wide: 'Alas, I cannot let your companion go. All the dictates of the law must be applied. She must answer for the lottery swindle. There are victims, there are witnesses. In this case an encounter with the courts cannot be avoided.'

'Oh!' the crop-headed girl exclaimed, so pitifully that Anisii's heart was wrung. 'Momchik, I don't want to go to prison!'

'It can't be helped, my girl; the law is the law,' the heartless swindler replied flippantly, edging gently towards the door. 'Don't you worry; I'll take care of you. I'll send you the most expensive lawyer in Russia, you'll see. May I go now, Erast Petrovich?'

'You rotter!' Mimi groaned. 'Stop! Where are you going?'

'I'm thinking of trying Guatemala,' Momos told her gleefully. 'I read in the newspapers they've had another coup. The Guatemalans have had enough of the republic; they're looking for a German prince to put on the throne. Perhaps I might suit?' And with a wave of farewell, he disappeared through the door.

*

The trial of the spinster Maria Nikolaevna Maslennikova, former actress of the St Petersburg Theatres, accused of fraud, criminal conspiracy and escaping from arrest, took place at the very end of April, in that blissful period after Easter when the branches are covered with succulent, swelling buds and the fresh grass is creeping untidily along the edges of roads that are still soft but beginning to dry out.

Her trial did not attract the attention of the broad public, since it was not a major case, but there were half a dozen or so reporters sitting in the courtroom – there had been vague but persistent rumours that the failed lottery swindle was connected in some way with the famous Jack of Spades, and so the editors had sent along their representatives just in case.

Anisii was one of the first to arrive and he took a place as close as possible to the dock. He was thoroughly agitated, since he had thought often during the previous two months about the jolly young lady Mimi and her unfortunate fate; and now it seemed that the final resolution had arrived.

In the meantime there had been quite a few changes in the life of the former courier. After Erast Petrovich had let the Jack go completely free, there had been an unpleasant scene at the Governor's residence. Prince Dolgorukoi had flown into an indescribable rage, refused to listen to anything and even shouted at the Court Counsellor, calling him a 'self-willed boy'. The Chief had immediately handed in his written resignation, but it had not been accepted because, when the Prince cooled down, he had realised just how much embarrassment he had been spared by the prudence of his Deputy for Special Assignments. The Jack of Spades' testimony concerning the case of Lord Pitsbrook would have shown the Prince up in an unfavourable light, not only to the people of Moscow but also to the Higher Spheres, in which the obdurate Governor-General had no few enemies who were only waiting for him to commit some blunder. And to become an object of fun was even worse than a blunder, especially if you were already seventy-six and there were others keen to take your place.

In fact, the Governor had come to the house on Malaya Nikitskaya Street, begged Erast Petrovich's pardon and even recommended him for yet another Order of St Vladimir – not for the Jack of Spades, of course, but for 'outstandingly zealous service and special work'. The Prince's generosity had even extended to Anisii: he had received a substantial financial reward, enough to settle into the new apartment, get a few treats for Sonya and acquire a complete set of uniforms. He had used to be plain, simple Anisii, but now he was His Honour Collegiate Registrar Anisii Pitirimovich Tulipov.

Today he had come to the court in his brand-new summer uniform, never worn before. Summer was still a long way off, but Anisii looked very impressive in his high-collared white jacket with gold trimming on the buttonholes.

When the accused was brought in, she noticed the white uniform immediately, smiled sadly, as if to an old acquaintance, and sat down with her head lowered. Mimochka's hair (Mimochka – that was how Anisii thought of her to himself) had not yet grown back properly and it was gathered into a simple little knot at the back of her head. The accused had put on a simple brown dress and she looked like a small grammar-school girl facing a strict school-council meeting.

When Anisii saw the jurors glancing sympathetically at the modest girl, his spirits rose slightly. Perhaps the sentence would not be too severe?

However, the prosecutor's opening address left him horrified. The counsel for the prosecution – a rubicund, heartless careerist – painted Mimochka's character in the most scandalous colours, described in detail the revolting cynicism of the 'charitable lottery' and demanded three years of penal servitude for the spinster Maslennikova, plus five years of exile in the less distant regions of Siberia.

The alcoholic actor who had played the part of the chairman of the lottery was released by the court because his guilt was so insignificant and he appeared as a witness for the prosecution. It looked as if Mimochka was destined to carry the can alone for everyone. She lowered her little golden head on to her folded hands and began crying silently.

Then Anisii took a decision. He would follow her to Siberia, find some place to live there and provide the poor girl with the moral support of his faithful devotion. Then, when she was released early, they would marry and then ... and then everything would be just fine.

'And what about Sonya?' his conscience asked. 'Will you put your only sister, an invalid needed by no one, in the poorhouse?'

'No,' Anisii answered his conscience. 'I'll throw myself at Erast Petrovich's feet – he's a noble man; he will understand.'

Things had worked out quite well for Sonya. Fandorin's new maid, the big-bosomed Palasha, had become very fond of the cripple. She looked after her and kept an eye on her, and wove her plaits for her. Sonya had even started saying a few words: 'ribbon' and 'comb'. The Chief would surely not abandon the helpless creature, and afterwards Anisii would take her to his place, just as soon as he was settled ...

At this point the judge gave the floor to the counsel for the defence and for the time being Tulipov set aside his desperate thoughts and gazed hopefully at the barrister.

To be quite honest, he did not look very promising: swarthy-skinned, with a long, drooping nose and a stoop. They said he had been hired from the famous St Petersburg firm of Rubinstein and Rubinstein by a person unknown and had the reputation of an expert in criminal matters. However, the defender's appearance was distinctly unprepossessing. When he stepped out to the front, sneezed loudly into a pink handkerchief and then hiccupped as well, Anisii was seized by foreboding. Oh, that mean rogue Momos had been too miserly to hire a good lawyer; he'd sent some mangy scruff, and a Jew into the bargain. Just look at the way those anti-Semitic jurors were glowering at him; they wouldn't believe a single word he said.

Tulipov's neighbour on the left, an impressive gentleman with a bushy beard and gold-rimmed spectacles who looked like a Kalmyk, examined the lawyer, shook his head and whispered conspiratorially to Anisii: 'He'll ruin the whole case, you'll see.'

The defender stood facing the jurors, pressed his hands to his sides and declared in a sing-song accent: 'Ah, Mr Judge and gentlemen of the jury, can you explain to me what this man has been talking about for the best part of an hour?' He jabbed his thumb derisively in the direction of the prosecutor. 'I would be interested to learn what all the commotion is about. On what is the money of honest taxpayers, such as you and I, being spent?'

The 'honest taxpayers' looked at this over-familiar windbag with evident distaste, but the barrister was not embarrassed in the least.

'What does the prosecution have?' he inquired sceptically. 'A certain swindler, whom, just between you and me, our valiant police have failed to find, organised a fraud. He hired this sweet, modest young lady to give out tickets, saying that the money would go to a good cause. Look at this young woman, gentlemen of the jury. I appeal to you: how is it possible to suspect such an innocent creature of such villainy?'

The jurors looked at the accused. Anisii looked too, and sighed. The case looked hopeless. Perhaps somebody else might have moved the court to pity, but not this hook-nose.

'Come now,' said the defender with a wave of his hand, 'she is as much a victim as the others. Even more so than the others, since the cashbox of the so-called lottery was arrested and all those who presented a ticket were given their money back. Do not ruin the life of this young creature, gentlemen of the jury; do not condemn her to a life among criminals.'

The lawyer sneezed again and pulled a heap of papers out of his briefcase.

'That's pretty feeble,' Anisii's bearded neighbour commented with cool, professional confidence. 'They'll find the girl guilty. How would you like a wager?' And he winked from behind his spectacles.

A fine sense of humour! Anisii moved away angrily, preparing for the worst.

But the defender had not finished yet. He pinched at his goatee beard in the manner of Lord Beaconsfield and genially pressed one hand to a shirt that was none too fresh.

'That is approximately the speech that I would have made to you, gentlemen of the jury, if there were anything to discuss here. But there is nothing to discuss, because I have here' – he shook the papers in the air – 'statements from all the plaintiffs. They are withdrawing their suits. Close the proceedings, Mr Judge. There is no case to be tried.' The barrister approached the judge and slapped the statements down on the table in front of him.

'But that's smart,' Anisii's neighbour whispered, growing excited. 'What will the prosecutor have to say to that?'

The prosecutor sprang to his feet and began shouting in a voice breaking under the weight of righteous indignation: 'This is plain bribery! And I shall prove it! The proceedings cannot be stopped! This is a case of public importance!'

The defender turned to the shouting man and began taunting him: '"Plain bribery"? What new Cato do we have here? It would have been cheaper to bribe you, Mr Prosecutor. Everybody knows that your rate is not very high. As it happens, by the way, I have one of your receipts here. Where is it now? Ah, here!' He pulled some other piece of paper out of his briefcase and thrust it under the judge's nose. 'For a mere one and a half thousand our prosecutor cancelled the bigamist Brutyan's sentence, and Brutyan fled.'

The prosecutor clutched at his heart and slumped down on to his chair. A hubbub broke out in the hall and the correspondents, who had so far been feeling bored, came to life and started scribbling in their notepads.

The judge rang his bell and gazed in confusion at the compromising receipt, as the disagreeable attorney turned awkwardly, and several photographic prints fell out of his inexhaustible briefcase, scattering on to the table.

Anisii could not see what was in those photographs, but the judge suddenly turned as white as chalk and gaped at them, his eyes wide in horror.

'I do apologise,' said the defender, and yet he appeared in no hurry to gather up the photographs from the table. 'They have absolutely nothing to do with our case here today. They are from another case, concerning the corruption of young boys.'

It seemed to Anisii that the barrister emphasised the words 'today' and 'another' in a somewhat strange manner, but then he did speak with a rather distinctive intonation, and Anisii could have imagined it.

'Well now, shall we close the case?' the advocate asked, looking the judge straight in the eye as he gathered up the photographs. 'On the basis that no crime has been committed, eh?'

A minute later the proceedings were declared concluded.

Anisii stood on the porch in a state of terrible agitation, waiting for the miraculous advocate to lead out his acquitted client.

And there they were: Mimochka was smiling to the left and the right, not looking miserable and pitiful any more. The stooping advocate was leading her along, arm in arm, and waving away the reporters with his other hand, which held the briefcase.

'Ah, I'm fed up with you all!' he exclaimed angrily as he helped his companion into the phaeton.

Anisii wanted to go up to Mimochka, but his neighbour from the courtroom, that interested commentator on the legal proceedings, stepped forward first.

'You'll go a long way, colleague,' he said to Mimochka's hook-nosed saviour, slapped him patronisingly on the shoulder, and strode away, tapping his cane heavily.

'Who was that?' Anisii asked an usher.

'Him, sir,' the usher replied in a voice filled with unbounded admiration, 'why, that was Fedor Nikiforich Plevako himself, the most brilliant lawyer in Russia. Gets people off without speaking more than a single sentence.'

At that moment, as Mimi plumped down on to the springy seat of the phaeton, she suddenly swung round and blew Anisii a kiss. The barrister also swung round. He looked sternly at the young lop-eared functionary in the white uniform jacket and suddenly did a very queer thing: he screwed up his face and stuck out a broad, bright-red tongue.

The carriage picked up speed, rumbling merrily over the cobblestones of the road.

'Stop! Stop!' Anisii shouted and went darting after it, but how could he possibly overtake it?

And what point was there, anyway?

THE DECORATOR

CHAPTER I

A Bad Beginning

Erast Petrovich Fandorin, the Governor-General of Moscow's Deputy for Special Assignments and a state official of the sixth rank, a knight of many Russian and foreign orders, was being violently sick.

The finely moulded but now pale and bluish-tinged features of the Collegiate Counsellor's face were contorted in suffering. One hand, in a white kid glove with silver press-studs, was pressed against his chest, while the other clawed convulsively at the air in an unconvincing attempt by Erast Petrovich to reassure his assistant, as if to say, 'Never mind, it's nothing; I shall be fine in a moment.' However, judging from the intensity with which his distress continued, it was anything but nothing.

Fandorin's assistant, Provincial Secretary Anisii Pitirimovich Tulipov, a skinny, unprepossessing young man of twenty-three, had never before had occasion to see his chief in such a pitiful state. Tulipov himself was in fact a little greenish round the gills, but he had resisted the temptation to vomit and was now secretly feeling proud of it. However, this ignoble feeling was merely fleeting, and therefore unworthy of our attention, but the unexpected sensitivity of his adored chief, always so cool-headed and not disposed to excessive displays of feeling, had alarmed Anisii quite seriously.

'G-Go ...' said Erast Petrovich, squeezing out the word as he wiped his purple lips with one glove. His constant slight stutter, a reminder of a concussion suffered long ago, had been become noticeably stronger as a result of his nervous discomfiture. 'G-Go in ... T-Take ... d-detailed ... notes. Photographs from all angles. And make sure they don't t-t-trample the evidence . . .'

He doubled over again, but this time the extended hand did not tremble – the finger pointed steadfastly at the crooked door of the little planking shed from which only a few moments earlier the Collegiate Counsellor had emerged as pale as a ghost with his legs buckling under him.

Anisii did not wish to go back into that grey semi-darkness, into that sticky smell of blood and offal. But duty was duty.

He filled his chest right up to the top with the damp April air (he didn't want his own stomach to start churning too), crossed himself and took the plunge.

The little hut was used for storing firewood, but there was hardly any left, because the cold season was already coming to an end. Quite a number of people had gathered inside: an investigator from the Public Prosecutor's Office, detectives from the Criminal Investigation Department, the district super-intendent of police, the local police inspector, a forensic medical expert, a photographer, local police constables, and also the yard-keeper Klimuk, first to discover the scene of the monstrous atrocity – that morning he had looked in to get some wood for the stove, seen it there, had a good long yell and gone running for the police.

There were two oil lamps burning, and shadows flickered gently across the low ceiling. It was quiet, except for a young constable gently sobbing and sniffing in the corner.

'Well now, and what do we have here?' forensic medical expert Egor Willemovich Zakharov purred curiously as he lifted some dark, bluish-crimson, porous object from the floor in a rubber-gloved hand. 'I do believe it's the spleen. Yes that's her, the little darling. Excellent. Into the little bag with her, into her little bag. And the womb too, the left kidney, and we'll have the full set, apart from a few odd little bits and pieces . . . What's that there under your boot, Monsieur Tulipov? Not the mesentery, is it?'

Anisii glanced down, started in horror and almost stumbled over the outstretched body of the spinster Stepanida An-dreichkina, aged thirty-nine years. This information, together with the nature of her occupation, had been obtained from the

154

yellow prostitute's card left lying neatly on her sundered chest. But there was nothing else neat to be observed in the post-humous appearance of the spinster Andreichkina.

One could assume that even in life her face had not been lovely to behold, but in death it had become nightmarish: it was livid blue, covered with blobs of powder, the eyes had slipped out of their sockets and the mouth was frozen in a soundless scream of horror. What could be seen below the face was even more horrific. Someone had slashed open the poor street-walker's body from top to bottom and from side to side, extracted all of its contents and laid them out on the ground in a fantastic design. By this time, though, Zakharov had already collected up almost the entire exhibition and put it away in little numbered bags. All that was left was the black patch of blood that had spread without hindrance and little scraps of the dress that had been either hacked or torn to shreds.

Leontii Izhitsin, the district prosecutor's Investigator for Espe-cially Important Cases, squatted down beside the doctor and asked briskly: 'Signs of intercourse?'

'That, my darling man, I'll particularise afterwards. I'll compose a little report portraying everything just the way it is, very prettily. In here, as you can see for yourself, we have been cast into the outer darkness.'

Like any foreigner with a perfect mastery of the Russian language, Zakharov was fond of peppering his speech with various quaint and whimsical turns of phrase. Despite his per-fectly normal surname, the expert was of English extraction. The doctor's father, also a medical man, had come to the kingdom of our late departed sovereign, put down roots and adapted a name that presented difficulty to the Russian ear – Zacharias – to local conditions, making it into 'Zakharov': Egor Willemovich had told them all about it on the way there in the cab. You could tell just from looking at him that he wasn't one of us Russians: lanky and heavy-boned, with sandy-coloured hair, a broad mouth with thin lips, and fidgety, constantly shifting that terrible pipe from one corner of his mouth to the other.

The investigator Izhitsin pretended to take an interest, clearly putting on a brave face, as the medical expert twirled yet another lump of tormented flesh between his tenacious fingers and inquired sarcastically: 'Well, Mr Tulipov, is your superior still taking the air? I told you we would have got by perfectly well without any supervision from the Governor's department. This is no picture for over-dainty eyes, but we've already seen everything there is to see.'

It was clear enough: Leontii Izhitsin was displeased; he was jealous. It was a serious matter to set Fandorin himself to watch over an investigation. What investigator would have been pleased?

'Stop that, Linkov, you're like a little girl!' Izhitsin growled at the sobbing policeman. 'Better get used to it. You're not destined for special assignments; you'll be seeing all sorts of things.'

'God forbid I could ever get used to such sights,' Senior Constable Pribludko muttered in a half-whisper: he was an old, experienced member of the force, known to Anisii from a case of three years before.

It wasn't the first time he'd worked with Leontii Izhitsin, either – an unpleasant gentleman, nervous and jittery, constantly laughing, with piercing eyes; always neat and tidy – his collars looked as if they were made of alabaster and his cuffs were even whiter – always brushing the specks of dust off his own shoulders; a man with ambitions, carving out a career for himself. Last Epiphany, though, he'd come a cropper with the investigation into the merchant Sitnikov's will. It had been a sensational case, and since it also involved the interests of certain influential individuals to some degree, any delay was unacceptable, so His Excellency Prince Dolgorukoi had asked Erast Petrovich to give the Public Prosecutor's Office a helping hand. But everyone knew the kind of assistance the Chief gave – he'd gone and untangled the entire case in one day. No wonder Izhitsin was furious. He could sense that yet again the victor's laurels would not be his.

'That seems to be all,' the investigator declared. 'So what now? The corpse goes to the police morgue, at the Bozhedomka Cemetery. Seal the shed, put a constable on guard. Have detectives question everyone living in the vicinity, and make it thorough – anything they've heard or seen that was suspicious. You, Klimuk. The last time you came to collect firewood was some time between ten and eleven, right?' Izhitsin asked the yard-keeper. 'And death occurred no later than two o'clock in the morning?' (That was to the medical expert Zakharov.) 'So what we have to look at is the period from ten in the evening to two in the morning.' And then he turned to Klimuk again. 'Perhaps you spoke to someone local? Did they tell you anything?'

The yard-keeper (a broad, thick beard, bushy eyebrows, irregular skull, with a distinctive wart in the middle of his forehead, thought Anisii, practising the composition of a verbal portrait) stood there, kneading a cap that could not possibly be any more crumpled.

'No, Your Honour, not at all. I don't understand a thing. I locked the door of the shed and ran to Mr Pribludko at the station. And they didn't let me out of the station until the bosses arrived. The local folk don't know a thing about it. That is, of course, they can see as lots of police have turned up ... that the gentlemen of the police force have arrived. But the locals don't know anything about this here horror,' said the yard-keeper, with a fearful sideways glance at the corpse.

'We'll check that soon enough,' Izhitsin said with a laugh. 'Right then, detectives, get to work. And you, Mr Zakharov, take your treasures away, and let's have a full evaluation, according to the book, by midday.'

'Will the gentlemen detectives please stay where they are.' Fandorin's low voice came from behind Izhitsin. Everybody turned around.

How had the Collegiate Counsellor entered the shed, and when? The door had not even creaked. Even in the semi-darkness it was obvious that Anisii's chief was pale and perturbed, but his voice was steady and he spoke in his usual reserved and courteous manner, a manner that did not encourage any objections.

'Mr Izhitsin, even the yard-keeper realised that it would not be good to spread gossip about this incident,' Fandorin told the investigator in a dry voice. 'In fact, I was sent here in order to ensure the very strictest secrecy. No questioning of the locals. And furthermore, I request – in fact I demand – that everyone here present must maintain absolute silence about the circumstances. Explain to the local people that . . . a st-streetwalker has hanged herself, taken her own life, a perfectly ordinary business. If rumours of what has happened here spread around Moscow, every one of you will be subject to official inquiry, and anyone found guilty of divulging information will be severely punished. I'm sorry, gentlemen, but th-those are the instructions that I was given, and there is good reason for them.'

At a sign from the doctor the constables were about to take the stretcher standing against the wall and place the corpse on it, but the Collegiate Counsellor raised his hand: 'Wait a m-moment. He crouched down beside the dead woman. 'What's this here on her cheek?'

Izhitsin, galled by the reprimand he had received, shrugged his narrow shoulders. 'A spot of blood; as you may have observed, there's plenty of blood here.'

'But not on her face.' Erast Petrovich cautiously rubbed the oval spot with his finger – a mark was left on the white kid leather of his glove. Speaking in extreme agitation, or so it seemed to Anissii, his chief muttered: 'There's no cut, no bite.'

The investigator Izhitsin watched the Collegiate Counsellor's manipulations in bewilderment. The medical expert Zakharov watched with interest.

Fandorin took a magnifying glass out of his pocket, peered from close up at the victim's face and gasped: 'The imprint of lips! Good Lord, this is the imprint of lips! There can be no doubt about it!'

'So why make such a fuss over that?' Izhitsin asked acidly. 'We've got plenty of marks far more horrible than that here.' He turned the toe of his shoe towards the open rib-cage and the gaping pit of the belly. 'Who knows what ideas a loony might get into his head?'

'Ah, how foul,' the Collegiate Counsellor muttered, addressing no one in particular.

He tore off his soiled glove with a rapid movement and threw it aside. He straightened up, closed his eyes and said very quietly: 'My God, is it really going to start in Moscow . . .?'

'What a piece of work is a man! How noble in reason! How infinite in faculties! In form and moving how express and admirable! In action how like an angel! In apprehension how like a god! The beauty of the world! The paragon of animals! And yet, to me, what is this quint-essence of dust?' No matter. What does it matter if the Prince of Denmark, an indolent and blasé creature, has no interest in man? I do! The Bard is half right: there is little angelic in the deeds of men, and it is sacrilege to liken the comprehension of man to that of God, but there is nothing in the world more beautiful than man. And what are action and apprehension but a chimera? Deception and vanity, truly the quintessence of dust? Man is not action, but body. Even the plants that are so pleasing to our eyes, the most sumptuous and intricate of flowers, can in no wise be compared with the magnificent arrangement of the human body. Flowers are primitive and simple, identical within and without, turn the petals whichever way you will. Looking at flowers is boring. How can the avidity of their stems, the primitive geometry of their inflorescences and the crude forms of their stamens rival the purple resilience of muscles, the elasticity of silky-smooth skin, the silvery mother-of-pearl of the stomach, the graceful curves of the intestines and the mysterious asymmetry of the liver?

How is it possible for the monotonous coloration of a blossoming poppy to match the variety of shades of human blood – from the shrill scarlet of the arterial current to the regal purple of the veins? How can the vulgar shade of the bluebell rival the tender blue pattern of the capillaries, or the autumnal colouring of the maple rival the deep blush of the menstrual discharge! The female body is more elegant and a hundred times more interesting than the male. The function of the female body is not coarse physical labour and destruction, but creation and nurturing. The elastic womb is like a precious pearl oyster. An idea! Some time I must lay open an impregnated womb to expose the maturing pearl within the shell – yes, yes, without fail! Tomorrow! I have been fasting too long already, since Shrovetide. My lips have shrivelled with repeating: 'Reanimate my accursed heart through this

159

sacrificial fast!' The Lord is kind and charitable. He will not be angry with me for lacking the strength to hold out six days until the Blessed Resurrection. And after all, the third of April is no ordinary day: it is the anniversary of the Enlightenment. It was the third of April then too. What date it was in the other style is of no importance. The important thing is the music of those words: the third of April.

I have my own fast, and my own Easter. When the fast is broken, let it be in style. No, I will not wait until tomorrow. Today! Yes, yes, lay out a banquet. Not merely to sate myself, but a surfeit. Not for my own sake, but to the glory of God.

For He it was who opened my eyes, who taught me to see and understand true beauty. More than that, to disclose it and reveal it to the world. And to disclose is to create. I am the Creator's apprentice.

How sweet it is to break the fast after a long abstinence. I remember each sweet moment; I know my memory will preserve it all down to the minutest detail, without losing a single sensation of vision, taste, touch, hearing or smell.

I close my eyes and I see it . . .

Late evening. I cannot sleep. Excitement and elation lead me along the dirty streets, across the empty lots, between the crooked houses and the twisted fences. I have not slept for many nights in a row. My chest is constricted, my temples throb. During the day I doze for half an hour or an hour and am woken by terrible visions that I cannot remember when awake.

As I walk along I dream of death, of meeting with Him, but I know that I must not die, it is too soon; my mission has not been completed.

A voice from out of the darkness: 'Spare the money for half a bottle.' Trembling, hoarse from drinking. I turn my head and see the most wretched and abominable of human beings: a degraded whore, drunk and in tatters, but even so, grotesquely painted with ceruse and lipstick. I turn away in squeamish disgust, but suddenly my heart is pierced by the familiar sharp pity. Poor creature, what have you done to yourself! And this is a woman, the masterpiece of God's art! How could you abuse yourself so, desecrate and degrade the gift of God, abase your precious reproductive system?

Of course, you are not to blame. A soulless, cruel society has dragged you through the mud. But I shall cleanse and save you. My heart is serene and joyful.

Who could have known it would happen? I had no intention of breaking the fast – if I had, my path would not have lain through these pitiful slums, but through the fetid lanes and alleys of Khitrovka or Grachyovka, where abomination and vice make their home. But l am overflowing with magnanimity and generosity, only slightly tainted by my impatient craving.

'I'll soon cheer you up, my darling,' I tell her. 'Come with me.' I am wearing men's clothes, and the witch thinks she has found a buyer for her rotten wares. She laughs hoarsely and shrugs her shoulders coyly: 'Where are we going? Listen, have you got any money? You might at least feed me, or better still buy me a drink.' Poor little lost sheep.

I lead her through the dark courtyard towards the sheds. I tug impatiently on one door, a second – the third is not locked.

The lucky woman breathes her cheap vodka fumes on my neck, and giggles: 'Well fancy that! He's taking me to the sheds; he's that impatient.'

A stroke of the scalpel, and I open the doors of freedom to her soul.

Liberation does not come without pain; it is like birth. The woman I now love with all my heart is in great pain; she wheezes and chews on the gag in her mouth, and I stroke her head and comfort her – 'Be patient.' My hands do their work deftly and quickly. I do not need light: my eyes see as well at night as they do during the day.

I lay open the profaned, filthy integument of the body, the soul of my beloved sister soars upwards and I am transfixed by awe before the perfection of God's machinery.

When I lift the hot bread-roll of the heart to my face with a tender smile, it is still trembling, still quivering, like a golden fish fresh from the water, and I kiss the miraculous fish on the parted lips of its aorta.

The place was well chosen, no one interrupts me, and this time the Hymn to Beauty is sung to the end, consummated with a kiss to her cheek. Sleep, sister; your life was revolting and horrible, the sight of you was an offence to the eye, but thanks to me you have become beautiful . . .

Consider that flower again. Its true beauty is not visible in the glade or in the flower-bed, oh no! The rose is regal on the bodice of a dress, the carnation in the buttonhole, the violet in a lovely girl's hair. The flower attains its glory when it has been cut; its true life is inseparable from death. The same is true of the human body. While it is alive, it cannot reveal its delightful arrangement in all its magnificence. I help the body to ascend its throne of glory. I am a gardener.

But no, a gardener merely cuts flowers, while I also create displays of intoxicating beauty from the organs of the body. In England a previously unheard-of profession is becoming fashionable nowadays – the decorator, a specialist in the embellishment and adornment of the home, the shop window, the street at carnival time.

I am not a gardener; I am a decorator.

CHAPTER 2

From Bad to Worse

Holy Week Tuesday, 4 April, midday

Those present at the emergency meeting convened by the Governor-General of Moscow, Prince Vladimir Andreevich Dolgorukoi, were as follows: the Head Police Master and Major-General of the Retinue of His Imperial Majesty, Yurovsky; the Public Prosecutor of the Chamber of Justice of Moscow, State Counsellor and Usher of the Chamber, Kozlyatnikov; the head of the Criminal Investigation Department of the police, State Counsellor Eichmann; the Governor-General's Deputy for Special Assignments, Collegiate Counsellor Fandorin; and the Investigator for Especially Important Cases of the Public Prosecutor's Office of Moscow, Court Counsellor Izhitsin.

'Oh this weather, this appalling weather, it's vile.' These were the words with which the Governor-General opened the proceedings. 'It's simply beastly, gentlemen. Overcast, windy, slush and mud everywhere and, worst of all, the River Moscow has overflowed its banks more than usual. I went to the Zamoskvorechie district – an absolute nightmare. The water's risen three and a half *sazhens*! It's flooded everything up as far as Pyatnitskaya Street. And it's no better on the left bank either. You can't get through Neglinny Lane. Oh, I shall be put to shame, gentlemen. Dolgorukoi will be disgraced in his old age!'

All present began sighing anxiously, and the only one whose face expressed a certain astonishment was the Investigator for Especially Important Cases. The Prince, who possessed exceptionally acute powers of perception, felt that perhaps he ought to explain.

163

'I see, young man, that you ... er ... Glagolev, is it? No, Luzhitsin.'

'Izhitsin, Your Excellency,' the Public Prosecutor prompted Prince Dolgorukoi, but not loudly enough – in his seventy-ninth year the Viceroy of Moscow (yet another title by which the all-powerful Vladimir Andreevich was known) was hard of hearing.

'Please forgive an old man,' said the Governor good-naturedly, spreading his hands. 'Well then, Mr Pizhitsin, I see you are in a state of ignorance ... Probably your position does not require you to know. But since we are having this meeting ... well then' – and the Prince's long face with its dangling chestnut-brown moustaches assumed a solemn expression – 'at Easter, Russia's first capital city will be blessed by a visit from His Imperial Highness. He will arrive without any pomp or ceremony – to visit and worship at the holy places of Moscow. We have been instructed not to inform the citizens of Moscow in advance, since the visit has been planned as an *impromptu*, so to speak. However, that does not relieve us of responsibility for the standard of his reception and the general condition of the city. For instance, gentlemen, this morning I received a missive from His Eminence Ioannikii, the Metropolitan of Moscow. His Reverence writes to complain that what is going on in the confectionery shops of Moscow before the holy festival of Easter is a downright disgrace: the shop windows and counters are stacked high with boxes of sweets and candy with pictures of the Last Supper, the Way of the Cross, Calvary and so forth. This is sacrilege, gentlemen! Please be so good, my dear sir,' said the Prince, addressing the Head Police Master, 'as to issue an order to the police today to the effect that a strict stop must be put to such obscenities. Destroy the boxes, donate their contents to the Foundlings' Hospital. Let the poor orphans have a treat for the holiday. And fine the shopkeepers to make sure they don't get me into any trouble before the Emperor's visit!'

The Governor-General nervously adjusted his curly wig, which had slipped a little to one side, and was about to say something else, but instead began coughing.

An inconspicuous door that led to the inner chambers immediately opened and a skinny old man dashed out from behind it, moving silently in felt overshoes with his knees bent. His bald cranium shone with a blinding brilliance and he had immense sideburns. It was His Excellency's personal valet, Frol Vedishchev. Nobody was surprised by his sudden appearance, and everybody present felt it appropriate to greet the old man with a bow or at least a nod for, despite his humble position, Vedishchev had the reputation in the ancient city of being an influential and in certain respects omnipotent individual.

He rapidly poured drops of some mixture from a small bottle into a silver goblet, gave them to the Prince to drink and disappeared with equal rapidity in the reverse direction without so much as glancing at anyone.

'Shank you, Frol, shank you, my dear,' the Governor-General mumbled to his favourite's back, shifted his chin to put his false teeth back in place and carried on without lisping any more. 'And so, if Erast Petrovich Fandorin would be so good as to explain the reason for the urgency of this meeting . . . You know perfectly well, my dear friend, that today every minute is precious to me. Well then, what exactly has happened? Have you taken care to make sure that rumours of this vile incident are not spread among the inhabitants of the city? That's all we need on the eve of the Emperor's visit . . .'

Erast Petrovich got to his feet and the eyes of Moscow's supreme guardians of law and order turned to look at the Collegiate Counsellor's pale, resolute face.

'Measures have been taken to maintain secrecy, Your Excellency,' Fandorin reported. 'Everybody who was involved in the inspection of the scene of the crime has been warned of the responsibility they bear and they have signed an undertaking not to reveal anything. Since the yard-keeper who found the body is an individual with an inclination to intemperate drinking and cannot answer for himself, he has been temporarily placed in a s-special cell at the Department of Gendarmes.'

'Good,' said the Governor approvingly. 'Then what need is there for this meeting? Why did you ask me to bring together the heads of the criminal investigation and police departments?

You and Pizhitsin could have decided everything between you?'

Erast Petrovich cast an involuntary glance at the investigator for whom the Governor had invented this amusing new name, but just at the moment the Collegiate Counsellor was not in the mood for jollity.

'Your Excellency, I did not request you to summon the head of the Criminal Investigation Department. This case is so disturbing that it should be classified as a crime of state importance, and in addition to the Public Prosecutor's Office it should be handled by the operations section of the gendarmes under the personal control of the Head Police Master. I would not involve the Criminal Investigation Department at all, there are too many incidental individuals there. That is one.'

Fandorin paused significantly. State Counsellor Eichmann started and was about to protest, but Prince Dolgorukoi gestured for him to remain silent.

'It seems I need not have bothered you, my dear fellow,' Dolgorukoi said amiably to Eichmann. 'Why don't you go and keep up the pressure on your pickpockets and swindlers, so that on Easter Sunday they break their fast at home in Khitrovka and, God forbid, don't show their noses outside. I am relying on you.'

Eichmann stood up and bowed without speaking, smiled with just his lips at Erast Petrovich and went out.

The Collegiate Counsellor sighed in the realisation that he had now acquired a lifelong enemy in the person of the head of Moscow's Criminal Investigation Department, but this case really was horrific, and no unnecessary risk could be justified.

'I know you,' said the Governor, looking anxiously at his trusted deputy. 'If you say "one", it means there will be a "two". Speak out; don't keep us on tenterhooks.'

'I greatly regret, Vladimir Andreevich, that the sovereign's visit will have to be cancelled,' Fandorin said in a very low voice, but this time the Prince heard him perfectly.

'How's that – "cancelled"?' he gasped.

The other individuals present reacted more violently to the Collegiate Counsellor's brash announcement.

'You must be out of your mind' exclaimed Head Police Master Yurovsky.

'It's absolutely incredible!' bleated the Prosecutor.

The Investigator for Especially Important Cases did not dare to say anything out loud, because his rank was too low to permit the taking of such liberties, but he did purse his plump lips as if he were outraged by Fandorin's insane outburst.

'What do you mean – cancelled?' Dolgorukoi repeated in a flat voice.

The door leading to the inner chambers opened slightly, and the valet's face emerged halfway from behind it.

The Governor began speaking with extreme agitation, hurrying so much that he swallowed syllables and even entire words: 'Erastpetrovich, it's not the first year . . . you . . . idle words . . . But cancel His Majesty's visit? Why, that's a scandal of unprecedented proportions! You've no idea what effort I . . . For me, for all of us, it's . . .'

Fandorin frowned, wrinkling his high, clear forehead. He knew perfectly well how long Dolgorukoi had manoeuvred and intrigued in order to arrange the Emperor's visit, and how the hostile St Petersburg 'camarilla' had plotted and schemed against it – they had been trying for twenty years to unseat the cunning old Governor from his enviable position! His Majesty's Easter *impromptu* would be a triumph for the Prince, sure testimony to the invincibility of his position. And next year His Excellency had a highly important anniversary: sixty years of service at officer's rank. With an event like that he could even hope for the Order of St Andrew. How could he suddenly turn around and ask for the trip to be cancelled!

'I understand all th-that, Your Excellency, but if it is not cancelled, things will be even worse. This case of mutilation is not the last.' The Collegiate Counsellor's face became more sombre with every word that he spoke. 'I am afraid that Jack the Ripper has moved to Moscow.'

Once again, as several minutes earlier, Erast Petrovich's declaration provoked a chorus of protests.

'What do you mean – not the last?' the Governor-General asked indignantly.

The Head Police Master and the Public Prosecutor spoke almost with a single voice: 'Jack the Ripper?'

Izhitsin gathered his courage and snorted. 'Stuff and nonsense!'

'What ripper's that?' Frol Vedishchev croaked from behind his little door in the natural pause that followed.

'Yes, yes, who is this Jack?' His Excellency gazed at his subordinates in obvious displeasure. 'Everybody knows; I'm the only one who hasn't been informed. It's always the same with you.'

'Your Excellency, he is a famous English murderer who kills streetwalkers in London,' the District Prosecutor explained in his pompous fashion.

'If you will permit me, Your Excellency, I will explain in detail.'

Erast Petrovich took a notebook out of his pocket and skimmed through several pages.

The Prince cupped one hand round his ear, Vedishchev put on a pair of spectacles with thick lenses and Izhitsin smiled ironically.

'As Your Excellency no doubt remembers, last year I spent several months in England in connection with a case with which you are familiar: the disappearance of the correspondence of Catherine the Great. Indeed, Vladimir Andreevich, you even expressed your dissatisfaction at my extended absence. I stayed in London longer than absolutely necessary because I was following very closely the attempts of the local police to find a monstrous killer who had committed eight brutal murders in the East End in the space of eight months, from April to December. The killer acted in a most audacious fashion. He wrote notes to the police, in which he called himself "Jack the Ripper" and on one occasion he even sent the commissioner who was in charge of the case half of a kidney that he had cut out of one of his victims.'

'Cut out? But what for?' the Prince asked in amazement.

'The Ripper's outrages had a tremendously distressing effect on the public, but not simply because of the murders. In a city as large and ill-favoured as London there is naturally no shortage of crimes, including those that involve bloodshed. But the manner in which the Ripper despatched his victims was genuinely monstrous. He usually cut the poor women's throats and then disembowelled them, like partridges, and laid out their entrails in a kind of nightmarish still life.'

'Holy Mother of God!' Vedishchev gasped and crossed himself.

'The abominations you speak of!' the Governor said with feeling: 'Well then, did they not catch the villain?'

'No, but since December the distinctive murders have ceased. The police have concluded that the criminal has either committed suicide or . . . left England.'

'And what else would he do except come to see us in Moscow?' said the Head Police Master, with a sceptical shake of his head. 'But if that is the case, finding and catching an English cut-throat is child's play.'

'Why are you so sure that he is English?' Fandorin asked, turning to the general. 'All the murders were committed in the slums of London, the home of many immigrants from the continent of Europe, including Russians. Indeed, in the first instance the English police suspected immigrant doctors.'

'And why doctors in particular?' Izhitsin asked.

'Because in every case the internal organs were extracted from the victims with great skill, with excellent knowledge of anatomy and also almost certainly with the use of a surgical scalpel. The London police were absolutely convinced that Jack the Ripper was a doctor or a medical student.'

Public Prosecutor Kozlyatnikov raised a well-tended white finger and the diamond ring on it glinted.

'But what makes you think that the spinster Andreichkina was killed and mutilated by the Ripper from London? As if we had no murderers of our own? Some son of a bitch got so tanked up on drink he didn't know what he was doing and imagined he was fighting some dragon or other. We have any number of those.'

The Collegiate Counsellor sighed and replied patiently: 'My dear sir, you've read the report from the forensic medical expert. No one in a drunken fury can dissect so precisely, and use "a cutting tool of surgical sharpness". That is one. And also, just as in the East End cases, there are none of the signs of sexual debauchery which are usual in crimes of this kind. That is two. The most sinister point is the imprint of a bloody kiss on the victim's cheek, and that is three. All of the Ripper's victims had that imprint – on the forehead, on the cheek, sometimes on the temple. Inspector Gilson, from whom I learned this detail, was not inclined to attach any importance to it, since the Ripper had plenty of other freakish whims. However, from the limited amount of information that forensic science possesses on maniacal murderers, we know that these fiends attach great significance to ritual. Serial killings with the features of manic behaviour are always based on some kind of "idea" that prompts the monster into repeatedly killing strangers. While I was in London, I tried to explain to the officers in charge of the investigation that their main task was to guess the maniac's "idea" and the rest was merely a matter of investigative technique. There can be no doubt at all that the typical features of Jack the Ripper's ritual and that of our Moscow murderer are identical in every respect.'

'But even so, it's just too fantastic,' said General Yurovsky with a shake of his head. 'For Jack the Ripper to disappear from London and turn up in a woodshed on Samotechnaya Street . . . And then, you must agree, cancelling the sovereign's visit just because some prostitute has been killed . . .'

Erast Petrovich's patience was clearly almost exhausted, because he said rather sharply: 'Permit me to remind Your Excellency that the case of Jack the Ripper cost the head of London's police his job, and the Home Secretary also lost his position, because they refused for too long to attach any importance to the murders of "some prostitutes or other". Even if we assume that we now have our own, home-grown Ivan the Ripper, that does not improve the situation. Once he has tasted blood, he won't stop. Just imagine the situation if the killer hands us another present like today's during the Emperor's visit! And if it comes out that it is not the first such crime? The old capital will have a fine Easter Sunday.'

Prince Dolgorukoi crossed himself in fright and General Yurovsky raised a hand to unbutton his gold-embroidered collar.

'It is a genuine miracle that this time we have managed to hush up such a fantastic case.' The Collegiate Counsellor ran his fingers over his foppish black moustache, seeming preoccupied. 'But have we really managed it?'

A deadly silence fell.

'Do as you wish, Prince,' Vedishchev said from behind his door, 'but he's right. Write to our father the Tsar. Tell him this and that, and there's been a bit of a muddle. It's to our own detriment, but for the sake of Your Majesty's peace of mind we humbly request you not to come to Moscow.'

'Oh, Lord.' The Governor's voice trembled pitifully.

Izhitsin stood up and, gazing loyally at his exalted superior, suggested a possible way out: 'Your Excellency, could you not refer to the exceptionally high water? As they say, the Lord of Heaven must take the blame for that.'

'Well done, Pizhitsin, well done,' said the Prince, brightening up. 'You have a good head. That's what I shall write. If only the newspapers don't manage to ferret out this business of the mutilation.'

Investigator Izhitsin glanced condescendingly at Erast Petrovich and sat down, but not in the same way as before, with half a buttock on a quarter of the stool, but fully at his ease, as an equal among equals.

However, the expression of relief that had appeared on the Prince's face was almost immediately replaced by dismay.

'It won't do any good! The truth will come out anyway. If Erast Petrovich says this won't be the last atrocity, then it won't be. He is rarely mistaken.'

Fandorin cast an emphatically quizzical glance at the Governor, as if to say: 'Ah, I see, so there are times when I am mistaken!'

At this point the Head Police Master began breathing heavily through his nose, lowered his head guiltily and said in a deep voice: 'I don't know if it's the last case or not, but it probably isn't the first. I am to blame, Governor; I didn't attach any importance to it, I did not wish to bother you over trifles. But today's murder looked too provocative altogether, and so I decided to report it to you in view of the Emperor's visit. However, I recall now that in recent times brutal murders of streetwalkers and female vagrants have probably been on the increase. During Shrovetide, I think it was, there was a report of a female beggar found on Seleznevskaya Street with her stomach slashed to ribbons. And before that, at the Sukharev Market, they found a prostitute with her womb cut out. We didn't even investigate the case of the beggar – there was no point – and we decided the prostitute's ponce had mutilated her in a drunken fit. We took the fellow in, but he still hasn't confessed; he's being stubborn.'

'Ah, General Yurovsky, how could you?' said the Governor, throwing his hands in the air. 'If we had launched an investigation straight away and set Erast Petrovich on the case, perhaps we might have already caught this villain! And we wouldn't have had to cancel His Highness's visit!'

'But Your Excellency, who could have known? – there was no deliberate deception. You know yourself what the city is like, and the people are blackguards; there's something of the kind every single day! I can't bother Your Excellency with every petty incident!' the General said, almost whining in his attempt to justify himself, and he looked round at the Public Prosecutor and the investigator for support, but Kozlyatnikov was gazing sternly at the chief of police and Izhitsin shook his head reproachfully, as if to say: 'This is not good.'

Collegiate Counsellor Fandorin interrupted the General's lament with a curt question: 'Where are the bodies?'

'Where else would they be but at the Bozhedomka? That's where they bury all the dissolutes, idlers and people without passports. If there are any signs of violence, they take them to the police morgue first, to Egor Zakharov, and after that they ship them over to the cemetery there. That's the procedure.'

'We have to carry out an exhumation,' Fandorin said, with a grimace of disgust. 'And with no delay. Check the records at the morgue to see which female individuals have recently – l-let's say, since the New Year – been brought in with indications of violent death. And exhume them. Check for similarities in the picture of the crime. See if there have been any similar incidents. The ground has not thawed out yet, the c-corpses ought to be perfectly preserved.'

The Public Prosecutor nodded: 'I'll issue instructions. You deal with this, Izhitsin. And how about you, Erast Petrovich – would you not care to be present? It would be most desirable to have your participation.'

Izhitsin grinned sourly – apparently he did not consider the Collegiate Counsellor's participation to be so very desirable.

Fandorin suddenly turned pale – he had remembered his recent shameful attack of nausea. He struggled with himself for a moment, but failed to master his weakness: 'I'll assign m-my assistant Tulipov to help Izhitsin. I think that will be adequate.'

The heavy job was finished after eight in the evening, by the light of flaming torches.

As a finishing touch, the ink-black sky began pouring down a cold, sticky rain and the landscape of the cemetery, which was bleak in any case, became dismal enough to make you want to fall face down into one of the excavated graves and sleep in the embrace of mother earth – anything not to see those puddles of filth, waterlogged mounds of soil and crooked crosses.

Izhitsin was giving the orders. There were six men digging: two of the constables who had been at the scene of the crime, kept on the investigation in order not to extend the circle of people who knew about the case, two long-serving gendarmes and two of the Bozhedomka gravediggers, without whom they would not have been able to manage the job. First they had thrown the thick, spongy mud aside with their spades and then, when the metal blades struck the unthawed ground, they had taken up their picks. The cemetery's watchman had showed them where to dig.

According to the list, since January of the current year, 1889, the police morgue had taken delivery of fourteen bodies of women bearing signs of 'death from stabbing or cutting with a sharp instrument'. Now they had extracted the dead women from their wretched little graves and dragged them back into the morgue, where they were being examined by Dr Zakharov and his assistant Grumov, a consumptive-looking young man with a goatee that looked as if it was glued on and a thin, bleating voice that suited him perfectly.

Anisii Tulipov glanced inside once and decided not to do it again – it was better out in the open air, under the grey April drizzle. However, after an hour or so, chilled and thoroughly damp, and with his sensibilities blunted somewhat, Anisii sought shelter again in the autopsy room and sat on a little bench in the corner. He was discovered there by the watchman Pakhomenko, who felt sorry for him and took him back to his hut to give him tea.

The watchman was a capital fellow with a kind, clean-shaven face and jolly wrinkles radiating from his clear, child-like eyes to his temples. Pakhomenko spoke the language of the people – it was fascinating to listen to, but he put in a lot of Ukrainian words.

'Working in a graveyard, you need a callous heart,' he said in his quiet voice, with a compassionate glance at the exhausted Tulipov. 'Any folk will grow sick and weary if they're shown their own end every day: Look there, servant of God, you'll be rotting just like that. But the Lord is merciful: he gives the digger calluses on his hand so he won't wear the flesh down to the bone, and them as is faced with human woes, he gives them calluses on their hearts too. So as their hearts won't get worn away. You'll get used to it too, mister. At first I was afraid – green as burdock I was; but here we are, supping our tea and gnawing on our bread. Never mind, you'll get used to it in time. Eat, eat . . .'

Anisii sat for a while with Pakhomenko, who had been around in his time and seen all sorts of things in all sorts of places. He listened to his leisurely yarns – about worshipping at holy places, about good people and bad people – and felt as if he had been thawed out somehow and his will had been strengthened. Now he could go back to the black pits, the rough wood coffins and the grey shrouds.

It was talking to the garrulous watchman and home-grown philosopher that gave Anisii the idea that redeemed his useless presence at the cemetery with interest. It happened like this.

As evening was coming on, some time after six, they carried the last of the fourteen corpses into the morgue. The cheerful Izhitsin, who had prudently dressed for the occasion in hunting boots and rubberised overalls with a hood, called the soaking-wet Anisii over to summarise the results of the exhumation.

In the autopsy room Tulipov gritted his teeth, reinforced the calluses on his heart and it was all right: he walked from one table to the next, looked at the revolting deceased and listened to the expert's summaries.

'They can take these three lovelies back: numbers two, eight and ten,' said Zakharov, pointing casually with his finger. 'Our staff have got something confused here. I'm not the one to blame. I only dissect the cases that are under special supervision; other-wise it's Grumov who pokes about inside them. I think he's a bit too fond of the hard stuff, the snake. And when he's drunk, he writes whatever comes into his head in the conclusions.'

'What are you saying, Egor Willemovich?' Zakharov's goat-bearded assistant protested resentfully. 'If I do occasionally indulge in strong drink, it's only a drop, to restore my health and my shattered nerves. Honestly, you should be ashamed.'

'Get away with you,' the gruff doctor said dismissively to his assistant and continued with his report. 'Numbers one, three, seven, twelve and thirteen are also not in our line either. The classic "jab in the side" or "slashed gizzard". Neat work, no excessive cruelty. Better take them away as well.' Egor Wil-lemovich puffed a blast of strong tobacco smoke out of his pipe and lovingly patted a macabre blue woman on her gaping belly. 'But I'll keep this Vasilisa the Beautiful and the other four. I have to check how precisely they were carved, how sharp the knife was and so on. At first I'd hazard a guess that numbers four and fourteen were our friend's handiwork. Only he must have been in a hurry, or else someone frightened him off and stopped the fellow from properly finishing off the work he loves.' The doctor grinned without parting his teeth, which were gripping the pipe that protruded from them.

Anisii checked the numbers against the list. It all fitted: number four was the beggar Maria Kosaya from Maly Tryokhs-vyatsky Lane. Number fourteen was the prostitute Zotova from Svininsky Lane. The same ones that the Head Police Master had mentioned.

For some reason the fearless Izhitsin was not satisfied with the pronouncements of the expert and started to check, almost sticking his nose into the gaping wounds and asking detailed questions. Anisii envied his self-possession and felt ashamed of his own uselessness, but he couldn't think of anything for himself to do.

He went outside into the fresh air, where the diggers were having a smoke

'Well, mister, was it worth all the digging?' asked Pak-homenko. 'Or are we going to dig some more?'

'There's no more digging to do,' Anisii responded gladly. 'We've dug them all up. It's strange, really. In three months in the whole of Moscow only ten streetwalkers were killed. And the newspapers say our city is dangerous.'

'Ha! Ten he says,' the watchman snorted. 'That's just how it looks. They're just the ones with names. But we stack the ones they bring us without names in the ditches?'

Anisii's heart started beating faster. 'What ditches?'

'What?' Pakhomenko asked in amazement. 'You mean the doctor didn't tell you? Come on, you can look for yourself.'

He led Anisii to the far side of the cemetery and showed him a long pit with a thin layer of earth sprinkled over the top.

'That's the April one. Just the beginning. And there's the March one, already filled in.' He pointed to a long mound of earth. And there's the February one, and there's the January one. But before that I can't tell; I wasn't here then. I've only been working here since Epiphany – I came here from the Optinaya Hermitage, from pilgrimage. Before me there was a Kuzma used to work here. I never saw him myself. At Christmas this Kuzma broke his fast with a bottle or two, tumbled into an open grave and broke his neck. That was the death God had waiting for him: You've been watching over graves, servant of God, so now you can die in one. The Lord likes to joke with us in the grave-yard. We're like his yard-keepers. The gravedigger Tishka at Srednokrestny—'

'So do they bury a lot of nameless women in the ditches?' Anisii asked, interrupting the talkative fellow. He had completely forgotten his damp boots and the cold.

'Plenty. Just last month it must be nigh on a dozen, or maybe more. A person without a name is like a dog without a collar. Take them to the knacker's yard – it's nobody's concern. Anyone who's lost their name is more like a flea than a human being.'

'And have there been any badly cut-up cases among the name-less women?'

The watchman twisted his face into a sad expression. 'Who's going to take a proper look at the poor darlings? They're lucky if the sexton from St John the Warrior rattles off a prayer over them, and sometimes I do, sinner that I am; I sing them "Eternal Peace". Oh, people, people . . .'

So much for the Investigator for Especially Important Cases, such a meticulous man, Anisii gloated to himself. Fancy missing something like that. He gestured to the watchman in a way that meant: 'Sorry, my friend, this is important,' and set off towards the cemetery office at a run.

'Come on, lads,' he shouted from a distance. 'There's more work to be done! Grab your picks and your shovels and let's get moving!'

Young Linkov was the only one to jump to his feet. Senior Constable Pribludko stayed sitting down, and the gendarmes actually turned away. They'd had enough of swinging picks and knocking themselves out in this unseemly work; the man giving the orders wasn't even their boss, and he wasn't so important anyway. But Tulipov felt he was responsible and he made the men move.

And, as it turned out, it was a good thing he did.

Very late in the evening – in fact it was really night, because it was approaching midnight already – Tulipov was sitting with his chief on Malaya Nikitskaya Street (such a fine outhouse with such fine rooms, with electric lighting and a telephone), eating supper and warming himself up with grog.

The grog was special, made with Japanese sake, red wine and prunes, prepared according to the oriental recipe of Masahiro Shibata, or Masa, Fandorin's servant. In fact, though, the Japanese did not behave or speak much like a servant. He was unceremonious with Erast Petrovich and did not regard Anisii as an important personage at all. In the line of physical exercise Tulipov was Masa's pupil and Anisii endured no little abuse and mockery from his strict teacher, and sometimes even thrashings disguised as training in Japanese fisticuffs. No matter what trick Anisii invented, no matter how he tried to shirk the practice of this hateful infidel wisdom, there was no way he could argue with his chief. Erast Petrovich had ordered him to master the techniques of ju-jitsu, and he had to do it, even if he was knocked out in the process. Only Tulipov did not make a very good sportsman. He was much more successful at getting himself knocked out.

'You squat hundred time this mornin'?' Masa asked menacingly when Anisii had had a little to eat and turned pink from the grog. 'You beat pams on iron stick? Show me pams.'

Tulipov hid his palms behind his back, because he was too lazy to pound them against the special metal stick a thousand times a day, and anyway, you know, it was painful. The tough calluses were simply not developing on the edges of Anisii's hands, and Masa abused him seriously for that.

'Have you finished eating? All right, now you can report on business to Erast Petrovich,' Angelina told him and took the supper things off the table, leaving just the silver jug with the grog and the mugs.

Angelina was lovely, a real sight for sore eyes. Light-blonde hair woven into a magnificent plait that was arranged in a bun on the back of her head, a clear, white-skinned face, large, serious grey eyes that seemed to radiate some strange light into the world around her. A special woman: you didn't meet many like her. A swan like that would never even glance at a shabby, lop-eared specimen like Tulipov. But Erast Petrovich was a fine partner in every possible respect, and women liked him. During the three years that Tulipov had been his assistant, several passions, each more lovely than the last, had reigned for a while in the outhouse on Malaya Nikitskaya Street before leaving, but there had never been one as simple, bright and serene as Angelina. It would be good if she stayed a bit longer. Or still better – if she stayed for ever.

'Thank you, Angelina Samsonovna,' said Anisii, looking at her tall, stately figure as she walked away.

A queen – that was the word for her, even though she came from a simple lower middle-class background. And the Chief always had queens. There was nothing so surprising about it: that was the kind of man he was.

Angelina Krasheninnikova had appeared in the house on Malaya Nikitskaya Street a year earlier. Erast Petrovich had helped the orphan in a certain difficult business, and afterwards she had clung to him. She obviously wanted to thank him in the best way she could and, apart from her love, she had nothing to give. It was hard now to remember how they had managed without her before. The Collegiate Counsellor's bachelor residence had become cosy and warm, welcoming. Anisii had always liked being here, but now he liked it even more. And with Angelina there, the Chief seemed to have become a bit gentler and simpler somehow. It was good for him.

'All right, Tulipov, now you're well fed and drunk, t-tell me what you and Izhitsin dug up over there.'

Erast Petrovich had an unusual, confused expression. His conscience is bothering him, Tulipov realised, for not going to the exhumation and sending me instead. But Anisii was only too happy if he could come in useful once in a blue moon and spare his adored chief unnecessary stress.

After all, he was pampered by the Chief in every way: provided with an apartment at public expense, a decent salary, interesting work. The greatest debt he owed him, one that could never be repaid, was for his sister Sonya, a poor cripple and imbecile. Anisii's heart no longer trembled for her, because while he was at work, Sonya was cared for with affection and fed. Fandorin's maid Palashka loved her and pampered her. Now she had even moved in with the Tulipovs. She would run to her master's house and help Angelina with the housework for an hour or two, then run back to Sonya – Tulipov's apartment was close by, on Granatny Lane.

Anisii began his report calmly, working up to the main point. 'Egor Zakharov found clear signs that two of the women had been brutally mutilated after they were dead. The beggar Marya Kosoi, who died in unexplained circumstances on the eleventh of February, had her throat cut and her abdominal cavity slit open; her liver is missing. The woman of easy virtue Alexandra Zotova, who was killed on the fifth of April (it was assumed by her pimp Dzapoev) also had her throat cut and her womb was cut out. Another woman, the gypsy Marfa Zhemchuzhnikova, killed by a person or persons unknown on the tenth of March, is a doubtful case: her throat was not cut, her stomach was slashed open from top to bottom and side to side, but all her organs are in place.'

At this point Anisii happened by chance to glance to one side and stopped in confusion. Angelina was standing in the doorway with one hand pressed to her full breasts and looking at him, her eyes wide with terror.

'Good Lord,' she said, crossing herself, 'what are these terrible things you're saying, Mr Tulipov?'

The Chief glanced round in annoyance. 'Angelina, go to your room. This is not for your ears. Tulipov and I are working.'

The beautiful woman left without a murmur and Anisii glanced reproachfully at his chief. You may be right, Erast Petrovich, but you could be a bit gentler. Of course, Angelina Samsonovna is not blue-blooded, she's not your equal, but I swear she'd be more than a match for any noble-born woman.

Any other man would make her his lawful wife without thinking twice. And he'd count himself lucky. But he didn't say anything out loud; he didn't dare.

'Signs of sexual intercourse?' the Chief asked intently, paying no attention to Tulipov's facial expression.

'Zakharov had difficulty in determining that. Even though the ground was frozen, some time had still passed. But there's something more important than all that!'

Anisii paused for effect and moved on to the main point. He told Erast Petrovich how on his instructions they had opened up the so-called 'ditches' – the common graves for the bodies without names. In all they had inspected more than seventy corpses. On nine of the bodies – and one of them was a man – there had been clear signs of savage abuse. The general picture was similar to today's: someone with a good knowledge of anatomy and access to a surgical instrument had severely mutilated the bodies.

'The most remarkable thing, Chief, is that three of the mutilated bodies were taken from last year's ditches!' Anisii declared, and then modestly added: 'I ordered them to dig up the ditches for November and December just to make sure.'

Erast Petrovich had listened to his assistant very attentively, but now he suddenly leapt up off his chair: 'December, you say, and November! That's incredible!'

'I was indignant about it too. How about our police, eh? A monster like that active all these months in Moscow, and we don't even hear a word about it! If it's a social outcast who gets killed, then it's none of the police's business – they just bury them and forget about them. You know, Chief, in your place I think I'd really give Yurovsky and Eichmann what for.'

But the Chief seemed upset about something else. He walked quickly across the room and back again and muttered: 'It couldn't have happened in December, let alone in November! He was still in London then!'

Tulipov blinked. He didn't understand what London had to do with anything – Erast Petrovich had not yet acquainted him with his theory about the Ripper.

Fandorin blushed as he recalled the insulted look he had given Prince Dolgorukoi earlier when the Governor had said that his Deputy for Special Assignments was rarely mistaken.

It seemed that Erast Petrovich was sometimes mistaken, and seriously so.

The delightful decision has been realised. Only God's providence could have helped me to implement it so soon.

The whole day was filled with a feeling of rapture and invulnerability – following yesterday's ecstasy.

Rain and slush, there was a lot of work in the afternoon, but I don't feel tired at all. My soul is singing, longing for open space, to wander through the streets and waste plots of the neighbourhood.

Evening again. I am walking along Protopopovsky Lane towards Kalanchevka Street. There's a woman standing there, a peasant woman, haggling with a cabby. She doesn't strike a deal, the cabby drives off and she's standing there, shuffling her feet in confusion. I look and see she has a huge, swollen belly. Pregnant, seven months at least. I feel my heart start to race: there it is, it has found me.

I walk closer – everything is right. Exactly the sort I need. Fat, with a dirty face. Her eyebrows and eyelashes have fallen out – she must have syphilis. It is hard to imagine a creature further removed from the concept of Beauty.

I start talking to her. She's come from the village to visit her husband. He's an apprentice in the Arsenal. I say the Arsenal is not far and promise to show her the way. She is not afraid, because today I am a woman. I lead her through the waste lots towards the Immerovsky horticultural establishment. It is dark and deserted there. While we are walking, the woman complains to me about how hard it is to live in the country. I sympathise with her.

I lead her to the river bank and tell her not to be afraid, there is great joy in store for her. She looks at me stupidly. She dies silently. There is only the whistle of the air from her throat and the gurgling of her blood.

I am impatient to lay bare the pearl within and I do not wait until the spasms have ceased.

Alas, a disappointment awaits me. When I open the incised womb with hands trembling in sweet anticipation, I am overcome by disgust.

The living embryo is ugly and nothing at all like a pearl. It looks exactly like the little monsters in jars of alcohol in Professor Lints's faculty: a little vampire just like them. It squirms and opens its mousy little mouth. I toss it away in disgust.

The conclusion: man, like a flower, must mature in order to become beautiful. It is clear now why I have never thought children beautiful: they are dwarfs with disproportionately large heads and under-developed reproductive systems.

The Moscow detectives have begun to stir – yesterday's decoration has finally made the police aware of my presence here. It's funny. I am more cunning and stronger; they will never unmask me. 'What an actor is going to waste,' said Nero. That applies to me.

But I throw the body of the woman and her mouse into the pond. There is no point in stirring things up unnecessarily, and the decoration was not satisfactory.

CHAPTER 3

The 'smopackadj'

From first thing in the morning Erast Petrovich locked himself away in his study to think, and Tulipov set out once again for the Bozhedomka – to have the October and September ditches opened up. He had suggested it himself: they had to determine when the Moscow killer had started his activities. The Chief had not objected. 'Why not?' he had said; 'You go,' but he was somewhere miles away, lost in thought – deducing.

It turned out to be dreary work, far worse than the previous day. The corpses that had been buried before the cold weather were severely decomposed and it was more than anyone could bear to look at them, let alone breathe the poisoned air. Anisii did puke a couple of times after all; he couldn't help himself.

'You see,' he said, with a sickly smile at the watchman, 'I still can't grow those calluses . . .'

'There are some as can't never grow them,' the watchman replied, shaking his head sympathetically. 'It's hardest of all for them to live in this world. But God loves them too. There you are now, mister, take a drop of this liquor of mine . . .'

Anisii sat down on a bench, drank the herbal infusion and chatted for a while with the cemetery philosopher about this and that; listened to his stories; told him about his own life – that mellowed his heart a little – and then it was back to digging the ditch.

Only it was all in vain. They didn't find anything new that was of use to the investigation in the old ditches.

Zakharov said acidly: 'A bad head gives the legs no rest, but it would be all right if it were only yours that suffered, Tulipov. Are you not afraid the gendarmes will accidentally tap you on the top of your head with a pick? And I'll write in my report, all in due order: the Provincial Secretary brought about his own death: he stumbled and smashed his bad head against a stone. And Grumov will witness it. We're sick and tired of you and your rotten flesh. Isn't that right, Grumov?'

The consumptive assistant bared his yellow teeth and wiped his bumpy forehead with his soiled shirt. He explained: 'Mr Zakharov is joking.' But that was all right: the doctor was a cynical, coarse man. What offended Anisii was having to suffer mockery from the repulsive Izhitsin.

The pompous investigator had rolled up at the cemetery at first light – somehow he'd got wind of Tulipov's operation. At first he'd been alarmed that the investigation was proceeding without him, but then he'd calmed down and turned cocky.

'Perhaps,' he said, 'you and Fandorin have some other brilliant ideas? Maybe you'd like to dig in the pits while I lead the investigation?'

And the rotten swine left, laughing triumphantly.

In sum, Tulipov returned to Malaya Nikitskaya Street empty-handed. He walked listlessly up on to the porch and rang the electric bell.

Masa opened the door, in a white gymnastic costume with a black belt and a band bearing the word for 'diligence' round his forehead. 'Hello, Tiuri-san. Le's do renshu.'

What – renshu, when he was so tired and upset he could barely even stand?

'I have an urgent report to give the Chief,' Anisii said, trying to be cunning, but Masa was not to be fooled.

He jabbed his finger at Tulipov's protruding ears and declared peremptorily: 'When you have urgen' repor you have goggrin' eye and red ear, annow eye small and ear aw white. Take off coat, take off shoes, put on trousers and jacket. We goin' run and shout.'

Sometimes Angelina would intercede for Anisii – she was the only one who could resist the pressure from the damned Japanese – but the clear-eyed lady of the house was nowhere to be seen, and the oriental tyrant forced poor Tulipov to change into his gymnastics suit right there in the hallway.

They went out into the yard. Jumping from foot to foot on the chilly ground, Anisii waved his hands around, yelled 'O-osu' to strengthen his prana and then the humiliation began. Masa jumped up on his shoulders from behind and ordered him to run in circles round the yard. The Japanese was not very tall, but he was stocky and solidly built, and he weighed four and a half *poods* at the very least. Somehow Tulipov managed to run two circles and then began to stumble.

But his tormentor spoke into his ear: *Gaman! Gaman!'* That was his favourite word. It meant 'Patience'.

Anisii had enough *gaman* for another half-circle, and then he collapsed. But not without an element of calculation: he collapsed right in front of a large dirty puddle so that this accursed eastern idol would go flying over his head and take a little swim. Masa went flying over the falling man's head all right, but he didn't come down with a splash in the puddle; he just put his hands down into it, then pushed off with his fingers, performed an impossible somersault in the air and landed on his feet on the far side of the watery obstacle.

He shook his round head in despair and said: 'Awri, go wash.'

Anisii was gone in a flash.

When his assistant reported in the study (after washing off the mud, changing his clothes and brushing his hair), Fandorin listened attentively. The walls were hung with Japanese prints, weapons and gymnastic equipment. Although it was already past midday, the Collegiate Counsellor was still in his dressing gown. He was not disappointed in the least by the lack of any result; in fact he even seemed rather glad. In any case, he did not express any particular surprise.

When his assistant stopped speaking, Erast Petrovich walked across the room, toying with his beloved jade beads and pronounced the phrase that always made Anisii's heart skip a beat: 'All right, l-let us think about this.'

The Chief clicked a small sphere of green stone and swayed the flaps of his dressing gown.

'Don't think that your little trip to the cemetery has been wasted,' he began.

On the one hand it was pleasant to hear this; on the other hand the phrase 'little trip' hardly seemed an entirely accurate description of the torture Anisii had suffered that morning.

'To be quite sure, we had to check if there were incidents involving the disembowelling of victims prior to November. When you told me yesterday that two mutilated corpses had been found in the common grave for December and in the November grave, at first I began to doubt my theory about the Ripper moving to Moscow.'

Tulipov nodded, since the previous day he had been given a detailed account of the bloody history of the British ogre.

'But today, having reviewed my London notes, I came to the conclusion that this hypothesis should not be abandoned. Would you like to know why?'

Anisii nodded again, knowing perfectly well that just at the moment his job was to keep quiet and not interrupt.

'Then by all means.' The Chief picked a notebook up off the table. 'The final murder attributed to the notorious Jack took place on the twentieth of December on Poplar High Street. By that time our Moscow Ripper had already delivered plenty of his nightmarish work to the Bozhedomka, which would seem to exclude the possibility that the English and Russian killers might be subsumed in the same person. However, the prostitute Rose Millet, who was killed on Poplar High Street, did not have her throat cut, and there were none of our Jack's usual signs of savagery. The police decided that the murderer had been frightened off by passers-by who were out late. But in the light of yesterday's discovery, I am willing to surmise that the Ripper had absolutely nothing to do with this death. Possibly this Rose Millet was killed by someone else, and the general hysteria that had gripped London following the previous killing led people to ascribe a new murder of a prostitute to the same maniac. Now for the previous murder, committed on the ninth of November.'

Fandorin turned over a page.

'This is Jack's work without a doubt. The prostitute Mary Jane Kelly was discovered in her own room on Dorset Street, where she normally received her clients. Her throat had been slit, her breasts had been cut off, the soft tissue on her thighs had been stripped away, her internal organs had been laid out neatly on the bed and her stomach had been cut open – it is conjectured that the killer consumed its contents.'

Anisii's stomach began churning again, as it had that morning at the cemetery.

'On her temple she had the bloody imprint of lips that is familiar to us from Andreichkina's corpse.'

Erast Petrovich broke off his reasoning at this point, because Angelina had come into the study: in a plain grey dress and black shawl, with locks of blonde hair dangling over her forehead – the fresh wind must have tugged them free. The Chief's lady-friend dressed in various styles, sometimes like a lady, but best of all she liked simple, Russian clothes like the ones she was wearing today.

'Are you working? Am I in the way?' she asked with a tired smile.

Tulipov leapt to his feet and hurried to reply before his chief: 'Of course not, Angelina Samsonovna. We're glad to see you.'

'Yes, yes,' said Fandorin with a nod. 'Have you come from the hospital?'

The beautiful woman lifted the shawl off her shoulders and pinned her rebellious hair in place. 'It was interesting today. Dr Bloom taught us how to lance boils. It turns out not to be hard at all.'

Anisii knew that Angelina, the kind soul, went to the Shtro-binderovsky Clinic on Mamonov Lane to help relieve the pain of the suffering. At first she had taken them presents and read the Bible to them, but then she had begun to feel that was not enough. She wanted to be of genuine benefit, to learn to be a nurse. Erast Petrovich had tried to dissuade her, but Angelina had insisted on having her own way.

A saintly woman, the kind that was the very foundation of Russia itself: prayer, help for one's neighbour, a loving heart. She might seem to be living in sin, but no impurity could stick to her. And it wasn't her fault that she found herself in the position of an unmarried wife, Anisii thought yet again, feeling angry with his chief.

Fandorin frowned. 'You've been lancing boils?'

'Yes,' she said with a joyful smile. 'For two poor old beggar women. It's Wednesday; they can come without having to pay. Don't worry, Erast Petrovich, I managed it very well, and the doctor praised me. I can already do a lot of things. And afterwards I read the Book of Job to the old women, for spiritual reinforcement.'

'You'd have done better to give them money,' Erast Petrovich said in annoyance. 'They're not interested in your book or your concern.'

Angelina replied: 'I did give them money, fifty kopecks each. And I have more need for this care and concern than they do. I'm far too happy living with you, Erast Petrovich. It makes me feel guilty. Happiness is good, but it's a sin to forget about those who are unhappy in your happiness. Help them, look at their sores and remember that your happiness is a gift from God, and not many people in this world are granted it. Why do you think there are so many beggars and cripples around all the palaces and mansions?'

'That's obvious enough: they give more there.'

'No, poor people give more than the rich. It's the Lord showing the fortunate people the unfortunate, saying: Remember how much suffering there is in the world and don't try to ignore it.'

Erast Petrovich sighed and made no attempt to reply to his mistress. He obviously couldn't think of anything to say. He turned towards Anisii and rattled his beads. 'Let's c-carry on. So, I am proceeding on the assumption that Jack the Ripper's last crime in England was the murder of Mary Jane Kelly, committed

189

on the ninth of November, and that he was not involved in the case of the twentieth of December. In the Russian style, the ninth of November is still the end of October, and so Jack the Ripper had enough time to get to Moscow and add a victim of his perverted imagination to the November ditch at Bozhedomka. Agreed?'

Anisii nodded.

'Is it very likely that two maniacs would appear in Europe who act in an absolutely identical fashion, following scenarios that coincide in every detail?'

Anisii shook his head.

'Then the final question, before we get down to business: is the likelihood I have already mentioned so slight that we can concentrate entirely on the basic hypothesis?'

Two nods, so energetic that Tulipov's celebrated ears swayed. Anisii held his breath, knowing that now a miracle would take place before his very eyes: an elegant thesis would emerge, conjured up out of nothing, out of the empty mist, complete with search methods, plan of investigative measures and perhaps even specific suspects.

'Let us sum up. For some reason so far unknown to us, Jack the Ripper has come to Moscow and set about eliminating the local prostitutes and vagrants in a most determined fashion. That is one.' The Chief clicked his beads to add conviction to his assertion. 'He arrived here in November last year. That is two (click!). He has spent the recent months in the city, or if he has gone away, then not for long. That is three (click!). He is a doctor or he has studied medicine, since he possesses a surgical instrument, knows how to use it and is skilled in anatomical dissection. That is f-four.'

A final click, and the Chief put the beads away in the pocket of his dressing gown, which indicated that the investigation had moved on from the theoretical stage to the practical.

'As you can see, Tulipov, the task does not appear so very complicated.'

Anisii could not yet see that, and so he refrained from nodding.

'Oh, come now,' Erast Petrovich said in surprise. 'All that's required is to check everyone who arrived in Russia from England and settled in Moscow during the period that interests us. Not even everybody, in fact – only those who are connected or have at some time been connected with medicine. And th-that's all. You'll be surprised when you see how narrow the range of the search is.'

Why indeed, how simple! Moscow was not St Petersburg; how many medical men could have arrived in the old capital from England in November?'

'So let's start checking the new arrivals registered at all the police stations!' said Anisii, leaping to his feet, ready to get straight down to work. 'Only twenty-four inquiries to make! That's where we'll find our friend: in the registers!'

Angelina had missed the beginning of Erast Petrovich's speech, but she had listened to the rest very carefully and she asked a very reasonable question: 'What if this murderer of yours didn't register with the police?'

'It's not very likely,' the Chief replied. 'He's a very thorough individual who has lived in one place for a long time and travels freely across Europe. Why would he take the unnecessary risk of infringing the provisions of the law? After all, he is not a political terrorist, or a fugitive convict, but a maniac. All of a maniac's aggression goes into his "idea"; he has no strength left over for any other activities. Usually they are quiet, unobtrusive people and you would never think that they c-carry all the torments of hell around inside their heads ... Please sit down, Tulipov. There's no need to go running off anywhere. What do you think I have been doing all morning, while you were disturbing the dead?' He picked up several sheets of paper, covered in formal clerk's handwriting, off the desk. 'I telephoned the district superintendents and asked them to obtain for me the registration details of everyone who arrived in Moscow directly from England or via any intermediary point. To be on the safe side, I asked for November as well as December – just a precaution: what if Rose Millet was killed by our Ripper after all, and your November discovery, on

191

the contrary, turns out to be the work of some indigenous cut-throat? It is hard to reach any firm conclusions on the pathology of a body that has been lying in the ground for five months, even if the ground was frozen. But those two bodies from December – that's a serious matter.'

'That makes sense,' Anisii agreed. 'The November corpse really wasn't exactly . . . Zakharov didn't even want to rummage inside it; he said it was profanation. In November the earth hadn't really frozen yet, so the body had rotted a bit. Oh, I beg your pardon, Angelina Samsonovna!' Tulipov exclaimed, alarmed in case his excessive naturalism had upset her. But apparently his alarm was needless: Angelina had no intention of fainting, and the expression in her grey eyes remained as serious and intent as ever.

'There, you see. But even over two months only thirty-nine people arrived here from England, including, by the way, myself and Angelina Samsonovna. But, with your permission, I won't include the t-two of us in our list.' Erast Petrovich smiled. 'Of the remainder, twenty-three did not stay in Moscow for long and therefore are of no interest to us. That leaves fourteen, of whom only three have any connection with medicine.'

'Aha!' Anisii exclaimed avidly.

'Naturally, the first to attract my attention was the doctor of medicine George Seville Lindsey. The Department of Gendarmes keeps him under secret surveillance, as it does all foreigners, so making inquiries could not have been any easier. Alas, Mr Lindsey does not fit the bill. It turned out that before coming to Moscow he spent only one and a half months in his homeland. Before that he was working in India, far from the East End of London. He was offered a position in the Catherine the Great Hospital, and that is why he came here. That leaves two, both Russian. A man and a woman.'

'A woman couldn't have done anything like this,' Angelina said firmly. 'There are all sorts of monsters amongst us women too, but hacking stomachs open with a knife – that takes strength. And we women don't like the sight of blood.'

'We are dealing here with a special kind of being, unlike ordinary people,' Fandorin objected. 'This is not a man and it is not a woman, but something like a third sex or, to put it simply, a monster. We can by no means exclude women. Some of them are physically strong too. Not to mention that at a certain level of skill in the use of a scalpel, no special strength is required. For instance' – he glanced at one of his sheets of paper – 'the midwife Elizaveta Nesvitskaya, a spinster twenty-eight years of age, arrived from England via St Petersburg on the nineteenth of November. An unusual individual. At the age of seventeen she spent two years in prison on political charges and was then exiled by administrative order to a colony in the Arkhangelsk province. She fled the country and graduated from the medical faculty of Edinburgh University. Applied to be allowed to return to her motherland. She returned. Her request for her medical diploma to be accepted as valid is under consideration by the Ministry of Internal Affairs, and in the meantime Nesvitskaya has set herself up as a midwife at the recently opened Morozov Gynaecological Hospital. She is under secret surveillance by the police. According to detectives' reports, although her right to work as a doctor has not yet been confirmed, Nesvitskaya is receiving patients from among the poor and impecunious. The hospital administration turns a blind eye and secretly even encourages her – no one wishes to waste their time on dealing with the poor. That is the information that we p-possess on Nesvitskaya.'

'During the time the Ripper committed his crimes, she was in London – that is one,' Tulipov began summarising. 'When the crimes were committed in Moscow, she was here – that is two. She possesses medical skills – that is three. From what we know, her personality seems to be unusual and not particularly feminine in its make-up – that is four. Nesvitskaya can certainly not be discounted.'

'Precisely. And in addition to that, let us not forget that in the London murders and in the murder of the spinster Andreichkina there are no indications of the sexual molestation which is usual when the maniac is a man.'

'And who's the other one?' asked Angelina.

'Ivan Stenich. Thirty years old. A former student of the medical faculty of the Moscow Imperial University. Excluded seven years ago "for immoral conduct". God only knows what was meant by that, but it looks as though it might fit our bill all right. He has held several jobs, been treated for psychological illness, travelled around Europe. Arrived in Russia from England on the eleventh of December. Since the New Year he has been working as a male nurse in the Assuage My Sorrows hospital for the insane.'

Tulipov slapped his hand on the table: 'Damned suspicious!'

'And so, we have t-two suspects. If neither of them is involved, then we shall follow the line suggested by Angelina Samsonovna – that when Jack the Ripper arrived in Moscow he managed to avoid the eyes of the police. And only if we are convinced that this too must be excluded will we then abandon the main hypothesis and start to search for a home-grown Ivan the Ripper who has never been to the East End in his life. Agreed?'

'Yes, but it *is* the same Jack anyway,' Anisii declared with conviction. 'Everything fits.'

'Who do you prefer to deal with, Tulipov – the male nurse or the midwife?' the Chief asked. 'I offer you the right to choose as the martyr of the exhumation.'

'Since this Stenich works in a mental hospital, I have an excellent excuse for making his acquaintance: Sonya,' said Anisii, expressing this apparently perfectly reasonable idea with more vehemence than cold logic required. A man – and one with a history of mental illness at that – appeared a more promising candidate for the Ripper than a runaway revolutionary.

'All right, then,' Erast Petrovich said with a smile. 'Off you go to Lefortovo, and I'll go to Devichie Polye, to see Nesvitskaya.'

In fact, however, Anisii was obliged to deal with both the former student and the midwife, because at that very moment the doorbell rang.

Masa entered and announced: 'Post.' Then he explained,

taking great satisfaction in pronouncing the difficult phrase: 'A smopackadj'.

The package was indeed small. Written on the grey wrapping paper in a hand that was vigorous but careless and irregular was: 'To His Honour Collegiate Counsellor Fandorin in person. Urgent and strictly secret.'

Tulipov felt curious, but his chief did not unwrap the package immediately.

'Did the p-postman bring it? There's no address written on it.'

'No, a boy. Hand to me and wan away. Should I catchim?' Masa asked in alarm.

'If he ran away, you won't catch him now.'

Underneath the wrapping paper there was a small velvet box, tied round with a red satin ribbon. In the box, resting on a napkin, there was a yellow object. For the first moment Anisii thought it was a forest mushroom, a milky cap. He looked closer and gasped.

It was a human ear.

The rumours have spread round Moscow.

Supposedly a werewolf has appeared in the city. If any woman puts her nose outside the door at night, the werewolf is there in a flash. He creeps along so quietly, with his red eye glinting behind the fence, and if you don't say your prayers in time, your Christian soul is done for – he leaps out and the first thing he does is sink his teeth into your throat, and then he tears your belly to shreds and munches and crunches on your insides. And apparently this werewolf has already bitten out countless numbers of women's throats, only the authorities are keeping it a secret from the people, because the Father-Tsar is afraid.

That's what they were saying today at the Sukharev Market.

That is about me, I am the werewolf who is prowling their city. It's funny. My kind don't simply appear in a place, they are sent to bring terrible or joyful news. And I have been sent to you, citizens of Moscow, with joyful news.

Ugly city and ugly people, I will make you beautiful. Not all of you, please forgive me – that would be too much. But many, many.

I love you, with all your hideous abominations and deformities. I only wish you well. I have enough love for all of you. I see Beauty under lice-ridden clothes, under the scabs on an unwashed body, under rashes and eruptions. I am your saviour and your salvatrix. I am your brother and sister, father and mother, husband and wife. I am a woman and I am a man. I am an androgyne, that most beautiful ancestor of humanity, who possessed the characteristics of both sexes. Then the androgynes were divided into two halves, male and female, and people appeared – unhappy, remote from perfection, suffering from loneliness.

I am your missing half. Nothing prevents me from reuniting with those of you whom I choose.

The Lord has given me intelligence, cunning, foresight and invulnerability. Stupid, crude, dull, grey people tried to catch the androgyne in London without even attempting to understand the meaning of the messages he sent to the world.

At first these pitiful attempts amused me. Then a bitter taste rose in my throat.

Perhaps my own land will receive the prophet, I thought. Irrational and mystical Russia, which has still not lost true faith, lured me to itself with its eunuch skoptsy sect, its schismatics, its self-immolations and its ascetics – and it seems to have deceived me. Now the same stupid, crude kind of people, devoid of imagination, are trying to catch the Decorator in Moscow. It amuses me; at night I shudder and shake in silent laughter. No one sees these fits of merriment, and if they did, no doubt they would think there was something wrong with me. Well certainly, if everyone who is not like them is mad; but in that case Christ is also mad, and all the holy saints, and all the insane geniuses of whom they are so proud.

In the daytime I am not different in any way from all the ugly, pitiful people with all their vain concerns. I am a virtuoso of mimicry; they could never guess that I am from a different race.

How can they disdain God's gift – their own bodies? My duty and my calling is to teach them a little about Beauty. I make the ugly beautiful. I do not touch those who are beautiful. They are not an offence against the image of God.

Life is a thrilling, jolly game. Cat and mouse, hide and seek. I hide and I seek. One-two-three-four-five, ready or not, I'm coming. If you're not hiding, it's not my fault.

CHAPTER 4

Tortoise, Setter, Lioness, Hare

Holy Week Wednesday, 5 April, afternoon

Anisii told Palasha to dress Sonya up in her holiday clothes. His sister, a full-grown adult but mentally retarded, was delighted and began gurgling in joy. For her, the poor imbecile, going on any trip was an event, wherever it was to, and she was particularly fond of visiting the 'dot' (in Sonya's language that meant 'doctor'). They talked to her patiently for a long time there; they always gave her a sweet or a spice cake; they put a cold metal thing against her chest and pressed her tummy so that it tickled and gazed into her mouth – and Sonya was happy to help by opening it wide enough for them to see everything inside.

They called a cabbie they knew, Nazar Stepanich. As always, at first Sonya was a little bit afraid of the calm horse Mukha, who snorted with her nostrils and jangled her harness, squinting with her bloody eyes at the fat, ungainly woman swaddled in shawls.

They drove from Granatny Lane to the Lefortovo district. Usually they went to a closer place, to Dr Maxim Khristoforich on Rozhdestvenka Street, to the Mutual Assistance Society; but this time they had to make the journey right across the city.

They had to drive around Trubnaya Street – it was completely flooded. When would the sunshine ever come and dry the ground out? Moscow looked dour and untidy. The houses were grey, the roads were dirty, the people all seemed to be wrapped in rags and hunched up against the wind. But Sonya seemed to like it. Every now and then she nudged her brother in the side with her elbow – 'Nisii, Nisii' – and pointed at the rooks in a tree, a water wagon, a drunken apprentice. But she prevented him from thinking. And he had a lot to think about – the severed ear, which the chief was dealing with in person, and his own difficult task.

The Emperor Alexander Society's Assuage My Sorrows Hospital, for the treatment of psychiatric, nervous and paralytic illnesses, was located on Hospital Square, beyond the River Yauza. He knew that Stenich was working as a male nurse with Dr Rozenfeld in department five, where they treated the most violent and hopeless cases.

After paying five roubles at the desk, Anisii took his sister to Rozenfeld. He began telling the doctor in detail about what had been happening with Sonya recently: she had begun to wake up crying in the night and twice she had pushed Palasha away, which had never happened before, and she had suddenly got into the habit of toying with a little mirror and staring into it for hours with her little piggy eyes.

It took a long time to tell the doctor everything. A man in a white coat came into the surgery twice. The first time he brought some boiled syringes, then he took the prescription for making up some tincture or other. The doctor spoke to him politely. So he had to be Stenich. Exhausted and pale, with immense eyes, he had grown his straight hair long, but he shaved his beard and moustache, which gave his face an almost medieval look.

Leaving his sister with the doctor to be examined, Anisii went out into the corridor and glanced in through a half-open door with the inscription 'Treatment Room'. Stenich had his back to him and was mixing up some green stuff in a small bottle. What could Anisii see from the back? Stooped shoulders, a white coat, patches on the back of his boots.

The Chief had taught him that the key to success lay in the first phrase of a conversation. If you could get the conversation going smoothly, then the door would open; you'd find out anything you wanted from the other person. The trick was to make sure you identified their type correctly. There weren't all that many types – according to Erast Petrovich there were exactly sixteen, and there was an approach for each of them.

Oh, if only he didn't get it wrong. He hadn't really mastered this tricky science completely yet. From what they knew about Stenich, and also from visual observation, he was a 'tortoise': an unsociable, suspicious type turned in on himself, living in a state of interminable internal monologue.

If that was right, then the correct approach was 'to show your belly' – that is, to demonstrate that you are defenceless and not dangerous and then, without even the slightest pause, to make a 'breach': to pierce through all the protective layers of alienation and caution, to take the other person by surprise, only without frightening him, God forbid, by being aggressive, or putting him off. You had to interest him, send a signal that seemed to say: You and I are berries from the same field, we speak the same language.

Tulipov mentally crossed himself and had a go. 'That was a good look you gave my idiot sister in the surgery just now. I liked it. It showed interest, but without pity. The doctor's just the opposite: he pities her all right, but he's not really all that interested in looking at her. Only the mentally ill don't need pity; they can be happier than we are. That's an interesting subject, all right: a being that looks like us, but is really quite different. And sometimes something might be revealed to an idiot that is a sealed book to us. I expect you think that too, don't you? I could see it in your eyes. You ought to be the doctor, not this Rozenfeld. Are you a student?'

Stenich turned round and blinked. He looked a little taken aback by the breach, but in the right kind of way, without feeling frightened or getting his back up. He answered curtly, in the way a tortoise was supposed to: 'I used to be.'

The approach had been chosen correctly. Now that the key was in the lock, according to the teachings of the Chief, he should grab it immediately and turn it until it clicked. There was a subtle point here: with a tortoise you had to avoid being too familiar, you mustn't narrow the distance between you, or he'd immediately withdraw into his shell.

'Not a political, are you?' asked Anisii, pretending to be disappointed. 'Then I'm a very poor reader of faces: I took you for a man with imagination; I wanted to ask you about my idiot sister ... These socialists are no good as psychiatrists – they're too carried away with the good of society, but they couldn't give a damn for the individual members of society, especially for imbeciles like my Sonya. Pardon my frankness, I'm a man who likes to speak directly. Goodbye, I'd better go and have a talk with Rozenfeld.'

He turned sharply to go away, in the appropriate manner for a 'setter' (outspoken, impetuous, with sharply defined likes and dislikes) – the ideal match for a tortoise.

'As you wish,' said the male nurse, stung to the quick. 'Only I've never concerned myself with the good of society, and I was excluded from the faculty for something quite different.'

'Aha!' Tulipov exclaimed, raising one finger triumphantly. 'The eye! The eye, it never deceives! I was right about you after all. You live according to your own judgement and follow your own road. It doesn't matter that you're only a medical assistant; I take no notice of titles. Give me a keen, lively man who doesn't judge things by the common standard. I've despaired of taking Sonya round the doctors. All of them just sing the same old tune: oligophrenia, the extreme stage, a hopeless case. But I sense that inside her soul is alive, it can be awakened. Will you not give me a consultation?'

'I'm not a medical assistant either,' Stenich replied, apparently touched by this stranger's frankness (and his flattery, of course – a man likes to be flattered). 'It's true that Mr Rozenfeld does use me as a medical assistant, but officially I'm only a male nurse. And I work without pay, as a volunteer. To make amends for my sins.'

Ah, so that's it, thought Anisii. That's where the glum look came from, and the resignation. I'll have to adjust my line of approach.

Speaking in the most serious voice he could muster, he said: 'You have chosen a good path for the exculpation of your sins. Far better than lighting candles in a church or beating your forehead against the church porch. May God grant you quick relief.'

'I don't want it quickly!' Stenich cried with unexpected ardour, and his eyes, which had been dull, were instantly aglow with fire and passion. 'Let it be hard, let it be long! That will be the best way, the right way! I . . . I don't talk with people often, I'm very reserved. And I'm used to being alone. But there's something in you that encourages frank talking. I feel like talking . . . Otherwise, I'm on my own all the time; my mind could go again soon.'

Anisii was truly amazed by the results of his chief's method! The key had fitted the lock, and fitted it so well that the door had swung open of its own accord. He didn't need to do anything else, just listen and agree with everything.

The pause unsettled the male nurse. 'Perhaps you don't have any time?' His voice trembled. 'I know you have problems of your own; you can't have time for other people's confessions . . .'

'A man with troubles of his own will understand another person's troubles better,' Anisii said jesuitically. 'What is eating at your soul? You can tell me. We're strangers; we don't even know each other's name. We'll have a talk and go our separate ways. What sin do you have on your soul?'

For just a moment Anisii dreamed of him dropping to his knees, bursting into sobs and saying: 'Forgive me, you good man, I am cursed, I bear the weight of bloody sin, I disembowel women with a scalpel.' And that would be it, case closed, and Tulipov would be rewarded by his superiors and, best of all, there'd be a word of praise from the Chief.

But no, Stenich didn't drop to his knees and he said something quite different: 'Pride. All my life I've been tormented by it. I took this job, this heavy, dirty work, in order to conquer it. I clean up the foul mess from the mad patients; no job is too disgusting for me. Humiliation and resignation – that's the best medicine for pride.'

'So you were excluded from the university for pride?' Anisii said, unable to conceal his disappointment.

'What? Ah, from the university. No, that was something different . . . I'll tell you – why not? – in order to humble my pride.' The male nurse blushed violently, turning bright red all the way up to the parting in his hair. 'I used to have another sin, a serious one: voluptuousness. I've overcome it now. Life has helped me. But in my young years I was depraved – not so much out of sensuality as out of curiosity. It's even viler, out of curiosity, don't you think?'

Anisii didn't know how to answer that, but it would be interesting to hear about the sin. What if there was a thread leading from this voluptuousness to the murder?

'I don't see any sin at all in sensuality,' he said aloud. 'Sin is when you hurt your neighbour. But who's hurt by a bit of sensuality, provided of course there's no violence involved?'

Stenich just shook his head. 'Ah, you're still young, sir. Have you not heard of the Sadist Circle? How could you? – you probably hadn't even finished grammar school then. It was exactly seven years ago this April . . . But in Moscow not many people know about the case. The rumours spread in medical circles, all right, but not much leaks out of them; it's a matter of *esprit de corps*, sticking together, a common front. Mind you, they threw me out . . .'

'What was that, the saddler's circle?' asked Anisii, pretending to be stupid but remembering that Stenich had been excluded for 'immoral behaviour'.

Senich laughed grimly. 'Not exactly. There were about fifteen of us, wild students in the medical faculty, and two girl students. It was a dark, oppressive time. A year earlier the nihilists had blown up the Tsar-Liberator. We were nihilists too, but without any politics. In those days, for politics we'd have been sentenced to hard labour or worse. But all they did was pack our leader Sotsky off to a penal battalion. With no trial, no fuss, by ministerial decree. Some of the others were transferred to non-medical faculties – pharmacists, chemists, anatomists – they weren't considered worthy of the exalted title of doctor. And some, like me, were simply flung out, if we couldn't find anyone highly placed to intercede for us.'

'That's a bit harsh, isn't it?' Tulipov asked with a sympathetic sigh. 'What on earth did you get up to?'

'Nowadays I tend to think it wasn't harsh at all. It was exactly right . . . You know, very young men who have chosen the path of medicine sometimes fall into a sort of cynicism. They become firmly convinced that man is not the image of God, but a machine made of joints, bones, nerves and various other bits of stuffing. On the early years of the course it's regarded as daring to take breakfast in the morgue and stand your bottle of beer on the stomach of a "piece of carrion" that's only just been sewn up. And there are jokes more vulgar than that – I won't tell you about them; they're disgusting. But these are all quite standard pranks: we went further. There were a few among us who had a lot of money, so we had the chance to cut loose. Simple debauchery wasn't enough for us any more. Our leader, the late departed Sotsky, had a fantastic imagination. He didn't come back from the penal battalion; he died there, or he would have carried on even further. We were especially fond of sadistic amusements. We'd find the ugliest streetwalker we could, pay her twenty-five roubles and then mock and torment her. We took it too far ... Once, in a fifty-kopeck bordello, when we'd had too much to drink, we took an old whore who would do anything for three roubles and worked her so hard she died ... The incident was hushed up and it never reached the courts. And everything was decided quietly, with no scandal. I was angry at first, because they'd shattered my life – I was studying on a pittance, giving lessons and sending my mother as much as I could ... But afterwards, years later, I suddenly realised I deserved it.'

Anisii screwed up his eyes.

'How do you mean – "suddenly"?'

'It just happened,' Stenich replied curtly and sternly. 'I saw God.'

There's something here, thought Tulipov. Probe here and I'll probably find the 'idea' the boss was talking about. How can I turn the conversation to England?

'I expect life has tossed you about quite a lot? Have you not tried seeking happiness abroad?'

'Happiness? No, I haven't looked for that. But I've searched for obscenities in various countries. And found more than enough, may the Lord forgive me.' Stenich crossed himself, facing the icon of the Saviour hanging in the corner.

Then Anisii asked in a simply, ... kind of voice: 'And have you ever been in England? That's my dream, but I'm obviously never going to get there. Everyone says it's an exceptionally civilised country.'

'Strange that you should ask about England,' said the repentant sinner, looking at Anisii intently. 'You're a strange gentleman altogether. Whatever you ask, it always hits the bull's eye. It was in England that I saw God. Until that moment I was living an unworthy, degrading kind of life. I was sponging off a certain crazy madcap. And then I decided to change everything all at once.'

'You said yourself that humiliation is good for conquering pride. So why did you decide to leave a humiliating life? That's not logical.'

Anisii had wanted to find out a bit more about Stenich's life in England, but he had committed a crude error: his question had put the tortoise on the defensive, and that was something he ought not to have done under any circumstances.

Stenich instantly withdrew into his shell: 'And who are you, to go interpreting the logic of my soul? What am I doing whinging to you like this anyway?'

The male nurse's gaze was suddenly inflamed with hate, his slim fingers began fumbling convulsively at the table. And on the table there happened to be a metal pan with various medical instruments. Anisii remembered that Stenich had been treated for mental illness, and he backed out into the corridor. Stenich wouldn't tell him anything else useful now.

But even so, certain things had been clarified.

Now he had a really long road to travel, from Lefortovo to the opposite extreme of Moscow, Devichie Polye, to the Timofei Morozov Gynaecological Clinic, financed by the resources of the rich Counsellor of Commerce, at the Moscow Imperial University. With all her disabilities Sonya was still a woman, and some female problems or other were sure to be found. And so the imbecile was to be useful to the inquiry yet again.

Sonya was in an agitated state – the 'dot' at Lefortovo had made a strong impression on her.

'Mer tap-tap, knee hop-hop, nofraid, sweety no,' she said boisterously, telling her brother about her adventures.

To anybody else, it was a meaningless jumble of sounds, but Anisii understood everything: the doctor had hit her knee with a little hammer, and her knee had jerked, only Sonya hadn't been afraid at all, but the doctor hadn't given her a sweet.

So that she wouldn't prevent him from concentrating, he stopped the cab at the Orphan's Institute and bought a large, poisonous-red sugar cockerel on a stick. Sonya stopped talking. She stuck her tongue out a good two inches and licked, staring around with her pale little eyes. So much had happened today, and she didn't know that there were still a lot of interesting things to come. She'd need a lot of attention in the evening; she'd be too excited to get to sleep for a long time.

They finally arrived. The generous Counsellor of Commerce had built a fine clinic, there was no denying that. The Morozov family had done a lot of good for the city in general. Recently the newspapers had written that Honorary Citizen Madam Morozova had organised working trips abroad for young engineers, in order to improve their practical knowledge. Now anyone who completed the full course at the Moscow Imperial Technical College could take a trip to England if he wanted, or even the United States – provided, of course, that he was Orthodox by faith and Russian by blood. It was a great thing. And here in the gynaecological clinic, consultation and treatment were free for the poor on Mondays and Tuesdays. Wasn't that remarkable?

Today, though, it was Wednesday.

Anisii read the announcement in the reception room: 'Consultation with the professor – ten roubles. Appointment with the doctor – five roubles. Appointment with the female doctor Roganova – three roubles.'

'A bit on the expensive side,' Tulipov complained to the attendant. 'My sister's retarded. Won't they take a retarded patient cheaper?'

At first the attendant replied sternly: 'It's not allowed. Come back on Monday or Tuesday.'

But then he looked at Sonya, standing there with her mouth open, and his heart softened.

'You could go to the obstetrical department, to Lizaveta Nesvitskaya. She's as good as a doctor, even though she's only called a midwife. She charges less, or nothing at all, if she takes pity on someone.'

This was excellent. Nesvitskaya was at work.

They walked out of the waiting room and turned into a small garden. As they were approaching the yellow, two-storey building of the obstetrical department, something dramatic happened. A window on the first floor slammed open and there was a loud tinkling of glass. Anisii saw a young woman climb up into the window, wearing just her nightdress, with her long black hair tangled across her shoulders.

'Go away, you torturers,' the woman howled. 'I hate you. You're trying to kill me!'

She looked down – the storeys in the building were tall and it was a long way to the ground – then she pressed her back against the stone wall and began edging along the parapet in small steps, away from the window. Sonya froze, watching with her mouth hanging open slackly. She'd never seen a wonder like this before.

Immediately several heads appeared at the window and began trying to persuade the black-haired woman not to play the fool and come back.

But it was clear that the woman was distressed. She was swaying, and the parapet was narrow. She was about to fall or jump. The snow below had melted, the earth was bare and covered with stones with some kind of iron rods sticking up out of it. It would be certain death or severe injury.

Tulipov looked to the left and the right. People were gaping, but the expression on all their faces was confusion. What should he do?

'Bring a tarpaulin, or at least a blanket!' he shouted to an orderly, who had come out for a smoke and frozen at the sight, with his small cigar clutched in his teeth. He started and went darting off, but he was unlikely to be in time.

A tall woman pushed her way through the people clustered at the window and climbed determinedly out on to the window sill – a white coat, steel pince-nez, hair pulled into a tight knot at the back of her head.

'Ermolaeva, don't be so stupid!' she shouted in a commanding voice. 'Your son's crying; he wants his milk!' And then she set off boldly along the parapet.

'It's not my son!' the dark-haired woman squealed. 'It's a foundling! Don't come near me, I'm afraid of you!'

The woman in the white coat took another step and reached out her hand, but Ermolaeva turned away and jumped with a howl.

The spectators gasped – at the very last instant the doctor had managed to grab the crazed woman just below the collar. The night-shirt tore, but it held. The dangling woman's legs were shamefully exposed, and Anisii began blinking rapidly, but immediately felt ashamed of himself – there was no time for that sort of thing now. The doctor grabbed hold of a drainpipe with one hand and held Ermolaeva with the other. Now she'd have to let the other woman go, or come tumbling down with her.

Anisii tore his greatcoat off his shoulders and waved to two men standing nearby. They stretched the coat out as far as it would go, and stood under the dangling woman.

'I can't hold on any longer! My fingers are slipping!' the iron doctor shouted, and at that very moment the black-haired woman fell.

The blow knocked them all down into a heap. Tulipov jumped up and shook his jarred wrists. The woman lay there with her eyes closed, but seemingly alive, and there was no sign of any blood. One of Anisii's helpers, who looked like a shop assistant, sat on the ground and whimpered, clutching his shoulder. Anisii's greatcoat was a sorry sight – it had lost both sleeves and the collar had split – a new greatcoat, he only had it made last autumn: forty-five roubles.

The woman doctor was already there – she must have moved

really fast. She squatted down over the unconscious woman, felt her pulse, rubbed her hands and feet: 'Alive and unhurt.'

To Anisii she said: 'Well done for thinking of using your coat.'

'What's wrong with her?'

'Puerperal fever. Temporary insanity. Rare, but it happens. What's wrong with you?' she said, turning to the shop assistant. 'Put your shoulder out? Come here.' She took hold of him with her strong hands and gave a sudden jerk – the shop assistant gave a loud gasp.

A female medical assistant ran up, caught her breath and asked: 'Lizaveta Andreevna, what shall we do with Ermolaeva?'

'Put her in the isolation ward – under three blankets; give her an injection of morphine. Let her sleep for while. And be careful not to take your eyes off her.' She turned to go.

'I was actually coming to see you, Miss Nesvitskaya,' Anisii said, thinking: The Chief was right not to exclude women from suspicion. A mare like this could easily choke you with her bare hands, never mind slicing you up with a scalpel.

'Who are you? What's your business?' The glance through the pince-nez was stern, not feminine at all.

'Tulipov, Provincial Secretary. Look, I've brought an imbecile for a consultation on women's matters. She seems to suffer a lot with her periods. Will you agree to take a look at her?'

Nesvitskaya looked at Sonya and asked briskly: 'An imbecile? Does she have a sex life? Are you cohabiting with her?'

'Of course not!' Anisii exclaimed in horror. 'She's my sister. She was born like this.'

'Can you pay? From those who can afford it I take two roubles for an examination.'

'I'll pay, with the greatest of pleasure,' Tulipov hastened to reassure her.

'If paying gives you that much pleasure, then why come to me and not to the doctor or the professor? All right, let's go to my surgery.'

She set off with rapid, broad strides. Anisii grabbed hold of Sonya's hand and followed her. He worked out his line of behaviour as he went.

There was no doubt about her type: a classic 'lioness'. The recommended approach was to act embarrassed and to mumble. That made lionesses soften.

The midwife's surgery was small and neat, with nothing superfluous: a gynaecological chair, a table and a chair. There were two brochures on the table: 'Problems of hygiene and women's clothing', written by A. N. Sobolev, docent of obstretics and women's ailments, and 'Proceedings of the Society for the Propagation of Practical Knowledge Among Educated Women'.

There was an advertisement hanging on the wall:

LADIES' HYGIENIC PADS

Manufactured from sublimated timber fibre

A very comfortable fastening, with the use of a belt, to be worn by ladies during difficult periods. The price of a dozen pads is one rouble. The price of the belt is from 40 kop. to 1 r. 50 kop.

Egorov's House, Pokrovka Street

Anisii sighed and began to mumble: 'You see, the reason I decided to come to you, Miss Nesvitskaya is . . . well, you see, I've heard that actually you have the highest possible qualifications, although you hold a position that doesn't correspond at all to the learning possessed by such a worthy individual . . . Of course, not that I have anything at all against the title of midwife . . . I didn't mean to belittle or, God forbid, express any doubts, on the contrary in fact . . .'

He thought he'd done really well, and even managed to blush a little, but Nesvitskaya's response astonished him: she took Anisii firmly by the shoulders and turned his face to the light

'Well now, well now, I know that look around the eyes. Would you be a police spy, then? You've started working with a bit of imagination now, even picked up an imbecile from somewhere. What else do you want from me? Why can't you just leave me in peace? If you're thinking of making something of my illegal practice, then the director knows all about it.' She pushed him away in disgust.

Tulipov rubbed his shoulders – she had a fierce grip. Sonya pressed herself against her brother in fright and began to whine; Anisii stroked her hair.

'Don't you be frightened. The lady's only joking, playing games. She's kind, she's a doctor . . . Elizaveta Andreevna, you're mistaken about me. I work in the chancellery of His Excellency the Governor-General. In a very modest position, of course, the lowest of the low, so to speak. Tulipov, Provincial Secretary. I have my identification with me, if you'd like me to show you it. Or is there no need?' He spread his arms timidly and smiled shyly.

Excellent! Nesvitskaya felt ashamed, and that was the very way to get a lioness to talk.

'I'm sorry, I see them everywhere . . . You must understand . . .' She picked up a *papyrosa* from the table with a trembling hand and lit it, but not straight away, only with the third match. So much for the iron doctor.

'I'm sorry I suspected you. My nerves are all shot. And then this Ermolaeva . . . Ah, yes, you saved Ermolaeva, I forgot . . . I must explain myself. I don't know why, but I'd like you to understand . . .'

'The reason you want to explain yourself to me, madame,' Anisii answered in his thoughts, 'is because you're a lioness, and I'm acting like a hare. Lionesses get on best of all with timid, defenceless little hares. Psychology, Lizaveta Andreevna.'

But together with his satisfaction, Tulipov also experienced a certain moral discomfort – he was no police spy, but he was still doing detective work and using his invalid sister as a cover. The doctor had been right.

She smoked the *papyrosa* quickly, in a few puffs, and lit another one.

Anisii waited, fluttering his eyelids pitifully.

'Smoke?' Nesvitskaya pushed the box of *papyrosas* towards him.

Tulipov generally didn't smoke, but lionesses like it when they can order people about, so he took one, inhaled the smoke and started to cough violently.

'Yes, they're a bit strong,' the doctor said with a nod. 'It's a habit. The tobacco's strong in the North, and in the summer there you can't get by without tobacco – all those mosquitoes and midges.'

'So you're from the North?' Anisii asked naively, clumsily shaking the ash off his *papyrosa*.

'No, I was born and brought up in St Petersburg. Until the age of seventeen I was my mother's little darling. But when I was seventeen, men in blue uniforms came for me in droshkies. They took me away from my mother and put me in a prison cell.'

Nesvitskaya spoke in short, abrupt phrases. Her hands weren't trembling any more; her voice had become harsh and her eyes had narrowed in anger – but it wasn't Tulipov she was angry with, that was clear.

Sonya sat down on a chair, slumped against the wall and began sniffing loudly – she was exhausted from all these new impressions.

'What did they arrest you for?' the hare asked in a whisper.

'For knowing a student who had once been in a house where revolutionaries sometimes used to meet,' Nesvitskaya said with a bitter laugh. 'There had just been another attempt on the life of the Tsar, and so they hauled in absolutely everybody. While they were getting to the bottom of things, I spent two years in solitary confinement. At the age of seventeen. I don't know how I managed not to go insane. Perhaps I did ... Then they let me out. But to make sure I didn't strike up any inappropriate acquaintances, they sent me into administrative exile – to the village of Zamorenka in the Arkhangelsk province. Under official surveillance. So I have special feelings about blue uniforms.'

'And where did you study medicine?' Anisii asked, with a sympathetic shake of his head.

'At first in Zamorenka, in the local hospital. I had to have something to live on, so I took a job as a nurse. And I realised that medicine was the thing for me. It's probably the only thing that makes any sense at all ... Later I ended up in Scotland and studied in the medical faculty, the first woman in the surgical department – they don't let women get ahead too easily there, either. I made a good surgeon. I have a strong hand; from the very beginning I was never afraid of the sight of blood, and I'm not disgusted by the sight of people's internal organs. They're even quite beautiful in their own sort of way.'

Anisii was on the edge of his seat. 'And you can operate?'

She smiled condescendingly: 'I can perform an amputation, and an abdominal operation, and remove a tumour. And instead of that, for all these months ...' She gestured angrily.

What 'instead of that'? Disembowelling streetwalkers in woodsheds?

Possible motives?

Tulipov slyly examined Nesvitskaya's unattractive, even rather coarse face. A morbid hatred of the female body? Very possible. Reasons? Her own physical unattractiveness and uncertain personal situation, being forced to carry out a midwife's duties, work that she did not like, the daily contemplation of patients whose lives as women had worked out happily. It could be almost anything, even including concealed latent insanity as a result of the injustice she had suffered and solitary confinement at a tender age.

'All right, let's take a look at your sister. I've been talking too long. It's not even like me.'

Nesvitskaya removed her pince-nez and wearily rubbed the bridge of her nose with her strong fingers, then for some reason massaged the lobe of her ear; and Anisii's thoughts naturally turned to the sinister ear in the box.

How was the Chief getting on? Had he managed to figure out who had sent the 'smopackadj'?

Again it is evening, the blessed darkness concealing me beneath its dusky wing. I am walking along a railway embankment. A strange excitement constricts my chest.

It is surprising how it throws one off balance to see acquaintances from a former life. They have changed, some are even unrecognisable, and as for me, it need hardly be said.

I am troubled by memories. Stupid, unnecessary memories. Everything is different now.

Standing at the crossing, outside the barrier, there is a young girl begging. Twelve or thirteen years old. She is shuddering from the cold, her hands are covered in red goose bumps, her feet are wrapped in some kind of rags. Her face is horrible, simply horrible: suppurating eyes, cracked lips, a runny nose. A miserable, ugly child of humanity.

How can I not pity such a creature? This ugly face can also be made beautiful. And there is really nothing I have to do. It is enough simply to reveal the true Beauty of its gaze.

I follow the girl. The memories are no longer troubling me.

CHAPTER 5

Fellow Students

Holy Week Wednesday, 5 April, afternoon and evening

After despatching his assistant on his errand, Erast Petrovich prepared himself for some intense thinking. The task appeared to be far from simple. Irrational enlightenment would be very welcome here, and so the right place to begin was with meditation.

The Collegiate Counsellor closed the door of his study, sat down on the carpet with his legs crossed and tried to rid himself of all thoughts of any kind – still his vision, shut off his hearing; sway on the waves of the Great Void from which, as on so many previous occasions, there would come the sound, at first barely audible, and then ever more distinct, and finally almost deafening, of the truth.

Time passed. Then it stopped passing. A cool calm began rising unhurriedly within him, from his belly upwards; the golden mist in front of his eyes grew thicker, but then the huge clock standing in the corner of the room churred and chimed deafeningly: bom-bom-bom-bom-bom!

Fandorin came to himself. Five o'clock already? He checked the time on his Breguet, because the grandfather clock could not be trusted – and he was right: it was twenty minutes fast.

Immersing himself in a meditative state for a second time proved harder. Erast Petrovich recalled that at five o'clock that afternoon he was due to take part in a competition of the Moscow Bicycle Enthusiasts' Club, to support the poor widows and orphans of employees of the military department. Moscow's strongest sportsmen and the bicycle teams of the Grenadier Corps were competing. The Collegiate Counsellor had a good

215

chance of repeating his success of the previous year and taking the main prize.

Alas, there was no time now for sports competitions.

Erast Petrovich drove away the inappropriate thoughts and began staring at the pale-lilac pattern of the wallpaper. Now the mist would thicken again, the petals of the printed irises would tremble, the flowers would begin breathing out their fragrance and satori would come.

Something was hindering him. The mist seemed to be carried away by a wind blowing from somewhere on his left. The severed ear was lying there, in the lacquered box on the table. Lying there, refusing to be forgotten.

Ever since his childhood, Erast Petrovich had been unable to bear the sight of tormented human flesh. He had lived long enough, seen all sorts of horrific things, taken part in wars and yet, strangely enough, he had still not learned to regard with indifference the things that human beings did to their own kind.

Realising that the irises on the wallpaper would not breathe out any scent today, Fandorin heaved a deep sigh. Since he had failed to arouse his intuition, he would have to rely on his reason. He sat down at the table and picked up his magnifying glass.

He began with the wrapping paper. It was just ordinary paper, the kind used to wrap all sorts of thing. Nothing to go on there.

Now for the handwriting. The writing was uneven and the letters were large with careless endings to their lines. If you looked closely, there were tiny splashes of ink – the hand had been pressed too hard against the paper. The writer was most probably a man in the prime of life. Possibly unbalanced or intoxicated. But he could not exclude the possibility of a woman with strong emotional and hysterical tendencies. In that regard he had to take into account the flourishes on the Os and the coquettish hooks on the capital Fs.

The most significant point was that they did not teach people to write like that in the handwriting classes in the grammar schools. What he had here was either someone educated at home, which was more typical of female individuals, or someone who had had no regular education at all. However, there was not a single spelling mistake. Hmm. This required a little thought. At least the writing was a clue.

Next – the velvet box. The kind in which they sold expensive cufflinks or brooches. Inside it there was a monogram: 'A. Kuznetsov, Kamergersky Way'. That was no help. It was a large jeweller's shop, one of the best known in Moscow. He could make inquiries, of course, but they would hardly come to anything – he could assume that they sold at least several dozen boxes of that kind a day.

The satin ribbon was nothing special. Smooth and red – the kind that gypsy women or merchants' daughters liked to tie their plaits with on holidays.

Using his magnifying glass, Erast Petrovich inspected the powder box (from 'Cluseret No. 6') with especial interest, holding it by the very edge. He sprinkled it with a white powder like talc, and numerous fingerprints appeared on the smooth lacquered surface. The Collegiate Counsellor carefully and precisely blotted them with a special, extremely thin paper. Fingerprints would not be accepted as evidence in court, but even so they would come in useful.

It was only now that Fandorin turned his attention to the poor ear. Judging from the sprinkling of freckles on both sides of the ear, its owner had been ginger-haired. The lobe had been pierced, and very carelessly: the hole was wide and long. Taking that into account, and also the fact that the skin was badly chapped by cold and wind, he could conclude, firstly, that the former owner of the object in question had worn her hair combed upwards; secondly, that she was not a member of the privileged classes; thirdly, that she had spent a lot of time out in the cold without wearing any hat. The final circumstance was especially noteworthy. It was well known that street girls touted their wares with their heads uncovered even during the cold season. It was one of the signs of their trade.

Biting his lip (he still couldn't manage to regard the ear as an object), Erast Petrovich turned the ear over with a pair of tweezers and began examining the cut. It was even, made with an extremely sharp instrument. Not a single drop of congealed blood. Which meant that when the ear was severed the ginger-haired woman had already been dead for at least several hours.

What was that slight blackening on the cut? What could have caused that? Defrosting, that was what! The body had been in an ice-room – that was why the cut was so perfect: when it had been made the tissues had still not completely thawed out.

A prostitute's body placed in an ice-room? What for? What kind of fastidiousness was this? That kind were always taken straight to the Bozhedomka and buried. If they were put in an ice-room, it was either in the medical-faculty morgue on Trubetskaya Street for educational purposes, or in the forensic morgue at Bozhedomka to help with a police investigation.

And now the most interesting question: who had sent him the ear and why?

First – why?

The London murderer had done the same thing the previous year. He had sent Mr Albert Lask, the chairman of the committee for the capture of Jack the Ripper, half of a kidney from the mutilated body of Catherine Eddows, which had been found on 30 September.

Erast Petrovich was convinced that this action had had a double meaning for the killer. The first, obvious meaning was a challenge, a demonstration of confidence in his own invulnerability, as if to say: No matter how hard you try, you'll never catch me. But there was probably a second underlying reason too: the typical masochistic desire of maniacs of this kind to be caught and punished: If you protectors of society really are all-powerful and ubiquitous, if Justice is the father and I am his guilty son, then here's the key for you; find me. The London police had not known how to use the key.

Of course, a quite different hypothesis was also possible. The terrible package had not been sent by the killer, but by some cynical joker who regarded the tragic situation as a pretext for a cruel jest. In London the police had also received a scoffing letter, supposedly written by the criminal. The letter had been signed 'Jack the Ripper', which was actually where the nickname had come from. The English investigators had concluded that it

218

was a hoax – probably because they had to justify the failure of their efforts to find the sender.

There was no point in complicating his task by making it a double one. At this moment it made no difference whether or not it was the killer who had sent the ear. All he needed to do at this moment was find out who had done it. It was very possible that the person who had severed the ear would turn out to be the Ripper. The Moscow trick with the small package differed from the London case in one substantial respect: the entire British capital had known about the murders in the East End, and in principle anybody at all could have 'joked' in that way. But in this case the details of yesterday's atrocity were only known to an extremely limited circle of individuals. How many of them were there? Very few, even if he included intimate friends and relatives.

And so, what details did he know of the person who had sent the 'small package'?

It was someone who had not studied in a grammar school, but had still received a good enough education to write the phrase 'Collegiate Counsellor' without any mistakes. That was one.

Judging from the box from Kuznetsov's and the powder box from Cluseret, the person involved was not poor. That was two.

This person was not only informed about the murders, but he knew about Fandorin's role in the investigation. That was three.

This person had access to the morgue, which narrowed the circle of suspects still further. That was four.

This person possessed the skills of a surgeon. That was five.

What else was there?

'Masa, a cab. And look lively!'

Zakharov came out of the autopsy room in his leather apron, his black gloves smeared with some brownish sludge. His face was puffy, he looked overhung and the pipe in the corner of his mouth had gone out.

'Ah, the eyes and ears of the Governor-General,' he muttered instead of a greeting. 'What is it – has somebody else been sliced up?'

'Mr Zakharov, how many prostitutes' bodies do you have in the ice-room?' Erast Petrovich asked curtly.

The forensic expert shrugged: 'On Mr Izhitsin's orders, they now bring in all the streetwalkers who have come to the end of their walk. In addition to our mutual friend Andreichkina, yesterday and today they've brought in another seven. Why – do you want to have a bit of fun?' Zakharov asked with a debauched grin. 'There are some very pretty ones. But probably none to suit your taste. You prefer the giblets, I think?' The pathologist could see perfectly well that Fandorin was not at ease, and he seemed to take pleasure in the fact.

'Show them to me.' The Collegiate Counsellor thrust his chin out stolidly, readying himself for the distressing sight.

The first thing that Fandorin saw in the spacious room lit by electric lights was the wooden shelves covered with glass jars with shapeless objects floating in them, and then he looked at the zinc-covered oblong tables. Projecting from one of them, beside the window, was the black neck of a microscope, and beside it a body was lying flat, with Zakharov's assistant working on it.

Erast Petrovich took a quick glance, saw that the body was male and turned away in relief.

'A deep firearms wound to the top of the head, Mr Zakharov, that's all,' the assistant said with a nasal twang, gazing curiously at Erast Petrovich, who was an almost legendary character in and around police circles.

'They brought that one in from Khitrovka,' Zakharov explained. 'But your little chicks are all over there, in the ice-room.' He pushed open a heavy metal door that breathed out a dense, chilly, repulsive stench. A switch clicked and the matte-glass globe on the ceiling lit up.

The doctor pointed. 'There are our heroines, on that side,' he said to Fandorin, who was feeling numb.

The initial impression was not at all horrific. Ingres's painting *The Turkish Bath*. A solid tangle of naked women's bodies, smooth lines, lazy immobility. Except that the steam was not hot, but frosty, and for some reason all the odalisques were lying down.

Then the details struck his eyes: the long crimson incisions, the blue patches, the sticky, tangled hair.

The forensic expert patted one of them, who looked like a mermaid, on her blue neck. 'Not bad eh? From a brothel. Consumption. In fact, there's only one violent death here: the one over there, with the big breasts; someone stove her head in with a rock. Two of them are suicides. Three of them died of hypothermia – froze to death when they were drunk. They bring them all in, no matter what. Teach a fool to pray and he won't know when to stop. But what's that to me. I don't have to do all that much.'

Erast Petrovich leaned down over one woman, thin, with a scattering of freckles on her shoulders and chest. He threw the long ginger hair back from the pitifully contorted, sharp-nosed face. Instead of a right ear the dead woman had a cherry-red hole.

'Well, who's been taking liberties here?' Zakharov asked in surprise and glanced at the tag attached to the woman's foot. 'Marfa Sechkina, sixteen years old. Ah, I remember: poisoned herself with phosphorous matches. Came in yesterday afternoon. But she still had both her ears, I remember that very well. So where's her right one got to?'

The Collegiate Counsellor took a powder box out of his right pocket, opened it without speaking and thrust it under the pathologist's nose.

Zakharov took the ear with a steady hand and held it against the cherry-red hole.

'That's it! So what does this mean?'

'That is what I would like you to tell me.' Fandorin held a scented handkerchief to his nose, feeling the nausea rising in his throat, and said: 'Come on, let's talk out there.'

They walked back into the autopsy room which now, despite the presence of the dissected corpse, Erast Petrovich found almost cosy.

'Three qu-questions. Who was here yesterday evening? Who have you told about the investigation and my participation in it? Whose writing is this?'

The Collegiate Counsellor set down the wrapping paper from the 'smopackadj' in front of Zakharov. He felt it necessary to add: 'I know that you did not write it – I am familiar with your handwriting. However, I trust you appreciate the significance of this correspondence?'

Zakharov turned pale; he had clearly lost any desire to play the clown.

'I'm waiting for an answer, Mr Zakharov. Shall I repeat the questions?'

The doctor shook his head and squinted at Grumov, who was pulling something greyish-blue out of the corpse's gaping belly with exaggerated zeal. Zakharov gulped and his Adam's apple twitched in his neck.

'Yesterday evening my colleagues from the old faculty called to see me. They were celebrating the anniversary of a certain ... memorable event. There were seven or eight of them. They drank some medical spirit here, in memory of the old student days ... It's possible that I might have blurted out something about the investigation – I don't exactly remember. Yesterday was a heavy day, I was tired, and the drink soon went to my head.' He stopped.

'The third question,' Fandorin reminded him: 'whose handwriting is it? And don't lie and tell me you don't know. The handwriting is quite distinctive.'

'I'm not in the habit of lying!' Zakharov snapped. 'And I recognise the writing. But I'm not a police informer; I'm a former Moscow student. You find out for yourself, without me.'

Erast Petrovich said in an unpleasant voice: 'You are not only a former student, but a current forensic medical expert, who has taken an oath. Or have you forgotten which investigation we are talking about here?' And then he continued in a very quiet, expressionless voice: 'I can, of course, arrange for the handwriting of everyone who studied in the same faculty as you to be checked, but that will take weeks. In that case your honour among your comrades would not suffer, but I would make sure that you were tried and deprived of the right to work in the state service. You've known me for some years already, Zakharov. I always mean what I say.'

Zakharov shuddered, and the pipe slid from left to right along the slit of his mouth. 'I'm sorry, Mr Court Counsellor, but I can't. Nobody would ever shake my hand again. Never mind the government service, I wouldn't be able to work in any area of medicine at all. But I'll tell you what ...' The forensic expert's yellow forehead gathered into wrinkles. 'Our revels are continuing this evening. We agreed to meet at seven at Burylin's place. He never completed the course, like many of our company in fact; but we get together from time to time ... I've just completed a job here; Grumov can finish up everything else. I was just about to have a wash, get changed and go. I have an apartment here. At the public expense, attached to the cemetery office. It's most convenient ... Well, if you like, I can take you with me to Burylin's place. I don't know if everyone who was here yesterday will come, but the person you're interested in will definitely be there, I'm certain of that ... I'm sorry, but that's all I can do. A doctor's honour.'

It was not easy for the pathologist to speak in such a plaintive manner; he was not accustomed to it, and Erast Petrovich decided to temper justice with mercy and not press him any harder. He merely shook his head in astonishment at the peculiarly elastic ethics of these people's *esprit de corps*: a man could not point out someone he had studied with as a likely killer, but there was no problem in bringing a detective along to a former fellow-student's house.

'You are complicating my task, but very well, let it be so. It's after eight already. Get changed and let's go.'

For most of their journey (and it was a long journey, to Yakimanka Street), they rode in silence. Zakharov was as gloomy as a storm cloud and he replied to questions reluctantly, but Fandorin did at least learn something about their host.

He was called Kuzma Savvich Burylin. He was a manufacturer, a millionaire from an old merchant family. His brother, who was many years older, had taken up the eunuch faith of the *skoptsy*. He had 'cut off his sin' and lived like a hermit, building up his capital. He had intended to 'purge' his younger brother as well, when he reached the age of fourteen, but on the very eve of the 'great mystery' the elder brother had died suddenly, and the youth had not only remained completely intact, but inherited an immense fortune. As Zakharov remarked acidly, a retrospective fear and the miraculous preservation of his manhood had marked Kuzma Burylin's life ever since. For the rest of his life he was doomed to demonstrate that he was not a eunuch, and he often went to excess in the process.

'Why did such a rich man join the medical faculty?' asked Fandorin.

'Burylin has studied all sorts of things – both here and abroad. He has a curious and unstable mind. He doesn't need a diploma, so he has never finished any course anywhere, but he was thrown out of the medical faculty.'

'What for?'

'There was good cause,' the forensic expert replied vaguely. 'You'll soon see for yourself what kind of individual he is.'

The illuminated entrance to Burylin's house, which faced the river, could be seen from a distance. It was the only house glowing with bright lights of different colours on the dark merchants' embankment, where they went to bed early during Lent and did not use any light unless they needed to. It was a big house, built in the absurd Mauritanian Gothic style: with little pointed turrets, chimeras and gryphons, but at the same time it had a flat roof and a round dome above the conservatory, even a watch-tower shaped like a minaret.

There was a crowd of idle onlookers outside the decorative gates, looking at the gaily illuminated windows and talking among themselves disapprovingly: an obscenity like this on Holy Week Wednesday, during the last week of the forty days of Lent! The muffled whining of gypsy violins drifted out of the house over the silent river, together with the jangling of guitars and jingling of little bells, peals of laughter and an occasional low growling.

They walked in and handed their outer garments to the doormen, and Erast Petrovich was surprised to see that beneath his tightly buttoned black coat, the forensic expert was wearing a white tie and tails.

Zakharov smiled crookedly at his glance of amazement. 'Tradition.'

They walked up a broad marble staircase. Servants in crimson livery opened tall gilded doors, and Fandorin saw before him a spacious hall, its floor covered with palms, magnolias and other exotic plants in tubs. It was the latest European fashion – to make your drawing room look like a jungle. 'The hanging gardens of Semiramis' it was called. Only the very rich could afford it.

The guests were distributed in leisurely style among the paradisiacal groves. Like Zakharov, everyone was in white tie and tails. Erast Petrovich's dress was dandyish enough – a beige American jacket, a lemon-yellow waistcoat, and a pair of trousers of excellent cut with permanent creases – but in this black-and-white congregation he felt like a Yuletide masker. Zakharov could at least have warned him what kind of clothes he was going to change into.

But then, even if Fandorin had come in tails, he still would not have been able to lose himself among the guests, because there were very few of them – perhaps a dozen. For the most part gentlemen of respectable and even prosperous appearance, although they were not at all old – about thirty, or perhaps a little older. Their faces were flushed from drinking, and some even looked a little confused – evidently for them this kind of merrymaking was not the usual thing. At the far end of the hall Fandorin could see another pair of gilded doors, which were closed, and from behind them he could hear the clatter of dishes and the sounds of a gypsy choir practising. A banquet was evidently in preparation inside.

The newcomers had arrived at the high point of a speech being given by a bald gentleman with a paunch and a gold pince-nez.

'Zenzinov – he was the top student. He's a full professor already,' Zakharov whispered, and Fandorin thought he sounded envious.

'... recalling our old pranks from those memorable days. That time, seven years ago, it fell on Holy Week Wednesday too, like today.'

For some reason the professor paused for a moment and shook his head bitterly. 'As they say: Out with your eye for remembering the past, but if you forget, out with both. And they also say: It will all work out in the end. And it has worked out. We've got old, turned fat and flabby. Thanks to Kuzma for still being such a wild man and occasionally shaking up us boring old disciples of Aesculapius.'

At that point everyone began laughing and cackling, turning towards a man who was sitting in an armchair in a stately pose with one leg crossed over the other and drinking wine from an immense goblet. Evidently he was Kuzma Burylin. An intelligent, jaundiced-looking face of the Tatar type – with broad cheekbones and a stubborn chin. His black hair was stuck up in a short French crop.

'It may have worked out for some, but not for everyone,' said a man with long hair and a haggard face, who did not look like the others. He was also wearing tails, but they were obviously not his own, and instead of a starched white shirt, he was definitely wearing a false shirt-front. 'You got away scot-free, Zenzinov. Of course, you were the faculty favourite. Others weren't so lucky. Tomberg became an alcoholic. They say Stenich went crazy. Sotsky died a convict. Just recently I keep thinking I see him everywhere. Take yesterday, for instance ...'

'Tomberg took to drink. Stenich went crazy, Sotsky died and Zakharov became a police corpse-carver instead of a doctor,' their host interrupted the speaker unceremoniously. However, he was looking not at Zakharov but at Erast Petrovich, and with distinct hostility.

'Who's this you've brought with you, Egorka, you English swine? Somehow I don't remember this bright spark as one of our medical brotherhood.'

Then the forensic expert, the Judas, demonstratively moved away from the Collegiate Counsellor and declared, as if everything were perfectly normal: 'Ah, this, gentlemen, is Erast Petrovich Fandorin, a very well-known individual in certain circles. He works for the Governor-General on especially important criminal cases. He insisted that I bring him here. I could not refuse – he is my superior. In any case, please make him welcome.'

The members of the brotherhood began hooting indignantly. Someone leapt out of his chair. Someone else applauded sarcastically.

'What the hell is this!'

'These gentlemen have gone too far this time!'

'He doesn't look much like a detective.'

These comments, and similar ones that assailed him from all sides, made Erast Petrovich blench and screw up his eyes. This business was taking an unpleasant turn. Fandorin stared hard at the perfidious forensic expert, but before he could say anything, the master of the house had dashed across to his uninvited guest in a couple of strides and taken him by the shoulders. Kuzma Savvich's grasp proved to be very powerful; there was no way to wriggle out of it.

'In my house there's only one superior: Kuzma Burylin,' the millionaire roared. 'Nobody comes here without an invitation, especially detectives. And anyone who does come will regret it later.'

'Kuzma, do you remember that bit in Count Tolstoy,' the long-haired man shouted, 'how they tied a constable to a bear and threw them in the river! Let's give this fop a ride too. And it will be good for your Potapich; he's been getting a bit dozy.'

Burylin threw his head back and laughed loudly. 'Oh, Filka, you delightful soul, that's what I value about you: your imagination. Hey! Bring Potapich here!'

Several of the guests who were not yet completely drunk tried to reason with their hosts, but two burly lackeys had already brought in a shaggy bear in a muzzle from the dining room, leading it on a chain. The bear was growling in annoyance and did not want to come; he kept trying to sit down on the floor, and the lackeys dragged him along, with his claws scraping along the highly polished parquet. A palm in a tub was overturned and went crashing to the floor, scattering lumps of earth.

'This is going too far! Kuzma!' Zenzinov appealed. 'After all, we're not boys any longer. You'll have to face the repercussions! In any case, I'm leaving if you don't stop this!'

'He's right,' some other reasonable individual chimed in, in support of the professor. 'There'll be a scandal, and nobody needs that.'

'Well, you can go to the devil then!' Burylin barked. 'But remember, you clyster tubes, I've engaged Madam Julie's establishment for the whole night. We'll go without you.'

After he said that, the voices of protest immediately fell silent.

Erast Petrovich stood there calmly. He did not say a word and did not make the slightest attempt to free himself. His blue eyes gazed without any expression at the wild merchant.

The master of the house gave brisk instructions to his lackeys. 'Turn Potapich's back this way, so he won't maul the detective. Have you brought the rope? And you turn your back this way, you state minion. Afonya, can Potapich swim?'

'Why, of course, Kuzma Savvich. In summer he's very fond of splashing about at the dacha,' a lackey with a forelock replied merrily.

'Well then, he can splash about a bit now. The water must be cold, it's only April. Well, why are you being so stubborn!' Burylin shouted at the Collegiate Counsellor. 'Turn round!'

He clutched Erast Petrovich' s shoulders with all his strength, trying to turn his back to the bear, but Fandorin did not budge an inch, as if he were carved out of stone. Burylin pushed and strained against him. His face turned crimson and the veins stood out on his forehead. Fandorin carried on calmly looking at his host, with just the faintest hint of a mocking smile in the corners of his mouth.

Kuzma Savvich grunted for a little longer but, realising that it looked extremely stupid, he removed his hands and gazed in astonishment at this strange official. The hall went very quiet.

'You're the one I want to see, my dear fellow,' said Erast Petrovich, opening his mouth for the first time. 'Shall we have a talk?'

He took the manufacturer's wrist between his finger and thumb and strode off rapidly towards the closed doors of the banqueting hall. Fandorin's fingers clearly possessed some special power, because his corpulent host grimaced in pain and minced after the man with black hair and white temples. The lackeys froze on the spot in bewilderment, and the bear slowly sat down on the floor and shook its shaggy head idiotically.

Fandorin looked back from the doorway. 'Carry on enjoying yourselves, gentlemen. Meanwhile Kuzma Savvich will explain a few things to me.'

The last thing Erast Petrovich noticed before he turned his back to the guests was the intense gaze of forensic medical expert Zakharov.

The table that was laid in the dining hall was a marvel to behold. The Collegiate Counsellor glanced in passing at the piglet dozing blissfully, surrounded by golden rings of pineapple, and the frightening carcass of the sturgeon in jelly, at the fancy towers of the salads, the red claws of the lobsters, and remembered that his unsuccessful meditation had left him without any dinner. Never mind, he comforted himself. Confucius said: 'The noble man satisfies himself by abstaining.'

In the far corner he could see the scarlet shirts and shawls of the gypsy choir. They saw the master of the house, and the elegant gentleman with a moustache leading him by the hand, and broke off their singing in mid-word. Burylin waved his hand at them in annoyance, as if to say: Stop staring, this is none of your business.

The female soloist, covered in necklaces of coins and ribbons, misunderstood his gesture and began singing in a chesty voice:

> *He was not her promised one,*
> *He was not her husband . . .*

The choir took up the tune in low voices, at only a quarter of full volume.

He brought his little darling
Into the timbered chamber . . .

Erast Petrovich released the millionaire's hand and turned to face him. 'I received your package. Should I interpret it as a confession?'

Burylin rubbed his white wrist. He looked at Fandorin curiously. 'Well, you really are strong, Mr Collegiate Counsellor. You wouldn't think so to look at you . . . What package? And a confession to what?'

'You see, you know my rank, although Zakharov didn't mention it today. You severed that ear; nobody else could have done it. You've studied medicine, and you visited Zakharov yesterday with your fellow students. He was certain that whoever else was here today, you would be. Is this your writing?' He showed the manufacturer the wrapping paper from the 'smopackadj'.

Kuzma Savvich glanced at it and laughed. 'Who else's? How did you like my little present? I told them to be sure to deliver it in time for dinner. Didn't choke on your bouillon, did you? No doubt you called a meeting and constructed hypotheses? Yes, I admit it, I like a joke. When the alcohol loosened Egorka Zakharov's tongue yesterday, I played a little prank. Have you heard about Jack the Ripper in London? He played a similar kind of trick on the police there. Egorka had a dead girl lying on the table – ginger-haired she was. I took a scalpel when he wasn't looking. I lopped off her ear, wrapped it in my handkerchief and slipped it in my pocket. His description of you was far too flowery, Mr Fandorin, you were this and you were that, and you could unravel any tangled thread. Well, Zakharov wasn't lying: you are a curious individual. I like curious individuals, I'm one myself.' The millionaire's narrow eyes glinted cunningly. 'I tell you what. You forget this little joke of mine – it didn't work anyway – and come along with us. We'll have a right royal time. Let me tell you in secret that I've thought up a most amusing wheeze for my old friends, the little doctors. Everything's all ready at Madam Julie's. Moscow will break its sides laughing when it finds out about it tomorrow. Come along with us, really. You won't be sorry.'

At this point the choir suddenly broke off its slow, quiet song and roared out as loud as it could:

Kuzya-Kuzya-Kuzya-Kuzya,
Kuzya-Kuzya-Kuzya-Kuzya,
Kuzya-Kuzya-Kuzya-Kuzya,
Kuzya-Kuzya-Kuzya-Kuzya,
Kuzya, drain your glass!

Burylin merely glanced over his shoulder, and the roaring stopped.

'Do you often go abroad?' Fandorin asked, apropos of nothing.

'This is the palace I often come to,' said his host, apparently not surprised by the change of subject. 'But I live abroad. I've no need to sit polishing the seat of my pants in the office here – I've got capable managers; they do things without me. In a big business like mine, there's only one thing you need: to understand people. Choose the right people and you can lie back and take it easy, the work does itself.'

'Have you been in England recently?'

'I often go to Leeds, and to Sheffield. I have factories there. I drop into the exchange in London. The last time was in December. Why do you ask about England?'

Erast Petrovich lowered his eyelids a little in order to soften the glint in his eyes. He picked a speck of dust off his sleeve and said emphatically: 'I am placing you under arrest for mutilating the body of the spinster Sechkina. Only administrative arrest for the time being, but in the morning there will be a warrant from the Public Prosecutor. Your appointed representative must deposit your bail no later than midday tomorrow. You are coming with me, and your guests can all go home. The visit to the bordello is cancelled. It's not good to bring such respectable d-doctors into disgrace like that. And you, Burylin, will enjoy a right royal time in the cells.'

As a reward for saving the girl, I was sent a dream last night.

I dreamed I was standing before the Throne of the Lord.

'Sit on my left hand,' the Father of Heaven said to me. 'Rest, for you bring people joy and release, and that is heavy work. They are foolish, my children. Their views are inverted: they see black as white and white as black, woe as happiness, and happiness as woe. When in my mercy I summon one of them to Me in their childhood, the others cry and pity the one I have summoned instead of feeling joy for him. When I let one of them live to a hundred years, until his body is weak and his spirit is extinguished as a punishment and a warning to the others, they are not horrified by his terrible fate, but envy it. After a bloody battle, those I have turned away rejoice, even if they have received injuries, while they pity those who have fallen, summoned by Me to appear before My face, and secretly even despise them for their failure. But they are the truly fortunate, for they are already with Me, the unfortunates are those who remain. What am I to do with people, tell Me, you kind soul? How am I to bring them to their senses?' And I felt sorry for the Lord, vainly craving the love of his foolish children.

CHAPTER 6

The Triumph of Pluto

Holy Week Thursday, 6 April

Today it fell to Anisii's lot to work with Izhitsin.

Late the previous evening, after an 'analysis' in the course of which it was determined that they now had more suspects than they required, the Chief had walked around the study for a while, clicked his beads and said: 'All right, Tulipov. We'll have to sleep on it. You go and rest; you've done more than enough running about for one day.'

Anisiii had expected the decision to be: put Stenich, Nesvitskaya and Burylin under secret observation, check all their movements for the last year and perhaps also set up some kind of investigative experiment. But no, the unpredictable Chief had come to a different conclusion. In the morning, when Anisii, shivering in the dreary drizzle, arrived at Malaya Nikitskaya Street, Masa handed him a note:

I am disappearing for a while. I shall try to come at this business from the other side. In the meantime, you work with Izhitsin. I am afraid he might botch things up with his excessive zeal. On the other hand, he may not be a very pleasant character, but he is tenacious, and he could just dig something up.

EF

Well, did you ever? And just what 'other side' could that be?

The pompous investigator was not easy to find. Anisii phoned the Public Prosecutor's office and they told him: 'He was called out by the Department of Gendarmes.' He called the Department of Gendarmes and they replied: 'He went out on urgent business that can't be discussed over the telephone.' The duty officer's voice sounded so excited that Tulipov guessed it had to be another murder. And a quarter of an hour later a messenger arrived from Izhitsin – it was the constable, Linkov. He had called at the Collegiate Counsellor's and not found him in, so he'd come round to Tulipov on Granatny Lane.

Linkov was terribly agitated. 'It's an absolute nightmare, Your Honour,' he told Anisii. 'The brutal murder of a juvenile. It's terrible, terrible . . .' He sniffed and blushed, evidently embarrassed by his own sensitivity.

Anisii looked at the ungainly, scrawny-necked policeman and saw straight through him: literate, sentimental, and no doubt he liked reading books; joined the police out of poverty, only this rough work wasn't for him, the poor lamb. Tulipov would have been the same if not for his fortunate encounter with Erast Petrovich.

'Come on, Linkov,' said Anisii, deliberately addressing the constable in a formal, polite tone. 'Let's go straight to the morgue; that's where they'll take her anyway.'

Deduction is a great thing. His calculation proved to be correct. Anisii had been sitting talking to Pakhomenko in his watchman's hut for no more than half an hour, enjoying a chat about life with the agreeable fellow, when three droshkies drove up to the gates, followed by a blind carriage with no windows, the so-called 'corpse-wagon'.

Izhitsin and Zakharov got out of the first droshky, a photographer and his assistant got out of the second, two gendarmes and a senior constable got out of the third. No one got out of the carriage. The gendarmes opened its shabby doors with the peeling paint and carried out something short on a stretcher, covered with a tarpaulin.

The medical expert was dour, chewing on his eternal pipe with exceptional bitterness, but the investigator seemed to be in lively spirits, almost even glad about something.

When he caught sight of Anisii, his face dropped: 'A-ah, there you are. So you already got wind of this? Is your chief here too?'

But when it turned out that Fandorin was not there and would not be coming, and so far his assistant did not really know anything, Izhitsin's spirits rose again. 'Well, now things will really start moving,' he told Tulipov, rubbing his hands energetically. 'So, it's like this. At dawn today the railway line patrolmen on the Moscow–Brest transfer line discovered the body of a juvenile female vagrant in the bushes close to the Novotikhvinsk level crossing. Zakharov has determined that death occurred no later than midnight. It's not very pretty, I warn you, Tulipov, it was an incredible sight!' Izhitsin gave a brief laugh. 'Just imagine it: the belly, naturally, had been completely gutted and the entrails hung all around on the branches, and as for the face . . .'

'What, another bloody kiss?' Anisii exclaimed excitedly.

The investigator burst out laughing and couldn't stop, he was helpless with laughter – obviously it was nerves.

'Oh, you'll be the death of me,' he said eventually, wiping away his tears. 'Fandorin and you and that kiss of yours. Please forgive my inappropriate merriment. When I show you, you'll understand. Hey, Silakov! Stop! Show him her face!'

The gendarmes put the stretcher down on the ground and turned back the edge of the tarpaulin. Anisii was expecting to see something particularly unpleasant: glassy eyes, a nightmarish grimace, the tongue lolling out of the mouth, but there was none of that. Under the tarpaulin there was some kind of black-and-red baked pudding with two round blobs: white, with a small dark circle in the centre.

'What is it?' Tulipov asked in surprise, feeling his teeth starting to chatter of their own accord.

'Seems like our joker left her without any face at all,' Izhitsin explained with morose humour. 'Zakharov says the skin was slit along the hair line and then torn off, like the peel off an orange. There's a kiss for you. And, best of all, now she can't be identified.'

Everything was still swimming and swaying in front of Anisii's eyes. The investigator's voice seemed to be coming from somewhere far in the distance.

'Anyway, the secret's out now. Those rogues of patrolmen

have blabbed to everyone they could. One of them was taken away in a faint. The rumours were already spreading round Moscow in any case. The Department of Gendarmes is flooded with reports of a killer who's decided to wipe out women completely. This morning they reported everything to St Petersburg, the whole truth, nothing kept back. The minister himself, Count Tolstoy, is coming. So there you have it. Looks like heads are going to roll. I don't know about you, but I'm quite fond of mine. Your chief can go on playing his game of deduction as long as he likes; he's safe enough, he has protection in high places. But I'll crack this one without deduction, by sheer determination and energy. This is no time for snivelling, I reckon.'

Tulipov turned away from the stretcher, gulped to dispel the murky veil that was clouding his eyes, and filled his lungs as full of air as he could. That was better.

Izhitsin couldn't be allowed to get away with that 'snivelling', and Anisii said in a flat, expressionless voice: 'My chief says determination and energy are good for chopping firewood and digging vegetable patches.'

'Exactly, my dear sir.' The investigator waved to the gendarmes to carry the body into the morgue. 'I'll damn well dig up the whole of blasted Moscow, and if it gets a bit messy, the result will justify it. If I don't get a result, my head's going to roll anyway. Have you been detailed to keep an eye on me, Tulipov? Do that then, but keep your comments to yourself. And if you feel like submitting a complaint, be my guest. I know Count Tolstoy; he appreciates determination and turns a blind eye to minor points of legality if liberties are taken in the interests of the case.'

'I have had occasion to hear that sort of thing from policemen, but such views sound rather strange coming from an official of the Public Prosecutor's Office,' said Anisii, thinking that was exactly what Erast Petrovich would have told Izhitsin if he had been in Anisii's place.

However, when the investigator simply shrugged off this dignified and restrained reprimand with a gesture of annoyance, Tulipov changed to an official tone of voice: 'Would you please stick closer to the point, Mr Court Counsellor. What is your plan?'

They went into the forensic medical expert's office and sat down at the desk, since Zakharov himself was working on the body in the autopsy theatre.

'Well, all right then,' said Izhitsin, giving this man he out-ranked a superior glance. 'So let's put our thinking caps on. Who does our belly-slasher kill? Streetwalkers, vagrants, beggars – that is, women from the lower depths of the city, society's discarded garbage. So now, let's remember where the killings have taken place. Well, there's no way to tell where the nameless bodies in the ditches were brought from. We know well enough that in such cases our Moscow police don't take too much trouble over the paperwork. But on the other hand, we do know where the bodies we dug out of the named graves came from.'

Izhitsin opened an exercise book with an oilcloth cover.

'Aha, look! The beggar Marya Kosaya was killed on the eleventh of February on Maly Tryokhsvyatsky Lane, at Sychugin's dosshouse. Her throat was cut, her belly was slit open, her liver is missing. The prostitute Alexandra Zotova was found on the fifth of February in Svininsky Lane, lying in the road. Again with her throat cut and her womb missing. These two are obvious clients.'

The investigator walked across to the police map of the city that was hanging on the wall and began jabbing at it with a long, pointed finger: 'So, let's take a look. Tuesday's And-reichkina was found just here, on Seleznyovskaya Street. Today's little girl was found by the Novotikhvinsk level crossing, right here. From one crime scene to the other it's no more than a *verst*. And it's the same distance to the Vypolzovo Tatar suburb as well.'

'What has the Tatar suburb got to do with anything?' Tulipov asked.

'Later, later,' said Izhitsin, with another impatient gesture. 'Just hold your horses . . . Now the two old bodies. Maly Tryokhs-vyatsky Lane – that's there. And there's Svininsky Lane. All in the same patch. Three hundred, maybe five hundred steps from the synagogue in Spasoglinishchevsky Lane.'

'But even closer to Khitrovka,' Anisii objected. 'Someone gets killed there every day of the week. That's no surprise: it's a hotbed of crime.'

'They get killed all right, but not like this! No, Tulipov, this smacks of something more than plain Christian villainy. I can sense a fanatical spirit at work in all these paunchings. An alien spirit. Orthodox folks get up to lots of beastly things, but nothing like this. And don't start with all that nonsense about the London Ripper being Russian and now he's come back for some fun and games in the land of his birth. That's rubbish! If a Russian can travel round cities like London, it means he comes from the cultured classes. And why would an educated man go rummaging in the stinking guts of some Manka Kosaya? Can you picture it?'

Anisii couldn't picture it and he shook his head honestly.

'Well then, you see. It's so obvious. You have to be a crackpot theoretician like your chief to abandon common sense for abstract intellectual postulates. But I, Tulipov, am a practical man.'

'But what about the knowledge of anatomy?' Anisii asked, dashing to his chief's defence. 'And the professional use of a surgical instrument? Only a doctor could have committed all these outrages!'

Izhitsin smiled triumphantly. 'That's where Fandorin is wrong! That hypothesis of his stuck in my throat from the very start. It does-n't hap-pen,' he said, hammering home every syllable. 'It simply doesn't happen, and that's all there is to it. If a man from respectable society is a pervert, then he'll think up something a bit more subtle than these abominations.' The investigator nodded in the direction of the autopsy room. 'Remember the Marquis de Sade. Or take that business last year with the notary Shiller – remember that? He got this bint blind drunk, stuck a stick of dynamite up her, you know where, and lit the fuse. An educated man – you can see that straight away; but a monster, of course. But only some low scum is capable of the loathsome abominations we're dealing with here. And as for the knowledge of anatomy and the surgical skill, you'll see that's all very easily explained, you know-alls.'

The investigator paused, raised one finger for dramatic effect and whispered: 'A butcher! There's someone who knows anatomy as well as any surgeon. Every day of the week he's separating out livers and stomachs and kidneys as neat and tidy as you like, every bit as precise as the late surgeon Pirogov. And a good butcher's knives are as sharp as any scalpel.'

Tulipov said nothing. He was shaken. The obnoxious Izhitsin was right! How could they have forgotten about butchers?

Izhitsin was pleased by Anisii's reaction. 'And now, about my plan.' He went up to the map again. 'Seems we have two focal points. The first two bodies were found over here, the last two – over here. What reason the criminal had for changing his area of activity we don't know. Perhaps he decided it was more convenient to commit murder in the north of Moscow than in the central district: waste lots, shrubs and bushes, not so many houses. To be on the safe side, I'm regarding all the butchers who live in either of the regions that interest us as possible suspects. I already have a list.' The investigator took out a sheet of paper and put it on the desk in front of Anisii. 'Only seventeen names in all. Note the ones that are marked with a six-pointed star or a crescent moon. This is the Tatar suburb, here in Vypolzovo. The Tatars have their own butchers, and real bandits they are. Let me remind you that it's less than a *verst* from the suburb to the shed where Andreichkina was found. It's the same distance to the railway crossing where the little girl's body was found. And here' – the long finger shifted across the map – 'in the immediate proximity of Tryokhsvyatsky and Svininsky Lanes, is the synagogue. That's where the kosher meat-carvers are, the filthy Yid butchers who kill the cattle in that barbarous fashion of theirs. Have you ever seen how it's done? Very much like the work of our good friend. Now do you get a whiff of where the case is heading?'

To judge from the pompous investigator's flaring nostrils, it was heading for a sensational trial, serious honours and breath-takingly rapid promotion.

'You're a young man, Tulipov. Your future's in your own hands. You can cling to Fandorin and end up looking stupid. Or you can work for the good of the cause and then I won't forget you. You're a smart lad, an efficient worker. I need helpers like you.'

Anisii was about to open his mouth to put the insolent fellow in his place, but Izhitsin was already carrying on with what he was saying: 'Of the seven butchers who interest us, four are Tatars and three are Yids. They're at the top of the list of suspects. But to avoid any reproaches of prejudice, I'm arresting the lot. And I'll give them a thorough working over. I have the experience for it, thank God.' He smiled rapaciously and rubbed his hands together. 'So right then. First of all I'll start by feeding the heathen scum salt beef, because they don't observe the Orthodox fast. They won't eat pork, so I'll order them to be given beef: we respect other people's customs. I'll give the Orthodox butchers a bit of salted herring. I won't give them anything to drink. Or let them sleep either. After they've been in for a night, they'll start howling, and in the morning, to make sure they don't get too bored, I'll call them out by turn and my lads will teach them a lesson with their "sticks of salami". Do you know what a "stick of salami" is?'

Tulipov shook his head, speechless.

'A most excellent little device: a stocking stuffed with wet sand. Leaves no marks, but it makes a great impression, especially applied to the kidneys and other sensitive spots.'

'But Mr Izhitsin, you're a university graduate!' Anisii gasped.

'Exactly, and that's why I know when to stick to the rules and when the interests of society allow the rules to be ignored.'

'And what if your theory's wrong and the Ripper isn't a butcher after all?'

'He's a butcher, who else could he be?' Izhitsin said with a shrug. 'Well, I've explained things convincingly enough, haven't I?'

'And what if it's not the guilty party that confesses, but the one with the weakest spirit? Then the real murderer will go unpunished!'

By this stage the investigator had become so insolent that he actually slapped Anisii on the shoulder: 'I've thought of that too. Of course, it won't look too good if we go and string up some Moshe or Abdul and then in three months or so the police discover another disembowelled whore. But this is a special case, bordering on a crime against the state – the Emperor's visit has been disrupted! And therefore, extreme measures are permissible.' Izhitsin clenched his fist so tight that his knuckles cracked. 'One of them will go to the gallows, and the rest will be exiled. By administrative order, with no publicity. To cold, deserted places where there aren't too many people to carve up. And even there the police will keep an eye on them.'

Anisii was horrified by the determined investigator's 'plan', although it was hard to deny the effectiveness of such measures. With a visit from the terrifying Count Tolstoy in the offing, the top brass would probably be frightened enough to approve the initiative, and the lives of a host of innocent people would be trampled into the dust. How could he prevent it? Ah, Erast Petrovich, where are you when you're needed?

Anisii gave a grunt, waggled his celebrated ears, mentally requested his chief's forgiveness for acting without due authority, and told Izhitsin about the previous day's investigative achievements. Just so he wouldn't get too carried away, let him be aware that, apart from his butchers, there were other, more substantial theories.

Leontii Izhitsin listened attentively without interrupting even once. His tense, nervous face first turned crimson, then began to turn pale, and at the end it came out in blotches, and his eyes had a drunken look.

When Tulipov finished, the investigator licked his thick lips with a whitish tongue and slowly repeated: 'A nihilist midwife? An insane student? A madcap merchant? Right, right . . .' Izhitsin leapt up off his chair and started running round the room and ruffling up his hair, doing irreparable damage to his perfect parting.

'Excellent!' he exclaimed, halting in front of Anisii. 'I'm very glad, Tulipov, that you have decided to collaborate openly with me. What secrets can there be between colleagues, after all; we're all doing the same job!'

Anisii felt a cold tremor run through his heart – he should have kept his mouth shut.

But there was no stopping the investigator now: 'All right, let's try it. I'll still arrest the butchers anyway, of course, but let them sit in cells for the time being. First let's get to work on your medicos.'

'How do you mean – "get to work"?' Anisii asked in panic, remembering the male nurse and the midwife. 'With the "salami stick"?'

'No; this class of people requires a different approach.'

The investigator thought for a moment, nodded to himself and put forward a new plan of action: 'Right then, this is what we're going to do. There's a different method for educated people, Tulipov. Education softens a man's soul, makes it more sensitive. If our belly-slasher comes from good society, then he's some kind of werewolf. During the day he's normal, like everyone else, and at night, in his criminal frenzy, it's as if he's possessed. That's where we'll catch him. I'll take the dear people in when they're normal and present them with the werewolf's handiwork. We'll see how their sensitive souls stand up to the sight. I'm sure the guilty party will break down. He'll see by the light of day what his alter ego gets up to and give himself away – he's bound to. That's psychology, Tulipov. Let's hold an investigative experiment.'

For some reason Anisii suddenly remembered a story his mother used to tell him when he was a child, keening in the plaintive voice of Petya-Petushka, the cock from the fairy-tale: 'The fox carries me off beyond the blue forests, beyond the high mountains, into her deep burrows . . .'

Chief, Erast Petrovich, things are looking bad, very bad.

Anisii did not participate in the preparations for the 'investigative experiment'. He stayed put in Zakharov's office, and in order not to think about the blunder he had committed, he began reading the newspaper lying on the desk – ploughing through it indiscriminately.

CONSTRUCTION OF THE EIFFEL TOWER COMPLETED

Paris. Reuters News Agency informs us that the gigantic and entirely useless structure of iron rods with which the French intend to astound visitors to the Fifteenth World Fair has finally been completed. This dangerous project is causing justified anxiety among the inhabitants of Paris. How can this interminable factory chimney be allowed to tower over Paris, dwarfing all the marvellous monuments of the capital with its ridiculous height? Experienced engineers express concern about whether such a tall and relatively slim structure, erected on a foundation only a third of its own height, is capable of withstanding the pressure of the wind.

A SWORD DUEL

Rome. The whole of Italy is talking about a sword duel that took place between General Andreotti and Deputy Cavallo. In the speech that he gave last week to veterans of the Battle of Solferino, General Andreotti expressed concern about Jewish dominance of the newspaper and publishing world of Europe. Deputy Cavallo, who is of Jewish origin, felt insulted by this entirely justified assertion and, speaking in parliament, he called the general a 'Sicilian ass', as a result of which the duel took place. In the second skirmish Andreotti was slightly wounded in the shoulder by a sword, after which the duel terminated. The opponents shook hands.

Anisii even read the advertisements: about a cooling glycerine powder, about a cream for galoshes, about the latest folding beds and nicotine-filtering cigarette holders. Overcome by a strange apathy, he spent a long time studying a picture with the following caption: 'The patented smell-free powder-closet using the system of mechanical engineer S. Timokhovich. Cheap and meets all the requirements of hygiene, can be located in any room in the home. At Adadurov's house near Krasnye Voroty you can observe the powder-closet in action. Can be rented out for dachas.'

After that he simply sat there and stared despondently out of the window.

Izhitsin, on the other hand, was a whirlwind of energy. Under his personal supervision they brought additional tables into the autopsy room, so that there were thirteen of them in all. The two gravediggers, the watchman and the constables carried three identified bodies out of the ice-room on stretchers, one of them the juvenile vagrant. The investigator gave several instructions for the bodies to be laid out this way or that way – he was striving for the maximum visual effect. Anisii simply shuddered when he heard Izhitsin's piercing, commanding tenor through the closed door:

'Where are you moving that table, you dolt! On three sides, I said, on three sides!' Or even worse: 'Not like that! Not like that! Open her belly up a bit wider! So what if it is all frozen together; use the spade, the spade! Right, now that's good.'

The prisoners were brought shortly after two in the afternoon, each one in a separate droshky with an armed guard.

Through the window Tulipov saw them bring the first one

into the morgue – a round-faced man with broad shoulders in a crumpled black tailcoat and a white tie that had slipped to one side – he could assume that he was the manufacturer Burylin, who hadn't managed to get home since being arrested the day before. About ten minutes later they brought Stenich. He was wearing a white coat (he must have come straight from the clinic) and glaring around like a trapped animal. Soon after that they brought in Nesvitskaya. She walked between two gendarmes with her shoulders held back and her head high. The midwife's face was contorted by an expression of hatred.

The door creaked and Izhitsin came into the office. His face was agitated and flaming red – a genuine theatrical entrepreneur on an opening night.

'For the moment our dear guests are waiting in the front office, under guard,' he told Anisii. 'Take a look and see if this is all right.'

Tulipov stood up listlessly and went into the dissection theatre.

In the middle of the wide room there was an empty space, surrounded on three sides by tables. Lying on each of them was a dead body covered by a tarpaulin. Standing along the walls behind the tables were the gendarmes, the constables, the gravediggers and the watchman: two men for each body. Zakharov was sitting on a chair beside the end table, wearing his perpetual apron and with his eternal pipe in his mouth. The forensic expert's face looked bored, even sleepy. Grumov was loitering behind him and a little to one side, like a wife with her everloving in a lower-middle-class photograph, except that he didn't have his hand on Zakharov's shoulder. The assistant had a dejected look – evidently the quiet man wasn't used to such large crowds in this kingdom of silence. The room smelled of disinfectant, but beneath the harsh chemical smell there was a persistent undercurrent: the sweet stench of decomposition.

On a separate, smaller table at one side there was a heap of paper bags. The prudent Izhitsin had provided for anything – somebody might easily be sick.

'I'll be here,' said Izhitsin, indicating the spot. 'They're here.

At my command these seven will take hold of one cover with their right hand and another cover with their left hand, and pull them off. It's a remarkable sight. You'll see it soon for yourself. I'm sure the criminal's nerves won't stand up to it. Or will they?' the investigator asked in sudden alarm, surveying his stage setting sceptically.

'They won't stand up to it,' Anisii replied gloomily. 'Not one of the three.'

His eyes met Pakhomenko's and the watchman gave him a sly wink, as if to say: Don't get upset, lad, remember that callus.

'Bring them in!' Izhitsin barked, turning towards the doors and then, hastily running into the centre of the room, he assumed a pose of stern inflexibility, with his arms crossed on his chest and one foot slightly advanced, his narrow chin jutting forward and his eyebrows knitted together.

They brought in the prisoners. Stenich immediately fixed his eyes on the terrible tarpaulins and tugged his head down into his hunched shoulders. He didn't even seem to notice Anisii and the others. Nesvitskaya, however, was not even slightly interested in the tables. She glanced round everybody there, rested her gaze on Tulipov and laughed contemptuously. Anisii blushed painfully. The captain of industry stood beside the table with the paper bags, leaning on it with one hand, and began turning his head this way and that curiously. Zakharov winked at him and Burylin nodded gently.

'I'm a forthright man,' Izhitsin began in a dry, piercing voice, emphasising every word. 'So I'm not going to beat about the bush here. In recent months there have been a number of brutal, monstrous murders in Moscow. The investigating authorities know for certain that these crimes were committed by one of you. I'm going to show you something interesting and look into your souls. I'm an old hand at detective work; you won't be able to fool me. So far the killer has only seen his or her own handiwork by night, while in the grip of insanity. But now you can see how lovely it looks by the light of day. All right!'

He waved his hand, and the tarpaulin shrouds seemed to slide to the floor by themselves. Linkov certainly spoiled the effect slightly – he tugged too hard, and the tarpaulin caught on the corpse's head. The dead head fell back on to the wooden surface with a dull thump.

It really was a spectacular sight. Anisii regretted he hadn't turned away in time, but now it was too late. He pressed his back against the wall, took three deep breaths, and it seemed to have passed.

Izhitsin did not look at the bodies. He stared avidly at the suspects, moving his eyes from one to the other in rapid jerks: Stenich, Nesvitskaya, Burylin; Stenich, Nesvitskaya, Burylin. And again, and again.

Anisii noticed that, although Senior Constable Pribludko was standing there motionless and stony-faced, the ends of his waxed moustache were quivering. Linkov was standing there with his eyes squeezed tight shut and his lips were moving – he was obviously praying. The gravediggers had expressions of boredom on their faces – they'd seen just about everything in their rough trade. The watchman was looking at the dead women in sad sympathy. His eyes met Anisii's and he shook his head very slightly, which surely meant: Ah, people, people, why do you do such things to each other? This simple human gesture finally brought Tulipov round. Look at the suspects, he told himself. Follow Izhitsin's example.

The former student and former madman Stenich was standing there cracking the knuckles of his slim fingers, with large beads of sweat on his forehead. Anisii would have sworn it was cold in there. Suspicious? No doubt about it!

But the other former student, Burylin, who had severed the ear, seemed somehow too calm altogether: he had a mocking smile hovering on his face and his eyes were glittering with evil sparks. No, the millionaire was only pretending that it all meant nothing to him – he'd picked up a paper bag from the table and was holding it against his chest. That was called an 'involuntary reaction' – the Chief had taught Anisii to take note of them in his very first lesson. A lover of the high life like Burylin could easily develop a thirst for new, intense sensations simply because he was so surfeited.

Now the woman of iron, Nesvitskaya, the former prison inmate, who had learned to love surgical operations in Edinburgh. An exceptional individual – you simply never knew what an individual like that was capable of and what to expect from her. Just look at the way her eyes blazed.

And the 'exceptional' individual immediately confirmed that she really was capable of acting unpredictably.

The deathly silence was shattered by her ringing voice: 'I know who your target is, Mister Oprichnik,' Nesvitskaya shouted at the investigator. 'How very convenient. A "nihilist" in the role of a bloodthirsty monster! Cunning! And especially spicy, because it's a woman, right? Bravo, you'll go a long way! I knew what kind of crimes your pack of dogs is capable of, but this goes far beyond anything I could have imagined!' The female doctor suddenly gasped and clutched at her heart with both hands, as if she'd been struck by sudden inspiration. 'Why, it was you! You did it yourselves! I should have realised straight away! It was your executioners who hacked up these poor women – why not? you've got no pity for "society's garbage"! The fewer of them there are, the simpler it is for you! You scum! Decided to play at Castigo, did you? Kill two birds with one stone, eh? Get rid of a few vagrants and throw the blame on the "nihilists"! Not very original, but most effective!' She threw her head back and laughed in scornful hatred. Her steel-rimmed pince-nez slid off and dangled on its string.

'Quiet!' Izhitsin howled, evidently afraid that Nesvitskaya's outburst would ruin his psychological investigation. 'Be silent immediately! I won't allow you to slander the authorities.'

'Murderers! Brutes! Satraps! Provocateurs! Scoundrels! Destroyers of Russia! Vampires!' Nesvitskaya shouted, and it was quite clear that her reserve of insults for the guardians of law and order was extensive and would not soon be exhausted.

'Linkov, Pribludko, shut her mouth!' the investigator shouted, finally losing all patience.

The constables advanced uncertainly on the midwife and took her by the shoulders, but they didn't seem to know how to go about shutting the mouth of a respectable-looking lady.

'Damn you, you animal!' Nesvitskaya howled, looking into Izhitsin's eyes. 'You'll die a pitiful death; your own intrigues will kill you!'

She threw up her hand, pointing one finger directly at the pompous investigator's face, and suddenly there was the sound of a shot.

Izhitsin jumped up in the air and bent over, clutching his head. Tulipov blinked: how was it possible to shoot anyone with your finger?

There was peal of wild laughter. Burylin waved his hands in the air and shook his head, unable to control his fit of crazy merriment. Ah, so that was it. Apparently, while everyone was watching Nesvitskaya, the prankster had quietly blown up a paper bag and then slammed it down against the table.

'Ha-ha-ha!' The captain of industry's smothered laughter soared up to the ceiling in an inhuman howling.

Stenich!

'I can't sta-a-and it!' the male nurse whined. 'I can't stand any more! Torturers! Executioners! Why are you tormenting me like this? Why? Lord, why, why?' His totally insane eyes slid across all of their faces and came to a halt, gazing at Zakharov, who was the only person there sitting down – sitting there silently with a crooked smile, his hands thrust into the pockets of his leather apron.

'What are you laughing at, Egor? This is your kingdom, is it? Your kingdom, your witch's coven! You sit on your throne and rule the roost! Triumphant! Pluto, the king of death! And these are your subjects!' He pointed to the mutilated corpses. 'In all their grace and beauty!' And then the madman started spouting rubbish that made no sense at all. 'Throw me out, unworthy! And you, you, what did you turn out to be worthy of? What are you so proud of? Take a look at yourself! Carrion crow! Corpse-eater! Look at him, all of you, the corpse-eater! And the little assistant? What a fine pair! One crow flies up to another; one crow says unto the other: "Crow, where can we dine together?"' And he started trembling and burst into peals of hysterical giggling.

249

The corners of the forensic expert's mouth bent down in a grimace of disapproval. Grumov smiled uncertainly.

A wonderful 'experiment', thought Anisii, looking at the investigator clutching his heart, and the suspects: one shouting curses, one laughing, one giggling. Well, damn you all, gentlemen.

Anisii turned and walked out. Phew, how good the fresh air was.

He called into his own apartment on Granatny Lane to check on Sonya and have a quick bowl of Palasha's cabbage soup, and then went straight to the Chief's house. What he was most anxious to learn about was what mysterious business Erast Petrovich had been dealing with today.

The walk to Malaya Nikitskaya Street was not very long – only five minutes. Tulipov bounded up on to the familiar porch and pressed the bell-button. There was no one there. Well, he supposed Angelina Samsonovna must be at church or in the hospital, but where was Masa? He felt a sharp stab of alarm: what if, while Anisii was undermining the investigation, the Chief had needed help and sent for his faithful servant?

He wandered back home listlessly. There were kids dashing about in the street and shouting. At least three of the urchins, the wildest, had black hair and slanting eyes. Tulipov shook his head, remembering that Fandorin's valet had the reputation of a sweetheart and a lady-killer among the local cooks, maids and laundrywomen. If things carried on like this, in ten years' time the entire district would be populated with Japanese brats.

He came back again two hours later, after it was already dark. Delighted to see light in the windows of the outhouse, he set off across the yard at a run.

The lady of the house and Masa were at home, but Erast Petrovich was absent, and it turned out that there hadn't been any news from him all day long.

Angelina didn't let her visitor go. She sat him down to drink tea with rum and eat éclairs, one of Anisii's great favourites.

'But it's the fast,' Tulipov said uncertainly, breathing in the heavenly aroma of freshly brewed tea, laced with the strong Jamaican drink. 'How can I have rum?'

'Oh, Anisii Pitirimovich, you don't observe the fast anyway,' Angelina said with a smile. She sat facing him, with her cheek propped on her hand. She didn't drink any tea or eat any éclairs. 'The fast should be a reward, not a deprivation. That's the only kind of fast the Lord needs. If your soul doesn't require it, then don't fast, and God be with you. Erast Petrovich doesn't go to church, he doesn't acknowledge the statutes of the Church, and it's all right – there's nothing terrible in that. The important thing is that God lives in his heart. And if a man can know God without the Church, then why coerce him?'

Anisii could hold back no longer, and he blurted out what had been on his mind for so long: 'Not all the statutes of the Church should be avoided. Even if it's not important to you, then you can think about the feelings of people close to you. Or else, well, see how it turns out. Angelina Samsonovna, you live according to the law of the Church, you observe all the rites, sin would never even dare come anywhere near you, but in the eyes of society . . . It's not fair, it's hurtful . . .'

He still wasn't able to say it directly and he hesitated, but clever Angelina had already understood him.

'You're talking about us living together without being married?' she asked calmly, as if it were a perfectly ordinary topic of conversation. 'Anisii Pitirimovich, you mustn't condemn Erast Petrovich. He has proposed to me twice, all right and proper. I was the one who didn't want it.'

Anisii was dumbstruck. 'But why not?'

Angelina smiled again, only this time not at Anisii, but at some thoughts of her own. 'When you love, you don't think about yourself. And I love Erast Petrovich. Because he's very beautiful.'

'Well that's true,' said Tulipov with a nod. 'A more handsome man would be hard to find.'

'That's not what I meant. Bodily beauty is not enduring. Smallpox, or a burn, and it's gone. Last year, when we were living in England, there was a fire in the house next door. Erast Petrovich went in to drag a puppy out of the flames and he got singed. His clothes were burned, and his hair. He had a blister on his cheek, his eyebrows and eyelashes all fell out. He was a really fine sight. His whole face could have been burned away. Only genuine beauty is not in the face. And Erast Petrovich really is beautiful.'

Angelina pronounced the last with special feeling, and Anisii understood what she meant.

'But I'm afraid for him. He has been given great strength, and great strength is a great temptation. I ought to be in church now: it's Great Thursday today, the commemoration of the Last Supper; but, sinner that I am, I can't read the prayers that I'm supposed to. I can only pray to our Saviour for him, for Erast Petrovich. May God protect him – against human malice, and even more against soul-destroying pride.'

At these words Anisii glanced at the clock and said anxiously: 'I must confess I'm more concerned about the human malice. It's after one in the morning and he's still not back. Thank you for the refreshments, Angelina Samsonovna; I'll be going now. If Erast Petrovich shows up, please be sure to send for me.'

As he walked home, Tulipov thought about what he'd heard. On Malaya Nikitskaya Street a saucy girl came dashing up to him under one of the gas lamps – a broad ribbon in her black hair, her eyes made up, her cheeks rouged.

'Good evening to you, interesting sir. Would you care to treat a girl to a little vodka or liqueur?' She raised and lowered her painted eyebrows and whispered passionately: 'And I'd be very grateful to you, handsome sir. I'd give you a time to remember for the rest of your life . . .'

Tulipov felt an ache somewhere deep inside him. The street-walker was good-looking – very good-looking, in fact. But since the last time he had given in to temptation, at Shrovetide, Anisii had renounced venal love. He felt awful afterwards, guilty. He ought to marry, but what could he do with Sonya?

Anisii replied with paternal sternness: 'You shouldn't be

wandering the streets at night. You never know, you might run into some crazy murderer with a knife.'

But the saucy girl wasn't bothered in the slightest. 'Oh, such concern. I don't reckon I'll get killed. We're watched – the boyfriend keeps an eye on us.'

And yes, there on the other side of the street, Anisii could see a silhouette in the shade. Realising he'd been spotted, the ponce came over unhurriedly, at a slovenly stroll. He was a very stylish specimen: beaver-fur cap pulled down over the eyes, fur coat hanging dashingly open, a snow-white muffler covering half his face and white spats as well.

He began speaking with a drawl, and a gold-capped tooth glinted in his mouth. 'I beg your pardon, sir. Either take the young lady or be on your way. Don't go wasting a working girl's time.'

The girl looked adoringly at her protector, and that angered Tulipov even more than her pimp's insolence.

'Don't you go telling me what to do!' Anisii said angrily. 'I'll drag you down to the station in no time.'

The ponce turned his head quickly to the left and the right, saw that the street was empty and inquired with an even slower, more menacing drawl: 'You sure the dragger won't come unstuck?'

'Ah, so it's like that, is it?' Anisii grabbed the rogue by his collar with one hand, and took his whistle out of his pocket with the other. There was a police constable's post round the corner on Tverskaya Street, and it was only a stone's throw to the gendarme station.

'Run for it, Ineska, I'll handle this!' the gold-toothed scoundrel said.

The girl immediately picked up her skirts and set off as fast as her legs would carry her, and the brazen ponce said in Erast Petrovich's voice: 'Stop blowing that thing, Tulipov. You've deafened me.'

The constable, Semyon Sychov, ran up, puffing and panting like a horse jangling its harness.

The Chief held out a fifty-kopeck piece to him: 'Good man, you're a fast runner.'

Semyon Lukich didn't take the money from the suspicious-looking man and glanced quizzically at Anisii.

'Yes, it's all right, Sychov, off you go my friend,' Tulipov said in embarrassment. 'I'm sorry for bothering you.'

Only then did Semyon Sychkov take the fifty kopecks, salute in a highly respectful manner and set off back to his post.

'How's Angelina – is she not sleeping?' Erast Petrovich asked, with a glance at the bright windows of the outhouse.

'No, she's waiting for you.'

'In that case, if you don't object, let's take a walk and have a little talk.'

'Chief, what's this masquerade in aid of? In the note it said you were going to approach things from the other side. What "other side" is that?'

Fandorin squinted at his assistant in clear disapproval. 'You're not thinking too well, Tulipov. "From the other side" means from the side of the Ripper's victims. I assumed that the women of easy virtue that our character seems to have a particular hatred for might know something we don't. They might have seen someone suspicious, heard something, g-guessed something. So I decided to do a bit of reconnaissance. These people aren't going to open up to a policeman or an official, so I chose the most appropriate camouflage. I must say that I've enjoyed distinct success in the role of a ponce,' Erast Petrovich added modestly. 'Several fallen creatures have volunteered to transfer to my protection, which has caused dissatisfaction among the competition – Slepen, Kazbek and Zherebchik.'

Anisii was not in the least surprised by his chief's success in the field of procuring – he was a really handsome fellow, and tricked out in full Khitrovka-Grachyovka chic too. Speaking aloud, he asked: 'Did you get any results?'

'I have a couple of things,' Fandorin replied cheerfully. 'Mamselle Ineska, whose charms, I believe, did not leave you entirely indifferent, told me an amusing little story. One evening a month and a half ago, she was approached by a man who said something strange: "How unhappy you look. Come with me and I'll bring you joy." But Ineska, being a commonsensical sort of girl, didn't go with him, because as he came up, she saw him hide something behind his back, and that something glinted in the moonlight. And it seems a similar kind of thing happened with another girl, either Glashka or Dashka. There was even blood spilt that time, but she wasn't killed. I'm hoping to find this Glashka-Dashka.'

'It must be him, the Ripper!' Anisii exclaimed excitedly. 'What does he look like? What does your witness say?'

'That's just the problem: Ineska didn't get a look at him. The man's face was in the shadow, and she only remembered the voice. She says it was soft, quiet and polite. Like a cat purring.'

'And his height? His clothes?'

'She doesn't remember. She admits herself that she'd taken a drop too much. But she says he wasn't a gent and he wasn't from Khitrovka either – something in between.'

'Aha, that's already something,' said Anisii, and he started bending down his fingers. 'Firstly, it is a man after all. Secondly, a distinctive voice. Thirdly, from the middle classes.'

'That's all nonsense,' the Chief said abruptly. 'The killer can quite easily change clothes for his n-nocturnal adventures. And the voice is suspicious. What does "like a cat purring" mean? No, we can't completely exclude a woman.'

Tulipov remembered Izhitsin' s reasoning. 'Yes, and the place! Where did he approach her? In Khitrovka?'

'No, Ineska's a Grachyovka lady, and her zone of influence takes in Trubnaya Square and the surrounding areas. The man approached her on Sukharev Square.'

'Sukharev Square fits too,' said Anisii, thinking. 'That's just ten minutes' walk from the Tatar suburb in Vypolzovo.'

'All right, Tulipov, stop.' The Chief himself actually stopped walking. 'What has the Tatar suburb to do with all this?'

Now it was Anisii's turn to tell his story. He began with the most important thing – Izhitsin's 'investigative experiment'.

Erast Petrocivh listened with his eyes narrowed. He repeated one word: 'Custigo?'

'Yes, I think so. That's what Nesvitskaya said. Or something like it. Why, what is it?'

'Probably "Castigo", which means "retribution" in Italian,'

Fandorin explained. 'The Sicilian police founded a s-sort of secret order that used to kill thieves, vagrants, prostitutes and other inhabitants of society's nether regions. The members of the organisation used to lay the blame for the killings on the local criminal communities and carry out reprisals against them. Well, it's not a bad idea from our midwife. You could probably expect that from Izhitsin.'

When Anisii finished telling him about the 'experiment', the Chief said gloomily: 'Yes, if one of our threesome is the Ripper, it won't be so easy to catch him – or her – now. Forewarned is forearmed.'

'Izhitsin said that if none of them gave themselves away during the experiment, he'd order them to be put under open surveillance.'

'And what good is that? If there are any clues, they will be destroyed. Every maniac always has something like a collection of souvenirs of sentimental value. Maniacs, Tulipov, are a sentimental tribe. One takes a scrap of clothing from the corpse, another takes something worse. There was one barbaric murderer, who killed six women, who used to collect their navels – he had a fatal weakness for that innocent part of the body. The dried navels become the most important clue. Our own "surgeon" knows his anatomy, and every time one of the internal organs is missing. I surmise that the killer takes them away with him for his collection.'

'Chief, are you sure the Ripper has to be a doctor?' Anisii asked, and he introduced Erast Petrovich to Izhitsin's butcher theory, and at the same time to his incisive plan.

'So he doesn't believe in the English connection?' Fandorin said in surprise. 'But the similarities with the London killings are obvious. No, Tulipov, this was all done by one and the same person. Why would a Moscow butcher go to England?'

'But even so, Izhitsin won't give up his idea, especially now, after his "investigative experiment" has failed. The poor butchers have been sitting in the lock-up since midnight. He's going to keep them there till tomorrow with no water and not let them sleep. And in the morning he's going to get serious with them.'

It was a long time since Anisii had seen the Chief's eyes glint so menacingly.

'Ah, so the plan is already being implemented?' the Collegiate Counsellor hissed through his teeth. 'Well then, I'll wager you that someone else will end up without any sleep tonight. And without a job too. Let's go, Tulipov. We'll pay Mr Pizhitsin a late visit. As far as I recall, he lives in a public-service apartment in the Court Department building. That's nearby, on Vozdvizhenskaya Street. Quick march, Tulipov, forward!'

Anisii was familiar with the two-storey building of the Court Department, where unmarried and seconded officials of the Ministry of Justice were accommodated. It was built in the British style, reddish brown in colour, with a separate entrance to each apartment.

They knocked at the doorman's lodge and he stuck his head out, half-asleep and half-dressed. For a long time he refused to tell his late callers the number of Court Counsellor Izhitsin's flat – Erast Petrovich looked far too suspicious in his picturesque costume. The only thing that saved the situation was Anisii's official cap with a cockade.

The three of them walked up the steps leading to the requisite door. The doorman rang the bell, tugged on his cap and crossed himself. 'Leontii Andreevich has a very bad temper,' he explained in a whisper. 'You gentlemen take responsibility for this.'

'We do, we do,' Erast Petrovich muttered, examining the door closely. Then he suddenly gave it a gentle push and it yielded without a sound.

'Not locked!' the doorman gasped. 'That Zinka, his maid – she's a real dizzy one. Nothing between the ears at all! You never know: we could easily have been burglars or thieves. Nearby here in Kislovsky Lane there was a case recently . . .'

'Sh-sh-sh,' Fandorin hissed at him, and raised one finger.

The apartment seemed to have died. They could hear a clock chiming, striking the quarter-hour.

'This is bad, Tulipov, very bad.'

Erast Petrovich stepped into the hallway and took an electric torch out of his pocket. An excellent little item, made in America:

you pressed a spring, electricity was generated inside the torch and it shot out a beam of light. Anisii wanted to buy himself one like it, but they were very expensive.

The beam roamed across the walls, ran across the floor and stopped.

'Oh, God in Heaven!' the doorman squeaked in a shrill voice. 'Zinka!'

In the dark room the circle of light picked out the unnaturally white face of a young woman, with motionless, staring eyes.

'Where's the master's bedroom?' Fandorin asked abruptly, shaking the frozen doorman by the shoulder. 'Take me there! Quickly!'

They dashed into the drawing room, from the drawing room into the study and through the study to the bedroom that lay beyond it.

Anybody might have thought that Tulipov had seen more than enough contorted dead faces in the last few days, but this one was more repulsive than anything he'd seen so far.

Leontii Andreevich Izhitsin was lying in bed with his mouth wide open.

The Court Counsellor's eyes were bulging out so incredibly far that they made him look like a toad. The beam of yellow light rushed back and forth, briefly illuminated some dark heaps of something around the pillow and darted away. There was a smell of decay and excrement.

The beam moved back to the terrible face. The circle of electric light narrowed and became brighter, until it illuminated only the top of the dead man's head.

On the forehead there was the dark imprint of a kiss.

It is astounding what miracles my skill can perform. It is hard to imagine a creature more repulsively ugly than that court official. The ugliness of his behaviour, his manners, his speech and his revolting features was so absolute that for the first time I felt doubt gnawing at my soul: could this scum really be as beautiful on the inside as all the rest of God's children?

And yet I managed to make him beautiful! Of course the male structure is far from a match for the female, but anybody who saw investigator Izhitsin after the work on him was completed would have had to admit that he was much improved in his new form.

He was lucky. It was the reward for his vim and vigour; and for making my heart ache with longing with that absurd spectacle of his. He awoke the longing – and he satisfied it.

I am no longer angry with him; he is forgiven. Even if because of him I have had to bury the trifles that were dear to my heart – the flasks in which I kept the precious mementoes that reminded me of my supreme moments of happiness. The alcohol has been emptied out of the flasks, and now all my mementoes will rot. But there is nothing to be done. It had become dangerous to keep them. The police are circling round me like a flock of crows.

It's an ugly job – sniffing things out, tracking people down. And the people who do it are exceptionally ugly. As if they deliberately choose that kind: with stupid faces and piggy eyes and crimson necks, and Adam's apples that stick out, and protruding ears.

No, that is perhaps unjust. There is one who is ugly to look at, but not entirely beyond redemption. I believe he is even rather likeable.

He has a hard life.

I ought to help the young man. Do another good deed.

CHAPTER 7

A Stenographic Report

Good Friday, 7 April

'... dissatisfaction and alarm. The sovereign is extremely concerned about the terrible, unprecedented atrocities that are being committed in the old capital. The cancellation of the Emperor's visit for the Easter service in the Kremlin is a quite extraordinary event. His Majesty has expressed particular dissatisfaction at the attempt made by the Moscow administration to conceal from the sovereign the series of murders, which, as it now appears, has been going on for many weeks. Even as I was leaving St Petersburg yesterday evening in order to carry out my investigation, the latest and most monstrous killing of all took place. The killing of the official of the Public Prosecutor's Office who was leading the investigation is an unprecedented occurrence for the entire Russian Empire. And the blood-chilling circumstances of this atrocity throw down a challenge to the very foundations of the legal order. Gentlemen, my cup of patience is overflowing. Foreseeing His Majesty's legitimate indignation, I take the following decision of my own volition and by virtue of the power invested in me ...'

The rain of words was heavy, slow, intimidating. The speaker surveyed the faces of those present gravely – the tense faces of the Muscovites and the stern faces of those from St Petersburg.

On the overcast morning of Good Friday an emergency meeting was taking place in Prince Vladimir Andreevich Dolgorukoi's study, in the presence of the Minister of Internal Affairs, Count Tolstoy, and members of his retinue, who had only just arrived from the capital.

This Orthodox champion of the fight against revolutionary devilment had a face that was yellow and puffy; the unhealthy skin sagged in lifeless folds below the cold, piercing eyes; but the voice seemed to be forged of steel – inexorable and imperious.

'. . . by the power I possess as minister, I hereby dismiss Major-General Yurovsky from his position as the High Police Master of Moscow,' the Count rapped out, and a sound halfway between a gasp and a groan ran through the top brass of the Moscow police.

'I cannot dismiss the district Public Prosecutor, who serves under the Ministry of Justice; however, I do emphatically recommend His Excellency to submit his resignation immediately, without waiting to be dismissed by compulsion . . .'

Public Prosecutor Kozlyatnikov turned white and moved his lips soundlessly, and his assistants squirmed on their chairs.

'As for you, Vladmir Andreevich,' the minister said, staring steadily at the Governor-General, who was listening to the menacing speech with his eyebrows knitted together and his hand cupped to his ear, 'of course, I dare not give you any advice, but I am authorised to inform you that the sovereign expresses his dissatisfaction with the state of affairs in the city entrusted to your care. I am aware that in connection with your imminent sixtieth anniversary of service at officer's rank, His Highness was intending to award you the highest order of the Russian Empire and present you with a diamond casket decorated with the monogram of the Emperor's name. Well, Your Excellency, the decree has been left unsigned. And when His Majesty is informed of the outrageous crime that was perpetrated last night . . .'

The Count made a rhetorical pause and total silence fell in the study. The Muscovites froze, because the cold breeze of the end of a Great Age had blown though the room. For almost a quarter of a century the old capital had been governed by Vladimir Andreevich Dolgorukoi; the entire cut of Moscow public-service life had long ago been adjusted to fit His Excellency's shoulders, to suit his grasp, that was firm yet did not constrain the comforts of life. And now it looked as if the old warhorse's end was near. The High Police Master and the Public Prosecutor dismissed from their posts without the sanction of the Governor-General of Moscow! Nothing of the kind had ever happened before. It was a sure sign that Vladimir Andreevich himself was spending his final days, or even hours, on his high seat. The toppling of the giant could not help but be reflected in the lives and careers of those present, and therefore the difference between the expressions on the faces of the Muscovites and those on the faces of the Petersburgians became even more marked.

Dolgorukoi took his hand away from his ear, chewed on his lips, fluffed up his moustache and asked: 'And when, Your Excellency, will His Majesty be informed of the outrageous crime?'

The minister narrowed his eyes, trying to penetrate the hidden motive underlying this question that appeared so simple-minded at first glance.

He penetrated it, appreciated it and laughed very quietly: 'As usual, from the morning of Good Friday the Emperor immerses himself in prayer, and matters of state, apart from emergencies, are postponed until Sunday. I shall be making my most humble report to His Majesty the day after tomorrow, before the Easter dinner.'

The Governor nodded in satisfaction. 'The murder of Court Counsellor Izhitsyn and his maid, for all the outrageousness of this atrocity, can hardly be characterised as a matter of state emergency. Surely, Minister, you will not be distracting His Imperial Highness from his prayers because of such a wretched matter? That would hardly earn you a pat on the back, I think?' Prince Dolorukoi asked with the same naive air.

'I will not.' The upward curls of the minister's grey moustache twitched slightly in an ironical smile.

The Prince sighed, sat upright, took out a snuff box and thrust a pinch into his nose. 'Well, I assure you that before noon on Sunday the case will have been concluded, solved, and the culprit exposed. A . . . a . . . choo!'

A timid hope appeared on the faces of the Muscovites.

'Bless you,' Tolstoy said morosely. 'But please be so good as to tell me why you are so confident? The investigation is in ruins. The official who was leading it has been killed.'

'Here in Moscow, my old chap, highly important investigations are never pursued along one line only,' Dolgorukoi declared in a didactic tone of voice. 'And for that purpose I have a special deputy, my trusted eyes and ears, who is well known to you: Collegiate Counsellor Fandorin. He is close to catching the criminal and in a very short time he will bring the case to a conclusion. Is that not so, Erast Petrovich?'

The Prince turned grandly towards the Collegiate Counsellor, who was sitting by the wall, and only the sharp gaze of the Deputy for Special Assignments could read the despair and entreaty in the protruding, watery eyes of his superior.

Fandorin got to his feet, paused for a moment and declared dispassionately: 'That is the honest truth, Your Excellency. I actually expect to close the case on Sunday.'

The minister peered at him sullenly. 'You "expect"? Would you mind giving me a little more detail? What are your theories, conclusions, proposed measures?'

Erast Petrovich did not even glance at Count Tolstoy, but carried on looking at the Governor-General.

'If Vladimir Andreevich orders me to, I will give a full account of everything. But in the absence of such an order, I prefer to maintain confidentiality. I have reason to suppose that at this stage in the investigation increasing the number of people who are aware of the details could be fatal to the operation.'

'What?' the minister exploded. 'How dare you? You seem to have forgotten who you are dealing with here!'

The gold epaulettes on shoulders from St Petersburg trembled in indignation. The gold shoulders of the Muscovites shrank in fright.

'Not at all.' And now Fandorin looked at the high official from the capital. 'You, Your Excellency, are an adjutant-general of the retinue of His Majesty, the Minister of Internal Affairs and Chief of the Corps of Gendarmes. And I serve in the chancellery of the Governor-General of Moscow and so do not happen to be your subordinate by any of the afore-mentioned lines. Vladimir Andreevich, is it your wish that I should give a full account to the minister of the state of how affairs stand in the investigation?'

Prince Dolgorukoi gave his subordinate a keen look and evi-dently decided that he might as well be hung for a sheep as a lamb. 'Oh, that will do. My dear minister, my old chap, let him investigate as he thinks best. I vouch for Fandorin with my own head. Meanwhile, would you perhaps like to try a little Moscow breakfast? I have the table already laid.'

'Well, your head it is, then,' Tolstoy hissed menacingly. 'As you will. On Sunday at precisely twelve thirty, everything will be included in my report in the presence of His Imperial Majesty. Including this.' The minister got up and stretched his bloodless lips into a smile. 'Well now, Your Excellency, I think we can take a little breakfast.'

The important man walked towards the door. As he passed Collegiate Counsellor Fandorin, he seared him with a withering glance. The other officials followed him, avoiding Erast Petro-vich by as wide a margin as possible.

'What are you thinking of, my dear fellow?' the Governor whispered, hanging back for a moment with his deputy. 'Have you taken leave of your senses? That's Tolstoy himself! He's vengeful and he has a long memory. He'll hound you to death; he'll find the opportunity. And I won't be able to protect you.'

Fandorin replied directly into his half-deaf patron's ear, also in a whisper: 'If I don't close the case before Sunday, neither you nor I will be here much longer. And as for the Count's vengeful nature, please do not be too concerned. Did you see the colour of his face? He won't be needing that long memory of his. Very soon he will be called to report, not to His Imperial Highness, but to a higher authority, the supreme one.'

'We all have to tread that path,' said Dolgorukoi, crossing

himself devoutly. 'We only have two days. You pull out all the stops, my dear chap. You'll manage it, eh?'

'I decided to provoke the wrath of that serious gentleman for a very excusable reason, Tulipov. You and I have no working theory. The murder of Izhitsin and his maid Matiushkina changes the whole picture entirely.'

Fandorin and Tulipov were sitting in a room for secret meetings located in one of the remote corners of the Governor-General's residence. The strictest instructions had been given that no one was to disturb the Collegiate Counsellor and his assistant. There were papers lying on the table covered in green velvet, and His Excellency's personal secretary was on continuous duty in the reception room outside the closed door, with a senior adjutant, a gendarme officer and a telephone operator with a direct line to the chancellery of the (now, alas, former) High Police Master, the Department of Gendarmes and the district Public Prosecutor (as yet still current). All official structures had been ordered to afford the Collegiate Counsellor the fullest possible cooperation. The Governor-General had taken the care of the formidable minister on his own shoulders – so that he would get in the way as little as possible.

Frol Vedishchev, Prince Dolgorukoi's valet, tiptoed into the study – he'd brought the samovar. He squatted modestly on the edge of a chair and waved his open hand through the air as if to say: I'm not here, gentlemen detectives; don't waste your precious attention on such small fry.

'Yes,' sighed Anisii, 'nothing's clear at all. How did he manage to reach Izhitsin?'

'Well that's actually no great puzzle. It happened like this . . .' Erast Petrovich strode across the room and took his beads out of his pocket with an accustomed gesture.

Tulipov and Vedishchev waited with bated breath.

'Last night, some time between half past one and two, someone rang the doorbell of Izhitsin's apartment. The doorbell is connected to the bell in the servant's room. Izhitsyn lived with his maid, Zinaida Matiushkina, who cleaned the apartment and his clothes and also, according to the statements of servants in the neighbouring apartments, fulfilled other duties of a more intimate character. However, it would seem that the deceased did not allow her into his bed and they slept separately. Which, by the way, corresponds perfectly to Izhitsin's well-known convictions concerning the "c-cultured" and "uncultured" classes. On hearing the ring at the door, Matiushkina threw on her shawl over her nightdress, went out into the entrance hall and opened the door. She was killed on the spot, in the entrance hall, by a blow to the heart with a sharp, narrow blade. Then the killer walked quietly though the drawing room and the study into the master's bedroom. He was asleep, there was no light – that was clear from the candle on the bedside table. The criminal appears to have managed without any light, a f-fact which is quite remarkable in itself, since, as you and I saw, it was absolutely dark in the bedroom. Izhitsin was lying on his back, and with a blow from an extremely sharp blade, the killer severed his trachea and his artery. While the dying man wheezed and clutched at his slit throat (you saw that his hand and the cuffs of his nightshirt were covered in blood), the criminal stood to one side and waited, drumming his fingers on the top of the secretaire.'

Anisii thought he was already used to everything, but this was too much, even for him. 'Oh come on, Chief, that's too much – the bit about the fingers. You told me yourself that when you're reconstructing a crime you mustn't fantasise.'

'God forbid, Tulipov; this no fantasy,' Erast Petrovich said with a shrug. 'Matiushkina really was a careless maid. There is a layer of dust on the top of the secretaire, and it has been marked by the numerous repeated impacts of fingertips. I checked the prints. They are a little blurred, but in any case they are not from Izhitsin's fingers ... I shall omit the details of the disembowelment. You saw the result of that procedure.'

Anisii shuddered and nodded.

'Let me draw your attention once again to the fact that, during the ... dissection, the Ripper somehow managed without any light. He obviously possesses the rare gift of being able to see in the dark. The criminal left without hurrying: he washed his hands in the washbasin and cleaned up the marks of his dirty feet in the rooms and the entrance hall with a cloth, and very thoroughly too. In general, he did not hurry. The most annoying thing is that everything indicates that you and I reached Vozdvizhenskaya Street only about a quarter of an hour after the killer left.' The Collegiate Counsellor shook his head in vexation. 'Those are the facts. Now for the questions and the conclusions. I will start with the questions. Why did the maid open the door to the visitor in the middle of the night? We don't know, but there are several possible answers. Was it someone they knew? If it was, then who knew them – the maid or the master? We don't know the answer. It is possible that the person who rang simply said that they had brought an urgent message. In his line of work Izhitsin must have received telegrams and documents at all times of the day and night, so the maid would not have been surprised. To continue. Why was her body not touched? And – even more interestingly – why was the victim a man, the first in all this time?'

'Not the first,' Anisii put in. 'Remember, there was a male body in the ditch at Bozhedomka too.'

It seemed like a useful and pertinent remark, but the Chief merely nodded 'yes, yes', without acknowledging Tulipov's retentive memory.

'And now the conclusions. The maid was not killed for the "idea". She was killed simply because, as a witness, she had to be disposed of. And so we have a departure from the "idea" and the murder of a man – and not just any man, but the man leading the investigation into the Ripper. An energetic, cruel man who would stop short at nothing. This is a dangerous turn in the Ripper's career. He is no longer just a maniac who has been driven insane by some morbid fantasy. He is now prepared to kill for new reasons that were previously alien to him – either out of the fear of exposure or c-confidence in his own impunity.'

'A fine business,' Vedishchev's voice put in. 'Streetwalkers won't be enough for this killer now. The terrible things he'll get up to! And I see you gentlemen detectives don't have a single clue to go on. Vladimir Andreevich and I will obviously be moving out of here. The devil take the state service – we could have a fine life in retirement – but Vladimir Andreevich won't be able to bear retirement. Without any work to do he'll just shrivel up and pine away. What a disaster, what a disaster ...'

The old man sniffed and wiped away a tear with a big pink handkerchief.

'Since you're here, Frol Grigorievich, sit quietly and don't interrupt,' Anisii said sternly. He had never before taken the liberty of talking to Vedishchev in that tone, but the Chief had not finished his conclusions yet; on the contrary, he was only just coming to the most important part, and then Vedishchev had stuck his oar in.

'However, at the same time, the departure from the "idea" is an encouraging symptom,' Fandorin said, immediately confirming his assistant's guess. 'It is evidence that we have already got very close to the criminal. It is now absolutely clear that he is someone who is informed about the progress of the investigation. More than that, this person was undoubtedly present at Izhitsin's "experiment". It was the investigator's first active move, and vengeance followed immediately. What does this mean? That in some way he himself was not aware of, Izhitsin annoyed or frightened the Ripper. Or inflamed his pathological imagination.'

As if in confirmation of this thesis, Erast Petrovich clicked his beads three times in a row.

'Who is he? The three suspects from yesterday are under surveillance, but surveillance is not imprisonment under guard. We need to check whether any of them could have evaded the police agents last night. To continue. We ourselves must personally investigate everybody who was present at yesterday's "investigative experiment". How many men were there in the morgue?'

Anisii tried to recall. 'Well, how many ... Me, Izhitsin,

Zakharov and his assistant, Stenich, Nesvitskaya, that, what's his name, Burylin, then the constables, the gendarmes and the men from the cemetery. I suppose about a dozen, or maybe more, if you count everybody.'

'Count everybody, absolutely everybody,' the Chief instructed him. 'Sit down and write a list. The names. Your impressions of each one. A psychological portrait. How they behaved during the "experiment". The most minute details.'

'Erast Petrovich, I don't know all of their names.'

'Then find out. Draw up a complete list for me; our Ripper will be on it. That is your task for today; get on with it. And meanwhile I'll check whether any member of our trio could have made a secret nocturnal outing.'

It's good to work with clear, definite instructions, when the task is within your ability and its importance is obvious and beyond all doubt.

From the residence the Governor's swift horses carried Tulipov to the Department of Gendarmes, where he had a talk with Captain Zaitsev, the commander of the mobile patrol company, about the two commandeered gendarmes, asking if he'd noticed anything strange about their characters, about their families and their bad habits. Zaitsev began to get alarmed, but Anisii reassured him. He said it was a top-secret and highly important investigation that required special supervision.

Then he drove to Bozhedomka. He called in to say hello to Zakhkarov, only it would have been better if he hadn't. The unsociable forensic specialist mumbled something unwelcoming and buried his nose in his papers. Grumov was not there.

Anisii also visited the watchman to find out about the grave-diggers. He didn't give the Ukrainian any explanations, and the watchman didn't ask any questions – he was a simple man, but he had a certain understanding and tact.

He went to see the gravediggers too, ostensibly to give them a rouble each as a reward for assisting the investigation.

He formed his own judgement about both of them. And that was it. It was time to go home and write out his list for the Chief.

When he finished the extensive document, it was already dark. He read it through, mentally picturing each person on it and trying to figure out if he fitted the role of a maniac or not.

The gendarme sergeant-major Siniukhin: an old trooper, a face of stone, eyes like tin – God only knew what he had in his soul.

Linkov. To look at, he wouldn't hurt a fly, but he made a very strange kind of constable. Morbid dreams, wounded pride, suppressed sensuality – there could be anything.

The gravedigger Tikhin Kulkov was an unpleasant character, with his haggard face and pockmarked jaw. What a face that man had – if you met someone like that in a deserted spot, he'd slit your throat without even blinking.

Stop! He'd slit your throat all right, but how could his gnarled and crooked hands manage a scalpel?

Anisii glanced at his list again and gasped. Beads of sweat stood out on his forehead and his throat went dry. Ah, how could he have been so blind? Why hadn't he realised it before? It was as if his eyes had been blinded by a veil. It all fitted! There was only one person in the entire list who could be the Ripper!

He jumped to his feet and dashed off, just as he was, without his cap or his coat, to see the Chief.

Masa was the only person in the outhouse: Erast Petrovich was out and so was Angelina, praying in the church. Yes, of course, today was Good Friday: that was why the church bells were tolling so sadly – for the procession of the Holy Shroud.

Ah, such bad luck! And there was no time to lose! Today's inquiries at Bozhedomka had been a mistake – he must have guessed everything! But perhaps that was for the best? If he'd guessed, then he'd be feeling anxious now, making moves. He had to be tracked down! Friday was almost over; there was only one day left!

Only one consideration made him doubt the correctness of

his inspiration, but there was a telephone in the house on Malaya Nikitskaya Street and that helped him resolve it. In the Meshchanskaya police district, which included Bozhedomka, Provincial Secretary Tulipov was well known and, despite the late hour, the reply to the question that was bothering him was given immediately.

The first thing Anisii felt was sharp disappointment: 31 October – that was too early. The last definite London killing had taken place on 9 November, so his theory didn't hold together. But today Tulipov's head was working quite remarkably well – if only it was always like this – and the catch was easily resolved.

Yes, the body of the prostitute Mary Jane Kelly had been discovered on the morning of 9 November, but by that time Jack the Ripper was already crossing the Channel! That killing, the most revolting of them all, could have been his farewell 'gift' to London, committed immediately before his departure for the continent. Anisii could check later to find out what time the night train left over there.

After that the whole thing simply fitted together by itself. If the Ripper left London on the evening of 8 November – that is, on 27 October in the Russian style – then he ought to have arrived in Moscow on precisely the thirty-first!

The mistake he and the Chief had made was that, when they checked the police passport offices, they had limited themselves to December and November and not taken the end of October into consideration. That accursed confusion of the two styles of date had thrown them off the track.

And that was it. The theory fitted down to the last jot and tittle.

He went back home for a moment: to put on something warm, get his 'Bulldog' and grab a quick bite of bread and cheese – there was no time to have a real supper.

While he was chewing, he listened to Palasha reading the Easter story from the newspaper to Sonya, syllable by syllable. The imbecile was listening intently, with her mouth half open. But who could tell if she really understood very much?

'In the provincial town of N,' Palasha read slowly, with feeling, 'last year on the eve of the glorious resurrection of Christ, a criminal escaped from the jail. He waited until all the townsfolk had gone to the churches for matins and crept into the apartment of a certain rich old woman who was respected by all, but who had not gone to the service because she was not well, in order to kill her and rob her.'

'Ooh!' said Sonya. My goodness, thought Anisii, she understands. And a year ago she wouldn't have understood a thing; she'd have just dozed off.

'At the very moment when the murderer was about to rush at her with an axe in his hand' – the reader lowered her voice dramatically – 'the first stroke of the Easter bell rang out. Filled with an awareness of the solemn holiness of that moment, the old woman addressed the criminal with the Christian greeting: "Christ is arisen, my good man!" This appeal shook the sinner to the very depths of his soul; it illuminated for him the deep abyss into which he had fallen and worked a sudden moral renewal within him. After several moments of difficult internal struggle, he walked over to exchange an Easter kiss with the old woman and then, breaking into uncontrollable sobbing . . .'

Anisii never learned how the story ended, it was time for him to rush away.

About five minutes after he had dashed off at breakneck speed, there was a knock at the door.

'Oh that crazy man,' Palasha said with a sigh; 'he's probably forgotten his gun again.'

She opened the door and saw that it wasn't him. It was dark outside – she couldn't see the face, but he was taller than Anisii. A quiet, friendly voice said: 'Good evening, my dear. Look, I wish to bring you joy.'

When the essential work had been completed – after the scene of the crime had been inspected, the bodies photographed and taken away, there was nothing left to do. And that was when Erast Petrovich began feeling really bad. The detectives had left and he was sitting alone in the small drawing room of Tulipov's modest apartment, gazing in a torpor at the blotches of blood on the cheerful bright-coloured wallpaper, and still he couldn't stop himself trembling. His head felt as empty as a drum.

An hour earlier Erast Petrovich had returned home and immediately sent Masa to fetch Tulipov. Masa had discovered the bloodbath.

At this moment Fandorin was not thinking of kind, affectionate Palasha, or even meek Sonya Tulipova, who had died a terrible death that could not possibly be justified by God or man. In the grief-stricken Erast Petrovich's head there was one short phrase hammering away over and over again: He won't survive this, he won't survive this, he won't survive this. There was no way that poor Tulipov could ever survive this shock. He would never see the nightmarish picture of the vicious mutilation of his sister's body, never see her round eyes opened wide in amazement; but he knew the Ripper's habits, and he would easily be able to imagine what Sonya's death had been like. And that would be the end of Anisii Tulipov, because no normal man could possibly survive something like that happening to people who were near and dear to him.

Erast Petrovich was in an unfamiliar state quite untypical of him: he could not think what to do.

Masa came in. Snuffling, he dragged in a rolled-up carpet and covered the terrible blotches on the floor, then he set about furiously scraping off the bloodstained wallpaper. That was right, the Collegiate Counsellor thought remotely, but it hardly did any good.

After a while Angelina also arrived. She put her hand on Erast Petrovich's shoulder and said: 'Anyone who dies a martyr's death on Good Friday will be in the Kingdom of Heaven, at the side of Christ.'

'That is no consolation to me,' Fandorin said in a dull voice, without turning his head. 'And it will hardly be any consolation to Anisii.'

But where was Anisii? It was already the middle of the night, and the boy hadn't slept a single wink last night. Masa said he'd called round without his cap, in a great hurry. He hadn't said anything or left a note.

It didn't matter: the later he turned up, the better.

Fandorin's head was absolutely empty. No surmises, no theories, no plans. A day of intensive work had produced very little. The questioning of the detectives who were keeping Nesvitskaya, Stenich and Burylin under surveillance, together with his own observations, had confirmed that, with a certain degree of cunning and adroitness, any one of the three could have slipped away and come back unnoticed by the police spies.

Nesvitskaya lived in a student hostel on Trubetskaya Street that had four exits or entrances, and the doors carried on banging until the dawn.

Following his nervous fit, Stenich was holed up in the Assuage My Sorrows clinic, to which the detectives had not been admitted. There was no way to check whether he had been sleeping or wandering round the city with a scalpel.

The situation with Burylin was even worse: his house was immense, with sixty windows on the ground floor, half of them concealed by the trees of the garden. The fence was low. It wasn't a house: it was a sieve, full of holes.

It turned out that any one of them could have killed Izhitsin. And the most terrible thing of all was that Erast Petrovich, convinced of the ineffectiveness of the surveillance, had cancelled it altogether. This evening the three suspects had had complete freedom of action!

'Don't despair, Erast Petrovich,' said Angelina. 'It's a mortal sin, and you especially have no right. Who else will find the killer, this Satan, if you just give up? There is no one apart from you.'

Satan, Fandorin thought listlessly. Ubiquitous, could be anywhere, any time, slip in through any opening. Satan changed faces, adopted any appearance, even that of an angel.

An angel. Angelina.

Freed from the control of his torpid spirit, his brain, so accustomed to forming logical constructions, obligingly joined the links up to form a chain.

It could even be Angelina – why couldn't she be Jack the Ripper?

She had been in England the previous year. That was one.

On the evenings when all the killings had taken place, she had been in the church. Supposedly. That was two.

She was studying medicine in a charitable society and already knew how to do many things. They taught them anatomy there too. That was three.

She was an odd individual, not like other women. Sometimes she would give you a look that made your heart skip a beat – but you couldn't tell what she was thinking about at such moments. That was four.

Palasha would have opened the door for her without thinking twice. That was five.

Erast Petrovich shook his head in annoyance, stilling the idling wheels of his insistent logic machine. His heart absolutely refused to contemplate such a theory, and the Wise One had said: 'The noble man does not set the conclusions of reason above the voice of the heart.' The worst thing was that Angelina was right: apart from him there was no one else to stop the Ripper, and there was very little time left. Only tomorrow. Think, think.

But his attempts to concentrate on the case were frustrated by that stubborn phrase hammering in his head: He won't survive this, he won't survive this.

The time dragged on. The Collegiate Counsellor ruffled up his hair, sometimes began walking around the room, twice washed his hands and face with cold water. He tried to meditate, but immediately abandoned the attempt – it was quite impossible!

Angelina stood by the wall, holding her elbows in her hands, watching with a sad insistence in her huge grey eyes.

Masa was silent too. He sat on the floor with his legs folded together, his round face motionless, his thick eyelids half-closed.

But at dawn, when the street was wreathed in milky mist,

there was the sound of hurrying feet on the porch, a determined shove made the unlocked door squeak open, and a gendarme officer came dashing into the room. It was Smolyaninov, a very capable, brisk young second lieutenant, with black eyes and rosy pink cheeks. 'Ah, this is where you are!' Smolyaninov said, glad to see Fandorin. 'Everybody's been looking for you. You weren't at home or in the department, or on Tverskaya Street! So I decided to come here, in case you were still at the scene of the murders. Disaster, Erast Petrovich! Tulipov has been wounded. Seriously. He was taken to the Mariinskaya Hospital after midnight. We've been looking for you ever since they informed us; just look how much time has gone by ... Lieutenant-Colonel Svershinsky went to the hospital immediately and all his adjutants were ordered to search for you. What's going on, eh, Erast Petrovich?'

Report by Provincial Secretary A.P. Tulipov
Personal Assistant to Mr E.P. Fandorin
Deputy for Special Assignments
of His Excellency the Governor-General of Moscow

8 April 1889, half past three in the morning

I report to your Honour that yesterday evening, while compiling the list of individuals suspected of committing certain crimes of which you are aware, I realised that it was absolutely obvious that the crimes indicated could only have been committed by one person, to whit, the forensic medical expert Egor Willemovich Zakharov.

He is not simply a doctor, but an anatomical pathologist – that is, cutting out the internal organs from human bodies is his standard, everyday work. That is one.

Constant association with corpses could have induced in him an insuperable revulsion for the whole human race, or else, on the contrary, a perverted adoration of the physiological arrangement of the human organism. That is two.

At one time he was a member of the Sadist Circle of medical

students, which testifies to the early development of depraved and cruel inclinations. That is three.

Zakharov lives in a public-service apartment at the police forensic morgue at Bozhedomka. Two of the murders (of the spinster Andreichkina and the unidentified beggar girl) were committed close to this place. That is four.

Zakharov often goes to England to visit his relatives, and he was there last year. The last time he came back from Britain was on 31 October last year (11 November in the European style) – that is, he could quite easily have committed the last of the London murders that was undoubtedly the work of Jack the Ripper. That is five.

Zakharov is informed of the progress of the investigation, and in addition, of all the people involved in the investigation, he is the only one who possesses surgical skills. That is six.

I could carry on, but it is hard for me to breathe and my thoughts are getting confused . . . I had better tell you about recent events.

After not finding Erast Petrovich at home, I decided there was no time to be lost. The day before I had been at Bozhedomka and spoken with the cemetery workers, which could not have escaped Zakharov's notice. It was reasonable to think that he would feel alarmed and give himself away somehow or other. To be on the safe side I took my gun with me – a Bulldog revolver that Mr Fandorin gave me as a present on my name day last year. That was a wonderful day, one of the best days in my life. But that has nothing to do with this case.

And so, about Bozhedomka. I got there by cab at ten o'clock in the evening; it was already dark. In the wing where the doctor has his quarters there was a light in one window, and I was glad that Zakharov had not run away. There was not a soul around. A dog started barking – they keep a dog on a chain by the chapel there – but I quickly ran across the yard and pressed myself against the wall. The dog went on barking for a while and then stopped. I put a crate by the wall (the window was high off the ground) and cautiously glanced inside. The lighted window was where Zakharov has his study. Looking in, I saw there were papers on the desk and the lamp was lighted. And he was sitting with his back to me, writing something, then tearing it up and throwing the pieces on the floor. I waited there for a long time, at least an hour, and he kept writing and tearing the paper up, writing and tearing it up. I wondered if I should arrest him. But I didn't have a warrant, and what if he was just writing some nonsense or other, or adding up some accounts? At seventeen minutes past ten (I saw the time on the clock), he stood up and went out of the room. He was gone for a long time. He started clattering something about in the corridor, then it went quiet. I hesitated about climbing inside to take a look at his papers, became agitated and let my guard down. Someone struck me in the back with something hot and I banged my forehead against the window sill as well. And then, as I was turning round, there was another burning blow to my side and one to my arm. I had been looking at the light, so I could not see who was there in the darkness, but I hit out with my left hand as Mr Masa taught me to do, and with my knee as well. I hit something soft. But I was a poor student for Mr Masa; I shirked my lessons. So that was where Zakharov had gone to from the study. He must have noticed me. When he started back to avoid my blows, I tried to catch up with him, but after I'd run a little distance, I fell down. I got up and fell down again. I took out my Bulldog and fired three shots into the air. I thought perhaps one of the cemetery workers would come running. I should not have fired. That probably only frightened them. I should have used my whistle. I didn't think of it; I was not feeling well. After that I do not remember very much. I crawled on all fours and kept falling. Outside the fence I lay down to rest and I think I fell asleep. When I woke up, I felt cold – very cold, although I had all my warm things on; I had especially put on a woolly jumper under my coat. I took out my watch and looked at it. It was already after midnight. That's it, I thought, the villain has got away. It was only then I remembered about my whistle. I started blowing

278

it. Soon someone came, I could not see who. They carried me. Until the doctor gave me an injection, I was in a kind of mist. But now it's better, you can see. I'm just ashamed of letting the Ripper get away. If only I had paid more attention to Mr Masa. I tried to do my best, Erast Petrovich. If only I'd listened to Mr Masa. If only . . .

POSTSCRIPT

At this point the stenographic recording had to be halted, because the injured man, who spoke in a lively and correct fashion at first, began rambling and soon fell into a state of unconsciousness, from which he never emerged. Dr K. I. Möbius was also surprised that Mr Tulipov had held on for so long with such serious wounds and after losing so much blood. Death occurred at approximately six o'clock in the morning and was recorded in the appropriate manner by Dr Möbius.

Lieutenant-Colonel of the Gendarmes Corps Sverchinsky
Stenographed and transcribed by Collegiate Registrar Arietti

A terrible night.

And the evening had begun so marvellously. The imbecile turned out wonderfully well in death – a real feast for the eyes. After this mas-terpiece of decorative art, it was pointless to waste any time on the maid, and I left her as she was. A sin, of course, but in any case there would never have been the same staggering contrast between external ugliness and internal Beauty.

My heart was warmed most of all by the awareness of a good deed accomplished: not only had I shown the youth the true face of Beauty, I had also relieved him of a heavy burden that prevented him from making his own life more comfortable.

And then it all finished so tragically.

The good young man was destroyed by his own ugly trade – sniffing things out, tracking people down. He came to his own death. I am not to blame for that.

I felt sorry for the boy and that led to sloppy work. My hand trembled.

The wounds are fatal, there is no doubt about that: I heard the air rush out of a punctured lung, and the second blow must have cut through the left kidney and the descending colon. But he must have suffered a lot before he died. This thought gives me no peace.

I feel ashamed. It is inelegant.

CHAPTER 8

A Busy Day

Holy Week Saturday, 8 April

The investigative group loitered at the gates of the wretched Bozhedomka Cemetery in the wind and the repulsive fine drizzle: Senior Detective Lyalin, three junior detectives, a photographer with a portable American Kodak, the photographer's assistant and a police dog-handler with the famous sniffer-dog Musya, known to the whole of Moscow, on a lead. The group had been summoned to the scene of the previous night's incident by telephone and given the strictest possible instructions not to do anything until His Honour Mr Collegiate Counsellor arrived, and they were now following their instructions strictly – doing nothing and shivering in the chilly embrace of the unseasonable April morning. Even Musya, who was so damp that she looked like a reddish-brown mop, was in low spirits. She lay down with her long muzzle on the soaking earth, wiggled her whitish eyebrows dolefully and even whined quietly once or twice, catching the general mood.

Lyalin, an experienced detective and a man who had been around a lot in general, was inclined by nature to scorn the caprices of nature and he wasn't bothered by the long wait. He knew that the Deputy for Special Assignments was in the Mariinskaya Hospital at that moment, where they were washing and dressing the poor wounded body of the servant of God Anisii, in recent times the Provincial Secretary Tulipov. Mr Fandorin was saying goodbye to his well-loved assistant; he would make the sign of the cross and then dash over to Bozhedomka in no time. It was only a five-minute journey anyway, and he presumed that the Collegiate Counsellor's horses were a cut above the old police nags.

No sooner had Lyalin had this thought than he saw a four-in-hand of handsome trotters with white plumes hurtling towards the wrought-iron gates of the cemetery. The coachman looked like a general, all covered in gold braid, and the carriage was resplendent, with its gleaming wet black lacquer and the Dolgorukoi crest on the doors.

Mr Fandonin jumped down to the ground, the soft springs swayed, and the carriage drove off to one side. It was evidently going to wait.

The newly arrived Chief was pale-faced and his eyes were burning brighter than usual, but Lyalin's keen eyes failed to discern any other signs of the shocks and sleepless nights that Fandorin had endured. On the contrary, he actually had the impression that the Deputy for Special Assignments' movements were considerably more sprightly and energetic than usual. Lyalin was about to offer his condolences, but then he looked a little more closely at His Honour's compressed lips and changed his mind. Extensive police experience had taught him it was best to avoid snivelling and just get on with the job.

'No one's been in Zakharov's apartment without you, according to instructions received. The employees have been questioned, but none of them has seen the doctor since yesterday evening. They're waiting over there.'

Fandorin glanced briefly in the direction of the morgue building, where several men were waiting, shifting from one foot to the other. 'I thought I made it clear: don't do anything. All right, let's go.'

Out of sorts, Lyalin decided. Which was hardly surprising in such sad circumstances. The man was threatened with the ruin of his career and now there was this upsetting business with Tulipov.

The Collegiate Counsellor ran lightly up on to the porch of Zakharov's wing and pushed at the door. It didn't yield – it was locked.

Lyalin shook his head – Dr Zakharov was a thorough man,

very neat and tidy. Even when he was making good his escape he hadn't forgotten to lock the door. A man like that wouldn't leave any stupid tracks or clues.

Without turning round, Fandorin snapped his fingers and the senior detective understood him without any need for words. He took a set of lock-picks out of his pocket, chose one that was the right length for the key, twisted and turned it for a minute or so, and the door opened.

The Chief walked swiftly round all the rooms, throwing out curt instructions as he went; his usual mild stammer had disappeared somehow, as if it had never existed. 'Check the clothes in the wardrobe. List them. Determine what is missing . . . Put all the medical instruments, especially the surgical ones, over there, on the table . . . There was a rug in the corridor – see that rectangular mark on the floor. Where has it gone to? Find it! What's this, the study? Collect all the papers. Pay especially close attention to fragments and scraps.'

Lyalin looked around and didn't see any scraps. The study appeared to be in absolutely perfect order. The agent was amazed once again by the fugitive doctor's strong nerve. He'd tidied everything up as neatly as if he were expecting guests. What scraps would there be here?

But just then the Collegiate Counsellor bent down and picked up a small, crumpled piece of paper from under a chair. He unfolded it, read it, and handed it to Lyalin.

'Keep it.'

There were only three words on the piece of paper: '*longer remain silent*'.

'Start the search,' Fandorin ordered and went outside.

Five minutes later, having divided up the sectors of the search among the detectives, Lyalin looked out of the window and saw the Collegiate Counsellor and Musya creeping through the bushes. Branches had been broken off and the ground had been trampled. That must be where the late Tulipov had grappled with the criminal. Lyalin sighed, crossed himself and set about sounding out the walls of the bedroom.

The search did not produce anything of great interest. A

pile of letters in English – evidently from Zakharov's relatives: Fandorin glanced through them rapidly, but didn't read them; he only paid attention to the dates. He jotted something down in his notebook, but didn't say anything out loud.

Detective Sysuev distinguished himself by discovering another scrap of paper, a bit bigger than the first, in the study, but its inscription was even less intelligible: *'erations of esprit de corps and sympathy for an old com'*.

For some reason the Collegiate Counsellor found this bit of nonsense interesting. He also looked very closely at the Colt revolver discovered in a drawer of the writing desk. The revolver had been loaded quite recently – there were traces of fresh oil on the drum and the handle. Then why hadn't Zakharov taken it with him, Lyalin wondered? Had he forgotten it, then? Or deliberately left it behind? But why?

Musya disgraced herself. Despite the mire, she went dashing after the scent pretty smartly, but then a massive, shaggy dog came flying out from behind the fence and started barking so fiercely that Musya squatted down on her hind legs and backed away, and after that it proved impossible to shift her from that spot. They put the watchman's dog back on its chain, but Musya had lost all her spirit. Sniffer-dogs are nervous creatures; they have to be in the right mood.

'Which of them is which?' Fandorin asked, pointing through the window at the cemetery employees.

Lyalin began reporting: 'The fat one in the cap is the supervisor. He lives outside the cemetery and has nothing to do with the work of the police morgue. Yesterday he left at half past five and he came this morning a quarter of an hour before you arrived. The tall consumptive-looking one is Zakharov's assistant; his name's Grumov. He's just got here from home recently as well. The one with his head lowered is the watchman. The other three are labourers. They dig the graves, mend the fence, take out the rubbish and so on. The watchman and the labourers live here and could have heard something. But we haven't questioned them in detail, since we were told not to.'

The Collegiate Counsellor talked with the employees himself.

He called them into the building and first of all showed them the Colt: 'Do you recognise it?'

The assistant Grumov and the watchman Pakhomenko testified (Lyalin wrote in his notes) that they were familiar with the weapon – they had seen it, or one just like it, in the doctor's apartment. However, the gravedigger Kulkov testified that he had never seen any 'revolvert' close up, but the previous month he had gone to watch the 'doctur' shooting rooks, and he had done it very tidily: every time he fired, rooks' feathers went flying.

The three shots fired last night by Provincial Secretary Tulipov had been heard by the watchman Pakhomenko and the labourer Khriukin. Kulkov had been in a drunken sleep and the noise had not wakened him.

Those who had heard the shots said they'd been afraid to go outside – how could you tell who might be wandering about in the middle of the night? – and they apparently had not heard any cries for help. Soon afterwards Khriukin had gone back to sleep, but Pakhomenko had stayed awake. He said that shortly after the shooting a door had slammed loudly and someone had walked rapidly towards the gates.

'What, were you listening then?' Fandorin asked the watchman.

'Of course I was,' Pakhomenko replied. 'There was shooting. And I sleep badly at nights. All sorts of thoughts come into my head. I was tossing and turning until first light. Tell me, pan general, has that young lad really passed away? He was so sharpeyed, and he was kind with simple folk.'

The Collegiate Counsellor was known always to be polite and mild-mannered with his subordinates, but today Lyalin could barely recognise him. The Chief gave no reply to the watchman's touching words and showed no interest at all in Pakhomeno's nocturnal thoughts. He swung round sharply and spoke curtly over his shoulder to the witnesses: 'You can go. No one is to leave the cemetery. But you, Grumov, be so good as to stay.'

Well, he was like a totally different man.

The doctor's assistant blinked in fright as Fandorin asked him:

'What was Zakharov doing yesterday evening? In detail, please.'

Grumov shrugged and spread his hands guiltily: 'I couldn't say. Yesterday Egor Willemovich was badly out of sorts; he kept cursing all the time, and after lunch he told me to go home. So I went. We didn't even say goodbye – he locked himself in his study.'

'"After lunch" – what time is that?'

'After three, sir.'

'"After three, sir",' the Collegiate Counsellor repeated, shaking his head for some reason, and clearly losing all interest in the consumptive morgue assistant. 'You can go.'

Lyalin approached the Collegiate Counsellor and delicately cleared his throat. 'I've jotted down a verbal portrait of Zakharov. Would you care to take a look?'

Fandorin didn't even glance at the excellently composed description; he just waved it away. It was rather upsetting to see such a lack of respect for professional zeal.

'That's all,' Fandorin said curtly. 'There's no need to question anyone else. You, Lyalin, go to the Assuage My Sorrows Hospital in Lefortovo and bring the male nurse Stenich to me on Tver-skaya Street. And Sysuev can go to the Yakimanka Embankment and bring the factory-owner Burylin. Urgently.'

'But what about the verbal portrait of Zakharov?' Lyalin asked, his voice trembling. 'I expect we're going to put him on the wanted list, aren't we?'

'No, we're not,' Fandorin replied absent-mindedly, and strode off rapidly towards his wonderful carriage, leaving the experienced detective totally bemused.

Vedishchev was waiting in the Collegiate Counsellor's office on Tverskaya Street. 'The final day,' Dolgorukoi's 'grey cardinal' said sternly instead of saying hello. 'We have to find that crazy Englishman. Find him and then report it, all right and proper. Otherwise you know what will happen.'

'And how do you come to know about Zakharov, Frol Gri-gorievich?' Fandorin asked, although he didn't seem particularly surprised.

'Vedishchev knows everything that happens in Moscow.'

'We should have included you in the list of suspects, then. You put His Excellency's cupping jars on and even let his blood, don't you? So practising medicine is nothing new to you.' The joke, however, was made in a flat voice and it was clear that Fandorin was thinking about something quite different.

'Poor old Anisii, eh?' Vedishchev sighed. 'That's really terrible, that is. He was a bright lad, our shorty. He should have gone a long way, from all the signs.'

'I wish you would go to your own room, Frol Grigorievich,' was the Collegiate Counsellor's reply to that. He was clearly not inclined to indulge in sentimentality today.

The valet knitted his grey eyebrows in a frown of annoyance and changed to an official tone of voice: 'I have been ordered to inform Your Honour that the Minister of the Interior left for St Petersburg this morning in a mood of great dissatisfaction and before he left he was being very threatening. I was also ordered to inquire if the inquiry will soon be closed.'

'Soon. Tell His Excellency that I need to carry out just two more interrogations, receive one telegram and make a little excursion.'

'Erast Petrovich, in Christ's name, will you manage it before tomorrow?' Vedishchev asked imploringly. 'Or we're all done for.'

Fandorin had no time to reply to the question, because there was a knock at the door and the duty adjutant announced: 'The prisoners Stenich and Burylin have been delivered. They are being kept in separate rooms, as ordered.'

'Bring Stenich in first,' Erast Petrovich told the officer, and pointed the valet towards the door with his chin. 'This is the first interrogation. That's all, Frol Grigorievich – go, I have no more time.'

The old man nodded his bald head submissively and hobbled towards the door. In the doorway he collided with a wild-looking man – skinny and jittery with long hair – but he didn't stare at him. He shuffled off rapidly along the corridor in his felt shoes, turned a corner and unlocked a closet with a key.

But it turned out not to be any ordinary closet: it had a concealed door in the inside corner. Behind the little door there was another small closet. Frol Grigorievich squeezed into it, sat down on a chair with a comfortable cushion on it, silently slid opened a small shutter in the wall and suddenly he was looking though glass at the whole of the secret study, and he could hear Erast Petrovich's slightly muffled voice: 'Thank you. For the time being you'll have to stay at the police station. For your own safety.'

The valet put on a pair of spectacles with thick lenses and pressed his face up close to the secret opening, but he only saw the back of the man leaving the room. So that was an interrogation, was it? – it hadn't even lasted three minutes. Vedishchev grunted sceptically and waited to see what would come next.

'Send in Burylin,' Fandorin ordered the adjutant.

A man with a fat Tatar face and insolent eyes came in. Without waiting to be invited, he sat down on a chair, crossed his legs and began swinging his expensive cane with a gold knob. It was obvious straight away that he was a millionaire.

'Well, are you going to take me to look at offal again?' the millionaire asked merrily. 'Only you won't catch me out like that. I have a thick skin. Who was that who went out? Vanka Stenich, wasn't it? Ooh, he turned his face away. As if he'd not had plenty of pickings from Burylin. He rode around Europe on my money, and he lived as my house guest. I felt sorry for him, the poor unfortunate. But he abused my hospitality. Ran away from me to England. Began to despise me – I was dirty and he decided he wanted a clean life. Well, let him go; he's a hopeless man – a genuine psychiatric case. Will you permit me to smoke a small cigar?'

All of the millionaire's questions went unanswered. Instead, Fandorin asked his own question, which Vedishchev didn't understand at all. 'At your meeting of fellow-students there was a man with long hair, rather shabby. Who is he?'

But Burylin understood the question and answered it willingly: 'Filka Rozen. He was thrown out of the medical faculty with me and Stenich, distinguished himself with honours in the line of immoral behaviour. He works as an assessor in a pawn shop. And he drinks, of course.'

'Where can I find him?'

'You won't find him anywhere. Before you came calling, like a fool I gave him five hundred roubles – turned sloppy in my old age, thinking of the old days. Until he's drunk it all to the last kopeck, he won't show up. Maybe he's living it up in some tavern in Moscow, or maybe in Peter, or maybe in Nizhny. That's the kind of character he is.'

For some reason this news made Fandorin extremely upset. He even jumped up off his chair, pulled those round green beads on a string out of his pocket and put them back again.

The man with the fat face observed the Collegiate Counsellor's strange behaviour with curiosity. He took out a fat cigar, lit it and scattered the ash on the carpet, the insolent rogue. But he didn't start asking questions; he waited.

'Tell me: why were you, Stenich and Rozen thrown out of the faculty, while Zakharov was only transferred to the anatomical pathology department?' Fandorin asked after a lengthy pause.

'It depended on who got up to how much mischief,' Burylin said with a laugh. 'Sotsky, the biggest hothead amongst us, actually got sent to a punitive battalion. I felt sorry for the old dog; he had imagination, even if he was a rogue. I was under threat too, but it was all right: money got me out of it.' He winked a wild eye and puffed out cigar smoke. 'The girl students, our jolly companions, got it in the neck too – just for belonging to the female sex. They were sent to Siberia, under police surveillance. One became a morphine addict, another married a priest – I made inquiries.' The millionaire laughed. 'And at that time Zakharka the Englishman wasn't really outstanding in any way – that's why he got off with a lesser punishment. "He was present and did not stop it" – that's what the verdict said.'

Fandorin snapped his fingers as if he had just received a piece of good news that he'd been expecting for ages, but then Burylin took a piece of paper folded into four out of his pocket.

'It's odd that you should ask about Zakharov. This morning I received a very strange note from him, just a moment before your dogs arrived to take me away. A street urchin brought it. Here, read it.'

Frol Grigorievich twisted himself right round and flattened his nose against the glass, but there was no point – he couldn't read the letter from a distance. Only it was clear from all the signs that this was a highly important piece of paper. Erast Petrovich' s eyes were glued to it.

'I'll give him some money, of course,' said the millionaire. 'Only there wasn't any special "old friendship" between the two of us; he's just being sentimental there. And what kind of melodrama is this: "Please remember me kindly, my brother"? What has he been up to, our Pluto? Did he dine on those girls that were lying on the tables in the morgue the other day?' Burylin threw his head back and laughed, delighted with his joke.

Fandorin was still examining the note. He walked across to the window, lifted the sheet of paper higher, and Vedishchev saw the scrawling, uneven lines of writing.

'Yes, it's such terrible scribble you can hardly even read it,' the millionaire said in his deep voice, looking round for somewhere to put the cigar he had finished smoking. 'As if it was written in a carriage or with a serious hangover.'

He didn't find anywhere. He almost threw it to the floor, but decided not to; he cast a guilty glance at the Collegiate Counsellor's back, wrapped the stub in his handkerchief and put it in his pocket. That's right.

'You can go, Burylin,' Erast Petrovich said without turning round. 'Until tomorrow you will remain under guard.'

The millionaire was highly incensed at that news. 'I've had enough; I've already spent one night feeding your police bedbugs! They're vicious beasts, and hungry. The way they threw themselves on an Orthodox believer's body!'

Fandorin wasn't listening. He pressed the bell button. The gendarme officer came in and dragged the rich man towards the door.

'But what about Zakharka?' Burylin shouted. 'He'll be calling for the money!'

'That's no concern of yours,' said Erast Petrovich, and he asked the officer: 'Has the reply to my inquiry arrived from the ministry?'

'Yes, sir.'

'Let me have it.'

The gendarme brought in some kind of telegram and went back out into the corridor.

The telegram produced a remarkable effect on Fandorin. He read it, threw it on to the desk and then suddenly did something very strange. He clapped his hands very quickly several times, and so loudly that Vedishchev banged his head against the glass in his surprise, and the gendarme, the adjutant and the secretary stuck their heads in at the door all at once.

'It's all right, gentlemen,' Fandorin reassured them. 'It's a Japanese exercise for focusing one's thoughts. Please go.'

And then even more wonders followed.

When the door closed behind his subordinates, Erast Petrovich suddenly started to get undressed. When he was left in just his underclothes, he took a travelling bag that Vedishchev hadn't noticed before out from under the desk and took a bundle out of the bag. The bundle contained clothes: tight striped trousers with footstraps, a cheap paper shirt-front, a crimson waistcoat and yellow check jacket.

The highly respectable Collegiate Counsellor was transformed into a pushy jerk, the kind that hover around the street girls in the evenings. He stood in front of the mirror, exactly a yard in front of Frol Vedishchev, combed his black hair into a straight parting, plastered it with brilliantine and coloured the grey at his temples. He twisted the ends of his slim moustache upwards and shaped them into two sharp points. (Bohemian wax, Frol Vedishchev guessed – he secured Prince Dolgorukoi's sideburns in exactly the same way, so that they stuck out like eagles' wings.)

Then Fandorin put something into his mouth and grinned, and a gold cap glinted on one tooth. He carried on pulling faces for a while and seemed perfectly content with his appearance.

The Yuletide masker took a small wallet out of the bag, opened it, and Vedishchev saw that it was no ordinary wallet: inside it he could see a small-calibre burnished steel gun barrel and a little drum like the one on a revolver. Fandorin put five shells into the drum, clicked the lid shut and tested the resistance of the lock with his finger – no doubt the lock played the role of a trigger. What will they think of next for killing a man? the valet thought, with a shake of his head. And where are you going dressed like a cheap dandy, Erast Petrovich?

As if he had heard the question, Fandorin turned towards the mirror and put on a beaver-fur cap, tilted at a dashing angle, winked familiarly and said in a low voice: 'Frol Grigorievich, light a candle for me at vespers. I won't get by without God's help today.'

Ineska was suffering very badly, in body and in spirit – in body, because last night Slepen, her former ponce, had waited for the poor girl outside the City of Paris tavern and given her a thorough beating for betraying him. At least the creep hadn't rearranged her face. But her stomach and sides were battered black and blue – she couldn't even turn over at night; she just lay there shifting about until morning, gasping and feeling sorry for herself. The bruises weren't the worst thing – they'd heal up soon enough, but poor Ineska's little heart was aching so badly she could hardly stand it.

Her boyfriend had disappeared, her fairy-tale prince, the handsome Erastushka; he hadn't shown his sweet face for two days now. And Slepen was as brutal as ever and always making threats. Yesterday she'd had to give her old pimp almost everything she earned, and that was no good; decent girls who stayed faithful didn't do that.

Erastushka had gone missing; that lop-eared short-arse must have handed him over to the police and her pretty dove was sitting in the lock-up in the first Arbat station, the toughest in the whole of Moscow. If only she could send her darling a present, but that Sergeant Kulebyako there was a wild beast. He'd put her inside again, the same as last year, threaten to take away her yellow ticket, and then she'd end up servicing the whole police district for free, down to the last snot-nosed constable. It still made her sick to remember it, even now. Ineska would gladly have accepted that kind of humiliation if she could just help her sweetheart, but after all, Erastushka wasn't just any boyfriend: he had brains, he was nice and clean, choosy; he wouldn't want to touch Ineska after that. Not that their passion had actually come to anything yet, so to speak; love was only just beginning, but from the very first glance Ineska had taken such a fancy to his lovely blue eyes and white teeth, she'd really fallen for him; terrible it was, worse than with that hairdresser Zhorzhik when she was sixteen, rot his pretty face, the lousy snake – if he hadn't drunk himself to death by now, of course.

Ah, if only he'd show up soon, her sweet honey-bunch. He'd put that vicious bastard Slepen in his place and he'd be sweet and gentle with Ineska, pamper her a bit. She'd found out what he'd told her to, and hidden some money in her garter too – three and a half roubles in silver. He'd be pleased; she had something to greet him and treat him with.

Erastik. It was such a sweet name, like apple jam. Her darling's real name was probably something simpler, but then Ineska hadn't been a Spanish girl all her life either; she'd been born into God's world as Efrosinya, plain simple Froska in the family.

Inessa and Erast – that had a real ring to it, like music it was. If only she could stroll arm-in-arm with him through Grachyovka, so that Sanka Myasnaya, Liudka Kalancha and especially that Adelaidka could see what a fine fancy-man Ineska had, and turn green with envy.

After that, they'd come to her apertiment. It might be small, but it was clean, and stylish too: pictures from fashion magazines stuck on the walls, a velvet lampshade, and a big, tall mirror; the softest down mattress ever, and lots of pillows, a whole seven of them – Ineska had sewn all the pillowcases herself

Then, just as she was thinking her very sweetest thoughts, her cherished dream came true. First there was a tactful knock at the door – tap-tap-tap – and then Erastushka came in, in his beaver-fur cap and white muffler, with his wool-cloth coat with the beaver collar, hanging open. You'd never think he was from the Kutuzka jail.

Ineska's little heart just stood still. She leapt up off the bed just as she was, in her cotton nightshirt, with her hair hanging loose, and threw herself on her sweetheart's neck. She only managed to kiss his lips once; then he took hold of her by the shoulders and sat her down at the table. He looked at her sternly.

'Right, tell me,' he said.

Ineska understood – those vicious tongues had already been wagging.

She didn't try to deny anything; she wanted everything to be honest between them. 'Beat me,' she said, 'beat me, Erastushka; I'm to blame. Only I'm not all that much to blame – don't you go believing just anyone. Slepen tried to force me' (she was fibbing there, of course, but not so much really) 'and I wouldn't give him it, and he gave me a real battering. Here, look.'

She pulled up her shirt and showed him the blue, crimson and yellow patches. So he would feel sorry for her.

But it didn't soften him. Erastushka frowned. 'I'll have a word with Slepen afterwards; he won't bother you again. Get back to the point. Did you find who I told you to? – the one who went with that friend of yours and barely came out alive?'

'I did, Erastushka, I found her; Glashka's her name. Glashka Beloboka from Pankratievsky Lane. She remembers the bastard all right – he nearly slit her throat open with that knife of his. Glashka still wraps a scarf round her neck, even now.'

'Take me to her.'

'I will, Erastushka, I'll take you, but let's have a bit of cognac first.' She took a bottle she'd been keeping out of the little cupboard, put her bright-coloured Persian shawl on her shoulders and picked up a comb to fluff up her hair and make it all glossy.

'We'll have a drink later. I told you: take me there. Business first.'

Ineska sighed, feeling her heart melting: she loved strict men – couldn't help herself. She went over and looked up into his beautiful face, his angry eyes, his curly moustache. 'I think my legs are giving way, Erastushka,' she whispered faintly.

But today wasn't Ineska's day for kissing and cuddling. There was a sudden crash and a clatter from a blow that almost knocked the door off its hinges, and there was Slepen standing in the doorway, evil drunk, with a vicious grin on his smarmy face. Oh the neighbours, those lousy Grachyovka rats, they'd told on her; they hadn't wasted any time.

'Lovey-doving?' he grinned. 'Forgotten about me, the poor orphan, have you?' Then the grin vanished from his rotten mug and his shaggy eyebrows moved together. 'I'll talk to you, Ineska, afterwards, you louse. Seems like you didn't learn your lesson. And as for you, mate, come out in the yard and we'll banter.'

Ineska rushed to the window – there were two of them in the yard: Slepen's stooges, Khryak and Mogila.

'Don't go!' she shouted. 'They'll kill you! Go away, Slepen, I'll make such a racket all Grachyovka'll come running' – and she had already filled her lungs with air to let out a howl; but Erastushka stopped her.

'Don't, Ineska, you heard what he said; let me have a talk with the man.'

'Erastik, Mogila carries a sawn-off under his coat,' Ineska explained to the dimwit. 'They'll shoot you. Shoot you and dump you in the sewer. They've done it before.'

But her boyfriend wouldn't listen; he wasn't interested. He took a big wallet out of his pocket, tortoiseshell. "Salright,' he said. 'I'll buy 'em off.' And he went out with Slepen, to certain death.

Ineska collapsed face down into the seven pillows and started whimpering – about her malicious fate, about her dream that hadn't come true, about the constant torment.

Out in the yard there were one, two, three, four quick shots, and then someone started howling – not just one person, a whole choir of them.

Ineska stopped whimpering and looked at the icon of the Mother of God in the corner, decorated for Easter with paper flowers and little coloured lamps. 'Mother of God,' Ineska asked her, 'work a miracle for Easter Sunday and let Erastushka be alive. It's all right if he's wounded; I'll nurse him well. Just let him be alive.'

The Heavenly Mediatress took pity on Ineska – the door creaked and Erastik came in. And not even wounded – he was as right as rain, and his lovely scarf hadn't even shifted a bit.

'There, I told you, Ineska; wipe that wet off your face. Slepen won't touch you any more; he can't. I put holes in both his grabbers. And the other two won't forget in a hurry either. Get dressed and take me to this Glashka of yours.'

And that dream of Ineska's did come true after all. She went strolling through the whole of Grachyovka on her prince's arm – she deliberately led him the long way round, though it was quicker to get to the Vladimir Road tavern, where Glashka lived, through the yards, across the rubbish tip and through the knacker's yard. Ineska had dressed herself up in her little velvet jacket and batiste blouse, and she'd put on her crêpe-lizette skirt for the first time and even her boots that were only for dry weather – she didn't care. She powdered her face that was puffy from crying and backcombed her fringe. All in all, there was plenty to turn Sanka and Liudka green. It was just a pity they didn't meet Adelaidka; never mind, her girlfriends would give her the picture.

Ineska still couldn't get enough of looking at her darling, she kept looking into his face and chattering away like a magpie: 'She has a daughter, Glashka does – a real fright she is. That's what the good folks told me: "You ask for the Glashka with the ugly daughter." '

'Ugly? What way is she ugly?'

'She has this birthmark that covers half her face – wine colour; it's a real nightmare. I'd rather put my head in a noose than walk around looking like that. In the next house to us, there was this Nadka used to live there, a tailor's daughter ...' But before she had time to tell him about Nadka, they'd already reached the Vladimir Road. They walked up the creaking staircase where the rooms were.

Glashka's room was lousy, not a patch on Ineska's apertiment. Glashka was there, putting on her make-up in front of the mirror – she was going out to work the street soon.

'Look, Glafira, I've brought a good man to see you. Tell him what he asks about that evil bastard that cut you,' Ineska instructed her, then sat sedately in the corner.

Erastik immediately put a three-rouble note on the table. 'That's yours, Glashka, for your trouble. What sort of man was he? What did he look like?'

Glashka was a good-looking girl, though in her strict way Ineska thought she didn't keep herself clean. She didn't even look at the money.

'Everyone knows his kind: crazy,' she answered and wiggled her shoulders this way and that.

She stuck the money up her skirt anyway – not that she was that interested, just to be polite. And she stared at Erast that hard, ran her peepers all over him, the shameless hussy, that Ineska's heart started fluttering.

'Men are always interested in me,' Glashka said modestly, to start her story. 'But that time I was really low. At Shrovetide I got these scabs all over my face, so bad I was scared to look in the mirror. I walked and walked and no one took any interest; I'd have been happy to do it for fifteen kopecks. That one's a big eater' – she nodded towards the curtain, from behind which they could hear the sound of sleepy snuffling. 'Plain terrible, it is. And anyway, this one comes up, very polite, he was—'

'That's right, that was the way he came up to me too,' Ineska put in, feeling jealous. 'And just think, my face was all scratched and battered then too. I had a fight with that bitch Adelaidka. No one would come near me, no matter what I said, but this one comes up all on his own. "Don't be sad," he says, "now I'll give you joy." Only I didn't do like Glashka did, I didn't go with him, because . . .'

'I heard that already,' Erastik interrupted her. 'You didn't get a proper sight of him. Keep quiet. Let Glafira talk.'

Glashka flashed her eyes, proud-like, at Ineska, and Ineska felt really bad. And it was her own stupid fault, wasn't it? – she'd brought him here herself

'And he says to me: "Why such a long face? Come with me,"

he says. "I want to bring you joy." Well, I was feeling happy enough already. I'm thinking, I'll get a rouble here, or maybe two, I'll buy Matryoshka some bread, and some pies. Oh, I bought them all right, didn't I?... had to pay the doctur a fiver afterwards, to have my neck stitched up.'

She pointed to her neck, and there, under the powder, was a crimson line, smooth and narrow, like a thread.

'Tell me everything in the right order,' Erastushka told her.

'Well, then, we come in here. He sat me on the bed – this one here – puts one hand on my shoulder and keeps the other behind his back. And he says – his voice is soft, like a woman's – "Do you think", he says, "that you're not beautiful?" So I blurts out: "I'm just fine, the face will heal up all right. It's my daughter that's disfigured for the rest of her life." He says, "What daughter's that?" "Over there," I say, "take a look at my little treasure," and I pulled back the curtain. As soon as he saw my Matryoshka – and she was sleeping then too; she's a sound sleeper, used to anything, she is – he started trembling, like, all over. And he says, "I'll make her into such a lovely beauty. And it'll make things easier for you too." I look a bit closer, and I can see he has something in his fist, behind his back, glinting like. Holy Mother, it was a knife! Sort of narrow and short.'

'A scalpel?' Erastik asked, using a word they didn't understand.

'Eh?'

He just waved his hand: Come on, tell me more.

'I give him such a clout and I start yelling: "Help! Murder!" He looked at me, and his face was terrible, all twisted. "Quiet, you fool! You don't understand your own happiness!" And then he slashes at me! I jumped back, but even so he caught me across the throat. Well then I howled so loud, even Matryoshka woke up. Then she starts in wailing, and she's got a voice like a cat in heat in March. And he just turned and scarpered. And that's the whole adventure. It was the Holy Virgin saved me.'

Glashka made the sign of the cross over her forehead and then straight off, before she'd even lowered her hands, she asked: 'And you, good sir, you're interested for business, are you, or just in general?' And she fluttered her eyelids, the snake.

But Erast told her, strict like: 'Describe him to me, Glafira. What does he look like, this man?'

'Ordinary. A bit taller than me, shorter than you. He'd be up to here on you.' And she drew her finger across the side of Erastushka's head, real slow. Some people have no shame!

'His face is ordinary too. Clean, no moustache or beard. I don't know what else. Show him to me, and I'll recognise him straight away.'

'We'll show him to you, we will,' Ineska's sweet darling muttered, wrinkling up his clear forehead and trying to figure something out. 'So he wanted to make things easier for you?'

'For that kind of help I'd unwind the evil bastard's guts with my bare hands,' Glashka said in a calm, convincing voice. 'Lord knows, we need the freaks too. Let my Matryoshka live – what's it to him?'

'And from the way he talked, who is he – a gentleman or a working man? How was he dressed?'

'You couldn't tell from his clothes. Could have worked in a shop, or maybe some kind of clerk. But he spoke like a gent. I remembered one thing. When he looked at Matryoshka, he said to himself: "That's not ringworm, it's a rare nevus matevus." Nevus matevus – that's what he called my Matryoshka; I remembered that.'

'Nevus maternus,' Erastik said, putting her right. 'In doctor's talk that means "birth mark".'

He knows everything, he's so bright.

'Erastik, let's go, eh?' Ineska said, touching her sweetheart's sleeve. 'The cognac's still waiting.'

'Why go?' that cheeky bitch Glashka piped up. 'Since you're already here. I can find some cognac for a special guest, it's Shutov; I've been keeping it for Easter. So what's that your name is, you handsome man?'

Masahiro Shibata was sitting in his room, burning incense sticks and reading sutras in memory of the servant of the state Anisii Tulipov, who had departed this world in such an untimely fashion, his sister Sonya-san and the maid Palashka, whom the Japanese had his own special reasons to mourn.

Masa had arranged the room himself, spending no small amount of time and money on it. The straw mats that covered the floor had been brought on a steamboat all the way from Japan, and they had immediately made the room sunny and golden, and the floor had a jolly spring under your feet, not like stomping across cold, dead parquet made out of stupid oak. There was no furniture at all, but a spacious cupboard with a sliding door had been built into one of the walls, to hold a padded blanket and a pillow, as well as the whole of Masa's wardrobe: a cotton yukata robe, broad white cotton trousers and a similar jacket for rensu, two three-piece suits, for winter and summer, and the beautiful green livery that the Japanese servant respected so very much and only wore on special festive or solemn occasions. On the walls to delight the eye there were coloured lithographs of Tsar Alexander and Emperor Mutsuhito. And hanging in the corner, under the altar shelf, there was a scroll with an ancient wise saying: 'Live correctly and regret nothing.' Standing on the altar today there was a photograph: Masa and Anisii Tulipov in the Zoological Gardens. It had been taken the previous summer: Masa in his sandy-coloured summer suit and bowler hat, looking serious, Anisii with his mouth stretched into a smile that reached the ears sticking out from under his cap, and behind them an elephant with ears just the same, except that they were a bit bigger.

Masa was distracted from mournful thoughts on the vanity of the search for harmony and the fragility of the world by the telephone.

Fandorin's servant walked to the entrance hall through the dark, empty rooms – his master was somewhere in the city, looking for the murderer, in order to exact vengeance; his mistress had gone to the church and would probably not be back soon because tonight was the main Russian festival of Easter.

'Harro,' Masa said into the round bell mouth. 'This is Mista Fandorin's number. Who is speaking?'

'Mr Fandorin, is that you?' said a metallic voice, distorted by electrical howling. 'Erast Petrovich?'

'No, Mista Fandorin not here,' Masa said loudly, so that he could be heard above the howling. They had written in the newspapers that new telephones had appeared with an improved system which transmitted speech 'without the slightest loss of quality, remarkably loudly and clearly'. They ought to buy one. 'Prease ring back rater. Would you rike to reave a message?'

'No thank—' The voice had gone from a howl to a rustle. 'I'll phone later.'

'Prease make yourself wercome,' Masa said politely, and hung up.

Things were bad, very bad. This was the third night his master had not slept, and the mistress did not sleep either; she prayed all the time – either in the church or at home, in front of the icon. She had always prayed a lot, but never so much as now. All this would end very badly, although it was hard to see how things could be any worse than they were already.

If only the master would find whoever had killed Tiuri-san and murdered Sonya-san and Palasha. Find him and give his faithful servant a present – give that person to Masa. Not for long, just half an hour. No, an hour would be better . . .

Engrossed in pleasant thoughts, he didn't notice the time passing. The clock struck eleven. Usually the people in the neighbouring houses were already asleep at this time, but today all the windows were lit up. It was a special night. Soon the bells would start chiming all over the city, and then different-coloured lights would explode in the sky, people in the streets would start singing and shouting, and tomorrow there would be a lot of drunks. Easter.

Perhaps he ought to go the church and stand with everyone and listen to the slow bass singing of the Christian bonzes. Anything was better than sitting all alone and waiting, waiting, waiting.

But he didn't have to wait any longer. The door slammed and he heard firm, confident footsteps. His master had returned!

'What, mourning all alone?' his master asked in Japanese, and touched him gently on the shoulder

Such displays of affection were not their custom, and the

301

surprise broke Masa's reserve; he sobbed and then broke into tears. He didn't wipe the water from his face – let it flow. A man had no reason to be ashamed of crying, as long as it was not from pain or from fear.

The master's eyes were dry and bright. 'I haven't got everything I'd like to have,' he said. 'I thought we'd catch him red-handed. But we can't wait any longer. There's no time. The killer is still in Moscow today, but after a while he could be anywhere in the world. I have indirect evidence: I have a witness who can identify him. That's enough; he won't wriggle out of it.'

'You will take me with you?' Masa asked, overjoyed by the good news. 'You will?'

'Yes,' his master said, with a nod. 'He is a dangerous opponent, and I can't take any risks. I might need your help.'

The telephone rang again.

'Master, someone phoned before. On secret business. He didn't give his name. He said he would call again.'

'Right then, you take the other phone and try to tell if it's the same person or not.'

Masa put the metal horn to his ear and prepared to listen.

'Hello. Erast Petrovich Fandorin's number. This is he,' the master said.

'Erast Petrovich, is that you?' the voice squeaked. Masa shrugged – he couldn't tell if it was the same person or someone else.

'Yes. With whom am I speaking?'

'This is Zakharov.'

'You!' The master's strong fingers clenched into a fist.

'Erast Petrovich, I have to explain things to you. I know everything is against me, but I didn't kill anyone, I swear to you!'

'Then who did?'

'I'll explain everything to you. Only give me your word of honour that you'll come alone, without the police. Otherwise I'll disappear, you'll never see me again and the killer will go free. Do you give me your word?'

'Yes,' the master answered without hesitation.

'I believe you, because I know you to be a man of honour. You have no need to fear: I am not dangerous to you, and I don't have a gun. I just want to be able to explain ... If you still are concerned, bring your Japanese along, I don't object to that. Only no police.'

'How do you know about my Japanese?'

'I know a great deal about you, Erast Petrovich. That's why you are the only one I trust ... Come immediately, this minute to the Pokrovskaya Gates. You'll find the Hotel Tsargrad on Rogozhsky Val Street, a grey building with three storeys. You must come within the next hour. Go up to room number fifty-two and wait for me there. Once I'm sure that only the two of you have come, I'll come up and join you. I'll tell you the whole truth, and then you can decide what to do with me. I'll accept any decision you make.'

'There will be no police, my word of honour,' the master said, and hung up.

'That's it, Masa, that's it,' he said, and his face became a little less dead. 'He will be caught in the act. Give me some strong green tea. I shan't be sleeping again tonight.'

'What weapons shall I prepare?' Masa asked.

'I shall take my revolver; I shan't need anything else. And you take whatever you like. Remember: this man is a monster – strong, quick and unpredictable.' And he added in a quiet voice: 'I really have decided to manage without any police.'

Masa nodded understandingly. In a matter like this, of course it was better without the police.

I admit that I was wrong: not all detectives are ugly. This one, for instance, is very beautiful.

My heart swoons sweetly as I see him close the ring around me. Hide and seek!

But I can facilitate his enlightenment a little. If I am not mistaken in him, he is an exceptional man. He won't be frightened, but he will appreciate the lesson. I know it will cause him a lot of pain. At first. But later he will thank me himself. Who knows, perhaps we shall become fellow-thinkers and confederates. I think I can sense a kindred spirit. Or perhaps two kindred spirits. His Japanese servant comes from a nation that understands true Beauty. The supreme moment of existence for the inhabitants of those distant islands is to reveal to the world the Beauty of their belly. In Japan, those who die in this beautiful way are honoured as heroes. The sight of steaming entrails does not frighten anyone there.

Yes, there will be three of us, I can sense it.

How weary I am of my solitude. To share the burden between two or even three would be unspeakable happiness. After all, I am not a god; I am only a human being.

Understand me, Mr Fandorin. Help me.

But first I must open your eyes.

CHAPTER 9

A Bad End to an Unpleasant Story

Easter Sunday, 9 April, night

Clip-clop, clip-clop, the horseshoes clattered merrily over the cobblestones of the street, and the steel springs rustled gently. The Decorator was riding through the Moscow night in festive style, bowling along to the joyful pealing of the Easter bells and the booming of the cannon. There had been illuminated decorations on Tverskaya Street, different-coloured little lanterns, and now on the left, where the Kremlin was, the sky was suffused with all the colours of the rainbow – that was the Easter firework display. The boulevard was crowded. Talking, laughter, sparklers. Muscovites greeting people they knew, kissing, sometimes even the popping of a champagne cork.

And here was the turn on to Malaya Nikitskaya Street. Here it was deserted, dark, not a soul.

'Stop, my good man, we're here,' said the Decorator.

The cabbie jumped down from the coachbox and opened the droshky's door, decorated with paper garlands. He doffed his cap and uttered the holy words: 'Christ is risen.'

'Truly He is risen,' the Decorator replied with feeling, throwing back the veil, and kissing the good Christian on his stubbly cheek. The tip was an entire rouble. Such was the bright holiness of this hour.

'Thank you, lady,' the cabby said with a bow, touched more by the kiss than by the rouble.

The Decorator's heart was serene and at peace.

The infallible instinct that had never deceived told him that this was a great night, when all the misfortunes and petty failures

305

would be left behind. Happiness lay very close ahead. Everything would be good, very good.

Ah what a tour de force had been conceived this time. As a true master of his trade, Mr Fandorin could not fail to appreciate it. He would grieve, he would weep – after all, we are all only human – but afterwards he would think about what had happened and understand; he was sure to understand. After all, he was an intelligent man and he seemed capable of seeing Beauty.

The hope of new life, of recognition and understanding, warmed the Decorator's foolish, trusting heart. It is hard to bear the cross of a great mission alone. Even Christ's cross had been supported by Simon's shoulder.

Fandorin and his Japanese were dashing at top speed on their way to Rogozhsky Val Street. They would waste time finding room number fifty-two and waiting there. And if the Collegiate Counsellor should suspect anything, he would not find a telephone in the third-class Hotel Tsargrad.

The Decorator had time. There was no need to hurry.

The woman the Collegiate Counsellor loved was devout. She was in the church now, but the service in the nearby Church of the Resurrection would soon be over, and at midnight the woman would certainly come home – to set the table with the Easter feast and wait for her man.

Decorative gates with a crown, the yard beyond them, and then the dark windows of the outhouse. Here.

Throwing back the flimsy veil, the Decorator looked around and slipped in through the wrought-iron gate.

It would take a moment or two to fiddle with the door of the outhouse, but that was an easy job for such agile, talented fingers. The lock clicked, the hinges creaked, and the Decorator was already in the dark entrance hall.

No need to wait for such well accustomed eyes to adjust to the darkness: it was no hindrance to them. The Decorator walked quickly round all the rooms.

In the drawing room there was a momentary fright caused by the deafening chime of a huge clock in the shape of Big Ben. Was it really that late? Confused, the Decorator checked the time with a neat lady's wristwatch – no, Big Ben was fast, it was still a quarter to the hour.

The place for the sacred ritual still had to be chosen.

The Decorator was on top form today, soaring on the wings of inspiration – why not right here in the drawing room, on the dinner table?

It would be like this: Mr Fandorin would come in from the entrance hall, turn on the electric light and see the delightful sight.

That was decided then. Now where did they keep their table-cloth?

The Decorator rummaged in the linen cupboard, selected a snow-white lace cloth and put it on the broad table with its dull gleam of polished wood.

Yes, that would be beautiful. Wasn't that a Meissen dinner service in the sideboard? The fine china plates could be laid out round the edge of the table and the treasures could be laid on them as they were extracted. It would be the finest decoration ever created.

So, the design had been completed.

The Decorator went into the entrance hall, stood by the window and waited, filled with joyful anticipation and holy ecstasy.

The yard was suddenly bright – the moon had come out. A sign, a clear sign! It had been overcast and gloomy for so many weeks, but now a veil seemed to have been lifted from God's world. What a clear, starry sky! This was truly a bright and holy Easter night. The Decorator made the sign of the cross three times.

She was here!

A few quick blinks of the eyelashes to brush away the tears of ecstasy.

She was here. A short figure wearing a broad coat and hat came in unhurriedly through the gate. When she approached the door, it was clearly a hat of mourning, with ... with a black gauze veil. Ah, yes, that was for the boy, Anisii Tulipov. Don't grieve, my dear, he and the members of his household are already with the Lord. They are happy there. And you too will be happy, only be patient a little longer.

'Christ is risen.' The Decorator greeted her in a quiet, clear voice. 'Don't be frightened, my dear. I have come to bring you joy.'

The woman, however, did not appear to be frightened. She did not cry out or try to run away. On the contrary, she took a step forwards. The moon lit up the entrance hall with an intense, even glow, and the eyes behind the veil glinted.

'Why are we standing here like two Moslem women in yashmaks?' the Decorator joked. 'Let's show our faces.' The Decorator's veil was thrown back, revealing an affectionate smile, a smile from the heart. 'And let's not be formal with each other. We're going to get to know each other very well. We shall be closer than sisters. Come now, let me look at your pretty face. I know you are beautiful, but I shall help you to become even more so.'

The Decorator reached out one hand, but the woman did not jump back; she waited. Mr Fandorin had a good woman, calm and acquiescent. The Decorator had always liked women like that. It would be bad if she spoiled everything with a scream of horror and an expression of fear in her eyes. She would die instantly, with no pain or fright. That would be the Decorator's gift to her.

One hand drew the scalpel out of the little case that was attached to the Decorator's belt at the back; the other threw back the fine gauze from the face of the fortunate woman.

The face revealed was broad and perfectly round, with slanting eyes. What kind of witchcraft was this? But there was no time to make any sense of it, because something in the entrance hall clicked and suddenly it was flooded with blindingly bright light, unbearable after the darkness.

With sensitive eyes screwed tightly shut against the pain, the Decorator heard a voice speaking through the darkness: 'I'll give you joy right now, Pakhomenko. Or would you prefer me to call you by your former name, Mr Sotsky?'

Opening his eyes slightly, the Decorator saw the Japanese

servant standing in front of him, fixing him with an unblinking stare. The Decorator did not turn round. Why should he turn round, when it was already clear that Mr Fandorin was behind him, probably holding a revolver in his hand? The cunning Collegiate Counsellor had not gone to the Hotel Tsargrad. He had not believed that Zakharov was guilty. Satan himself must have whispered the truth to Fandorin.

Eloi, Eloi, lama sabacthani? Or perhaps You have not abandoned me, but are testing the strength of my spirit?

Then let us test it.

Fandorin would not fire, because his bullet would go straight through the Decorator and hit the Japanese.

Thrust the scalpel into the short man's belly. Briefly, just below the diaphragm. Then, in a single movement, swing the Japanese round by his shoulders, shield himself with him and push him towards Fandorin. The door was only two quick bounds away, and then they would see who could run faster. Not even the fierce wolfhounds of Kherson had been able to catch convict number 3576. He'd manage to get away from Mr Collegiate Counsellor somehow.

Help me, O Lord!

His right hand flew forward as fast as an uncoiling spring, but the sharp blade cut nothing but air – the Japanese jumped backwards with unbelievable ease and struck the Decorator's wrist with the edge of his hand; the scalpel went flying to the floor with a sad tinkling sound, and the Asiatic froze on the spot again, holding his arms out slightly from his sides.

Instinct made the Decorator turn round. He saw the barrel of a revolver. Fandorin was holding the gun low, by his hip. If he fired from there, the bullet would take the top of the Decorator's skull off and not touch the Japanese. That changed things.

'And the joy I will bring you is this,' Fandorin continued in the same level voice, as if the conversation had never been interrupted. 'I spare you the arrest, the investigation, the trial and the inevitable verdict. You will be shot while being detained.'

He has abandoned me. He truly has abandoned me, thought

the Decorator, but this thought did not sadden him for long; it was displaced by a sudden joy. *No, He has not abandoned me! He has decided to be merciful to me and is calling me, taking me to Himself! Release me now, O Lord.*

The front door creaked open and a desperate woman's voice said: 'Erast, you mustn't!'

The Decorator came back from the celestial heights that had been about to open to him, down to earth. He turned round curiously and in the doorway he saw a very beautiful, stately woman in a black mourning dress and a black hat with a veil. The woman had a lilac shawl on her shoulders; in one hand she was holding a package of pashka Easter dessert and in the other a garland of paper roses.

'Angelina, why did you come back?' the Collegiate Counsellor said angrily. 'I asked you to stay in the Hotel Metropole tonight!'

A beautiful woman. She would hardly have been much more beautiful on the table, soaking in her own juices, with the petals of her body open. Only just a little bit.

'I felt something in my heart,' the beautiful woman told Fandorin, wringing her hands. 'Erast Petrovich, don't kill him; don't take the sin on your soul. Your soul will bend under the weight of it and snap.'

This was interesting. Now what would the Collegiate Counsellor say?

His cool composure had vanished without a trace; he was looking at the beautiful woman in angry confusion. The Japanese had been taken aback too: he was shaking his shaven head either at his master or his mistress with a very stupid expression.

Well, this is a family matter; we won't intrude. They can sort things out without our help.

In two quick bounds the Decorator had rounded the Japanese, and then it was five steps to the door and freedom – and Fandorin couldn't fire because the woman was too close. *Goodbye, gentlemen!*

A shapely leg in a black felt boot struck the Decorator across

the ankle, and the Decorator was sent sprawling, with his forehead flying towards the doorpost.

A blow. Darkness.

Everything was ready for the trial to begin.

The unconscious accused was sitting in an armchair in a
woman's dress, but without any hat. He had an impressive purple
bump coming up on his forehead.

The court bailiff, Masa, was standing beside him with his arms
crossed on his chest.

Erast Petrovich had appointed Angelina as the judge and taken
the role of prosecutor on himself.

But first there was an argument.

'I can't judge anyone,' said Angelina. 'The Emperor has judges
for that; let them decide if he is guilty or not. Let them pronounce
sentence.'

'What s-sentence?' Fandorin asked with a bitter laugh. He had
started to stammer again after the criminal had been detained –
in fact even more than before, as if he were trying to make up
for lost time. 'Who needs a scandalous t-trial like that? They'll
be only too glad to declare Sotsky insane and put him in a
madhouse, from which he will quite definitely escape. No bars
will hold a man like this. I was going to kill him, in the way one
kills a mad dog, b-but you stopped me. Now decide his fate
yourself, since you interfered. You know what this monster has
done.'

'What if it's not him? Are you quite incapable of making a
mistake?' Angelina protested passionately.

'I'll prove to you that he, and no one else, is the murderer.
That's why I'm the prosecutor. You judge f-fairly. I couldn't find
a more merciful judge for him in the whole wide world. And if
you don't want to be his judge, then go to the Metropole and
don't get in my way.'

'No, I won't go away,' she said; 'let there be a trial. But in a
trial there's a counsel for the defence. Who's going to defend
him?'

'I assure you that this gentleman will not allow anyone else to take on the role of counsel for the defence. He knows how to stand up for himself. Let's begin.'

Erast Petrovich nodded to Masa, and the valet stuck a bottle of smelling salts under the nose of the man in the chair.

The man in the woman's dress jerked his head and fluttered his eyelashes. The eyes were dull at first, then they turned a bright sky-blue colour and acquired intelligence. The soft features were illuminated by a good-natured smile.

'Your name and title?' Fandorin said sternly, trespassing somewhat on the prerogatives of the chairman of the court.

The seated man examined the scene around him. 'Have you decided to play out a trial? Very well, why not. Name and title? Sotsky ... former nobleman, former student, former convict number 3576. And now – nobody.'

'Do you admit that you are guilty of committing a number of murders?' Erast Petrovich began reading from a notepad, pausing after each name: 'The prostitute Emma Elizabeth Smith on the third of April 1888 on Osborne Street in London; the prostitute Martha Tabram on the seventh of August 1888 near George Yard in London; the prostitute Mary Ann Nichols on the thirty-first of August 1888 on Back Row in London; the prostitute Ann Chapman on the eighth of September 1888 on Hanbury Street in London; the prostitute Elizabeth Stride on the thirtieth of September 1888 in Berner Street in London; the prostitute Catherine Eddows also on the thirtieth of September 1888 on Mitre Square in London; the prostitute Mary Jane Kelly on the ninth of November 1888 on Dorset Street in London; the prostitute Rose Millet on the twentieth of December 1888 on Poplar High Street in London; the prostitute Alexandra Zotova on the fifth of February 1889 in Svininsky Lane in Moscow; the beggar Marya Kosaya on the eleventh of February 1889 in Maly Tryokhsvyatsky Lane in Moscow; the prostitute Stepanida Andreichkina on the night of the third of April on Seleznyovsky Lane in Moscow; an unidentified beggar girl on the fifth of April 1889 near the Novotikhvinsk level crossing in Moscow; Court Counsellor Leontii Izhitsin and his maid Zinaida Matiushkina on the night of the fifth of April 1889 on Vozdvizhenskaya Street in Moscow; the spinster Sophia Tulipova and her nurse Pelageya Makarova on the seventh of April 1889 on Granatny Lane in Moscow; the Provincial Secretary Anisii Tulipov and the doctor Egor Zakharov on the night of the seventh of April at the Bozhedomka Cemetery in Moscow – in all eighteen people, eight of whom were killed by you in England and ten in Russia. And those are only the victims of which the investigation has certain knowledge. I repeat the question: do you admit that you are guilty of committing these crimes?'

Fandorin's voice seemed to have been strengthened by reading out the long list. It had become loud and resonant, as if the Collegiate Counsellor were speaking to a full courtroom. The stammer had also disappeared in some mysterious fashion.

'Well, that, my dear Erast Petrovich, depends on the evidence,' the accused replied amiably, apparently delighted with the proposed game. 'Well, let's say that I don't admit it. I'm really looking forward to hearing the opening address from the prosecution. Purely out of curiosity. Since you've decided to postpone my extermination.'

'Well then, listen,' Fandorin replied sternly. He turned over the page of his notepad and continued speaking, addressing himself to Pakhomenko–Sotsky, but looking at Angelina most of the time.

'First, the prehistory. In 1882 there was a scandal in Moscow that involved medical students and students from the Higher Courses for Women. You were the leader, the evil genius of this depraved circle and, because of that, you were the only member of it who was severely punished: you were sentenced to four years in a convict battalion – without any trial, in order to avoid publicity. You cruelly tormented unfortunate prostitutes who had no right of redress, and fate repaid you with equal cruelty. You were sent to the Kherson military prison, which is said to be more terrible than hard labour in Siberia. The year before last, following an investigation into a case of the abuse of power, the senior administrators of the punishment battalion were put on trial. But by then you were already far away . . .'

Erast Petrovich hesitated and then continued after a brief

pause: 'I am the prosecutor and I am not obliged to seek excuses for you, but I cannot pass over in silence the fact that the final transformation of a wanton youth into a ravenous, bloodthirsty beast was facilitated by society itself. The contrast between student life and the hell of a military prison would drive absolutely anyone insane. During the first year there you killed a man in self-defence. The military court acknowledged the mitigating circumstances, but it increased your sentence to eight years and when you were sent to the guardhouse, they put shackles on you and subjected you to a long period of solitary confinement. No doubt it was owing to the inhuman conditions in which you were kept that you turned into an inhuman monster. No, Sotsky, you did not break, you did not lose your mind, you did not try to kill yourself. In order to survive, you became a different creature, with only an external resemblance to a human being. In 1886 your family, who had turned their backs on you long before, were informed that convict Sotsky had drowned in the Dnieper during an attempted escape. I sent an inquiry to the Department of Military Justice, asking if the fugitive's body had been found. They replied that it had not. That was the answer I had been expecting. The prison administration had simply concealed the fact of your successful escape. A very common business.'

The accused listened to Fandorin with lively interest, neither confirming what he said nor denying it.

'Tell me, my dear prosecutor: what was it that made you start raking through the case of the long-forgotten Sotsky? Forgive me for interrupting you, but this is an informal court, although I presume the verdict will be binding and not subject to appeal.'

'Two of the individuals who were included in the list of suspects had been your accomplices in the case of the Sadist Circle, and they mentioned your name. It turned out that forensic medical expert Zakharov, who was involved in the inquiry, had also belonged to the group. I realised straight away that the criminal could only be receiving news of the inquiry from Zakharov, and I was going to take a closer look at the people around him, but first I took the wrong path and suspected the factory-owner Burylin. Everything fitted very well.'

'And why didn't you suspect Zakharov himself?' Sotsky asked, in a voice that sounded almost offended. 'After all, everything pointed to him, and I did everything I could to help things along.'

'No, I couldn't think that Zakharov was the murderer. He besmirched his name less than the others in the Sadist Circle case; he was only a passive observer of your cruel amusements. And in addition, Zakharov was frankly and aggressively cynical and that kind of character is not typical of maniacal killers. But these are circumstantial points; the main thing is that last year Zakharov only stayed in England for a month and a half, and he was in Moscow when most of the London murders took place. I checked that at the very beginning and immediately excluded him from the list of suspects. He could not have been Jack the Ripper.'

'You and your Jack the Ripper,' said Sotsky, with an irritated twitch of his shoulder. 'Well, let us suppose that while Zakharov was staying with relatives in England he read a lot in the news-papers about the Ripper and decided to continue his work in Moscow. I noticed just now that you count the number of victims in a strange manner. Investigator Izhitsin came to a different conclusion. He put thirteen corpses on the table, and you only accuse me of ten killings in Moscow. And that's including those who died after the "investigative experiment"; otherwise there would only be four. Your numbers don't add up somewhere, Mr Prosecutor.'

'On the contrary,' said Erast Petrovich, not even slightly per-turbed by this unexpected outburst. 'Of the thirteen bodies exhumed with signs of mutilation, four had been brought directly from the scene of the crime: Zotova, Marya Kosaya, Andreichkina and the unidentified girl, and you had also not managed to process two of your February victims according to your special method – clearly, someone must have frightened you off. The other nine bodies, the most horribly mutilated of all, were extracted from anonymous graves. The Moscow police are, of course, far from perfect, but it is impossible to imagine that no one paid any attention to bodies that had been mutilated in such a monstrous fashion. Here in Russia many people are murdered, but more simply, without all these fantasies. When they found Andreichkina slashed to pieces, look what an uproar it caused immediately. The Governor-General was informed straight away, and His Excellency assigned his Deputy for Special Assignments to investigate. I can say without bragging that the Prince only assigns me to cases that are of exceptional importance. And here we have almost ten mutilated bodies and nobody has made any fuss? Impossible.'

'Somehow I don't understand,' said Angelina, speaking for the first time since the trial had begun. 'Who did such things to these poor people?'

Erast Petrovich was clearly delighted by her question – the stubborn silence of the 'judge' had rendered the examination of the evidence meaningless.

'The earliest bodies were exhumed from the November ditch. However, that does not mean that Jack the Ripper had already arrived in Moscow in November.'

'Of course not!' said the accused, interrupting Fandorin. 'As far as I recall, the latest London murder was committed on Christmas Eve. I don't know if you will be able to prove to our charming judge that I am guilty of the Moscow murders, but you certainly won't be able to make me into Jack the Ripper.'

An icy, disdainful smile slid across Erast Petrovich's face, and he became stern and sombre again. 'I understand the meaning of your remark perfectly well. You cannot wriggle out of the Moscow murders. The more of them there are, the more monstrous and outrageous they are, the better for you – you are more likely be declared insane. But for Jack's crimes the English would be certain to demand your extradition, and Russian justice would be only too delighted to be rid of such a bothersome madman. If you go to England, where things are done openly, nothing will be hushed up in our Russian fashion. You would swing from the gallows there, my dear sir. Don't you want to?' Fandorin's voice shifted down an octave, as if his own throat had been caught in a noose. 'Don't even hope that you can leave your career in London behind you. The apparent mismatch of the dates is easily explained. "Watchman Pakhomenko" appeared at the Bozhedomka Cemetery shortly after the New Year. I assume that Zakharov got you the job for old times' sake. Most likely you met in London during his most recent visit. Of course, Zakharov did not know about your new amusements. He simply thought that you had escaped from prison. How could he refuse to help an old comrade whom life had treated so harshly? Well?'

Sotsky did not reply; he merely shrugged one shoulder as if to say: I'm listening, go on.

'Did things get too hot for you in London? Were the police getting too close? All right. You moved to your native country. I don't know what passport you used to cross the border, but you turned up in Moscow as a simple Ukrainian peasant, one of those godly wandering pilgrims, of whom there are so many in Russia. That's why there is no information about your arrival from abroad in the police records. You lived at the cemetery for a while, settled in, took a look around. Zakharov obviously felt sorry for you; he gave you protection and money. You went for quite a long time without killing anybody – more than a month. Possibly you were intending to start a new life. But you weren't strong enough. After the excitement in London, ordinary life had become impossible for you. This peculiarity of the maniacal mind is well known to criminal science. Once someone has tasted blood, he can't stop. At first you took the opportunity offered by your job to hack up bodies from the graves; it was winter, so the bodies buried since the end of November had not begun to decompose. You tried a man's body once, but you didn't like it. It didn't match your "idea" somehow. By the way, what is your idea? Can you not tolerate sinful, ugly women? "I want to give you joy," "I will help to make you more beautiful" – do you use a scalpel to save fallen women from their ugliness? Is that the reason for the bloody kiss?'

The accused said nothing. His face became solemn and remote, the bright blue of his eyes dimmed as he half-closed his eyelids.

'And then lifeless bodies weren't good enough any longer. You made several attempts which, fortunately, were unsuccessful, and committed two murders. Or was it more?' Fandorin suddenly shouted out, rushing at the accused, shaking him so hard by the shoulders that his head almost flew off.

'Answer me?'

'Erast!' Angelina shouted. 'Stop it!'

The Collegiate Counsellor started away from the seated man, took two hasty steps backwards and hid his hands behind his back, struggling to control his agitation. The Ripper, not frightened at all by Erast Petrovich's outburst, sat without moving, staring at Fandorin with an expression of calm superiority.

'What can you understand?' the full, fleshy lips whispered almost inaudibly.

Erast Petrovich frowned in frustration, tossed a lock of black hair back off his forehead and continued his interrupted speech: "On the evening of the third of April, a year after the first London murder, you killed the spinster Andreichkina and mutilated her body. A day later the juvenile beggar became your victim. After that, events moved very quickly. Izhitsin's "experiment" triggered a paroxysm of excitation which you discharged by killing and disembowelling Izhitsin himself, at the same time murdering his entirely innocent maid. From that moment on, you deviate from your "idea" and you kill in order to cover your tracks and avoid retribution. When you realised that the circle was closing in, you decided it would be more convenient to shift the blame on to your friend and protector Zakharov. Epecially since the forensic specialist had begun to suspect you – he must have put a few facts together, or else he knew something that I don't. In any case, on Friday evening Zakharov was writing a letter addressed to the investigators, in which he intended to expose you. He kept tearing it up and starting again. His assistant Grumov said that Zakharov locked himself in his office shortly after three, so he was struggling with his conscience until the evening, struggling with the understandable, but in the present instance entirely inappropriate, feelings of honour and *esprit de corps*, as well as simple compassion for a comrade whom life had treated harshly. You took the letter and collected all the torn pieces. But there were two scraps that you failed to notice. On one it said *"longer remain silent"* and on the other *"erations of esprit de corps and sympathy for an old com"*. The meaning is obvious: Zakharov was writing that that he could no longer remain silent, and attempting to justify harbouring a murderer by referring to considerations of *esprit de corps* and sympathy for an old comrade. That was the moment when I was finally convinced that the killer had to be sought among Zakharov's former fellow students. Since it was a matter of "sympathy", then it had to be one of those whose lives had gone badly. That excluded the millionaire Burylin. There were only three left: Stenich, the alcoholic Rozen and Sotsky, whose name kept coming up in the stories that the former "sadists" told me. He was supposed to be dead, but that had to be verified.'

'Erast Petrovich, why are you certain that this doctor, Zakharov, has been killed?' Angelina asked.

'Because he has disappeared, although he had no need to,' replied Erast Petrovich. 'Zakharov is not guilty of the murders and he had believed that he was sheltering a fugitive convict, not a bloody killer. But when he realised who he had been sheltering, he was frightened. He kept a loaded revolver beside his bed. He was afraid of you, Sotsky. After the murders in Granatny Lane you returned to the cemetery and saw Tulipov observing Zakharov's office. The guard dog did not bark at you; he knows you very well. Tulipov was absorbed in his observation work and failed to notice you. You realised that suspicion had fallen on Zakharov and decided to exploit the fact. In the report he dictated just before he died, Tulipov states that shortly after ten Zakharov went out of his study and there was some sort of clattering in the corridor. Obviously the murder took place at that very moment. You entered the house silently and waited for Zakharov to come out into the corridor for something. And that is why the rug disappeared from the corridor. It must have had bloodstains on it, so you removed it. When you were finished with Zakharov, you crept outside and attacked Tulipov from behind, inflicting mortal wounds and leaving him to bleed to death. I presume you saw him get up, stagger to the gates and then collapse again. You were afraid to go and finish him, because you knew that he had a weapon, and in any case you knew that his wounds were fatal. Without wasting any time, you dragged Zakharov's body out and buried it in the cemetery. I even know exactly where. You threw it into the April ditch for unidentified bodies and sprinkled earth over it. By the way, do you know how you gave yourself away?'

Sotsky started, and the calm, resigned expression was replaced once again by curiosity, but only for a few moments. Then the invisible curtain came down again, erasing all trace of living feeling.

'When I talked to you yesterday morning, you said you hadn't slept all night, that you had heard the shots, and then the door slamming and the sound of footsteps. That was supposed to make me think that Zakharov was alive and had gone into hiding. But in fact it made me think something else, If the watchman Pakhomenko's ears were sharp enough to hear footsteps from a distance, why could he not hear the blasts that Tulipov gave on his whistle when he came round? The answer is obvious: at that moment you were not in your hut; you were some distance away from the spot – for instance, at the far end of the cemetery, where the April ditch happens to be. That is one. If Zakharov had been the killer, he could not have gone out through the gates, because Tulipov was lying there wounded and had still not come round. The killer would certainly have finished him off. That is two. So now I had confirmation that Zakharov, who I already knew could not be the London maniac, was not involved in Tulipov's death. If he had nonetheless disappeared, it meant that he had been killed. If you lied about the circumstances of his disappearance, it meant that you were involved in it. And I remembered that both murders that were committed according to the "idea", the prostitute Andreichkina and the young beggar, were committed within fifteen minutes' walking distance of the Bozhedomka Cemetery – it was the late investigator Izhitsin who first noticed that, although he drew the wrong conclusions from it. Once I put these facts together with the fragments of phrases from the letter, I was almost certain that the "old comrade" with whom Zakharov sympathised and whom he did not wish to give away was you. Because of your job you were involved in the exhumation of the bodies and you knew a lot about how the investigation was developing. That is one. You were present at the "investigative experiment". That is two. You had access to the graves and the ditches. That is three. You knew Tulipov – in fact you were almost friends. That is four. In the list of those present at the experiment drawn up before he died, you are described as follows.'

Erast Petrovich walked across to the table, picked up a sheet of paper and read from it: 'Pakhomenko, the cemetery watchman. I don't know his first name and patronymic, the labourers call him "Pakhom". Age uncertain: between thirty and fifty. Above average height, strongly built. Round, gentle face, without a moustache or beard. Ukrainian accent. I have had several conversations with him on various subjects. I have listened to the story of his life (he was a wandering pilgrim and has seen a lot of things) and told him about myself. He is intelligent, observant, religious and kind. He has assisted me greatly in the investigation. Perhaps the only one of them whose innocence could not possibly be in the slightest doubt.'

'A nice boy,' the accused said, touched, and his words made the Collegiate Counsellor's face twitch, while the dispassionate court guard whispered something harsh and hissing in Japanese.

Even Angelina shuddered as she looked at the man in the chair.

'You made use of Tulipov's revelations on Friday when you entered his apartment and committed a double murder,' Erast Petrovich continued after a brief pause. 'And as for my ... domestic circumstances, they are known to many people, and Zakharov could have told you about them. So today or, in fact, yesterday morning already, I had only one suspect left: you. But I still had a few things to do. Firstly, establish what Sotsky looked like, secondly, ascertain whether he really was dead and, finally, find witnesses who could identify you. Stenich described Sotsky to me as he was seven years ago. You have probably changed greatly in seven years, but height, the colour of the eyes and the shape of the nose are not subject to change, and all of those features matched. A telegram from the Department of Military Justice which included the details of Sotsky's time in prison and his supposedly unsuccessful attempt to escape, made it clear that the convict could quite well still be alive. My greatest difficulty was with witnesses. I had high hopes of the former "sadist" Filipp Rozen. When he spoke about Sotsky in my presence, he used a strange phrase that stuck in my memory. "He's dead, but I keep thinking I see him everywhere. Take yesterday . . ." He never finished the phrase – someone interrupted him. But on that "yesterday", that is, on the fourth of April, Rozen was with Zakharov and the others at the cemetery. I wondered if he might have seen the watchman Pakhomenko there and spotted a resemblance to his old friend. Unfortunately, I wasn't able to locate Rozen. But I did find a prostitute you tried to kill seven weeks ago at Shrovetide. She remembered you very well and she can identify you. At that stage I could have arrested you; there were enough solid clues. That is what I would have done if you yourself had not gone on the offensive. Then I realised that there is only way to stop someone like you . . .'

Sotsky appeared not to notice the threat behind these words. At least, he did not show the slightest sign of alarm – on the contrary, he smiled absent-mindedly at his own thoughts.

'Ah yes, and there was the note that was sent to Burylin,' Fandorin remembered. 'A rather clumsy move. The note was really intended for me, was it not? The investigators had to be convinced that Zakharov was alive and in hiding. You even tried to imitate certain distinctive features of Zakharov's handwriting, but you only reinforced my conviction that the suspect was not an illiterate watchman but an educated man who knew Zakharov well and was acquainted with Burylin. That is – Sotsky. Your telephone call when you took advantage of the technical shortcomings of the telephone to pretend to be Zakharov could not deceive me either. I have had occasion to use that trick myself. Your intention was also quite clear. You always act according to the same monstrous logic: if you find someone interesting, you kill those who are most dear to him. That was what you did in Tulipov's case. That was what you wanted to do with the daughter of the prostitute who had somehow attracted your perverted attention. You mentioned my Japanese servant very specifically – you clearly wanted him to come with me. Why? Why, of course, so that Angelina Samsonovna would be left at home alone. I would rather not think about the fate that you had in mind for her. I might not be able to restrain myself and . . .'

Fandorin broke off and swung round sharply to face Angelina: 'What is your verdict? Is he guilty or not?'

Pale and trembling, Angelina said in a quiet but firm voice: 'Now let him speak. Let him justify himself if he can.'

Sotsky said nothing, still smiling absent-mindedly. A minute passed, and then another, and just when it began to seem that the defence would not address the court at all, the lips of the accused moved and the words poured out – clear, measured, dignified words, as if it were not this man in fancy dress with a woman's face who was speaking, but some higher power with a superior knowledge of truth and justice.

'I do not need to justify anything to anyone. And I have only one judge – our Heavenly Father, who knows my motives and my innermost thoughts. I have always been a special case. Even when I was a child, I knew that I was special, not like everybody else. I was consumed by irresistible curiosity, I wanted to understand everything in the wonderful structure of God's world, to test everything, to try everything. I have always loved people, and they felt that and were drawn to me. I would have made a great healer, because nature gave me the talent to understand the sources of pain and suffering, and understanding is equivalent to salvation – every doctor knows that. The one thing I could not stand was ugliness; I saw it as an offence to God's work – ugliness enraged me and drove me into a fury. One day, in a fit of such fury, I was unable to stop myself in time. An ugly old whore, whose very appearance was sacrilege against the name of the Lord, according to the way that I thought then, died as I was beating her with my cane. I did not fall into that fury under the influence of sadistic sensuality, as my judges imagined – no, it was the holy wrath of a soul imbued through and through with Beauty. From society's point of view it was just one more unfortunate accident – gilded youth has always got up to worse things than that. But I was not one of their privileged favourites, and they made an example of me to frighten the others. The only one, out of all of us! Now I understand that God had decided to choose me, I *am* the only one. But that is hard to understand at the age of twenty-four. I was not ready. For an educated man of sensitive feelings, the horrors of prison – no, a hundred times worse than that, the horrors of disciplinary confinement – are impossible to describe. I was subjected to cruel humiliation, I was the most abused and defenceless person in the entire barracks. I was tortured, subjected to rape, forced to walk around in a woman's dress. But I could feel some great power gradually maturing within me. It had been present within my being from the very beginning, and now it was putting out shoots and reaching up to the sun, like a fresh stalk breaking up through the earth in the spring. And one day I felt that I was ready. Fear left me and it has never returned. I killed my chief tormentor – killed him in front of everyone, grabbed hold of his ears with my hands and beat his half-shaved head against a wall. I was put in shackles and kept in the punishment cell for seven months. But I did not weaken or fall into consumptive despair. Every day I became stronger and more confident; my eyes learned to penetrate the darkness. Everyone was afraid of me – the guards, the officers, the other convicts. Even the rats left my cell. Every day I strained to understand what this important thing was that was knocking at the door of my soul and not being admitted. Everything around me was ugly and repulsive. I loved Beauty more than anything else in the world, and in my world there was absolutely none. So that this would not drive me insane, I remembered lectures from university and drew the structure of the human body on the earth floor with a chip of wood. Everything in it was rational, harmonious and beautiful. That was where Beauty was, that was where God was. In time God began to speak to me, and I realised that He was sending down my mysterious power. I escaped from the jail. My strength and stamina knew no bounds. Even the wolfhounds that were specially trained to hunt men could not catch me, the bullets did not hit me. I swam along the river at first, then across the estuary for many hours, until I was picked up by Turkish smugglers. I wandered around the Balkans and Europe. I was put in prison several times, but the prisons were easy to escape from, much easier than the Kherson fortress. Eventually I found a good job. In Whitechapel in London. In a slaughterhouse. I butchered the carcasses. My knowledge of surgery came in useful then. I was well respected and earned a lot; I saved money. But something was maturing within me again, as I looked at the beautiful displays of the rennet bags, the livers, the washed intestines for making sausages, the kidneys, the lungs. All this offal was put into bright, gay packaging and sent to the butchers' shops. Why does man show himself so little respect? I thought; surely the belly of the stupid cow, intended for the processing of coarse grass, is not more worthy of respect than our internal apparatus, created in the likeness of God? My enlightenment came a year ago, on the third of April. I was walking home from the evening shift. On a deserted street, where not a single lamp was lit, a repulsive hag approached me and suggested I should take her into one of the gateways. When I politely declined, she moved very close to me, searing my face with her filthy breath, and began shouting coarse obscenities. What a mockery of the image of God, I thought. What were all her internal organs working for day and night? Why was the tireless heart pumping the precious blood? Why were the myriads of cells in her organism being born, dying and being renewed again? What for? And I felt an irresistible urge to transform ugliness into Beauty, to look into the true essence of this creature who was so unattractive on the outside. I had my butcher's knife hanging on my belt. Later I bought a whole set of excellent scalpels, but that first time an ordinary butcher's instrument was enough. The result far surpassed all my expectations. The hideous woman was transformed! In front of my eyes she became beautiful! And I was awestruck at such obvious evidence of a miracle from God.'

The man in the chair shed a tear. He tried to continue, but just waved his arm and did not say another word.

'Is that enough for you?' Fandorin asked. 'Do you declare him guilty?'

'Yes,' Angelina whispered, and crossed herself. 'He is guilty of all these atrocities.'

'You can see for yourself that he cannot be allowed to live. He brings death and grief. He must be exterminated.'

Angelina started. 'No, Erast Petrovich. He is insane. He needs treatment. I don't know if it will work, but it has to be tried.'

'No, he isn't insane,' Erast Petrovich replied with conviction. 'He is cunning and calculating; he possesses a will of iron and he is exceptionally enterprising. What you see before you is not a madman, but a monster. Some people are born with a hump or a harelip. But there are others whose deformity is not visible to the naked eye. That kind of deformity is the most terrible kind. He is only a man in appearance, but in reality he lacks the most important, the most distinctive feature of a human being. He lacks that invisible, vital string that dwells in the human soul, sounding to tell a man if he has acted well or badly. It is still present even in the most inveterate villain. Its note may be weak, perhaps almost inaudible, but it still sounds. In the depths of his soul a man always knows the worth of his actions, if he has listened to that string even once in his life. You know what Sotsky has done, you heard what he said, you can see what he is like. He does not have the slightest idea that this string exists; his deeds are prompted by a completely different voice. In olden times they would have called him a servant of the devil. I put it more simply: he is not human. He does not repent of anything. And he cannot be stopped by ordinary means. He will not go to the gallows, and the walls of an insane asylum will not hold him. It will start all over again.'

'Erast Petrovich, you said that the English will demand his extradition,' Angelina exclaimed pitifully, as if she were clutching at her final straw. 'Let them kill him, only not you!'

Fandorin shook his head. 'The handover is a long process. He'll escape – from prison, from a convoy, from a train, from a ship. I cannot take that risk.'

'You have no trust in God,' she said sadly, hanging her head. 'God knows how and when to put an end to evil deeds.'

'I don't know about God. And I cannot be an impartial observer. In my view, that is the worst sin of all. No more, Angelina, I've decided.'

Erast Petrovich spoke to Masa in Japanese: 'Take him out into the yard.'

'Master, you have never killed an unarmed man before,' his servant replied agitatedly in the same language. 'You will suffer. And the mistress will be angry. I will do it myself.'

'That will not change anything. And the fact that he is unarmed makes no difference. To hold a duel would be mere showmanship. I should kill him just as easily even if he were armed. Let us do without any cheap theatrics.'

When Masa and Fandorin took the condemned man by the elbows to lead him out into the yard, Angelina cried out: 'Erast, for my sake, for our sake!'

The Decorator glanced back with a smile: 'My lady, you are a picture of beauty, but I assure you that on the table, surrounded by china plates, you would be even more beautiful.'

Angelina squeezed her eyes shut and put her hands over her ears, but she still heard the sound of the shot in the yard – dry and short, almost indistinguishable against the roaring of the firecrackers and the rockets flying into the starry sky.

Erast Petrovich came back alone. He stood in the doorway and wiped the sweat from his brow. His teeth chattered as he said: 'Do you know what he whispered? "Oh Lord, what happiness".'

They stayed like that for a long time: Angelina sitting with her eyes closed, the tears flowing out from under her eyelids; Fandorin wanting to go to her, but afraid.

Finally she stood up. She walked up to him, put her arms round him and kissed him passionately several times – on the forehead, on the eyes, on the lips.

'I'm going away, Erast Petrovich; remember me kindly.'

'Angelina ...' The Court Counsellor's face, already pale, turned ashen grey. 'Surely not because of that vampire, that monster...'

'I'm a hindrance to you; I divert you from your own path,' she interrupted, not listening to him. 'The sisters have been asking me to join them for a long time now, at the Boris and Gleb Convent. It is what I should have done from the very beginning, when my father passed away. And I have grown weak with you. I wanted a holiday. But that is what holidays are like: they don't last for long. I shall watch over you from a distance. And pray to God for you. Follow the promptings of your own soul, and if something goes wrong, don't be afraid: I will make amends through prayer.'

'You can't go into a c-convent,' Fandorin said rapidly, almost incoherently. 'You're not like them; you're so vital and passionate. You won't be able stand it. And without you, I won't be able to go on.'

'You will; you're strong. It's hard for you with me. It will be easier without me... And as for me being vital and passionate the sisters are just the same. God has no need of cold people. Forgive me, goodbye. I have known for a long time we should not be together.'

Erast Petrovich stood in silent confusion, sensing that there were no arguments that could make her alter her decision. And Angelina was silent too, gently stroking his cheek and his grey temple.

Out of the night, from the dark streets, so out of tune with this farewell, there came the incessant pealing of the Easter bells.

'It's all right, Erast Petrovich,' said Angelina. 'It's all right. Do you hear? Christ is risen.'